THE JOHNSTOWN TRAGEDY

GOD IN ITS MIDST

". . . But God doesn't own this side alone; He owns the other side too, and all is well whether we are on this side or the other. Are your dear ones saved or lost? The only answer to that question is found in whether they trusted in God or not. Trust in the Lord and verily ye shall dwell in the land and be fed."

Chaplain Maguire
Protestant Memorial - Johnstown, Pennsylvania
June 9th, 1889

i

DEDICATION.

TO THE

SURVIVING SUFFERERS

OF THE

APPALLING CALAMITY AT JOHNSTOWN

AND

NEIGHBORING VILLAGES

THIS WORK

WHICH RELATES THE THRILLING STORY

OF THE GREAT DISASTER

IS DEDICATED.

THE
JOHNSTOWN HORROR!!!

OR

VALLEY OF DEATH,

BEING

A COMPLETE AND THRILLING ACCOUNT OF THE AWFUL
FLOODS AND THEIR APPALLING RUIN.

CONTAINING

Graphic Descriptions of the Terrible Rush of Waters; the
great Destruction of Houses, Factories, Churches, Towns,
and Thousands of Human Lives; Heart-rending Scenes
of Agony, Separation of Loved Ones, Panic-
stricken Multitudes and their Frantic
Efforts to Escape a Horrible Fate.

COMPRISING

THRILLING TALES OF HEROIC DEEDS; NARROW ESCAPES
FROM THE JAWS OF DEATH; FRIGHTFUL HAVOC BY
FIRE; DREADFUL SUFFERINGS OF SURVIVORS;
PLUNDERING BODIES OF VICTIMS, ETC.
TOGETHER WITH

Magnificent Exhibitions of Popular Sympathy; Quick
Aid from every City and State; Millions of Dollars
Sent for the Relief of the Stricken Sufferers.

By JAMES HERBERT WALKER,
THE WELL KNOWN AUTHOR

THE JOHNSTOWN TRAGEDY

GOD IN ITS MIDST

Mark S Mirza

BASED ON THE 1889 VERSION OF
THE JOHNSTOWN HORROR
BY
JAMES HERBERT WALKER

CTM Publishing Inc.
Atlanta, GA

Trade Paperback: ISBN 978-1-7322442-0-7
Kindle: ISBN 978-0-9972365-9-0
ePub: ISBN 978-0-9972365-8-3

Published by CTM Publishing, Inc.
850 Piedmont Ave NE, Suite # 1506
Atlanta, GA 30308

wwwMarkMirza.com

Ordering Information:

Special discounts are available on quantity purchases by corporations, associations, educators, and others. For details, contact the publisher at the above listed address.

U.S. trade bookstores and wholesalers:
Please contact CTM Publishing, Inc. Tel: (404) 606-2322; or email Mark@CTMPrayer.org

Table of Contents

based on the 1889 edition
but adjusted for this edition

Preface from the 1889 Edition

The whole country has been profoundly startled at the Terrible Calamity which has swept thousands of human beings to instant death at Johnstown and neighboring villages. The news came with the suddenness of a lightning bolt falling from the sky. A romantic valley, filled with busy factories, flourishing places of business, multitudes of happy homes and families, has been suddenly transformed into a scene of awful desolation. Frightful ravages of Flood and Fire have produced in one short hour a destruction which surpasses the records of all modern disasters. No calamity in recent times has so appalled the civilized world. What was a peaceful, prosperous valley a little time ago is today a huge sepulcher, filled with the shattered ruins of houses, factories, banks, churches, and the ghastly corpses of the dead.

This book contains a thrilling [exhilarating, galvanizing] description of this awful catastrophe, which has shocked both hemispheres. It depicts with graphic power the terrible scenes of the great disaster and relates the fearful story with masterly effect.

The work treats of the great storm which devastated the country, deluging large sections, sweeping away bridges, swelling rivulets to rivers, prostrating forests, and producing incalculable damage to life and property; of the sudden rise in the Conemaugh River and tributary streams, weakening the dam thrown across the fated valley, and endangering the lives of 50,000 people; of the heroic efforts of a little band of men to stay the flood and avert the direful calamity; of the swift ride down the valley to warn the inhabitants of their impending fate, and save them from instant death; of the breaking away of the imprisoned waters after all efforts had failed to hold them back; of the rush and roar of the mighty torrent, plunging down the valley with sounds like advancing thunder, reverberating like the booming of cannon among the hills; of the frightful havoc attending the mad flood descending with incredible velocity, and a force which nothing could resist; of the rapid rise of the waters, flooding buildings, driving the terrified inhabitants to the upper stories and roof in the desperate effort to escape their doom; of hundreds of houses crashing down the surging river, carrying men, women and children beyond the hope of rescue; of a night of horrors, multitudes dying amid the awful terrors of flood and fire, plunged under the wild torrent, buried in mire, or consumed in devouring flames; of helpless creatures rending the air with pitiful screams crying aloud in their agony, imploring help with outstretched hands, and finally sinking with no one to save them.

Whole families were lost and obliterated, perishing together in a watery tomb, or ground to atoms by floating timbers and wreck; households were suddenly bereft; some of fathers, others of mothers, others of children, neighbors and friends; frantic efforts were made to rescue the victims of the flood, render aid to those who were struggling against death, and mitigate the terrors of the horrible disaster. There were noble acts of heroism, strong men and frail women and children putting their own lives in peril to save those of their loved ones.

The terrible scene at Johnstown bridge, where thousands were consumed was the greatest funeral pyre known in the history of the world. It was ghastly work; that of recovering the bodies of the dead; dragging them from the mire in which they were imbedded, from the ruins in which they were crushed, or from the burning wreck which was consuming them. Hundreds of bodies were mutilated and disfigured beyond the possibility of identifying them, all traces of individual form and features utterly destroyed. There were multitudes of corpses awaiting coffins for their burial, putrefying under the sun, and filling the air with the sickening stench of death. There were ghouls who robbed the bodies of the victims, stripping off their jewels-even cutting off fingers to obtain rings, and plundering pockets of their money.

The burial of hundreds of the known and unknown, without minister or obsequies, without friend or mourner, without surviving relatives to take a last look or shed a tear, was one of the appalling spectacles. There was the breathless suspense and anxiety of those who feared the worst, who waited in vain for news of the safety of their friends, and at last were compelled to believe that their loved ones had perished.

The terrible shock attending the horrible accounts of the great calamity, was followed by the sudden outburst and exhibition of universal grief and sympathy. Dispatches from the President, Governors of States, and Mayors of Cities, announced that speedy aid would be furnished. The magnificent charity that came to the rescue with millions of dollars, immense contributions of food and clothing, personal services and heroic efforts, is one impressive part of this graphic story. Rich and poor alike gave freely, many persons dividing their last dollar to aid those who had lost their all.

These thrilling scenes are depicted, and these wonderful facts are related, in *The Johnstown Horror*, by eye-witnesses who saw the fatal flood and its direful effects. No book so intensely exciting has ever been issued. The graphic story has an awful fascination and will be read throughout the land.

2018 Heavenly Foreword

Hello, my name is Nesah[1], and I am honored to write this forward for one of my Guardian Angels, Hael[2]. I am his immediate supervisor and an undersecretary to Michael the Archangel.

It is with great honor, great pleasure, and even greater trepidation that I write this forward.

Many of us were concerned when the author of "The Pray-ers" introduced Hael, one of our fellow angels to the world in 2016. While we are proud of him and grateful to our Lord for allowing this author to give some insights into Hael's life as a Guardian Angel we were also fearful that a book like this would occur, bringing unwarranted focus upon us, rather than on the Lord as it belongs.

However, the Creator of heaven and earth has given His approval for this book, so it is with great pleasure and much editing that I introduce to you one of the many challenges we have as Guardian Angels.

One of the challenges has been one we did not consider. Hael, in his zeal has shared a few things that our editors are uncomfortable with and so they have redacted those words from Hael's. But to keep Hael's thoughts shared with you, we have chosen to show the redacting as follows: ███████. We hope you will understand.

Hael will tell you his story of an incredible tragedy that happened nearly one and a half mortal centuries ago in the United States of America. I am not sure why Hael chose this tragedy, there are and have been many all over the world during these last 6000 years that he could have chosen. I believe that he chose this because the majority of this book is made up by a book in public domain that he was able to use and not have to write everything from scratch. We may be angels, but there are some things that we must do as slowly as, well, mortal people.

Nevertheless, all of us here in heaven, on the Guardian Angel side, are honored to have you read this. We would ask you only one thing. Be good Bereans[3] and compare everything that you read from Hael, to the Word of God.

Approximately two thirds of the book is from 1889 and the rest is from Hael. You will instantaneously see which parts are Hael's because he will

---

[1] pronounced NEH-su, "E" as in net, "u" as in up
[2] pronounced hay-EL, "a" as in Day, "E" as in net
[3] Acts 17:11

begin those sections with his name and then a brief tease, I.E. "HAEL: CHRIST LIKE BRAVERY"

Also, his words will be *written in italics* so that you can see the parts added to the original book.

I would like to say "enjoy the book" but I cannot, for it will be a painful book to read. What I will say though, is that this sobering book should cause your "trust-muscle" to be strengthened as you trust God Almighty to strengthen your faith in the midst of tragedies.

Honored,

Nesah
Nesah

Immediate Supervisor to Hael
Undersecretary to Michael the Archangel

2018 Earthly Foreword

On the afternoon of May 31, 1889, our nation witnessed one of the greatest tragedies and loss of human life as flood waters swept down the Allegheny Mountains, engulfing the town of Johnstown, Pennsylvania. The angry wall of water descended upon residents after a dam burst several miles upstream, and the town was overrun by a flood that had power to destroy buildings, homes, streets, and thousands of lives. But it did not have enough power to destroy faith.

Survivors talked of the breadth of the destruction, having witnessed the menacing flood wreak havoc upon everything and everyone in its path. The writer of the 1889 account, after reviewing the severity of the devastation, stated hopelessly that "desolation reigns." The collapsed buildings, mounds of rubble, and upended earth were second only to the thousands of destroyed lives. The steely pangs of death reached deep and wide into the peaceful community, leaving no family untouched.

In this remarkable presentation of the tragedy of the Johnstown flood, Mark Mirza weaves fresh life and new thoughts into the events surrounding the horrific scenes left in the wake of the destructive flood. Mirza reminds us that tragic events—whether they be long ago such as the flood in Johnstown or something more recent like 9-11 or Gulf Coast hurricanes—can also be reminders of God's mercy and grace. Like those who witnessed the Johnstown flood, have you ever wondered about God's presence and purpose when desolation seemed to reign everywhere?

Even when pain and suffering appear in our lives, our faith reminds us the God still sits enthroned above the heavens. When observing death, destruction, and devastation, we need to remember what Mirza writes: "There is nothing that occurs on earth that does not run through His fingers first."

Where are the fingers of God during hurricanes, acts of terrorism, death, and disease? And where was God during the overwhelming destruction of the Johnstown flood? That's what this book talks about.

Mirza introduced the angel Hael to readers in his first novel, *The Pray-ers*, and the nine-foot-tall angel returns to provide us some "stories behind the story" that illustrate how God can be in the midst of such misery and despair. Like all angels, Hael works at the behest and beckoning of Almighty God, yet he is able to see things that we humans can neither see nor understand. Hael's immediate supervisor, an angel named Nesah, provides some introductory insight before we are provided a look behind some of the scenes and lost lives of the Johnstown flood.

All of this, of course, is a literary device used by Mirza to introduce themes of faith, sovereignty, and mercy. Mirza is careful not to make this book more about angels than about God, and the observations of Hael are inserted into the text of the original 1889 record, challenging the reader to see God and spiritual principles at work. Even during calamity and disasters, there are lessons to learn about greed, grief, comfort, trust, desperation, wickedness, and grace.

The question this book explores is not a new one—where is God when tragedy strikes? One option is that God is unaware. The depths of despair that some people face during catastrophe reaffirm the mistaken notion that God set the world in motion and has now turned his attention to other things. Humans are left alone in this world, having to make the best of what comes their way. This view, of course, represents a limited and unbiblical view of God, yet many people reach for this option when trying to pick up the pieces of their shattered lives. But is God more than a detached, disinterested deity who has left us alone to make it on our own?

A second option is that God is simply unable to change the natural course of tragic events. Hurricanes, tornadoes, acts of terrorism, and disasters of all sorts are simply the natural result of sin introduced into the world, and God is unable to alter their course once they start. Many people come to this conclusion because if God is good and powerful, then he would certainly not allow suffering as it is seen today. The fact that a good God allows such tragedy to take place must mean he is powerless and unable to stop it. After all, what does it say about God if he is able to prevent horrific scenes like as the Johnstown flood, yet chooses not to prevent them from happening?

The third option, which Mirza presents in this book, is that God is unnoticed. Working in ways we may neither see nor understand, God is in the midst of tragedy, accomplishing his work and meting out mercy because he both sees and understands. Beneath the suffering, devastation, and pain of this world, we discover that we have not been forsaken nor forgotten by God. Because of his grace, we find peace among pain and hope amid hopelessness. That's what happened during the Johnstown flood, and that's what can happen in our lives today.

The town of Johnstown was swallowed up and consumed by the flood in 1889, but the faith and trust of its survivors was not. The sweeping carnage, the unspeakable misery, and the stacks of decaying and decomposing bodies all speak of devastation and ruin. But Mirza invites you into the realm of the angel Hael, describing scenes behind the historical record and urging us to notice God and his grace in the midst of it all.

Dr. John Waters
Sr. Pastor First Baptist Church
Statesboro, Georgia
Past President of the Georgia Baptist Convention

Introduction

In this introduction, I trust that you will see various reasons I asked for permission to write this tome. I am very grateful to the author that introduced me and a friend of mine to the world recently in Book 1 "Troubles" of this three-part series of "The Pray-ers." He is still writing books 2 and 3. By the way, I have been looking over his shoulder at his writing, and frankly while his stories are very creative, he's got to get-on-the-ball I think you would say and get them done. He's moving a little too slowly.

Anyway, since his introduction of us to mortals, some serious questions have been popping up in the prayers we hear in heaven's courts. You are all looking forward to the return of Jesus to earth, as we are also, but I fear that you have forgotten a key issue surrounding Jesus' Second Coming.

You see, we in heaven, as angels, keep hearing prayers asking the Lord to get rid of the persecution of Christians, the natural disasters you all have to face, their tragic results, and all kinds of things like this.

Let me tell you why this is so bothersome to me and to my fellow angels here in heaven. We remember what I fear many of you have forgotten. Paul stated plainly that "all who desire to live godly lives in Christ Jesus will be persecuted, while evil men and imposters go from bad to worse, deceiving and being deceived. But as for you, continue in the things you have learned and firmly believed."[1]

As I and my fellow angels hear your prayers, our hearts hurt for you, for you are praying as if God is not in control. It sounds to us like you are not praying trusting Him. Rather you are praying questioning His sovereignty and giving Him advice. Have you forgotten that He spoke the words and the worlds leapt into existence?

Let me tell you how to read this book, or how not to read this book. I intend to give you footnotes every time I use a Scripture. These are only there for your convenience. <u>Do not</u> tell yourself that you have to look each one of them up while you are reading.

These occasional footnotes are there because as you are reading you will recognize a phrase or sentence, and knowing that it came from Scripture, you may want to look it up. That's when you look down at the footnotes. There's a second time you will want to use the footnotes and that will be when you choose to be a good Berean[2] as Nesah suggested when he wrote his Foreword above.

---

[1] 2 Timothy 3:12-14a
[2] Acts 17:11

I started writing this about one earth month before Hurricane Harvey hit the USA, in 2017. As the facts of destruction, heroes, thieves, and senseless death enter the modern news and your social media, I am seeing numerous parallels in 2017 compared to this 1889 tragedy. I believe you will too.

I intend to tell you of this tragedy by using the earliest book written on this subject, just a few months after the event in 1889, "The Johnstown Horror, or The Valley of Death." While this book gives you graphic descriptions of the destruction that occurred, I will include some periodic back stories on what you are reading.

I have one goal in this book, and that is for you to see God in the midst of tragedies, hence the title, "The Johnstown Tragedy, God In Its Midst"

I intend to walk a fine line in sharing with you what is happening from our perspective, perhaps even taking a little bit of narrative flexibility, or creative license to broaden your understanding of our job as guardian angels. To use the phrase "Guardian Angels" isn't quite accurate, for the truth is God Almighty is already your protector[1] whether we are there or not. He uses us, and we gratefully serve Him. I think you will see our service and see that we are honored to perform it. Believe me, we are merely His servants, doing what He expects of us.[2]

There is a secondary reason I am writing this book. I am sure that difficulties are coming your way. I say that without hesitation not because God Almighty has shared with any of us the future, after all I didn't know about Hurricane Harvey when I started this book. But we have been watching you for 6000 years, and, well, if you would like to know what I'm talking about just go back to the Book of Judges. What you are living today is, in part, and only by application, portions of the Book of Judges.

The author that I mentioned before, that introduced me to the world, likes to say when he is teaching about prayer that he sees in the churches "men and women that are scared to death of death." He is accurate in that statement for we see it also. As much as we try to comfort you, for God gives us many, many opportunities to encourage you, to strengthen you and to comfort you, even in all that we do, we see an incredible sense of fear of death.

Many of you live in an affluent society where the evil one is encouraging you to focus upon what you can have or what you do have here on Earth, rather than what you are aspiring to in heaven. Your focus is on this Earth as if this Earth is

---

[1] Psalm 46
[2] Luke 17:10

your home. *Those of you that are saved by the blood of the Son need to remember that Earth is not your home! You are merely sojourners there.*[1]

Let me not waste any more time. As you see this story unfold before your mind, remember one thing the psalmist said in chapter 103 verse 19: your Father and our God is enthroned above the heavens and He is Sovereign over everything."

Servant of The King,

Hael

Hael,
Guardian Angel

---

[1] 1 Chronicles 29:15, Psalm 39:12, 119:19, 1 Peter 2:11

CHAPTER I
THE APPALLING NEWS

THE APPALLING NEWS

On the advent of Summer, June 1st, the country was horror-stricken by the announcement that a terrible calamity had overtaken the inhabitants of Johnstown, and the neighboring villages. Instantly the whole land was stirred by the startling news of this great disaster. Its appalling magnitude, its dreadful suddenness, its scenes of terror and agony, the fate of thousands swept to instant death by a flood as frightful as that of the cataract of Niagara, awakened the profoundest horror. No calamity in the history of modern times has so appalled the civilized world.

The following graphic pen-picture will give the reader an accurate idea of the picturesque scene of the disaster:

Away up in the misty crags of the Alleghanies some tiny rills [streams] trickle and gurgle from a cleft in the mossy rocks. The drippling waters, timid perhaps in the bleak and lonely fastness of the heights, hug and coddle one another until they flash into a limpid pool. A score of rivulets from all the mountain side babble hither over rocky beds to join their companions. Thence in rippling current they purl and tinkle down the gentle slopes, through bosky nooks sweet with the odors of fir tree and pine, over meads dappled with the scarlet snap-dragon and purple heath buds, now pausing for a moment to idle with a wood encircled lake, now tumbling in opalescent cascade over a mossy lurch, and then on again in cheerful, hurried course down the Appalachian valley.

None stays their way. Here and there perhaps some thrifty Pennsylvania Dutchman coaxes the saucy stream to turn his mill-wheel and every league or so it fumes and frets a bit against some rustic bridge. From these trifling tourneys though, it emerges only the more eager and impetuous in its path toward the towns below.

THE FATAL RIVER

Coming nearer, step by step, to the busy haunts of men, the dashing brook takes on a more ambitious air. Little by little it edges its narrow banks aside, drinks in the waters of tributaries, swells with the copious rainfall of the lower valley. From its ladder in the Alleghanies it catches a glimpse of the steeples of Johnstown, red with the glow of the setting sun. Again, it spurts and spreads as if conscious of its new importance, and the once tiny rill expands into the dignity of a river, a veritable river, with a name of its own. Big with this sounding symbol of prowess it rushes on as if to sweep by the teeming town in a flood of majesty. To its vast surprise the way is barred. The hand of man has dared to check the will of one that up to now has known no curb save those the forest gods imposed. For an instant the waters, taken aback by this strange audacity, hold themselves in leash. Then, like Erlking in the German legends, they broaden out to engulf their opponent. In vain they surge with crescent surface against the barrier of stone. By day, by night, they beat and breast in angry impotence against the ponderous wall of masonry that man has reared, for pleasure and profit, to stem the mountain stream.

THE AWFUL RUSH OF WATERS

Suddenly, maddened by the stubborn hindrance, the river grows black and turgid. It rumbles and threatens as if confident of an access of strength that laughs at resistance. From far up the hillside comes a sound, at first soft and soothing as the Fountains of Lindaraxa, then rolling onward it takes the voluminous quaver of a distant waterfall. Louder and louder, deeper and deeper, nearer and nearer comes an awful crashing and roaring, till its echoes rebound from the crags of the Alleghanies like peals of thunder and boom of cannon.

On, on, down the steep valley trumpets the torrent into the river at Jamestown. Joined to the waters from the cloud kissed summits of its source, the exultant Conemaugh, with a deafening din, dashes its way through the barricade of stone and starts [shocks] like a lemon on its path of destruction.

Into its maw [voracious throat] it sucks a town. A town with all its hundreds of men and women and children, with its marts of business, its

22

homes, its factories and houses of worship. Then, insatiate still, with a blast like the chaos of worlds dissolved, it rushes out to new desolation, until Nature herself, awe stricken at the sight of such ineffable woe, blinds her eyes to the uncanny scene of death, and drops the pall of night upon the earth.

HAEL: ROARING LION

Below, the writer seems to nearly romanticize the destruction calling it a "Thunderbolt from Jove" referring to Jupitar who is of Roman mythology and is called the god of the sky. Let me share what this writer did not see, nor could he have, even if he had been in Johnstown on that fateful, infamous, and tragic day.

A demonic horde had gathered in the Alleghanies, not because they knew what would happen, but simply because we have been at this struggle for the heart and mind of man for some six thousand of your years. When tragedies occur, the demons' entire focus is to bring horror into the life of the dying, or those about to die. They each act as roaring lions seeking someone to devour.[1] Our job, is to comfort the saved while they are in peril.

To look back in my memory of this date, and to see the lives of men, women, boys and girls my heart aches even now, for not all were saved. As this book progresses I will show you a picture that is hardly romantic, and yet while demons attempted to bring horror, and in many cases did so, you will read about wonderful faith, and more than that, trust. Yes, a trust in the Almighty, even in the midst of tragedy that men and women in your churches of today, in the twenty-first century, have sorely missed.

DESTRUCTION DESCENDED AS A BOLT OF JOVE

A fair town in a western valley of Pennsylvania, happy in the arts of peace and prospering by its busy manufacture, suddenly swept out of existence by a gigantic flood and thousands of lives extinguished as by one fell stroke-such has been the fate of Johnstown.

Never before in this country has there happened a disaster of such appalling proportions. It is necessary to refer to those which have occurred

---

[1] 1 Peter 5:8

in the valleys, the great European rivers, where there is a densely crowded population, to find a parallel.

HAEL: DEATH TOLL COMPARISON

And the writer is correct, never had there been more Americans lost in one day on American soil than this day, May 31st, 1889, and it would not be until your infamous 9/11 on September 11, 2001 that more lives were lost in one day in your country.

As this is being written the death toll from Hurricane Harvey has reached 45. If it reaches 50, it will still be 44 times LESS than the death toll of the Johnstown Flood. The estimated death toll of the Johnstown Flood is 2200, but we can tell you that it was higher. However, using the known number above, Hurricane Harvey is barely 2% of the deaths that occurred in Johnstown, Pennsylvania on May 31st, 1889.

THE HORRORS UNESTIMATED

At first the horror was not all known. It could only be imperfectly surmised. Until a late hour on the following night there was no communication with the hapless city. All that was positively known of its fate was seen from afar. It was said that out of all the habitations, which had sheltered about twelve thousand people before this awful doom had befallen, only two were visible above the water. All the rest, if this be true, had been swallowed up or else shattered into pieces and hurled downward into the flood-vexed valley below.

What has become of those twelve thousand inhabitants? Who can tell until after the waters have wholly subsided?

Of course, it is possible that many of them escaped. Much hope is to be built upon the natural exaggeration of first reports from the sorely distressed surrounding region and the lack of actual knowledge, in the absence of direct communication. But what suspense must there be between now and the moment when direct communication shall be opened!

If you watched the news media on that day back in September 2001 when the Twin Towers came down, early estimates were based on the number of people normally in the towers, and visiting. Many of your newscasters were concerned that as many as 20,000 (or higher) may have lost their life. This was not the case of course, but easily could have been.

Why was the death toll on 9/11 not higher? Do you remember the World Series Earthquake of 1988 in the San Francisco bay area? It occurred at rush hour and yet there were incredibly few deaths, even when the freeways pancaked onto each other.

Why did so many more people live, here in Johnstown, than the early expectations? There is only one word that explains it, "mercy." The mercy of God, my dear readers. You will ask, where was God? And I will recount to you numerous cases where He showed Himself in Johnstown, just as He did on 9/11, just as He did during the World Series and just as He has done during Hurricane Harvey.

HEEDLESS OF FATE

The valley of the Conemaugh in which Johnstown stood lies between the steep walls of lofty hills. The gathering of the rain into torrents in that region is quick and precipitate. The river on one side roared out its warning, but the people would not take heed of the danger impending over them on the other side, [known as] the great South Fork dam, two and a half miles up the valley [as the crow flies, or 14 miles up via the winding Conemaugh River] and looming [70] feet in height from base to top. Behind it were piled the waters, a great, ponderous mass, like the treasured wrath of fate. Their surface was about three hundred feet above the deserted town.

If Noah's neighbors thought it would be only a little shower the people of Johnstown were yet more foolish. The railroad officials had repeatedly told them that the dam threatened destruction. They still perversely lulled themselves into a false security. The blow came, when it did, like a flash. It was as if the heavens had fallen in liquid fury upon the earth. It was as if ocean itself had been precipitated into an abyss. The slow but inexorable march of the mightiest glacier of the Alps, though comparable, was not equal to this in force. The whole of a Pyramid, shot from a colossal catapult, would not have been the petty charge of a pea shooter [compared] to it. Imagine Niagara, or a greater [falls] even than Niagara, falling upon an ordinary collection of brick and wooden houses.

HAEL: STEWARDSHIP

The writer will bring up in various ways an issue that each Christian needs to take stock of in their life, and that is stewardship. We all are to be good stewards of that which is entrusted to us. Even in Heaven we angels are to do and accomplish the following as good stewards:

And on earth, each of you need to take responsibility for stewardship of your own life. Later testimony would come out that:

The towns people did not take the potential of a dam break seriously.

Many would mock the idea of the dam breaking, even when they were told on that day!

My friends, have we not seen the same thing in Houston? How many people arrogantly chose to stay in their homes when told to leave?

The same thing occurred during the Mt. Saint Helens volcanic eruption, the most famous being Harry Truman who refused to leave his lodge located at Spirit Lake. While he was eventually given special permission to stay, that too was poor stewardship exhibited by people in leadership roles.

AN INCONCEIVABLE FORCE

The South Fork Reservoir was [among] the largest in the United States, and it contained millions of tons of water. When its fetters were loosened, crumbling before it like sand, a building or even a rock that stood in its path presented as much resistance as a card house. The dread execution was little more than the work of an instant.

The flood passed over the town as it would over a pile of shingles, covering over or carrying with it everything that stood in its way. It bounded down the valley, wreaking destruction and death on each hand and in its fore.

Torrents that poured down out of the wilds of the mountains swelled its volume.

All along from the point of its release it bore debris and corpses as its hideous trophies. In a very brief time it displayed some of both, as if in hellish glee, to the horrified eyes of Pittsburg, seventy-eight miles west of the town of Johnstown that had been, having danced them along on its exultant billows or rolled them over and over in the depths of its dark current all the way through the Conemaugh, the Kiskiminitas and the Allegheny river.

It was like a fearful monster, gnashing its dripping jaws in the scared face of the multitude, in the flesh of its victims.

One eye-witness of the effects of the deluge declares that he saw five hundred dead bodies. Hundreds were counted by others. It will take many a day to make up the death roll. It will take many a day to make up the reckoning of the material loss.

If any pen could describe the scenes of terror, anguish and destruction which have taken place in Conemaugh Valley it could write an epic greater than the "Iliad." The accounts that come tell of hairbreadth escapes, heartrending tragedies and deeds of heroism almost without number,

A Climax of Horror

As if to add a lurid touch of horror to the picture that might surpass all the rest a conflagration came to mock those who were in fear of drowning with a death yet more terrible. Where the ruins of Johnstown [and the ruin of towns further up the river that were swept down into Johnstown], composed mainly of timber, [but including men and women swept down with the torrent] had been piled up forty feet high against a railroad bridge below the town a fire was started and raged with eager fury. It is said that scores of persons were burned alive, their piercing cries appealing for aid to hundreds of spectators who stood on the banks of the river, but could do nothing.

Western Pennsylvania is in mourning. Business in the cities is virtually suspended and all minds are bent upon this great horror, all hearts convulsed with the common sorrow.

As spectators had opportunity, they tried to untangle the incredible pile, but it contained homes so badly mangled one could not tell where one began and the other ended. There were thousands and thousands of feet of barbed wire, one of the main products made in the Cambria Steel Mill. Trees and poles, uprooted and broken as if they were small twigs broken in one's hand, wound around and trapped people, too numerous for the onlookers to save.

As the shrieks went up there came a sound from what the spectators surmised as a small family. They couldn't see them, for the family had been on a roof and when it careened into the pile another building covered them. They could be heard but not seen. The father of four, with his wife by his side saw the fire as they slammed into the forty-foot-tall pile.

I will let my fellow guardian angel tell what happened.

I placed myself on the roof of Dr. Jones' home intent on ministering[1] to them and strengthening[2] them throughout this horrific journey. Dr. Jones brought his family during the previous week from Pittsburgh to visit his sister living in South Fork, just a short distance down river from the dam.

The four children, aged six through thirteen had enjoyed the steep hills that Dr. Jones' sister lived on. They had a great time as I watched them find branches to slide down the hills, especially when it started to rain heavily. It brings a great smile to my face even now as I remember those last few days.

The house, built many years earlier sat just above the railroad tracks and so near the water that the children enjoyed the South Fork Creek as well as the slippery valley walls.

Their mother Mrs. Jones, spent the first day wanting to make a good impression and she could not comprehend how her children got their clothes so dirty. Embarrassed that her children were making a mess of Gertrude's home (Dr. Jones' sister) she barred her children from playing outside after the first day. Gertrude watched Mrs. Jones silently for the whole of that first day and prayed all night for her, although Mrs. Jones had no idea. The next morning Gertrude pulled Mr. Jones aside and shared her plan with him which he heartily agreed to.

Later that morning when Mrs. Jones made her way out of the bedroom Gertrude sidled up to her and put her arms around the mother of four, "Would you give me the honor of letting your kids run around and enjoy the outdoors like my brother and I used to?"

---

[1] Matthew 4:11
[2] Luke 22:43

Gertrude then looked at her sister-in-law and noticed tears running down her cheek. "Oh Gertrude," she said and turned to hug her. "It seems like all night long I asked the Lord how to broach that very idea with you. I don't know what happened but somewhere in the middle of the night I awoke with this terrible guilt that my children were missing a wonderful memory, and my selfishness was the cause. After your brother left our room this morning I prayed that the Lord would allow me to figure out how to let the children outside again. Thank you, Gertrude, thank you."

When the torrent of debris and water made its way into East Conemaugh and swept up the house, Gertrude was in the kitchen getting hot chocolate ready for the end of the afternoon Bible study regimen that her brother kept his kids to. When she heard that loud and terrible sound and felt the ground shake she dropped the glass hot water pot. She had turned to yell to the family to exit the home and climb up the mountain, but when the glass pot fell it broke and the scalding water splashed onto her legs doubling her over in pain and taking every word from her mouth that she had planned to give as a warning.

In the living room Dr. Jones and his family had no idea that the South Fork dam had burst and that a fifty-foot wave of water, preceded by an equally tall wave of debris would hit their home in a matter of minutes.

When the children heard the sound, they jumped up, for their father had not started the Bible study yet. They ran upstairs so as to get a better view of this new adventure. The children were out the sitting room and up the stairs before Mrs. Jones could react. She had no idea what was happening and as she started to panic, Mr. Jones consoled her. When they heard the glass break in the kitchen they both froze.

I had the opportunity to wrap my wings around them both giving them comfort for a few moments as Dr. Jones whispered up a short prayer for wisdom.[1] And then he remembered the old dam. Sensing a renewed strength, he pulled away from his wife. "Go upstairs to the highest point, get the kids up there now. I'll be right behind you. Something is wrong with Gertrude. I will get her and bring her up with you.

Mr. Jones watched his wife make her way wobbly up the stairs as the shaking of the home intensified. When he entered the kitchen, he didn't see Gertrude, so he called out to her. He heard a muffled cry from the floor near the stove and went over to get her, but at that very moment a loud crash enveloped the back side of the house. Both Gertrude and her brother looked behind her, for where stood the back of the home, with its indoor porch and all of the children's soiled clothes

---

[1] James 1:5

29

waiting to be washed, a four-foot-wide pine tree crashed through the back of the house as if it were cutting through paper.

As if in slow motion, the back of the kitchen, where Gertrude lay, started to disintegrate. Before Dr. Jones could move to his sister, she too was gone. Dr. Jones and I both saw a slight smile begin to appear on her face before she disappeared. What Dr. Jones could not see, but I did, was that her Guardian Angel had encircled her with his wings, began to hum a melodious tune and comforted her. I asked him later about her smile and he said the Holy Spirit of Comfort[1] had implanted that scene of her blessing her sister-in-law a few mornings earlier. That is what was in her mind when she left this world and opening her eyes saw Jesus standing at the right hand of the Father, welcoming her into glory.

Moving quickly Dr. Jones ran upstairs to his wife and children who were huddled in a corner whimpering with chests heaving. I was allowed to break off a corner of the roof where they were huddled, just as Dr. Jones came forward and as I knew he would, he hoisted his wife and children on to the top of the roof where we all stayed. As the roof careened back and forth down the river, raising and lowering in height based on the large swell of water compressed between the steep valley, we made our way into Woodvale where the kids and parents heard screaming and crying, and somewhat unaccountably, saw children and families along the side of the mountain. They had turned to look at the raging water, as if in a stadium watching as spectators would. It was an odd and eerie sight, even for me.

About twenty minutes later, after much rocking and weaving and jostling on the roof we made it into Johnstown and that is where the truly frightful event began to unfold. As I wrapped my wings around his family and they experienced some comfort I could see the homes standing up against the bridge below town that we were going to run into. Dr. Jones saw it too and had his children lay face down grabbing onto the roof shingles as best they could. Six-year-old little Gertie (named for Dr. Jones' sister) was praying on her knees balancing as best she could when the roof stopped suddenly. Her momentum drove the little pray-er into the water before Dr. Jones could react. As he saw her bob up and down in the water, moving way too fast for him to catch her, he noticed that she had somehow landed on a floor that was also being carried along in the undulating waters. As he watched her he cocked his head to one side thinking, how curious, and how like little Gertie to stay in prayer. And as our Lord does so often, even in that tragic moment He allowed Dr. Jones a moment of peace. A number of minutes later when Gertie opened her eyes, a little tentative, for something felt different, she

---

[1] Acts 9:31

saw Jesus standing there reaching out his nail-scarred hands as an angel carried her to Him. And next to Jesus was Auntie Gertrude.

Dr. Jones now saw the next challenge, the water course they were on would take them into a mountain of debris that had begun to settle at the railroad track bridge they had been on just a few days before. He yelled for his kids and wife to hold on tight when the corner of their roof struck a building and sliced into that building like it were a piece of thin paper. With a sigh of relief Dr. Jones knew that because they had their heads down they were all safely wrapped into another building. It was too low to stand up in, but they were safe, for the time being.

This is Hael interjecting a couple of sentences. You may remember that when the author of The Pray-ers introduced me to the world he gave away a bit of a tightly held secret that I feel I need to acknowledge. You see, our normal stature is that we are 9' tall. However, God the Creator has given us an interesting body function. We can fit ourselves into whatever location our charges happen to be in. I'm not really sure how this works, but in the automobile driven by Dr. Dale (The Pray-ers, Book 1, Troubles) I am able to scrunch my body into a small convertible. This is the same thing done here, by the Jones' guardian angel.

Two hours later, still in a water free pocket, but now freezing and teeth chattering due to their water-logged clothes, Dr. Jones heard the first explosion. He would have no idea that this explosion meant the pile of debris, including people both dead and alive, would bring a fire that would consume the whole pile, burn for days and leave a stench of burning human flesh for weeks afterwards. All he knew was that his wife and three of his children were safe, and he trusted that the Lord reigned.

They were not able to dig their way out, for they had no hand tools. And yet they heard many other people around them, screaming and crying which is what they too wanted to do. But Dr. Jones, a wise husband and father encouraged his kids to tell him their verses they had been memorizing. Periodically he would ask his kids to be silent so he could hear what was going on, and then he would call out, but the muffled reverberation in their watertight pocket kept the sound in, even as the air somehow circulated to allow them fresh air. Once in a while he and his family could hear a rush of air enter their space circle around and die in a corner.

When, after another hour, he felt the heat increase rapidly and he knew what would be there soon. Hael, these next few minutes were incredibly difficult for me, but as I encircled the family with my wings strengthening and encouraging them, Mrs. Jones started to sing:

> *What a Friend we have in Jesus*
> *All our sins and griefs to bear!*
> *What a privilege to carry*

> *Everything to God in prayer!*
> *Oh, what peace we often forfeit,*
> *Oh, what needless pain we bear,*
> *All because we do not carry*
> *Everything to God in prayer!*

People all around them began to stop whimpering and listened. Some tried to sing but were too scared.

> *Have we trials and temptations?*
> *Is there trouble anywhere?*
> *We should never be discouraged—*
> *Take it to the Lord in prayer.*
> *Can we find a friend so faithful,*
> *Who will all our sorrows share?*
> *Jesus knows our every weakness;*
> *Take it to the Lord in prayer.*

> *Are we weak and heavy-laden,*
> *Cumbered with a load of care?*
> *Precious Savior, still our refuge—*
> *Take it to the Lord in prayer.*
> *Do thy friends despise, forsake thee?*
> *Take it to the Lord in prayer!*
> *In His arms He'll take and shield thee,*
> *Thou wilt find a solace there.*

Here is where the onlookers from the banks heard the singing too. Amazed, many tried to sing, but couldn't for they saw the fires glowing unmercifully toward the enclave of sound.

As the Jones family sang the last verse, five of us were prepared for the inevitable task of carrying them to Glory and yet we were allowed to participate with them and hum as they sang.

Watching their bravery, then, and now as I am remembering it Hael, I have rarely seen trusting Christians like the Jones family. They completely trusted the Lord. Even in the midst of death. Oh Hael, what they can teach the church today. The church that is so scared to death of death. What a contrast. What a contrast.

> *Blessed Savior, Thou hast promised*
> *Thou wilt all our burdens bear;*
> *May we ever, Lord, be bringing*
> *All to Thee in earnest prayer.*

Soon in glory bright, unclouded,
There will be no need for prayer—
Rapture, praise, and endless worship
Will be our sweet portion there.

As they sang the last line I could hear demons carrying other souls to their final resting place too. Grateful that the Jones' could not hear the cackling demons enjoying themselves all five of us were ready when the top of the building they were in blew off as if by a great wind and the small puffs of air that for hours had been their life now sucked in the flames that were their death.

The flames that brought their death came in so quickly and were so efficient in death that they were still holding on to one another when we carried them to the throne room. Their bodies were buried so deep that it would be weeks later that their charred unrecognizable bodies would be pulled from this pile. Those digging them up would never know for sure how many were in this pile: three, four, five?

One thing is certain though, while in their temporary resting place here on earth they would be deposited as "Unknown Family of Unknown Number," their bodies will be reunited in that great day, for the Father will raise them from the dead and reunite them with their spiritual body.

For so it will be with the resurrection of the dead:

Sown in corruption, raised in incorruption;
sown in dishonor, raised in glory;
sown in weakness, raised in power;
sown a natural body, raised a spiritual body.
For not only is there a natural body, but there is also a spiritual body[1]

As they gave up this life on earth, quickly closing their eyes in fright, as is the human reaction we were holding each of them, taking them across the Jordan into the waiting arms of Jesus.

I never cease to be amazed by these events, and even now Hael, I am reminded of watching this precious family open their eyes almost simultaneously and seeing Jesus with His arms outstretched. They realized instantly that their faith was

---

[1] 1 Corinthians 15:42-44

honored by the One who was pierced[1] for them and now, as then, He ever liveth to make intercession for those on earth.[2]

And nearly as quickly, they saw the happy faces of little Gertie and Gertrude standing there in white robes, smiling and welcoming the rest of the family to their home, their new home, their real home. They would no longer be sojourners in a world not their home.[3]

HEARTRENDING SCENES AND HEROIC STRUGGLES FOR LIFE.

Another eye-witness describes the calamity as follows: A flood of death swept down the Alleghany Mountains yesterday afternoon and last night. Almost the entire city of Johnstown is swimming about in the rushing, angry tide. Dead bodies are floating about in every direction, and almost every piece of movable timber is carrying from the doomed city a corpse of humanity, drifting with the raging waters. The disaster overtook Johnstown about six o'clock last evening.

As the train bearing the writer sped eastward, the reports at each stop grew more appalling. At Derry, a group of railway officials were gathered who had come from Bolivar, the end of the passable portion of the rail westward. They had seen but a small portion of the awful flood, but enough to allow them to imagine the rest. Down through the Packsaddle came the rushing waters. The wooded heights of the Alleghanies looked down in wonder at the scene of the most terrible destruction that ever struck the romantic valley of the Conemaugh.

The water was rising when the men left at six o'clock at the rate of five feet an hour. Clinging to improvised rafts, constructed in the death battle from floating boards and timbers, were agonized men, women and children, their heartrending shrieks for help striking horror to the breasts of the onlookers. Their cries were of no avail. Carried along at railway speed on the breast of this rushing torrent, no human ingenuity could devise a means of rescue.

With pallid face and hair clinging wet and damp to her cheek, a mother was seen grasping a floating timber, while on her other arm she held her babe, already drowned. With a death-grip on a plank a strong man just

---

[1] Isaiah 53:5
[2] Hebrews 7:25
[3] Psalm 105:12, Hebrews 11:9

giving up hope cast an imploring look to those on the bank, and an instant later he had sunk into the waves. Prayers to God and cries to those in safety rang above the roaring waves.

The special train pulled into Bolivar at half-past eleven last night, and the trainmen were there notified that further progress was impossible. The greatest [anxious] excitement prevailed at this place, and parties of citizens are out all the time endeavoring to save the poor unfortunates that are being hurled to eternity on the rushing torrent.

HAEL: PROFFERED PRAYERS

It is amazing to us the prayers we hear during tragedies like this. It is, in many cases beautiful and amazing, and yet in others the prayers are heartbreaking, even for us who have been alongside you for these past six thousand years.

We often hear shrieks for "mercy" from the God of Mercy, and He is always there to give it.

We see the humbleness of a person resolved to seeing their maker very soon, bowing his or her head and accepting the coming inevitability.

And then there are those who have never completely trust the Lord to "always act in their best interest," similar to King Hezekiah of old in 2 Kings chapter 20. The attitude of these pray-ers are more along the lines of demanding from God what they want rather than trust God for what He intends in their life. God will sometimes answer you based on what you want, but it will be to your own peril, as He did for Hezekiah.

God gave him fifteen more years[1] but much evil and poor judgment came with it.

As the Apostle Paul read through this section of this book he called me over to remind me of something that he wrote two thousand years earlier. By the way, Paul heard about the writing of this book in our ▓▓▓▓▓▓▓ meeting where it came out.

Anyway, I came up to him and said, "I know, I know Paul, I should have alluded to Romans chapter 1 where you remind the humans . . ."

And to my surprise he interrupted me and said, "No, Hael. I want you to remind them that I knew fears within and troubles without. But it is the humble that

---

[1] 2 Kings 20:6

God comforts.[1] *That is the message my brothers and sisters on earth need to be reminded of my friend."*

And he is right. The moment I recorded the conversation with him there came upon me a peace that told me this is what you needed to hear. When you find yourself struggling, humble yourselves.

There is another prayer that we hear during tragedies, and it always hurts our hearts more than you could know. It is the prayer of the arrogant unsaved. Still in the midst of tragedy they are unwilling to accept the loving arms of the savior.

If the editors will allow me, I want to share a reality, stated clearly about Christians but alluded to for the unsaved, namely, that when Christians die, we angels are there to not merely escort you to heaven but to carry you to heaven.[2] *My friends, if we are there to carry you to heaven, what meets the unsaved to carry them to where they will spend eternity? Just think about it.*

Here's my point, even in the midst of being overwhelmed by demons preparing to take this unsaved soul to his resting place too often they still exhibit an arrogance that comes out of his or her mouth, it just astonishes us. The Father is not willing that any should perish[3] *and His arms open until that last moment as Jesus demonstrated on the cross.*[4] *Pride going before a fall*[5] *is never more real than at the time of death. It is such a tragedy and so unnecessary.*

ATTEMPTS AT RESCUE

The tidal wave struck Bolivar just after dark, and in five minutes the Conemaugh rose from six to forty feet and the waters spread out over the whole country. Soon houses began floating down, and clinging to the debris were men, women and children shrieking for aid. A large number of citizens at once gathered on the county bridge, and they were reinforced by a number from Garfield, a town on the opposite side of the river.

They brought a number of ropes and these were thrown over into the boiling [undulating] waters as persons drifted by in efforts to save some poor beings. For half an hour all efforts were fruitless, until at last, when the rescuers were about giving up all hope, a little boy, astride a shingle roof, managed to catch hold of one of the ropes. He caught it under his left

---

[1] 2 Corinthians 7:5-6
[2] Luke 16:22
[3] 2 Peter 3:9
[4] Luke 23:42-43
[5] Proverbs 16:18

arm and was thrown violently against an abutment, but managed to keep hold, and was successfully pulled on to the bridge amid the cheers of the onlookers. His name was Hessler and his rescuer was a trainman named Carney. The lad was at once taken to the town of Garfield and was cared for. The boy was aged about sixteen. His story of the frightful calamity is as follows:

THE ALARM

"With my father I was spending the day at my grandfather's house in Cambria City. In the house at the time were Theodore, Edward and John Kintz, and John Kintz, Jr.; Miss Mary Kintz, Mrs. Mary Kintz, wife of John Kintz, Jr.; Miss Treacy Kintz, Mrs. Rica Smith, John Hirsch and four children, my father and myself. Shortly after five o'clock [3:30] there was a noise of roaring waters and screams of people. We looked out the door and saw persons running. My father told us to never mind, as the waters would not rise further.

"But soon we saw houses being swept away, and then we ran up to the floor above. The house was three stories, and we were at last forced to the top one. In my fright I jumped on the bed. It was an old fashioned one, with heavy posts. The water kept rising and my bed was soon afloat. Gradually it was lifted up. The air in the room grew close and the house was moving. Still the bed kept rising and pressed the ceiling. At last the posts pushed against the plaster. It yielded, and a section of the roof gave way. Then suddenly I found myself on the roof, and was being carried downstream.

SAVED

"After a little this roof began to part, and I was afraid I was going to be drowned, but just then another house with a shingle roof floated by, and I managed to crawl on it, and floated down until nearly dead with cold, when I was saved. After I was freed from the house I did not see my father. My grandfather was on a tree, but he must have been drowned, as the waters were rising fast. John Kintz, Jr., was also on a tree. Miss Mary Kintz and Mrs. Mary Kintz I saw drown. Miss Smith was also drowned. John Hirsch was in a tree, but the four children were drowned. The scenes were terrible. Live bodies and corpses were floating down with me and away from me. I would see persons, hear them shriek, and then they would disappear. All along the line were people who were trying to save us, but they could do nothing, and only a few were caught."

This boy's story is but one incident, and shows what happened to one family. No one knows what has happened to the hundreds who were in the path of the rushing water. It is impossible to get anything in the way of news save meager details.

An eye-witness at Bolivar Block Station tells a story of unparalleled heroism that occurred at the lower bridge which crosses the Conemaugh at this point. A. Young, with two women was seen coming down the river on a part of a floor. At the upper bridge, a rope was thrown down to them. This they all failed to catch. Between the two bridges he was noticed to point towards the elder woman, who, it is supposed, was his mother. He was then seen to instruct the women how to catch the rope that was lowered from the other bridge. Down came the raft with a rush. The brave man stood with his arms around the two women.

UNAVAILING COURAGE

As they swept under the bridge he seized the rope. He was jerked violently away from the two women, who failed to get a hold on the rope. Seeing that they would not be rescued, he dropped the rope and fell back on the raft, which floated on down the river. The current washed their frail craft in toward the bank. The young man was enabled to seize hold of a branch of a tree. He aided the two women to get up into the tree.

He held on with his hands and rested his feet on a pile of driftwood. A piece of floating debris struck the drift, sweeping it away. The man hung with his body immersed in the water. A pile of drift soon collected, and he was enabled to get another insecure footing. Up the river there was a sudden crash, and a section of the bridge was swept away and floated down the stream, striking the tree and washing it away. All three were thrown into the water and were drowned before the eyes of the horrified spectators just opposite the town of Bolivar.

Early in the evening a woman with her two children were seen to pass under the bridge at Bolivar clinging to the roof of a coal house. A rope was lowered to her, but she shook her head and refused to desert the children. It was rumored that all three were saved at Cokeville, a few miles below Bolivar. A later report from Lockport says that the residents succeeded in rescuing five people from the flood, two women and three men. One man succeeded in getting out of the water unaided. They were taken care of by the people of the town.

The railroader below would never know that Gertie had been in the arms of the savior by this time, but her influence on his life is immeasurable. The vision of her would haunt him in his sleep, encourage him during the day, and eventually call him to the ministry with a focus on encouraging prayer everywhere he taught. Many townspeople would be unaccustomed to his poor English and consider him unlearned. And correct they would be. But he would always be known by us in heaven and by the demons in hell as a man constantly contending for his parishioners in his prayers, that they would stand mature and fully assured in everything God willed for them.[1]

In heaven, we see how God uses your events and we see that Romans 8:28 is still true. He works everything out for the better for those who love Him and are called according to His purposes. Why did little Gertie get swept off of the roof she shared with her family as recorded a few pages earlier? I don't know all of the reasons, but I know one. And it begins with a railroad man. There would become many a devoted pray-er[2] due to him, but as you can see now, it would be in part because of little Gertie.

A CHILD'S FAITH

A little girl passed under the bridge just before dark. She was kneeling on a part of a floor and had her hands clasped as if in prayer. Every effort was made to save her, but they all proved futile. A railroader who was standing by remarked that the piteous appearance of the little waif brought tears to his eyes. All night long the crowd stood about the ruins of the bridge which had been swept away at Bolivar. The water rushed past with a roar, carrying with it parts of houses, furniture and trees. The flood had evidently spent its force up the valley. No more living persons were being carried past. Watchers with lanterns remained along the banks until daybreak, when the first view of the awful devastation of the flood was witnessed.

Along the bank lay remnants of what had once been dwelling houses and stores; here and there was an uprooted tree. Piles of drift lay about, in some of which bodies of the victims of the flood will be found. Rescuing parties are being formed in all towns along the railroad. Houses have been

----

[1] Colossians 4:12
[2] Colossians 4:2

thrown open to refugees, and every possible means is being used to protect the homeless.

WRECKING TRAINS TO THE RESCUE

The wrecking trains of the Pennsylvania Railroad are slowly making their way east to the unfortunate city. No effort was being made to repair the wrecks, and the crews of the trains were organized into rescuing parties, and an effort will be made to send out a mail train this morning. The chances are that they will go no further east than Florence. There is absolutely no news from Johnstown. The little city is entirely cut off from communication with the outside world. The damage done is inestimable. No one can tell its extent.

The little telegraph stations along the road are filled with anxious groups of men who have friends and relatives in Johnstown. The smallest item of news is eagerly seized upon and circulated. If favorable they have a moment of relief, if not their faces become more gloomy. Harry Fisher, a young telegraph operator who was at Bolivar when the first rush began, says: "We knew nothing of the disaster until we noticed the river slowly rising and then more rapidly. News then reached us from Johnstown that the dam at South Fork had burst. Within three hours [it actually took less than one hour from moment of the dam breach for] the water in the river to rise at least twenty feet. Shortly before six o'clock ruins of houses, beds, household utensils, barrels and kegs came floating past the bridges. At eight o'clock the water was within six feet of the roadbed of the bridge. The wreckage floated past without stopping for at least two hours. Then it began to lessen, and night coming suddenly upon us we could see no more. The wreckage was floating by for a long time before the first living persons passed. Fifteen people that I saw were carried down by the river. One of these, a boy, was saved, and three of them were drowned just directly below the town. It was an awful sight and one that I will not soon forget."

Hundreds of animals lost their lives. The bodies of horses, dogs and chickens floated past. The little boy who was rescued at Bolivar had two dogs as companions during his fearful ride. The dogs were drowned just before reaching the bridge. One old mule swam past. Its shoulders were torn, but it was alive when swept past the town.

SAVED FROM A WATERY GRAVE TO PERISH BY FLAMES

After a long, weary ride of eight or nine miles over the worst of country roads New Florence, fourteen miles from Johnstown, was reached. The road bed between this place and Bolivar was washed out in many places. The trackmen and the wreck crews were all night in the most dangerous portions of the road.

The last man from Johnstown brought the information that scarcely a house remained in the city. The upper portion above the railroad bridge had been completely submerged. The water dammed up against the viaduct [as its width reduced the water's center, calming the torrent slightly] the wreckage and debris finishing the work that the torrent had failed to accomplish. The bridge at Johnstown proved too stanch for the fury of the water. It is a heavy piece of masonry, and was used as a viaduct by the old Pennsylvania Canal. Some of the top stones were displaced.

The story reached here a short time ago that a family consisting of father and mother and nine children were washed away in a creek at Lockport. The mother managed to reach the shore, but the husband and children were carried out into the Conemaugh to drown. The woman is crazed over the terrible event.

HAEL: JESUS WEPT

Contrary to what you may think I am saying in this book, there is neither a right way, nor a wrong way to walk through disasters. Our Creator God knows each of you personally and intimately and is fully able to walk with you in your incredible pain.

What a tragedy like this tells us is how He truly is alongside you, guarding you along the way so that where you end up, physically, emotionally and spiritually is a location that He has already prepared for you.[1] The issue for you my friend, is to trust God.

Look at the shortest verse in the Bible[2] where Jesus weeps because he sees the pain his friends are going through with the death of Lazarus. Now remember, Jesus had already planned on raising Lazarus from the dead.[3] Why then did He weep? For one reason, because of His empathy for His friends, NOT as I've heard well meaning, but misinformed pastors say, because He didn't want to make Lazarus go through death a second time.

---

[1] Exodus 23:20
[2] John 11:35
[3] John 11:4

41

*Sorry, I got a little distracted there. Here's my point, Jesus wept, and so can you!
Don't let anyone else tell you that you've wept for a loved one long enough. Jesus
knows what you are going through.*

A NIGHT OF HORROR

After night settled down upon the mountains the horror of the scenes was
enhanced. Above the roar of the water could be heard the piteous appeals
from the unfortunate as they were carried by. To add also to the terror of
the night, a brilliant illumination lit up the sky. This illumination could be
plainly seen from this place [fourteen miles from where it burns].

A message received from Sang Hollow stated that this light came from a
hundred burning wrecks of houses that were piled upon the Johnstown
Bridge. A supervisor from up the road brought the information that the
wreckage at Johnstown was piled up forty feet above the bridge.

The startling news came in that more than a thousand lives had been lost.
This cannot be substantiated. By actual count one hundred and ten people
had been seen floating past Sang Hollow before dark. Forty-seven were
counted passing New Florence and the number had diminished to eight at
Bolivar. The darkness coming on stopped any further count, and it was
only by the agonizing cries that rang out above the waters that it was
known that a human being was being carried to death.

AN IRRESISTIBLE TORRENT

The scenes along the river were wild in the extreme. Although the water
was subsiding, still as it dashed against the rocks that filled the narrow
channel of the Conemaugh its spray was carried high up on the shore. The
towns all along the line of the railroad from Johnstown west had received
visitations. Many of the houses in New Florence were partially under
water. At Bolivar, the whole lower part of the town was submerged.

The ride over the mountain road gave one a good idea of the cause of this
disaster. Every creek was a rushing river and every rivulet a raging torrent.
The ground was water soaked, and when the immense mountain district
that drains into the Conemaugh above South Fork is taken into
consideration the terrible volume of water that must have accumulated can
be realized. Gathering, as it did, within a few minutes, it came against the
breast of the South Fork dam with irresistible force. The frightened
inhabitants along the Conemaugh describe the flood as something awful.

The first rise came almost without warning, and the torrent came roaring down the mountain passes in one huge wave, several feet in height [twenty-five to forty feet]. After the first swell the water continued to rise at a fearful rate.

DAYLIGHT BRINGS NO RELIEF

The gray morning light does not seem to show either hope or mitigation of the awful fears of the night. It has been a hard night for everybody. The overworked newspaper men, who have been without rest and food since yesterday afternoon, and the operators who have handled the messages are already preparing for the work of the day. There has been a long wrangle over the possession of a special train for the press between rival newspaper men, and it has delayed the work of others who are anxious to get further east.

Even here, so far from the washed-out towns, seven bodies have been found. Two were in a tree, a man and a woman, where the flood had carried them. The country people are coming into the town in large numbers telling stories of disaster along the river banks in sequestered places.

HAEL: HINDERING THE WORK

I am so glad that this writer brought up this little incident. It went without being reported by most because of the poor light it sheds on the press.

In the USA, during this modern time you have similar issues going on between "powerful-people" who are in the press, in government, and in business. And we see that their selfish actions actually hinder the progress of completing the humanitarian works that need to be accomplished.

I want to discuss this through the grid of Scripture though. I refuse to even think about specific instances. No, the bigger issue is what the Word says. Listen carefully, "Your struggle isn't with flesh and blood."[1] And I know, I experience the same frustration too, you want to look up to God and say, with all due respect, "Father, aren't You listening to this argument. Of course, my struggle is with flesh and blood."

---

[1] Ephesians 6:12

But my friends, this is a spiritual battle, and it is defeated through prayer. So, be a true intercessor who stands in the gap until through you comes the answer.[1] This is how you are to deal with these challenges. I know that it goes completely against the grain of what you want to do, but as someone in your time has said, "you need to learn to eat humble pie" overlooking issues, and trusting God to step in. Remember, His throne is above the heavens and He is sovereign over all.[2] So trust Him!

FLOATING HOUSES

John McCarthey, a carpenter, who lives in Johnstown, reached here about four o'clock. He left Johnstown at half-past four yesterday afternoon and says the scene then was indescribable. The people had been warned early in the morning to move to the highlands, but they did not heed the warning, although it was repeated a number of times up to one o'clock, when the water poured into Cinder street several feet deep [two hours later the dam broke and one hour later a wall of debris followed by water rushed into town].
Then the houses began rocking to and fro, and finally the force of the current carried buildings across streets and vacant lots and dashed them against each other, breaking them into fragments. These building were full of the people who had laughed at the cry of danger. McCarthey says that in some cases he counted as many as fifteen persons clinging to buildings. McCarthey's wife was with him. She had three sisters, who lived near her. They saw the house in which these girls lived carried away, and then they could endure the situation no longer and hurried away. The husband feared his wife would go crazy. They went inland along country roads until they reached here.

It is said to be next to impossible to get to Johnstown proper today in any manner except by rowboat. The roads are cut up so that even the countrymen refuse to travel over them in their roughest vehicles. The only hope is to get within about three miles by a special train or by hand car.

---

[1] Paraphrased Leonard Ravenhill, Revival Praying, Bethany House, 1962, 2005, page 46
[2] Psalm 103:19

This is a very unpopular subject in your time, the 21st Century, because so many people want to stay away from those three difficult words, "I was wrong." But as much as you will not like it, it must be addressed.

A few weeks after the calamity in Johnstown, many will seek reparations from the people who owned the fishing club and were responsible for the dam. I will stay away from the legalese but let me just tell you about a townsman, Mr. Elder who did not put the blame entirely onto the owners of the dam even though he lost a wife, a daughter, a house and everything he owned. He said that the townspeople "have always looked at the dam as a potential problem, so we all must be partially to blame."

This is the very reason Mr. McCarthey's wife is near "going crazy" as of the writing of the original book in 1889.

You would have no way of knowing this, but there was another family in Johnstown by a similar name, the McCarthy's, and they too had four sisters. Let me tell you about them. This Mrs. McCarthy did "go crazy" and spent her remaining days with Mr. McCarthy looking after her 24 hours per day. He could not work and they lived as poor folks until she died many years later.

But now you need to know why this happened. The McCarthy's were seemingly very godly people. He was an elder at the Methodist church and she an organist. They both taught Sunday School and were very well respected in the community.

There were four sisters, the eldest being Mrs. McCarthy. Under the leadership of the two eldest, Mrs. McCarthy and Josephine, the sisters opened a day care. "After all," Mrs. McCarthy would always say, "You never know when Providence might need some help, financially I mean. We're working hard, making money so we can be good stewards of our resources."

Now friends, readers, this would be alright if it were not for her underlying attitude. Slipping into this "holy facade" was a complete and total lack of trust in God. These sisters never accepted the premise that if they sought first His kingdom and His righteousness that He would take care of all of the details[1] in their lives. No! These ladies preferred to worry about every one of their tomorrows today so that the care they gave to the children was horrendous. Let me give you a simple example which is completely cogent to this book. When they did not want the children in their care to get dirty by going too near the streams their retort always centered around the dam.

---

[1] Matthew 6:33

"Don't go out there too close to the creek," they would say, "for the dam may break and you will be washed away!"

Now the unfortunate truth is that the entire town mocked the safety of the dam. Even the few people who formally tried to deal with its safety never brought the issue to a conclusion. Were specific decisions, poorly made, impactful to the dam's safety? Certainly. Could people have been to some extent liable? Absolutely. But were the townspeople also partially to blame? Of course.

Regarding the McCarthy's though, I cannot judge the sisters without casting some of the blame on Mr. McCarthy who refused to see this lack of trust in God in his wife. This seemingly godly couple was not!

How they demonstrated they were not godly is clearly seen by one word. Mrs. McCarthy ushered it out of her mouth over and over again. "Why?"

All she could ever ask the Lord, for years upon years was, "why Lord? Why did You let this happen to me and my sisters?"

This may sound harsh, and so I apologize, but God does NOT owe you an explanation about anything! "Why," is not the question to ask, rather, "What Lord do You want me to learn?"

But there is a reason many people do not ask the "what" question, and it is because it requires them to humble themselves before their Creator. They don't mind giving God advice, but they do not want to give Him permission to tell them ANYTHING He wants to. And this is dangerous. It can end in an unsound mind, as in the case of Mrs. McCarthy.

My utterances about the "why" questions may have eclipsed the point of responsibility I wanted to make here, so hear me clearly. The people of the town were also responsible for they were poor stewards of the town leaders. And in your political climate of the 21st Century this is very apropos.

THE DEAD CAST UP

Nine dead bodies have been picked up within the limits of this borough since daylight. None of them has yet been recognized. Five are women. One woman, probably twenty-five years old, had clasped in her arms a babe about six months old. The body of a young man was discovered in the branches of a huge tree which had been carried down the stream. All the orchard crops and shrubbery along the banks of the river have been destroyed.

The body of another woman has just been discovered in the river here. Her foot was seen above the surface of the water and a rope was fastened about it.

A ROOF AS A RAFT

John Weber and his wife, an old couple, Michael Metzgar and John Forney were rescued near here early this morning. They had been carried from their home in Cambria City on the roof of the house. There were seven others on the roof when it was carried off, all of whom were drowned. They were unknown to Weber, having drifted on to the roof from floating debris. Weber and wife were thoroughly drenched and were almost helpless from exposure. They were unable to walk when taken off the roof at this place. They are now at the hotel here.

Hundreds of people from Johnstown and up river towns are hurrying here in search of friends and relatives who were swept away in last night's flood. The most intense excitement prevails. The street corners are crowded with pale and anxious people who tell of the calamity with bated breath. Squire Bennett has charge of the dead bodies, and he is having them properly cared for. They are being prepared for burial, but will be held here for identification.

Four boys, have just come from the river bank above here. They say that on the opposite side a number of bodies can be seen lying in the mud. They found the body of a woman on this side badly bruised.

R. B. Rodgers, Justice of the Peace at Nineveh, has wired the Coroner at Greensburg that one hundred dead bodies have been found at that place, and he asks what is to be done with them. From this one can estimate that the loss of life will reach over one thousand [the official count will be just over 2200 dead].

A report has just been received that twenty persons are on an island near Nineveh and that men and women are on a partly submerged tree.

A report has just reached here that at least one hundred people were consumed in the flames at Johnstown last night, but it cannot be verified here. The air is filled with thrilling and most incredible stories, but none of them have as yet been confirmed. It is certain, however, that even the worst cannot be imagined.

Warnings Remembered Too Late

It is very evident that more lives have been lost because of foolish incredulity than from ignorance of the danger. For more than a year there have been fears of an accident of just such a character. The foundations of the dam were considered to be shaky early last spring and many increasing leakages were reported from time to time.

According to people who live in Johnstown and other towns on the line of the river, ample time was given to the Johnstown folks by the railroad officials and by other gentlemen of standing and reputation. In dozens, yes, hundreds of cases, this warning was utterly disregarded, and those who heeded it early in the day were looked upon as cowards, and many jeers were uttered by lips that now are cold among the rank grass beside the river.

There has grown up a bitter feeling among the surviving sufferers against those who owned the lake and dam, and damage suits will be plentiful by and by.

The dam in Stony Creek, above Johnstown, broke about noon yesterday and thousands of feet of lumber passed down the stream. It is impossible to tell what the loss of life will be, but at nine o'clock the Coroner of Westmoreland county sent a message out saying that 100 bodies had been recovered at Nineveh, halfway from here to Johnstown. Sober minded people do not hesitate to say that 1,200 is moderate.

HAEL: TIME OF DAM BREAK

The dam actually broke at about 3:15 and emptied the lake in 36 minutes. The velocity of water leaving the lake has been likened to the velocity of water at Niagara Falls. Saying it another way, the water that headed toward Johnstown below would have been gushing down the valley like the running of Niagara Falls for 36 minutes.[1]

There is another point that history speaks to which this writer could not know. Namely, there would be very few lawsuits and none of them would win over the owners of the club on Lake Conemaugh.

---

[1] The Johnstown Flood, David McCullough, Simon & Schuster, 1968

FIRE'S AWFUL WORK

"How can anybody tell how many are dead?" said a railroad engineer this morning. "I have been at Long Hollow with my train since eleven o'clock yesterday, and I have seen fully five hundred persons lost in the flood."

J. W. Esch, a brave railroad employee, saved sixteen lives at Nineveh.

The most awful culmination of the awful night was the roasting of a hundred or more persons in mid-flood. The ruins of houses, old buildings and other structures swept against the new railroad bridge at Johnstown, and from an overturned stove or some such cause the upper part of the wreckage caught fire.

There were crowds of men, women and children on the wreck, and their screams were soon heard. They were literally roasted on the flood. Soon after the fire burned itself out other persons were thrown against the mass. There were some fifty people in sight where the ruins suddenly broke up and were swept under the bridge into the darkness.

The latest news from Johnstown is that but two houses could be seen in the town. It is also said that only three houses remain in Cambria City.

The first authentic news was from W. N. Hays, of the Pennsylvania Railroad Company, who reached New Florence at nine o'clock. He says the valley towns are annihilated.

DESTRUCTION AT BLAIRSVILLE

The flood in the Conemaugh River at this point is the heaviest ever known here. At this hour the railroad bridge between here and Blairsville intersection has been swept away, and also the new bridge at Coketon, half a mile below. It is now feared that the iron bridge at the lower end of this town will go. A living woman and dead man, supposed to be her husband, were seen going under the railroad bridge. They were seen to come from under the bridge safely, but shortly disappeared and were seen no more.

A great many families lose their household goods. The river is running full of timber, houses, goods, etc. The loss will be heavy. The excitement here is very great. The river is still rising. There are some families below the town in the second story of their houses who cannot get out. It is feared that if the water goes much higher the loss of life will be very great. The railroad company had fourteen cars of coal on their bridge when it went down, and all were swept down the river.

The town bridge has just succumbed to the seething floods, whose roar can be heard a long distance. The water is still rising and it is thought that the West Pennsylvania Railroad will be without a single bridge. It is reported that a man went down with the Blairsville bridge while he was adjusting a headlight.

Havoc about Altoona

The highest and most destructive flood that has visited this place for fifty years occurred yesterday. It has been raining continuously for the past twenty-four hours. The Juniata river is ten feet above low water mark and is still rising. The lower streets of Gaysport bordering on the river bank are submerged, and the water is two feet deep on the first floors of the houses there. The water rose so rapidly that the people had to be removed from the houses in boats and wagons. Three railroad trestles and a number of bridges over the streams have been carried away, and railroad travel between this place and the surrounding towns has been interrupted.

Property of all kinds was carried off. The truck gardens and grain fields along the river were utterly destroyed, and the fences carried away. The iron furnaces and rolling mills at this place and Duncanville were compelled to shut down on account of the high water. Keene & Babcock lost 300,000 brick in the kiln ready to burn, G. W. Rhodes 350,000, and Joseph Hart I5,000. It is estimated that the flood has done over $50,000 damage in this vicinity. The fences of the Blair County Agricultural Society were destroyed.

Hael: Barn Building

Luke records for us a very salient parable. Let me just place it here:

[16] Then He told them a parable: "A rich man's land was very productive. [17] He thought to himself, 'What should I do, since I don't have anywhere to store my crops? [18] I will do this,' he said. 'I'll tear down my barns and build bigger ones and store all my grain and my goods there. [19] Then I'll say to myself, you have many goods stored up for many years. Take it easy; eat, drink, and enjoy yourself.'

[20] "But God said to him, 'You fool! This very night your life is demanded of you. And the things you have prepared—whose will they be?'

---

[1] Editor's Note: Approximately $1,250,000 in 2018 dollars.

[21] "That's how it is with the one who stores up treasure for himself and is not rich toward God."[1]

When you read this passage, the focus is clear, namely, "Where do you put your trust?"

Notice Jesus' words before the parable and after the parable. He's teaching on what you are putting your trust in, the things of this world, IE other people's opinion[2], one's inheritance[3] and worry over the basics of life[4].

Let me finish with what Jesus said because I think this sums it all up: "For where your treasure is, there your heart will be also."[5]

ALARM AT YORK

Last night was one of great alarm here. It rained steadily all day, some of the showers being severe. The great flood of 1884 is forcibly recalled. Many families are moving out. At half-past one A. M. a general alarm was sounded on the bells of the city.

The flood in the Susquehanna River here reached its greatest height about six o'clock this morning, when all bridges save one were under water. Business places and residences in the low section were flooded to a great extent, and the damage in this city alone amounts to $25,000 so far. The injury to the Spring Grove paper mills near this city is heavy. By noon the water had fallen sufficiently to restore travel over nearly all the bridges.

A number of bridges in the county have been swept away, and the loss in the county exclusive of the city is estimated at $100,000.

In attempting to catch some driftwood James McIlvaine lost his balance and fell into the raging current and was drowned.

Seven bodies have been taken from the water and debris on the river banks at New Florence. One body has also been taken from the river at this point, that of a young girl. None of them have been identified.

The whole face of the country between here and New Florence is under water, and houses, bridges and buildings fill the fields and even perch upon

---

[1] Luke 12:16-21 (HCSB)
[2] Luke 12:8-12
[3] Luke 12:13-15
[4] Luke 12:22-34
[5] Luke 12:34

the hillside all the way to Johnstown. Great flocks of crows are already filling the valley, while buzzards are almost as frequently seen. The banks of the river are lined with people who are looking as well for booty as for bodies. Much valuable property was carried away in the houses as well as from houses not washed away.

The river has fallen again into its channel, and nothing in the stream itself except its red, angry color shows the wild horror of last night. It has fallen fully twenty feet since midnight, and by tonight it will have attained its normal depth.

HAEL: LOOTING

As mentioned earlier, there are a number of things that I will delete as the records do not show the accusations made in 1889 to be true. But the reality of looting is evident, both here in 1889 and in Houston in 2017. So, what do we do about it?

Answer? A little later in this book you will read about Mordechai Milford and how he dealt with the following precept, promise and prayer from the Word and then his prayer based on what he learned.

Precept (Principle)

Let him that stole steal no more: but rather let him labour, working with his hands the thing which is good, that he may have to give to him that needeth.[1]

Promise (from God)

I have shewed you all things, how that so labouring ye ought to support the weak, and to remember the words of the Lord Jesus, how He said, It is more blessed to give than to receive.[2]

Prayer (to God)

Remember not the sins of my youth, nor my transgressions.[3]

Oh Lord, thank You for the labor that You have given me to do, whether it be glamorous or not isn't the point, that I have the opportunity to take care of my needs, and those of some others, I thank You. What I have done in the past, You

------

[1] Ephesians 4:28
[2] Acts 20:35
[3] Psalm 25:7

have forgiven me of, what I do now, I do to be the good steward that You have called me to.

I think Mordechai's story (coming later) will add some specific insight to the reality of tragedies.

PAINFUL SCENES

At all points from Greensburg to Long Hollow, the limit of the present trouble, scores of people throng the stations begging and beseeching railroad men on the repair trains to take them aboard, as they are almost frenzied with anxiety and apprehension in regard to their friends who live at or near Johnstown. Strong men are as tearful as the women who join in the request.

Pitiable sights and scenes multiply more and more rapidly. The Conemaugh is one great valley of mourning. Those who have not lost friends have lost their house or their substance, and apparently the grief for the one is as poignant as for the other.

THEY WERE WARNED

The great volume of water struck Johnstown about half-past five in the afternoon [actually shortly after 4:00]. It did not find the people unprepared, as they had had notice from South Fork that the dam was threatening to go. Many, however, disregarded the notice and remained in their houses in the lower part of the city and were caught before they could get out.

Superintendent Pitcairn, of the Pennsylvania Railroad, who has spent the entire day in assisting not only those who were afflicted by the flood, but also in an attempt to reopen his road, went home this morning. Before he left he issued an order to all Pennsylvania Railroad employees to keep a sharp lookout for bodies, both in the river and in the bushes, and to return them to their friends.

Assistant Superintendent Trump is still on the ground near Lone Hollow directing the movements of gravel and construction trains, which are arriving as fast as they can be fitted up and started out. The roadbeds of both the Pennsylvania and the West Pennsylvania railroads are badly damaged, and it will cost the latter, especially from the Bolivar Junction to

Saltsburg, many thousands of dollars to repair injuries to embankments alone.

In Pittsburg, there was but one topic of conversation, and that was the Johnstown deluge. Crowds of eager watchers all day long besieged the newspaper bulletin boards and rendered streets impassable in their vicinity. Many of them had friends or relatives in the stricken district, and "Names!" "Names!" was their cry. But there were no names. The storm which had perhaps swept away their loved ones had also carried away all means of communication and their vigil was unrewarded. It is not yet known whether the telegraph operator at Johnstown is dead or alive. The nearest point to that city which can be reached tonight is New Florence, and the one wire there is used almost constantly by orders for coffins, embalming fluid and preparing special cars to carry the recovered dead to their homes.

Along the banks of the now turbulent Allegheny were placed watchers for dead bodies, and all wreckage was carefully scanned for the dead. The result of this vigilance was the recovery of one body, that of a woman floating down on a pile of debris. Seven other bodies were seen, but could not be reached owing to the swift moving wreckage by which they were surrounded.

A HEARTRENDING SIGHT

A railroad conductor who arrived in the city this morning said: "There is no telling how many lives are lost. We got as far as Bolivar, and I tell you it is a terrible sight. The body of a boy was picked up by some of us there, and there were eleven bodies recovered altogether. I do not think that anyone got into Johnstown, and it is my opinion that they will not get in very soon. No one who is not on the grounds has any idea of the damage done. It will be at least a week before the extent of this flood is known, and then I think many bodies will never be recovered."

Assistant Superintendent Wilson, of the West Pennsylvania Railroad, received the following dispatch from Nineveh today:

"There appears to be a large number of people lodged in the trees and rubbish along the line. Many are alive. Rescuing parties should be advised at every station."

Another telegram from Nineveh said that up to noon 175 bodies had been taken from the river at that point. The stage of water in the Allegheny this afternoon became so alarming that residents living in the low-lying district began to remove their household effects to a higher grade. The tracks of the Pittsburgh and Western Railroad are under water in several places, and great inconvenience is felt in moving trains.

CRIMINAL NEGLIGENCE

It was stated at the office of the Pennsylvania Railroad early this morning that the deaths would run up into the thousands rather than hundreds, as was at first supposed. Dispatches received state that the stream of human beings that was swept before the floods was pitiful to behold. Men, women and children were carried along frantically shrieking for help. Rescue was impossible.

Husbands were swept past their wives, and children were borne along at a terrible speed to certain death before the eyes of their terrorized and frantic parents. It was said at the depot that it was impossible to estimate the number whose lives were lost in the flood. It will simply be a matter of conjecture for several days as to who was lost and who escaped.

The people of Johnstown were warned of the possibility of the bursting of the dam during the morning, but very few if any of the inhabitants took the warning seriously. Shortly after noon [actually 3:15] it gave Way about five miles [as the crow flies but 14 miles per the route of the river] above Johnstown, and sweeping everything before it burst upon the town with terrible force [after this wall of water had slammed and pushed its way thru four previous towns, carrying these town's debris in front of its wake as it reached Johnstown].

Everything was carried before it, and not an instant's time was given to seek safety. Houses were demolished, swept from their foundations and carried in the flood to a culvert near the town. Here a mass of all manner of debris soon lodged, and by evening it had dammed the water back into the city over the tops of many of the still remaining chimneys.

THE DAM ALWAYS A MENACE

Assistant Superintendent Trump, of the Pennsylvania, is at Conemaugh, but the officials at the depot had not been able to receive a line from him until as late as half-past two o'clock this morning. It was said also that it will be impossible to get a train through either one way or the other for at least two or three days. This applies also to the mails, as there is absolutely no way of getting mails through.

"We were afraid of that lake," said a gentleman who had lived in Johnstown for years, "we were afraid of that lake seven years ago. No one could see the immense height to which that artificial dam had been built without fearing the tremendous power of the water behind it. I doubt if there was a man or woman in Johnstown who at some time or other had not feared and spoken of the terrible disaster that has now come.

"People wondered and asked why the dam was not strengthened, as it certainly had become weak, but nothing was done, and by and by they talked less and less about it as nothing happened, though now and then some would shake their heads as though conscious that the fearful day would come some time when their worst fears would be transcended by the horror of the actual occurrence.

CONVERTED INTO A LAKE

"Johnstown is in a hollow between two rivers, and that lake must have swept over the city at a depth of forty feet. It cannot be, it is impossible, that such an awful thing could happen to a city of ten thousand inhabitants, and if it has, thousands have lost their lives, and men are to blame for it, for warnings have been uttered a thousand times and have received no attention."

The body of a Welsh woman, sixty years of age, was taken from the river near the suspension bridge, at ten o'clock this morning. Four other bodies were seen but owing to the mass of wreckage which is coming down they could not be recovered, and passed down the Ohio River.

A citizens' meeting has been called to devise means to aid the sufferers. The Pennsylvania Railroad officials have already placed cars on Liberty street for the purpose of receiving provisions and clothing, and up to this hour many prominent merchants have made heavy donations.

HAEL: DONATION

When word of the tragedy in Johnstown reached Pittsburgh, Thaddeus Beaulton, the owner of Beaulton's Mercantile was counting his meager income for the day. This was the sixth day in a row of extremely low sales. The rainy season this year had been bad and rain always adversely affected income.

He had mortgaged his home this year, for this was now the third year running where weather was bad. When he and his wife Abigail built their home they both agreed that they would never mortgage it, for they had each seen their parents lose their homes when they could not pay their mortgage. However, this next month's payment would barely be made. If sales remained like this they would not make the following month's payment.

So when word of the South Fork dam break and all of the incredible devastation and need reached his ears, a demon sidled up alongside and whispered gently, as an angel of light,[1] "do you see how god has supplied for your needs?"

Putting aside his accounting and furrowing his brow Thaddeus Beaulton arose and allowed himself to devise a plan to help financially secure himself, his wife, and his family. After all, "Providence had answered his prayers for help."

He sent a message home to his wife informing her that he would be working late tonight. As the plan formed in his mind and the arguments in his brain grew and grew, they eclipsed rational thinking and rather than sensing the Holy Spirit pricking his heart, he took that "uncomfortableness" as reassurance that he moved, "in God's will," after all, "this was God's provision for him."

He had no idea that what was really occurring had to do with his own high-minded ideas being raised against the knowledge of what God would have him do. And far from taking these thoughts captive, instead he encouraged the thoughts in his mind.[2]

On Saturday morning, June 1ˢᵗ, he was up early, smiling cheerfully while reading a new early edition of the Pittsburgh Dispatch and all of the horrors then known of the death and destruction up-river from Pittsburgh.

His wife, noticing his excitement and not knowing about the tragedy yet, welcomed him to the table for breakfast. "Oh, my husband, it is good to see you smiling before work for a change. You have been so upset these last few weeks. I am praying for you."

And with that she kissed him on the top of the head as he sat down to eat. She entered the kitchen to refill his coffee and when she returned he had already finished eating and put on his hat and raincoat. Sensing the need to allow him to go, she said, "good-bye my husband. I will be in the store soon."

He rushed out the door with his coffee and a grunt, saying something about expecting to be busy today.

Sitting down to open her Bible and pray she found herself in Acts chapter twenty. Ever since reading her fellow countryman's story, The Autobiography of

---

[1] 2 Corinthians 11:14
[2] 2 Corinthians 10:5

George Müeller, she began each day with her Bible open, letting the Word of God direct her prayers, just as he had.

Today, as she found herself watching Paul say goodbye to his Ephesian friends,[1] it was not until verse thirty-five that she sensed the Lord focusing her thoughts.

Just then, as if being struck across the side of the head she immediately thought of Thaddeus, "you must hurry to the store, he needs your help."

As she started to close her Bible and get up the feeling urgency eased for a moment and going back to the verse she reread it, the only words she saw were, ". . . labouring ye ought to support the weak, and to remember the words of the Lord Jesus, how He said, It is more blessed to give than to receive."[2]

"Oh Lord," she got to her knees, "what are You trying to teach me? What do You not want me to miss?"

Staying on her knees in silence she waited on the Lord for what seemed like minutes when one of her children bounded into the sitting room. "Odd," she thought, for her children were never up this early on a Saturday. "Hmm," she continued, "what meaneth this?"

Getting up to take care of her children's breakfast she briefly saw the newspaper and its headline, something about a tragedy. The children continued to make their way downstairs and so she took no more notice of the article, except to acknowledge a small check in her spirit.

Ninety minutes later she crossed from the residences into downtown, walking toward their store. As she approached she saw a large sign in front of the store, "Help Flood Victims, Reduced Costs For You To Give."

Very proud of her husband Mrs. Beaulton walked into the store with a smile on her face. Her husband, surrounded by many people there to purchase and give as much as they could, looked up at her with a wary face. She didn't know why, but again, she felt a strange check in her spirit. Taking a quick look around and assessing the needs she immediately headed for the back storage to get more blankets, cooking utensils and first-aid equipment boxes which were nearly depleted. As she stocked the items the signage caught her eye, again causing an odd troubling in her heart. But she needed to keep moving.

Next, she brought out additional bolts of cloth, and then she saw it. She stopped and froze and looked questioningly at a husband who had seen her reaction. She

---

[1] Acts 20:17
[2] Acts 20:35

saw him immediately drop his gaze from her face. The entire day they scarcely said a word to each other.

She knew what he had done, and he knew that she knew what he had done.

All day long in his inner ear he kept replaying the argument, "god has provided this situation for you, Thaddeus."

And all the while in her inner ear she kept hearing the same thing. But each time she heard it she remembered her prayer verse today, ". . . labouring ye ought to support the weak, and to remember the words of the Lord Jesus, how He said, It is more blessed to give than to receive." Each time this verse returned to her she started to become angry at her husband, and just as quickly she remembered Ephesians 6:12 and would tell herself, "My struggle isn't with Thaddeus, my struggle isn't with Thaddeus."

At one point after lunch she could hardly contain herself and went outside, into the rain, crossing the street, and turning she looked back at the building and the huge sign. Looking up to God she nearly screamed, "Of course my struggle is with flesh and blood Lord, look what he has done!" Not content to stop she went on, "Father of all, my creator and sustainer, He has raised the prices on EVERYTHING IN THE STORE. He has lied to our customers and friends. How could you let him do this?"

Now exhausted she headed back to the store, "Lord, I am sorry, what would You have me to do?"

Throughout the rest of the day, her continual refrain when anger arose in her became the same thing, "Oh Lord, that is not where You want my thoughts. Where would You have my thoughts?"

And at the end of the day, just as she picked up her coat and hat from the storage room, it seemed the Lord said, "This is what I would have you do. . ."

Just then a loud knocking came from the back door. As she opened the door, Mr. Fletcher stood there with two wagon loads of goods. "Mr. Beaulton sent a message to me in a rush this afternoon to bring him supplies to replenish what had been sold today."

As he paused, the calm wife said, "Oh Mr. Fletcher, there has been some mistake, these goods were to be taken to the Pennsylvania Railroad car that is collecting merchandise for the flood victims. My husband wanted to donate it. Let me sign for it and I will trust you to take it there for us. Can you do that? My husband is so busy he cannot get to it."

Surprised, and then a little bewildered Mr. Fletcher said, "Mrs. Beaulton, I do declare, I am honored to be your friend. Yes, I will take care of this for you."

And with that she left, through the front door, smiling to her husband for the first time today. Noticing her smile he breathed a sigh of relief.

"Oh, I am so glad she is no longer mad at me," he said to himself.

Some hours passed by when a sheepish Mr. Beaulton finally came home. The kids were reading the Bible with their mother and all jumped up to hug him. He sat on the floor with them, something noticed by his wife for he rarely did that. And as the children were reading, they passed the large family Bible for him to read. Although lost in thought he picked up exactly where they left off.

Acts chapter twenty, verse thirty-five, ". . . labouring ye ought to support the weak, and to remember the words of the Lord Jesus, how He said, It is more blessed to give than to receive."

Breathing deeply his throat started to constrict and he lowered his head and stopped reading. After a pause he asked his children to explain the meaning of the verse, a tear escaped his eye as they spoke. And when they had finished giving their understanding of the verse he looked at all of them and said, "I am very proud of you for trusting the Lord to give us the opportunity to give to those less fortunate than us." And then looking at his quiet, humble wife he said again, "I am very proud of you."

And somewhere in the unseen world two opposite reactions occurred. In one case a demon stomped off cursing and in the other, an angel wiped a tear from his eye.

ANXIETY OF THE PEOPLE

The difficulty of obtaining definite information added tremendously to the [anxious] excitement and apprehension of the people in Pittsburgh who had relatives and friends at the scene of the disaster.

Members of the South Fork Club, and among them some of the most eminent men in the Pittsburgh financial and mercantile world, were in or near Johnstown, and several of them were accompanied by their wives and families. There happened to be also quite a number of residents of Johnstown in Pittsburgh, and when the news of the horror was confirmed, and the railroads bulletined the fact that no trains would go east, the scene at Union Depot was profoundly pathetic and exciting. But two trains were sent out by the Pennsylvania road from the Union station at Pittsburgh.

A dispatch states that the Cambria Iron Company's plant on the north side of the Conemaugh River at Johnstown is a complete wreck. Until this dispatch was received it was not thought that this portion of the plant had been seriously injured. It was known that the portion of the plant located on the south bank of the river was washed away, and this was thought to be the extent of the damage to the property of that immense corporation. The plant is said to be valued at $5,000,000[1].

CHAPTER II
Death and Desolation

The terrible situation on the second day after the great disaster only intensifies the horror. As information becomes more full and accurate, it does not abate one tittle of the awful havoc. Rather it adds to it, and gives a thousand-fold terror to the dreadful calamity.

Not only do the scenes which are described appear all the more dreadful, as is natural, the nearer they are brought to the imagination, but it seems only too probable that the final reckoning in loss of life and material wealth will prove far more stupendous than has even yet been supposed.

The very greatness of the destruction prevents the possibility of an accurate estimate. Beneath the ghastly ruins of the once happy towns and villages along the pathway of the deluge, who shall say how many victims lie buried? Amid the rocks and woods that border the broad track of the waters, who shall say how many lie bruised and mangled and unrecognizable, wedged between boulders or massed amid debris and rubbish, or hidden beneath the heaped-up deposits of earth, and whether all of them shall ever be found and given the last touching rites?

Already the air of the little valley, which four days ago was smiling with all the health of nature and the contentment of industrious man, is waxing pestiferous with the awful odor of decaying human bodies. Buzzards, invited by their disgusting instinct, gather for a promised feast, and sit and glower on neighboring perches or else circle round and round in the blue empyrean over the location of unfriended corpses, known only to their keen sense of smell or vision.

But another kind of buzzard, more disgusting, more hideous, more vile, has hastened to this scene of woe and anguish and desolation to exult over it to his profit. Thugs and thieves in unclean hordes have mysteriously turned up at Johnstown and its vicinity, as hyenas in the desert seem to spring bodily out of the deadly sand whenever the corpse of a gallant warrior, abandoned by his kind, lies putrefying in the night.

There is a cry from the afflicted community for the policing of the devastated region, and there is no doubt it is greatly needed.

Yet, as simply told as possible, there are many incidents of this great tragedy which nothing has ever surpassed or ever can surpass in impressiveness. It is a consolation, too, that human nature at such times does betray here and there a gleam of that side of it which gives forth a reflection of the ideal manhood or womanhood. Bits of heroism and of tender devotedness scattered throughout this dark, dismal picture of destruction and despair light it up with wonderful beauty, and while they bring tears to the eyes of the sternest reader, will serve as a grateful relief from the pervading hue of horror and blackness.

There is the very gravest need of vigorous relief measures in favor of the survivors of the flood. A spontaneous movement in that direction has been begun, but as yet lacks the efficiency only to be derived from a general and organized cooperation.

COMPLETE ANNIHILATION

When Superintendent Pitcairn telegraphed from Johnstown to Pittsburgh Friday night that the town was annihilated he came very close to the facts of the case, although he had not seen the ill-fated city. To say that Johnstown is a wreck is but stating the facts of the case. Nothing like it was ever seen in this country. Where long rows of dwelling houses and business blocks stood forty-eight hours ago, ruin and desolation now reign supreme.

The losses, however, are as nothing compared to the frightful sacrifices of precious human lives. During Sunday, Johnstown has been drenched with the tears of stricken mortals, and the air is filled with sobs that come from breaking hearts. There are scenes enacted here every hour and every minute that affect all beholders profoundly. When brave men die in battle, for country or for principle, their loss can be reconciled to the stern destinies of life. When homes are torn asunder in an instant, and the loved ones hurled from the arms of loving and devoted mothers, there is an element of sadness connected with the tragedy that touches every heart.

The loss of life is simply dreadful. The most conservative people declare that the number will reach 5000, while others confidently assert that 8000 or 10,000 have perished.

HOW JOHNSTOWN LOOKS AFTER FLOOD AND FIRE HAVE DONE THEIR WORST

An eye-witness writing from Pittsburgh says: We have just returned from a trip through what is left of Johnstown. The view from beyond is almost impossible to describe. To look upon it is a sight that neither war nor catastrophe can equal. House is piled upon house, not as we have seen in occasional floods of the Western rivers, but the remains of two and four storied buildings piled upon the top of one another.

The ruins of what is known as the Club House are in perhaps the best condition of any in that portion of the town, but it is certainly damaged beyond possibility of repair. On the upper floor five bodies are lying unidentified. One of them, a woman of genteel birth, judging by her dress, is locked in one of the small rooms to prevent a possibility of spoliation by wreckers, who are flocking to the spot from all directions and taking possession of everything they can get hold of.

Here and there bodies can be seen sticking in the ruins. Some of the most prominent citizens are to be seen working with might and main to get at the remains of relatives whom they have located.

There is no doubt that, wild as the estimates of the loss of life and damage to property hive been, it is even larger than there is any idea of.

Close on to 2,000 residences lie in kindling wood at the lower end of the town.

FREAKS OF THE FLOOD

An idea of the eccentricity of the flood may be gathered from the fact that houses that were situated at Woodvale and points above Johnstown are piled at the lower end of the town, while some massive houses have been lifted and carried from the lower end as far as the cemetery at the extreme upper portion of the town. All through the ruin are scattered the most costly furniture and store goods of all kinds.

THIEVES ARE BUSY

I stood on the keyboard and strings of a piano while I watched a number of thieves break into the remnants of houses and pilfer them, while others again had got at a supply of fine groceries and had broken into a barrel of fine brandy, and were fairly steeping themselves in it. I met quite a number of Pittsburghers in the ruins looking for friends and relatives. If the skiffs which were expected from Pittsburgh were there they would be of vast assistance in reaching the ruins, which are separated by the stream of water descending from the hills. A great fear is felt that there will be some difficulty in restoring the stream to its proper channel. Its course now lies right along Main street, and it is about two hundred yards wide.

Something should be done to get the bodies of the dead decently taken care of. The ruins are reeking with the smell of decaying bodies. Right at the edge of the ruins the decaying body of a stout woman is lying like the remains of an animal, without any one to identify and take care of it.

FIENDS IN HUMAN FORM

To one who saw bright, bustling Johnstown a week ago the sight of its present condition must cause an [anxious] thrill of horror, no matter how callous he might be. I doubt if any incident of war or flood ever caused a more sickening sight. Wretchedness of the most pathetic kind met the gaze on every side.

Unfaithfulness runs riot. If ever military aid was needed now is the time. The town is perfectly overrun with thieves, many of them from Pittsburgh. They seem to operate in regular organized bands. In Cambria City, this morning they entered a house, drove out the occupants at the point of revolvers and took possession. They can be constantly seen carrying large quantities of plunder to the hills.

The number of drunken men is remarkable. Whiskey seems marvelously plenty. Men are actually carrying it around in pails. Barrels of the stuff are constantly located among the drifts, and men are scrambling over each other and fighting like wild beasts in their mad search for it.

At the cemetery, at the upper end of the town, I saw a sight that rivals the inferno. A number of ghouls had found a lot of fine groceries, among them a barrel of brandy, with which they were fairly stuffing themselves. One huge fellow was standing on the strings of an upright piano singing a profane song, every little while breaking into a wild dance. A half dozen others were engaged in a hand-to-hand fight over the possession of some treasure stolen from a ruined house, and the crowd around the barrel were yelling like wild men.

The cry for help increases every hour.

HAEL: THE DEMONIC HORDE

And the demonic horde is seen by us in the realm that your humanity does not see. To watch them influence men to drink, as you would say in the 21st century, "get stinking drunk" so that these men cannot help the people that are dying, is a constant battle in our minds.

Often I want the Lord to just send the demons to their final home, their final place of torment. But I hold my tongue (this is becoming more autobiographical than I'm comfortable with) because I trust the Creator, my Almighty God and your Father. I have seen Him take completely worthless men and make them fishers of men.

So I trust that He works all things for the better, for those who love Him and are called to His purposes.[1] There are many men in heaven that submitted themselves to the Lord, even after the evil ones deceived them into drink.

Yet though I have quoted this verse I am reminded that it does not hold true to those who never submit themselves to the Messiah Jesus. While there may be many in heaven whose lives were changed after the demons deceived them into drink, there are many in hell who cannot say that things worked out for the better for them.

WATCHED THEIR FRIENDS DIE

The fire in the drift above the bridge is still burning fiercely and will continue to do so for several days. The skulls of six people can be seen sticking up out of the ruins just above the east end of the bridge. Nothing but the blackened skulls can be seen. They are all together.

The sad scenes will never all be written. One lady told me this morning of seeing her mother crushed to pieces just before her eyes and the mangled body carried off down the stream. William Varner lost six children and saved a baby about eighteen months old. His wife died just three weeks ago. An aged German, his wife and five daughters floated down on their house to a point below Nineveh, where the house was wrecked. The five daughters were drowned, but the old man and his wife stuck in a tree and hung there for twenty-four hours before they could be taken off.

DIED KISSING HER BABE

One of the most pitiful sights of this terrible disaster came to my notice this afternoon, when the body of a young lady was taken out of the Conemaugh River. The woman was apparently quite young, though her features were terribly disfigured. Nearly all the clothing except the shoes was torn off the body. The corpse was that of a mother, for although cold in death the woman clasped a young male babe apparently not more than a

---

[1] Romans 8:28

year old, tightly in her arms. The little one was huddled close up to its mother's face, who when she realized their terrible fate: had evidently raised the babe to her lips to imprint upon its little lips the last motherly kiss it was to receive in this world. The sight was a pathetic one and turned many a stout heart to tears.

Among the miraculous escapes to be recorded in connection with the great disaster is that of George J. Leas and his family. He resided on Iron street. When the rush of water came there were eight people on the roof. The little house swung around off its moorings and floated about for nearly half an hour before it came up against the bank of drift above the stone bridge. A three-year-old girl with sunny golden hair and dimpled cheeks prayed all the while that God would save them, and it seemed that God really answered the prayer of this innocent little girl and directed the house against the drift, enabling every one of the eight to get off. Mrs. Leas carried the little girl in her arms, and how she got off she doesn't know. Every house around them, she said, was crushed, and the people either killed or drowned.

HAEL: INCREDULOUS ABOUT PRAYER

Even as I pause here to insert a few lines I hear my editors saying, "Hael, be careful what you write."

The author of this rewrite, the one who introduced me to the world in his first novel, The Pray-ers likes to say when he preaches, "The unsaved will act like the unsaved, expect them to. Our concern is with the Christians who act like the unsaved."

It is surprising to me how often the above example played out during this horrific devastation. Let me tell you about Brother Hannity who lived in the area of Johnstown that was well up the hill. Being secure in their location, when the flooding started in the morning and then continued into the afternoon he and his wife Geraldine did not vary their structured life. Just before supper they sat in their family circle to review the week's memory verses. It appeared that little Martha had memorized the passage and she was sharing it with the family when the yelling and screaming began. As people ran by their home and saw them sitting in their entry near the log fire, they yelled for them to take to the hills. But arrogant Bro. Hannity and Sis. Geraldine reassured the children that everything would be fine, so they moved not!

They moved not, until the forces of nature moved them. And with one swift movement their sturdy home was moving upon the waters. As one they all ran to the top floor where they were able to climb out onto the roof. As the waters of the massive flood continued into the valley, pulling the little home along with it, the entire family yelled and screamed for help. The entire family, that is, except young Martha. Since the house was not bobbing up and down much she got onto her knees and prayed her memory verses. . .

[2]And Jesus called a little child unto Him, and set him in the midst of them, [3]And said, Verily I say unto you, Except ye be converted, and become as little children, ye shall not enter into the kingdom of heaven. [4]Whosoever therefore shall humble himself as this little child, the same is greatest in the kingdom of heaven.[1]

[1]I love the Lord, because He hath heard my voice and my supplications. [2]Because He hath inclined His ear unto me, therefore will I call upon Him as long as I live. [3]The sorrows of death compassed me, and the pains of hell got hold upon me: I found trouble and sorrow.[2]

Listening to her daughter babble on Sis. Gertrude turned to yell at her daughter to shut up but this impetuous little girl continued, giving no heed to her mother's gesticulations.

[4]Then called I upon the name of the Lord; O Lord, I beseech Thee, deliver my soul. [5]Gracious is the Lord, and righteous; yea, our God is merciful. [6]The Lord preserveth the simple: I was brought low, and He helped me. [7]Return unto thy rest, O my soul; for the Lord hath dealt bountifully with thee. [8]For Thou hast delivered my soul from death, mine eyes from tears, and my feet from falling. [9]I will walk before the Lord in the land of the living.[3]

When they walked off the roof safely, the only one who did not seem surprised was Martha, and why would she? She trusted the Lord to do as He said He would for her.

If they even took the time to pray, too many parents would end their prayer, "if it be Your will Lord." But that completely contradicts the Lord saying we should "believe we already have that which we have asked of Him."[4]

---

[1] Matthew 18: 2-4
[2] Psalm 116:1-3
[3] Psalm 116:4-9
[4] Mark 11:24, John 15:7, 1 John 5:14-15

Forgive me for being so exercised by this example, but to their deathbeds Bro. Hannity and Sis. Geraldine considered themselves, "lucky to live as long as they did." It made and still makes me sick. And unfortunately, Martha's childlike faith was eventually ripped from her heart too. But what would one expect from parents who taught, "trust the Lord with one's whole heart,"[1] but demonstrated with their lives a lack of complete trust, a lack of childlike faith.

Little Martha kept the faith in childhood and lost it in adulthood.

THUGS AT THEIR WORK

One of the most dreadful features of this catastrophe has been the miserable weakness displayed by the authorities of Johnstown and the surrounding boroughs. Johnstown needed them sadly for forty-eight hours. There is supposed to be a Burgess, but like most burgesses he is a shadowy and mythical personage. If there had been concerted and intelligent action the fire, in the debris at the dam could have been extinguished within a short time after it started. Too many cooks spoiled this ghastly broth.

Even now if dynamite or some other explosive was intelligently' applied the huge mass of wreckage which has up to the present time escaped the flame, and no doubt contains a number of bodies, could be saved from fire.

This, however, is a matter of small import compared with the immunity granted the outrageous and open graveyard robbery and disgusting thievery which have thriven bravely since Friday morning.

Dozens of barrels of strong liquor have been rescued from among the ruins of saloons and hotels and the contents of the same have been freely indulged in. This has led to an alarming debauchery, which is on the increase. All day the numbers of the drunken crowd have been augmented from time to time by fresh arrivals from the surrounding districts.

An employee of J. L. Gill, of Latrobe, says he and thirty-five other men were in a three-story building in Johnstown last night. They had been getting out logs for the Johnstown Lumber Company. The man says that the building was swept away, and all the men were drowned except Gill and his family.

---

[1] Proverbs 3:5

If the above few paragraphs sounded like what you see and experience in the 21st Century, I'd like to arrest those thoughts and correct this 1889 writer. Unlike a number of your real-life examples, these city officials, who were still alive, jumped into action quickly and accomplished much, as will be seen in future anecdotes.

As for the ghastly fire, it could not have been stopped, unfortunately.

HANDLING THE DEAD

The recovery of bodies has taken up the time of thousands all day. The theory now is that most of those killed by the torrent were buried beneath the debris. Today's work in the ruins in a large degree justifies this assumption. I saw six bodies taken out of one pile of rubbish not eight feet square.

The truth is that bodies are almost as plentiful as logs. The whirl of the waters puts the bodies under and the logs and boards on top. The rigidity of arms standing out at right angles to the bloated and bruised bodies show that death in ninety-nine out of a hundred cases took place amid the ruins- that is after the wreck of houses had closed over them.

Dr. D. G. Foster, who has been here all day, is of the opinion that most of the victims were killed by coming into violent contact with objects in the river and not by drowning. He found many fractured skulls and on most heads blows that would have rendered those receiving them instantly unconscious, and the water did the rest.

HAEL: AN OLD MERCY

You may find this hard to accept, but being rendered, "instantly unconscious" because of the severe head trauma, as in the above paragraph, was a mercy from the Lord performed on many, many of the dead.

HANDLING THE DEAD (CONTINUED)

Not fewer than three hundred bodies have been taken from the river and rubbish today. It has been the labor of all classes of citizens, and marvelous work has been accomplished. The eastern end of Main street, through which the waters tore most madly and destructively, and in which they left their legacy of wrecked houses, fallen trees and dead bodies in a greater degree than in any other portion of the city, has been cleared and the remains of over fifty have been taken out.

All over town the searchers have been equally successful. As soon as a body is found it is placed on a litter and sent to the Morgue, where it is washed and placed on a board for several hours to await identification.

The Morgue is the Fourth-ward school house, and it has been surrounded all day by a crowd of several thousand people. At first the crowd were disposed to stop those bearing the stretchers, uncover the remains and view them, but this was found to be prolific not only of great delay, also scenes of agony that not even the bearers could endure.

Now a litter is guarded by a file of soldiers with fixed bayonets, and the people are forced aside until the Morgue is reached. It is astonishing to find how small a number of injured are in the city. Few survived. It was death or nothing with the demon of the flood.

Now that an adequate idea of what has befallen them has been reached, and the fact that a living has still to be made, that plants must be taken care of, that contracts must be filled, the business people of the city are giving their attention to the future. Vice President and Director James McMillan, of the Cambria Iron Company, says their loss has been well-nigh incalculable. They are not daunted, but will tomorrow begin the work of clearing up the ruins of their mills preparatory to rebuilding and repairing their works. They will also immediately rebuild the Gautier Iron Works. This is the disposition of all.

"Our pockets are light," they say, "but if nothing happens all of us will be in business again." The central portion of Johnstown is as completely obliterated as if it had never had foundation. The river has made its bed upon the sites of hundreds of dwellings, and a vast area of sand, mud and gravel marks the old channel.

It is doubtful whether it will be possible even to reclaim what was once the business portion of the city. The river will have to be returned to its old bed in order to do this.

Among the lost is H. G. Rose, the District Attorney of Cambria county, whose body was among the first discovered.

Governor Foraker, of Ohio, this afternoon sent five hundred tents to this city. They will be pitched on the hillside tomorrow. They are sadly needed, as the buildings that are left are either too damp or too unsafe for occupancy.

BURYING THE DEAD

The work of burying the dead began this morning and has been kept up till late this evening. The bruising of the bodies by logs and trees and other debris and other exposure in the water have tended to hasten decomposition, which has set in in scores of cases, making interment instantly necessary.

Bodies are being buried as rapidly as they are identified. The work of Pittsburgh undertakers in examining the dead has rendered it possible to keep all those embalmed two or three days longer, but this is desirable only in cases where identification is dubious, and no claimants appear at all.

Today the cars sent out from Pittsburgh with provisions for the living were hastily cleared in order to contain the bodies of the dead intended for interment in suburban cemeteries and in graveyards handy to the city.

Formality is dispensed with. In some instances, only the undertaker and his assistants are present, and in others only one or two members of the family of the dead.

The dead are more plentiful than the mourners.

Death has certainly dealt briefly with the stricken city. "Let the dead bury the dead" has been more nearly exemplified in this instance than in any other in this country's history. The magnitude of the horror increases with the hours. It is believed that not less than two thousand of the drowned found lodgment beneath the omnium gatherum in the triangle of ground that the Conemaugh cut out of the bank between the river and the Pennsylvania Railroad bridge.

HAEL: HUMAN'S DEATH

I have sought some counsel about writing this portion. Our ▮▮▮▮▮▮ ▮▮▮▮▮▮ Department, here in heaven has been very helpful in this regard. While I want you to have a sense of what the Christian experiences at death, it has been suggested to me to begin with the unsaved. You will recall sometime earlier I asked, "what meets the unsaved dead to carry them to their final resting place?"

Let me enlarge slightly on the picture of the agony an unsaved person goes through as they are leaving the earthly realm for that place made for sataN and his demons.[1] Contrast the picture with the saved person who enters their eternal rest with wonder and excitement, because loving angels are carrying that Christian to his or her Saviour. The unsaved person, on the other hand is escorted, excuse me, carried to their final abode and their journey is not pleasant. For the Christian, the sting of death has been taken away.[2]

But there is a logical question that you should have, and I want to try to explain it. I actually saw this visual just recently when Dr. Dale (my current Christian I am guarding) went on a hiking weekend with his wife Margie. They are on a trek up portions of the Appalachian Trail every few days.

After walking an entire day, seeing the beautiful country and wild animals they came to a stream. Now recognize, they are high up in the Appalachians. The water is bitterly cold. As I watched them pull off their hiking boots and socks Margie just plunged her feet right in. Dale however, did something different. Watching his wife, he started to step into the cold water just as comfortably, but the moment his toe hit the water he stopped. The bitterly cold water, even just on his toes caused his entire body to halt, for just a moment though for in the next moment his toes were used to the water and he comfortably slid the rest of his foot into the creek.

That is how it is when you die, yes there can be pain, but we as angels are there with you and what you experience in death is quickly calmed by what you see and experience in heaven. Hence, the Christian's life immediately after death is incredibly different from the unsaved soul.

I hope that helps, it's the best I can do. It is critical that you understand this reality of death for the next section by this 1889 author will be very painful otherwise.

THE GREATEST FUNERAL PYRE IN HISTORY

The victims were not upon it, but were parts of it.

Whole houses were washed into the apex of the triangle. Hen coops, pigsties and stables were added to the mass. Then a stove ignited the mass and the work of cremation began. It was a literal breast of fire. The smoke arose in a huge funnel-shaped cloud, and at times it changed to the form of

---

[1] Matthew 25:41
[2] 1 Corinthians 15:55

an hour glass. At night, the flames united would light up this misty remnant of mortality. The effect upon the living, both ignorant and intelligent, was the same. That volume of smoke with its dual form, produced a feeling of awe in many that was superior in most cases to that felt in the awful moment of the storm's wrath on Friday.

Hundreds stood for hours regarding the smoke and wondering whether it foreboded another visitation more dire than its predecessor.

The people hereabouts this morning awoke to find that nothing was left but a mass of ashes, calcined human bones, stoves, old iron and other approximately indestructible matter, from which only a light blue vapor was arising. General Hastings took precautions to prevent the extension of the fire to another huge pile, a short distance away, and this will be rummaged today for bodies of flood victims.

The Pittsburgh undertakers have contributed more to facilitate the preparation of the dead for the graves than all others besides.

There was a disposition on the part of many thieves to raid the houses, and do an all-around thieving business, but the measures adopted by the police had a tendency to frighten them off in nearly every case.

One man was caught in the act of robbing the body of an old woman, but he protested that he had got nothing and was released. He immediately disappeared, and it was found afterward that he had taken $100 from the pocket of the corpse.

Yesterday and this morning a thriving business was had in collecting hams, shoulders, chickens and even furniture. One man had thieves in his employ, and while to some of them he was paying regular salaries, others were doing the work for a drink of whiskey. The authorities stopped this thing very suddenly, but not until a number of the people threatened to lynch the organizer. In one or two instances very narrow escapes from the rope were made.

Thousands of coffins and rough boxes have already arrived, and still the supply is short. They are brought in marked to some undertaker, who has a list of his dead, and as fast as the coffins come he writes the name of its intended tenant and tells the friends (when there are any) where to find it.

How a Funeral Takes Place

Two of them go after it, and, carrying it between them to the Morgue or to their homes, place the body in it and take it to the burial grounds.

One unfortunate feature of the destruction is the fact that someone has been drowned from nearly every house in the city, and teams are procurable only with the greatest difficulty.

Dead horses are seen everywhere. In one stable two horses, fully harnessed, bridled and ready to be taken out, stand dead in their stable, stiff and upright. In a sand pile near the Pennsylvania Railroad depot a horse's hind feet, rump and tail are all that can be seen of him. He was caught in the rapidly running waters and had been driven into the sand.

The following telegram from Johnstown has been received at Pittsburg:

"For God's sake tell the sight-seers to keep away from Johnstown for the present. What we want is people to work, not to look on [said the] "Citizen's Committee." Three trains have already been sent out with crowded cargoes of sight-seers. At every station along the road excited crowds are waiting for an opportunity to get aboard.

That's what would have happened to the owners of South Fork Fishing Club if they had put in an appearance.

There is great indignation among the people of Johnstown at the wealthy Pittsburghers who own South Fork. They blame them severely for having maintained such a frightfully dangerous institution there. The feeling among the people was intense. If any of the owners of the dam had put in an appearance in Johnstown they would have been lynched.

The dam has been a constant menace to this valley ever since it has been in existence, and the feeling, which has been bitter enough on the occasion of every flood hitherto, after this horrible disaster is now at fever heat.

Without seeing the havoc created no idea can be given of the area of the desolation or the extent of the damage.

ONLY ONE LEFT TO MOURN

An utterly wretched woman stood by a muddy pool of water, trying to find some trace of a once happy home. She was half crazed with grief, and her eyes were red and swollen. As I stepped to her side she raised her pale and haggard face, crying:

"They are all gone. Oh God be merciful to them. My husband and my seven dear little children have been swept down with the flood and I am left alone. We were driven by the raging flood into the garret, but the waters followed us there. Inch by inch it kept rising until our heads were crushing against the roof. It was death to remain. So I raised a window and one by one placed my darlings on some driftwood, trusting to the Great Creator. As I liberated the last one, my sweet little boy, he looked at me and said:

"Mamma, you always told me that the Lord would care for me; will he look after me now?"

"I saw him drift away with his loving face turned toward me, and with a prayer on my lips for his deliverance he passed from sight forever. The next moment the roof crashed in and I floated outside to be rescued fifteen hours later from the roof of a house in Kernville. If I could only find one of my darlings, I could bow to the will of God, but they all are gone. I have lost everything on earth now but my life, and I will return to my old Virginia home and lay me down for my last great sleep."

A handsome woman, with hair as black as a raven's wing, walked through the depot, where a dozen or more bodies were awaiting burial. Passing from one to another, she finally lifted the paper covering from the face of a woman, young and with traces of beauty showing through the stains of muddy water. With a cry of anguish, she reeled backward, to be caught by a rugged man who chanced to be passing. In a moment or so she had calmed herself sufficiently to take one more look at the features of her dead. She stood gazing at the unfortunate as if dumb. Finally turning away with another wild burst of grief she said:

"And her beautiful hair all matted and her sweet face bruised and stained with mud and water."

The dead woman was the sister of the mourner. The body was placed in a coffin a few minutes later and sent away to its narrow house.

These incidents are but fair samples of the scenes familiar to every turn in this stricken city.

CHAPTER III
The Horror Increases

During the night thirty-three bodies were brought to one house. As yet the relief force is not perfectly organized, and bodies are lying around on boards and doors. Within twenty feet of where this was written the dead body of another woman lies.

Provision has been made by the Relief Committee for the sufferers to send dispatches to all parts of the country. The railroad company has a track through to the bridge. The first train arrived about half-past nine o'clock this morning. A man in a frail craft got caught in the rapids at the railroad bridge, and it looked as if he would increase the already terrible list of dead, but fortunately he caught on a rock, where he now is and is liable to remain all day.

The question on every person's lips is: Will the Cambria Iron Company rebuild? The wire mill is completely wrecked, but the walls of the rolling mill are still standing. If they do not resume it is a question whether the town will be rebuilt.

The worst part of this disaster has not been told. Indeed, the most graphic description that can be written will not tell half the tale. No pen can describe, nor tongue tell the vastness of this devastation.

I walked over the greater part of the wrecked town this morning, and one could not have pictured such a wreck, nor could one have imagined that an entire town of this size could be so completely swept away.

A. J. Haws, one of the prominent men of the town, was standing on the hillside this morning, taking a view of the wreck. He said:

"I never saw anything like this, nor do I believe anyone else ever did. No idea can be had of the tremendous loss of property here. It amounts up into the millions. I am going to leave the place. I never will build here."

I heard the superintendents and managers of the Cambria Iron Works saying they doubted if the works will be rebuilt. This would mean the death blow to the place. Mr. Stackhouse, first vice-president of the iron works, is expected here today. Nothing can be done until a meeting of the company is held.

The 1889 author has no source of comparison, and you reading this in the 21ˢᵗ century only have the pictures you have seen on the internet of isolated pockets of the earth being deluged.

But reading the above paragraphs took me back to another deluge, one that God said He would never repeat.[1] You will know this as Noah's flood, I know it as a great worldwide upheaval. As you were watching one area destroyed due to Hurricane Harvey, and another destroyed due to Hurricane Irma, we in heaven watched the entire world destroyed some 4500 mortal years ago.

To me the most fascinating part of Noah's deluge came from watching the Creator God's reaction. He sent the deluge because every intent of man's heart was evil continually.[2] In your Bible you read that God regretted that He had made man.[3] But friends, you often miss the next phrase, where the Word says that God grieved. All that I can say is that out of His unfathomable love for you He grieved heavily in His heart for the ones that He had made as special to Himself.

You have a relationship with Him that we do not have and that we at times long to have.[4] I don't think that you fully comprehend the excruciating pain our Lord went through, sending this deluge in Noah's day. We were so, what's the right word, "fearful" for God? No, we were, yes, we were consumed with agony for Him, watching Him wipe mankind off the face of the earth.[5]

And yet, this wonderful Creator knew that you would continue to live the way you did before the flood, and He still made a covenant to save your species. Look back at the passage already referred to:

[12]When the Lord smelled the pleasing aroma, He said to Himself, "I will never again curse the ground because of man, even though man's inclination is evil from his youth. And I will never again strike down every living thing as I have done.

[13]As long as the earth endures,
seedtime and harvest, cold and heat,

---

[1] Genesis 8:21-22
[2] Genesis 6:5
[3] Genesis 6:6
[4] 1 Peter 1:12
[5] Genesis 6:7

summer and winter, and day and night
will not cease."[1]

Look at the promise to you humans, even though you will be inclined to evil from
your youth God will make sure the seasons and the opportunities to make a living
continue on. In another passage the Son says, "He will not leave you as orphans,
but will send His Holy Spirit to live among you."[2]

Do you have any idea how much the Creator loves you? I don't think you do.

Let me end with this, I fear that you miss the tenderness with which God loves
you.

The modern author of this book says the following all of the time, and he's right,
"Prayer is completely illogical, except for ONE thing! God wants to have a
relationship with you. That is why He developed prayer, so that you could
dialogue with Him."

One of your contemporary pastors, Dr. Charles F. Stanley has edited a Bible that
he calls his Life Principles Bible. You may not realize this, but this is his very
first principle: "Our intimacy with God – His highest priority for our lives –
determines the impact of our lives." After fifty years of ministry this pastor is
telling you what the most important principle is to God, intimacy with Him.

Since I've gone this far I suppose I should take another step here. How much time
do you spend in prayer? How much time do you spend with the Lord compared
to the time you spend with social media and other forms of entertainment? My
friends, you act like you have forgotten that this is not your home. The truth is
you are merely sojourners on earth.[3]

I'm sorry, maybe I've gone too far, but I have been here for six millennia
watching all y'all:

I was here when Adam and Eve were in the Garden and sataN rebelled and the
subsequently they rebelled.

I saw our Creator's heart break for the fallen angels who joined lucifeR and
mankind joined him making him the god of their evil and vileness.

I saw the deluge and then periodic catastrophes that the Lord both brought and
allowed so that mankind would turn to Him.

And I see these same things again, and you are missing it!

---

[1] Genesis 8:21-22 (HCBS)
[2] John 14:18
[3] 1 Peter 2:11

How many times do we watch and listen to you pray that God will fix other people. Do you not realize that He wants you to focus on YOUR humbleness? He has the address of the unsaved and the backslidden. He will get ahold of them when it is their time. YOU ARE His concern. You are!

I'm sorry, I know that I've again gone too far. But He hurts when He causes you suffering and pain, and you do not see it. You don't see the way ███████████

███████████████████████████████████ *that*

we see in heaven. But you will one day, and then you will grieve. And do you know what He will do when He sees you, His chosen people grieving? I know because I have seen it for six thousand years. Do you know what He will do? He will wipe away your tears.[1]

PREPARATIONS FOR BURIAL

Adjutant General Hastings, who is in charge of the relief corps at the railroad station, has a force of carpenters at work making rough boxes in which to bury the dead. They will be buried on the hill, just above the town, on ground belonging to the Cambria Iron Company. The graves will be numbered. No one will be buried that has not been identified without a careful description being taken [and even with these precautions one out of every three dead persons found will never be identified]. General Hastings drove fifty-eight miles across the country in order to get here, and as soon as he came took charge. He has the whole town organized, and in connection with L. S. Smith has commenced the building of bridges and clearing away the wrecks to get out the dead bodies.

General Hastings has a large force of men clearing private tracks of the Cambria Iron Company in order that the small engines can be put to work bringing up the dead that have been dragged out of the river at points below.

The bodies are being brought up and laid out in freight cars. Mr. Kittle, of Ebensburg, has been deputized to take charge of the valuables taken from the bodies and keep a registry of them, and also to note any marks of identification that may be found. A number of the bodies have been stripped of rings or bracelets and other valuables.

---

[1] Revelation 21:4

Over six hundred corpses have now been taken out on the south side of Stony Creek, the greater portion of which have been identified.

SEND US COFFINS

Preparations for their burial are being carried on as rapidly as possible, and "coffins, coffins," is the cry. No word has been received anywhere of any being shipped. Even rough boxes will be gladly received. Those that are being made, and in which many of the bodies are being buried, are of rough unplaned boards. One hundred dead bodies are laid out at the soap factory, while two hundred or more people are gathered there that are in great distress. Boats are wanted. People have the greatest difficulty in getting to the town.

STRUGGLING FOR ORDER

Another account from Johnstown on the second day after the disaster says:

The situation here has not changed, and yesterday's estimates of the loss of life do not seem to be exaggerated. Six hundred bodies are now lying in Johnstown, and a large number have already been buried. Four immense relief trains arrived last night, and the survivors are being well cared for.

Adjutant General Hastings, assisted by Mayor Sanger, has taken command at Johnstown and vicinity. Nothing is legal unless it bears the signature of the former. The town itself is guarded by Company H, Sixth regiment, Lieutenant Leggett in command. New members were sworn in by him, and they are making excellent soldiers.

Special police are numerous, and the regulations are so strict that even the smoking of a cigar is prohibited. General Hastings expresses the opinion that more troops are necessary.

Mr. Alex Hart is in charge of the special police. He has lost his wife and family. Notwithstanding his great misfortune he is doing the work of a Hercules in his own way.

HAEL: COMFORTED TO COMFORT

Mr. Hart's distress in this situation is indeed sorrowful to behold. I will let his Guardian Angel tell you what happened.

My charge and his wife and three children started to escape up the steeply sloping valley along with many others, nearly all of whom were saved from this tragedy. He had to carry his wife for she had just broken her leg a few weeks earlier. Carrying her in his arms he kept looking over his shoulder to make sure his children, aged seven, nine and ten, were following. Because of their age and the steepness of the grade he and his family went upwards much slower than those around him. After three minutes of strenuous climbing up the valley wall and through small torrents of water on the bare hill, a tremor made its way across the incline they were traversing. Mr. Hart now realized that he had another problem, the bare mountainside was giving way.

His wife Elizabeth could feel the tremor too. "Put me down, Alex," she yelled, "and get the children."

He hesitated and saw a tree just twenty yards away. Apologizing to his wife he threw her over his shoulder, she screamed in pain, but trusted him. He immediately picked up seven-year-old Harry with his other hand and ran to the tree.

Setting Elizabeth and Harry down gently he turned back to nine and ten-year-old Margaret and Billy who had stopped to rest. Alex turned and took two steps towards them calling and waving with his arms. He hadn't taken a third step when he saw the ground give way.

He didn't know that as the two children were standing there, exhausted, two of my team of angels had put their wings around the children and hummed to them as they perished. They were then carried to the Father.

Stunned and unable to move he stood there in the rain, nothing could be done and he knew it. Mr Hart dreaded to turn around, for he heard Elizabeth yelp as she was unable to scream. He knew she had seen the same thing he did. Again he would have no idea that I did this, but I wrapped my wings around him for when he finally did turn around, the tree, Elizabeth, and Harry were also gone. He stood on a small island of hard ground, the channels of rainwater going by him. He was alone.

My poor Mr. Hart stood there for what seemed to him like hours, but it was only a few minutes. He then walked slowly, in utter dismay, up the valley.

A pragmatic man, he searched his mind for memory verses he could focus upon. He started, "though I walk through the valley of. . ." and then stopped, disgusted and started to cry, louder than I have ever heard him cry before. I believe that more tears escaped his eyes than rain hit his head.

After a few more minutes of ambling up the valley, tripping and falling, getting angrier and angrier, for there was also at hand a demonic spirit speaking discouragement into Alex's heart, I heard the sound that occurs when the Holy Spirit is moving.[1] It is a sound that only we hear, but it is powerful and when the already defeated demon hears this he knows that the Spirit is moving, and he knows that his deception is thwarted.

Some minutes later, as he still traversed up the steep slope, the Holy Spirit reminded Alex Hart of 2 Corinthians 1:4 where Paul wrote that we are often comforted by Him so that we can comfort others in the self-same way. For many months after the flood, Alex would just begin to cry for no apparent reason. But Alex had known the reason the first time these crying spells came upon him. God was preparing him to comfort others.

He was nearly to the top of the hill he was climbing, some forty-five minutes after the death of his family. Alex suddenly remembered the great Apostle Paul saying that yes, they had troubles without and fears within,[2] just like he did just then. But it was the next verse that held Alex's heart, for Paul went on to make clear who it is that God comforts, namely, the humble.[3]

He knew that, because he had just taught it the weekend before in the Sunday School class for his church, the Johnstown First Presbyterian Church. He would humble himself before the Lord, just as Job had and God would comfort him.

On the other side of the Jordan, Elizabeth stood next to Jesus, His nail scarred hand holding hers as she held Billy's hand, and he held Margaret's held Harry's. They all watched Mr. Hart reach the top of the steep valley. He looked up into the rain coming from heaven, and closing his eyes he wept again, but the children and Elizabeth knew that he would be alright. God, the Spirit, had already comforted him, and their dad, her husband would comfort others in the self-same way,[4] as he did when he was put in charge of the Special Police.

Firemen and Soldiers Arriving

Chief Evans, of the Pittsburgh Fire Department, arrived this evening with engines and several hose carts, with a full complement of men. A large number of Pittsburgh physicians came on the same train.

A squad of Battery B, under command of Lieutenant Brown, the forerunners of the whole battery, arrived at the improvised telegraph office

---

[1] Ezekiel 1:24
[2] 2 Corinthians 7:5
[3] 2 Corinthians 7:6
[4] 2 Corinthians 1:4

at half-past six o'clock, Lieutenant Brown went at once to Adjutant General Hastings and reported for duty.

A portion of the police force of Pittsburgh and Alleghany are on duty, and better order is maintained than prevailed yesterday. Communication has been restored between Cambria City and Johnstown by a foot bridge.

The work of repairing the tracks between Sang Hollow and Johnstown is going on rapidly, and trains will probably be running by tomorrow morning. Not less than fifteen thousand strangers are here.

The unruly element has been put down and order is now perfect. The Citizen's Committee are in charge and have matters well organized.

A proclamation has just been issued that all men who are able to work must report for work or leave the place. "We have too much to do to support idlers," says the Citizen's Committee, "And will not abuse the generous help that is being sent by doing so." From tomorrow, all will be at work.

Money now is greatly needed to meet the heavy pay rolls that will be incurred for the next two weeks. W. C. Lewis, Chairman of the Finance Committee, is ready to receive the same.

FALL OF THE WALL OF WATER

Mr. Crouse, proprietor of the South Fork Fishing Club Hotel, came to Johnstown this afternoon. He says: "When the dam of Conemaugh Lake broke the water seemed to leap, scarcely touching the ground. It bounded down the valley, crashing and roaring, carrying everything before it. For a mile its front seemed like a solid wall twenty feet high."

Freight Agent Dechert, said that when the great wall that held the body of water began to crumble at the top, he sent a message begging the people of Johnstown for God's sake to take to the hills. He reports no serious accidents at South Fork.

Richard Davis ran to Prospect Hill when the water raised. As to Mr. Dechert's message, he says just such have been sent down at each flood since the lake was made. The warning so often proved useless that little attention was paid to it this time. "I cannot describe the mad rush," he said. "At first it looked like dust. That must have been the spray. I could see houses going down before it like a child's play blocks set on edge in a row. As it came nearer I could see houses totter for a moment, then rise and the next moment be crushed like egg shells against each other."

James McMillin, vice-president of the Cambria Iron Works, was met this afternoon. In a conversation he said:

"I do not know what our loss is. I cannot even estimate, as I have not the faintest idea what it may be. The upper mill is totally wrecked, damaged beyond all possibility of repairs. The lower mill is damaged to such an extent that all machinery and buildings are useless.

"The mills will be rebuilt immediately. I have sent out orders that all men that can must report at the mill tomorrow to commence cleaning up. I do not think the building was insured against a flood. The great thing we want is to get the mill in operation again."

The Gautier Wire Works was completely destroyed. The buildings will be immediately rebuilt and put in operation as soon as possible. The loss at this point is complete. The land on which it stood is today as barren and desolate as if it were in the midst of the Sahara Desert.

The Cambria Iron Company loses its great supply stores. The damage to the stock alone will amount to $50,000.

The building was valued at $150,000 and is a total loss. The company offices which adjoins the store was a handsome structure. It was protected by the first building, but nevertheless is almost totally destroyed.

The Dartmouth Club, at which employees of the works boarded, was carried away in the flood. It contained many occupants at the time. None were saved.

Estimates of the losses of the Cambria Iron Company given are from $2,000,000 to $2,500,000. But little of this can be recovered.

History of the Works

The Cambria Iron Works at Johnstown were built in 1853. It was the second largest plant of its kind in the country, and was completely swept away. Its capacity of finished steel per annum was 180,000 net tons of steel rails and 20,000 net tons of steel in other shapes. The mill turned out steel rails, spike bars, angles, flats, rounds, axles, billets and wire rods. There were nine Siemens and forty-two reverbatory heating furnaces, one seven ton and two 6,000 pound hammers and three trains of rolls.

The Bessemer Steel Works made their first blow July 10, 1871, and they contained nine gross ton converters, with an annual capacity of 200,000 net tons of ingots. In 1878 two, fifteen gross tons Siemens open hearth steel furnaces were built, with an annual capacity of 20,000 net tons of ingots.

The Cambria Iron Company also owns the Gautier Steel Works at Johnstown, which were erected in 1878.

The rolling mill produced annually 30,000 net tons of merchant bar steel of every size and for every purpose. The wire mill had a capacity alone of 30,000 tons of fence wire.

There are numerous bituminous coal mines near Johnstown, operated by the Cambria Iron Company, the Euclid Coal Company and private persons. There were three woolen mills, employing over three hundred hands and producing an annual product valued at $300,000[1].

Awful Work of the Flames

Fifty acres of town swept clean. One thousand two hundred buildings destroyed. Eight thousand to ten thousand lives lost[2].

That is the record of the Johnstown calamity as it looked to me just before dark last night. Acres of the town were turned into cemeteries, and miles of the river bank were involuntary storage rooms for house hold goods.

From the half-ruined parapet at the end of the stone railroad bridge, in Johnstown proper, one sees sights so gruesome that none but the soulless can command his emotions.

At my right is a fiery pit that is now believed to have been the funeral pyre of almost a thousand persons.

HAEL: BUILD ANOTHER BARN

My friends, as I read the previous two sections from our 1889 author I am again reminded of Jesus' parable of the rich man who built another barn, which I related to you earlier. I want to remind you of a different aspect of that parable. Let the Holy Spirit speak to you through Christ's words:

---

[1] Editor's note: $1,250,000 in 2017 dollars

[2] Hael's note: *[the final official number, well after this original book printed, totaled 2,209 souls. But when we in heaven add up those escorted to heaven and then add the ones taken to hell, the number is inflated from 2,209 to* ███████*]*

[16]Then He told them a parable: "A rich man's land was very productive. [17]He thought to himself, 'What should I do, since I don't have anywhere to store my crops? [18]I will do this,' he said. 'I'll tear down my barns and build bigger ones and store all my grain and my goods there. [19]Then I'll say to myself, You have many goods stored up for many years. Take it easy; eat, drink, and enjoy yourself.' [20]"But God said to him, You fool! This very night your life is demanded of you. And the things you have prepared—whose will they be? [21]That's how it is with the one who stores up treasure for himself and is not rich toward God."[1]

May I just point out a small portion of one verse to you? Look at verse 20 where God says to him, "You fool." I know you mortals. I have been watching you for some 6,000 of your years, and I know this about you, you do NOT want to be considered a fool. So think about this. The God of heaven, the One who created heaven and earth, the One who controls the elements, He is the One calling you a fool. Please, please my dear friends, be sobered by His words.

Note one more thing, God isn't calling a person a fool because he is a good steward building a bigger barn when business is good, no! He is calling a person a fool who is rich on earth but "NOT rich toward God."

Ask yourself my friend, are you rich toward God?

STREETS OBLITERATED

The fiercest rush of the current was straight across the lower, level part of Johnstown, where it entirely obliterated Cinder, Washington, Market, Main and Walnut streets. These streets were from a half to three quarters of a mile in length, and were closely crowded along their entire course with dwellings and other buildings, and there is now no more trace of streets or houses than there is at low tide on the beach at Far Rockaway.

In the once well populated boroughs of Conemaugh and Woodvale there are tonight literally but two buildings left, one the shell of the Woodvale Woolen Mill and the other a sturdy brick dwelling.

The buildings which were swept from twenty out of the thirty acres of devastated Johnstown were crowded against the lower end of the big stone bridge in a mass 200 yards wide, 500 yards broad and from 60 to100 feet deep. They were crushed and split out of shape and packed together like playing cards.

---

[1] Luke 12:16-21 (HCBS)

89

When you realize that in nearly every one of these buildings there were at least one human being, while in some there were as many as seventy-five, it is easy to comprehend how awful it was when this mass began to burn fiercely last night. It was known that a large number of persons were imprisoned in the debris, for they could be plainly seen by those on shore, but it was not until people stopped to think and to ask themselves questions, which startled them in a ghastly way, that the fact became plain that instead of a pitiful hundred or two of victims at least a thousand were in that roaring, crackling, loathsome, blazing mass upon the surface of the water and in the huge, inaccessible arches of the big bridge.

HAEL: GOD IS RELIABLE

The author's description above is appalling and gruesome, but it is accurate. And so I have left it because I know you people, as you see the gruesomeness of life, you can see the reliability of our Lord. To that end I will share with you the Psalmist's words that are true, even in the midst of great tragedy. "The one who lives under the protection of the Most High dwells in the shadow of the Almighty."[1]

I know that from your perspective this seems impossible, but that is the deception of the evil one. Jesus took away the sting of death which allows you to meet death victoriously.[2] Hold on to that truth as you read the next section.

CHARRED BODIES

Charred bodies could be seen here and there all through the glowing embers. The fire is spreading toward a large block of crushed buildings further up the stream. There is a broad stretch of angry water above and below, while over there, just opposite the end of the bridge, is the ruin of the great Cambria Iron Works, which have been damaged to the extent of over $1,000,000.

The Gautier Steel Works have been wiped away, and are represented by a loss of $1,000,000 and a big hole.

The Holbert House, owned by Renford Brothers, has entirely disappeared. It was a five-story building, was the leading hotel of Johnstown, and

---

[1] Psalm 91:1
[2] 1 Corinthians 15:55-57

contained a hundred rooms. Of the seventy-five guests who were in it when the flood came, only eight have been saved. Most of them were crushed by the fall of the walls and flooring.

Hundreds of searching parties are looking in the muddy ponds and among the wreckage for bodies and they are being gathered in ghastly heaps.

In one building among the bloated victims, I saw a young and well-dressed man and woman, still locked in each other's arms, a young mother with her babe pressed with delirious tenacity to her breast, and on a small pillow was a tiny babe a few hours old, which the doctors said must have been born in the water. It is said that 720 bodies have so far been recovered, or have been located.

The coroner of Westmoreland county is ordering coffins by the carload.

HAEL: THE NEWLYWEDS AND THE NEW MOTHER

Our 1889 author gives you the visual that he sees, but I am honored to tell you what he did not see. I will let the two guardian angels tell you their experience, for the newlyweds and then for the new mother.

I had spent the morning near my newlyweds. They were delighting in one another as freely as the Song of Solomon wanted them to. When they first arrived in Johnstown Wednesday night for their honeymoon they were disappointed to see the weather so gloomy, disappointed that is, until they spent that first night together.

Hael just wants me to tell you what occurred, but I would like to say something first. I see more and more couples living together now in the 21st century, and I have to tell you, as one who has observed this in humans since time began, YOU SO MUCH MORE enjoy your first nibblings of intimacy when you have abstained from sex before marriage. Alright, I'm done preaching.

Anyway, the young brilliant pastor, James, whose calling took him from school to marriage and then to his first pastorate, all in the same week, married Madelyn on Wednesday so they could be in his church to preach on Sunday, three days hence. They would not make it, and the church where they were to be ministering had no idea they were in Johnstown so of course they spoke very judgmentally about him for weeks.

On that fateful day, James and Madelyn loved on each other all morning long, had a late breakfast, in bed of course, and were giggled at by the room attendants who knew the newlyweds were enjoying themselves, as well they should.

The harder it would rain, the more the couple would laugh. They started a touching game at 10:00 PM the night before. When they heard the sound of the rain change intensity, James would get up from the bed, no longer ashamed of his nakedness in front of his wife, go to the window, and turn and joyfully say, "I'm sorry my dear, we must stay in bed a bit longer."

They would both laugh, he would return to bed and they would enjoy themselves all over again.

Even as a mature angel I can tell you that it was sweet. I am to this day so proud of this newlywed couple. I knew what would happen on that fateful day, for I had already been given my assignment. But to watch them enjoying themselves, to recognize what an incredible couple in ministry they would be, I had a tendency to wonder why the Lord would allow them to pass from earth to heaven on this day.

And then the Lord opened a beautiful insight to me, which now that I am writing this I have to admit that He has done before. But He reminded me that He gave James and Madelyn this wonderful time together, before they went to heaven and then allowed me to wrap my wings around them, in comfort, as they faced death together.

Hi, I'm another of the Lord's Guards assigned to you.

"Hael, thank you for the opportunity to share with your readers."

My story of the new mother is exactly the same, from the perspective of our Creator giving pleasure in a way that is unique to an individual's situation. You see, the new mother lived in Pittsburg, but her husband worked for a month at a time in Johnstown. A month earlier the Holy Spirit had prompted her and her husband to be in Johnstown during those last few weeks of her seventh month of pregnancy, so she could accompany him back home, where they would have their baby.

As is God's providence however, He added a personal twist of fate for Elizabeth, her husband George and their baby Henry.

She too arrived in Johnstown on Wednesday night and in fact, was assigned to the newlywed's railroad car. While she did her share of blushing, watching the two who were so anxious to get to their hotel room, she too longed for her hotel room as her husband George would be there. Her husband arrived late to their room but as was his custom, gently awakened her by stroking her cheeks. She would always open her eyes, which he loved to watch her do and then she would reach up to him, leaning up at the same time and draw him into a loving embrace, kissing him passionately.

Now if you are wondering what that looked like with her seven plus months pregnant, I will have to confess that it sometimes looked funny, but true to the loving man that George was, he soon learned that he needed to help her so when she would open her eyes he would reach around her and pull her toward him, and, gently lay himself to her side. Again, it was very, very sweet, and occasionally funny.

On the afternoon of the fateful day, George was allowed to be at the hotel with Elizabeth and as the water rose higher and higher her anxiety grew greater and greater. George started to recite to her, from his memory, a few of her favorite Psalms.

About 3:30 PM she had been lying down, and in agony every few minutes. Now the pain started to come more often and more often. Elizabeth knew what was about to happen, but oblivious George, being more impacted by his reading than her, had no clue.

Again, in the midst of this terrible tragedy it was somehow cute, personal, and very intimate. Finally, there was an evil sounding crunch of carnage that startled the two of them. They had heard people around them yelling and screaming but they had made up their minds they would trust their Savior for their lives and the life of their baby for they knew they could not run and George would not leave his wife.

When they heard the carnage, Henry entered the world. George did the best he could with the baby, and Elizabeth directed him from her face-up prone position. After a few moments, a scared and weak Elizabeth joyfully held her baby. The proud papa kneeling beside them on the floor grinned from ear to ear. They cooed into the child's ears and into one another's.

As I knew their time had come, a fellow angel appeared and wrapped his comforting wings around George as I did around Elizabeth and her baby Henry. George told Elizabeth how much he loved her and was leaning upwards to kiss her when a tree seemed to fly through the wall and George was no longer there. Out of a natural reflex Elizabeth gripped the smiling baby Henry and pulled away from the scene, and just then the floor her bed was on buckled and gave way. As she dropped into eternity she held all the tighter onto baby Henry.

While the writer of the 1889 book saw the physical beings, Elizabeth and baby Henry, and sees that as the end, I can tell you a tiny bit more of the story. You see, when I carried Elizabeth and baby Henry over Jordan, there was George, standing next to Jesus, robed in white, welcoming his wife and child into heaven.

———————

IN THE RAGING WATERS

A dispatch from Derry says: In this city, the poor people in the raging waters cried out for aid that never came. More than one brave man risked his life in trying to save those in the flood. Every hour details of some heroic action are brought to light. In many instances, the victims displayed remarkable courage and gave their chances for rescue to friends with them. Sons stood back for mothers and were lost while their parents were taken out. Many a son went down to a watery grave that a sister or a father might be saved. Such instances of sacrifice in the face of fearful danger are numerous.

THE FORCE OF THE WATERS

One can estimate the force of the water when it is known that it carried locomotives down the mountain side and turned them upside down where they are now lying. Long trains of cars have been derailed and carried great distances from the railroads [one hundred yards to one and a half miles in some cases].

The first sight that greeted the men at nine this morning was the body of a beautiful woman lying crushed and mangled under the ponderous wheels of a gondola car. The clothing was torn to shreds. Dr. Berry said that he never saw such intense pain pictured on a face before.

TERRIBLE STORIES.

At this time of writing it is impossible to secure the names of any of the lost. Every person one meets along the road has some horrible tale of drowned and dead bodies recovered.

One thousand people or more were buried and crushed in the great fire. The flats below Conemaugh are full of cars with many dead bodies lying under them. At Sang Hollow a man named Duncan sat on the roof of a house and saw his father and mother die in the attic below him. The poor fellow was powerless to help them, and he stood there wringing his hands and tearing his hair.

A man was seen clinging to a tree, covered with blood. He was lost with the others.

Long after dark the flames of fire shot high above the burning mass of timber, lighting the vast flood of rushing waters on all sides.

THE DEAD

Dead bodies are being picked up. The train master, E. Pitcairn, has been working manfully directing the rescuing of dead bodies at Nineveh. In a ten-acre field seventy-five bodies were taken out within a half mile of each other. Of this number only five were men, the rest being women and children. Many beautiful young girls, refined in features and handsomely dressed, were found, and women and young mothers with their hair matted with roots and leaves are constantly being removed.

The wrecking crew which took out these bodies are confident that 150 bodies are lying buried in the sand and under the debris on those low-lying bottom lands. Some of the bodies were horribly mangled, and the features were twisted and contorted as if they had died in the most excruciating agony. Others are found lying stretched out with calm faces.

Many a tear was dropped by the men as they worked away removing the bodies. An old lady with fine gray hair was picked up alive, although every bone in her body was broken. Judging from the number of women and children found in the swamps of Nineveh, the female portion of the population suffered the most.

HAEL: TWO SISTERS' DEATHS

Note the account above of the features being "twisted and contorted as if they had died in the most excruciating agony. Others are found lying stretched out with calm faces." This reminds me of two sisters, both were Christians and are in heaven right now. But both met their death very differently.

Miss Molly and Miss Emma were known in South Fork as the Spinster Sisters. They were twins born in 1831 when this area was known as the rough far west region of the Unites States. They were born of sturdy hard-working parents who just barely made a living, raising chickens and cattle. The girls grew up knowing the hard labor that sons would have done, had their mother been able to have additional children after the girls were born. But the birth of twins out in the beautiful, but lonely far west ruined her ability to have any more children.

And so, the two girls were the "boys" their father wanted and needed. Miss Molly and Miss Emma were visiting family in Pittsburg when their parents died together in a flood in 1862 that occurred because the same dam weakened and broke. Being unmarried and thirty-one years old, they decided to stay on in South Fork, after all, Molly had become very active in her church.

Miss Molly and Miss Emma were identical twins. Standing next to one another, you couldn't tell them apart, but that is where the similarity ended. The moment they moved apart you could see instantly the activity that Miss Molly would endeavor to accomplish. But Miss Emma's heart was very different.

When Miss Molly was teaching a Bible study, making a dinner and organizing the young boys to clean the yard where they were to feast after church, Miss Emma contented herself to play with the children, tidy the house, and read their parent's Bible, allowing it to direct what she prayed about and how she prayed.

That morning and afternoon were exactly what you would expect, Miss Molly entered Johnstown before the sun and walked the grounds where numerous flags awaited the soon coming parade. She had two or three boys with her sending them as dispatch riders to accomplish this item and accomplish that item.

Miss Emma stayed close to Molly but would break away to encourage a little child she saw who might be up early on this historic and exciting day. Alert to the feelings of those around her she always watched the boys her sister would give orders to and calm their nerves when they realized Miss Molly had just demanded what they feared would be beyond their ability.

Miss Molly ordered people, and Miss Emma encouraged people.

Miss Molly handled her women's Bible study the same way: she told them how to live and what to do. And then she demonstrated it, "showing what a real Proverbs 31 woman does" she would often say.

One Sunday morning Miss Molly felt so bad from a head cold that she could not get out of bed to go to church. Fearing that her women would begin to believe that they too did not need to go to church, she sent her sister, Miss Emma to conduct the Bible study.

"Emma," she said, "I know that you surely cannot teach the women like I do, nevertheless, I need your help and expect you to teach the women for me."

After a calm smile, confident Miss Emma replied softly, "I'll do my best sister."

It was the last time Miss Molly ever asked her sister to lead the study, for the next Sunday when Miss Molly sat with her ladies and Miss Emma took her usual place behind Molly, the class began to tell her how much they enjoyed Miss Emma.

"It was like we were sitting at the feet of Jesus,"[1] one woman explained.

On the fateful day of the flood which tore their mortal lives from them, they were hiking alongside the swift moving Conemaugh River. The trail they were

---

[1] Luke 10:38-42

walking on got closer and closer to the normally tranquil river and immediately their trail disappeared under the raging water so the sisters started to climb up the steep ravine. They had left Johnstown heading back home to South Fork when they heard it. They had never heard a sound like this before. As it came toward them they expected to see bolts and shafts of lightning all around them. For the sound was as if thousands of cracking lightning bolts were being hurled down by God Himself.

As they stopped to take a rest the two sisters saw a dirty mist churning toward them. They looked in shocked amazement for what seemed like an eternity but could only have been a few seconds. They saw trees being turned over in a large wave of dust and debris.

The debris would rise to the top of the wave and then come sharply, and forcefully down upon the earth below, with a deafening sound. They turned to look at one another, realizing at the same time that they would not escape this, and here in the midst of the ultimate turmoil, a life-threatening event, the differences in the two sisters became evident.

While Miss Emma fell to her knees she raised her hands and lifted her face to heaven. Remembering the words of Job, she cried out, for she had to yell to hear herself above the roar coming so close to her. "Oh Father, with nothing I came into this world, and with nothing I leave this world."

With her arms raised she lowered her head in submission to God. The debris flying around her was so thick that she shut her eyes. When she opened them again she saw Jesus standing and welcoming her into His kingdom, and standing next to him were her mother and father.

A few feet away from Miss Emma, who had just hit her knees, Miss Molly had a decidedly different reaction. When her sister went to her knees, she turned and hurled herself in the opposite direction. While running and jumping as quickly as she could the sound got closer and closer.

Looking up to the heavens as she ran she said anxiously, "Why have you done this Lord?" She then felt the crush of the churning debris pick her up and pound her into the ground. Although a fellow angel had her surrounded by his wings she felt an intense agony so all pervasive that she did not want to open her eyes, yet when she did, she saw Emma, already robed in white, standing next to Jesus along with their parents.

A Fatal Tree

Mr. O'Conner was at Sang Hollow when the flood began. He remained there through the afternoon and night, and he states that there was a fatal tree on the island against which a number of people were dashed and instantly killed. Their bodies were almost tied in a knot doubled over the tree by the force of the current. Mr. O' Conner says that the first man who came down had his brains knocked out against this obstruction. In fact, those who hit the tree met the same fate and were instantly killed under the pile of driftwood collected there. He could give no estimate of the number lost at this point but says that it is certainly large.

Braves Death for His Family

One of the most thrilling [shocking] incidents of the disaster was the performance of A. J. Leonard, whose family reside in Morrellville, a short distance below this point.

He was at work here, and hearing that his house had been swept away determined at all hazards to ascertain the fate of his family. The bridges having been carried away he constructed a temporary raft and clinging to it as close as a cat to the side of a fence, he pushed his frail craft out in the raging torrent and started on a chase which, to all who were watching, seemed to mean an embrace in death.

Heedless of cries "For God's sake go back, you will be drowned," and "Don't attempt it," he persevered. As the raft struck the current he threw off his coat and in his shirt sleeves braved the stream. Down plunged the boards and down went Leonard, but as it rose he was seen still clinging. A mighty shout arose from the throats of the hundreds on the banks, who were now deeply interested, earnestly hoping he would successfully ford the stream.

Down again went his bark, but nothing, it seemed, could shake Leonard off. The craft shot up in the air apparently ten or twelve feet, and Leonard stuck to it tenaciously. Slowly but surely, he worked his boat to the other side of the stream, and after what seemed an awful suspense he finally landed amid ringing cheers of men, women and children.

The last seen of him he was making his way down a mountain road in the direction of the spot where his house had lately stood. His family consisted of his wife and three children.

An Angel in the Mud

The Pennsylvania Railroad Company's operators at Switch Corner, which is near Sang Hollow, tell thrilling stories of the scenes witnessed by them on Friday afternoon and evening. Said one of them:

"In order to give you an idea of how the tidal wave rose and fell, let me say that I kept a measure and timed the rise and fall of the water, and in forty-eight minutes it fell four and a half feet.

"I believe that when the water goes down about seventy-five children and fifty grown persons will be found among the weeds and bushes in the bend of the river just below the tower.

"There the current was very strong, and we saw dozens of people swept under the trees, and I don't believe that more than one in twenty came out on the other side."

"They found a little girl in white just now," said one of the other operators.

"Good God!" said the chief operator, "she isn't dead, is she!"

"Yes; they found her in a clump of willow bushes, kneeling on a board, just about the way we saw her when she went down the river." Turning to me he said:

"That was the saddest thing we saw all day yesterday. Two men came down on a little raft, with a little girl kneeling between them, and her hands raised and praying. She came so close to us we could see her face, and that she was crying. She had on a white dress and looked like a little angel. She went under that cursed shoot in the willow bushes at the bend like all the rest, but we did hope she would get through alive."

"And so, she was still kneeling," he said to his companion, who had brought the unwelcome news.

"She sat there," was the reply, "as if she were still praying, and there was a smile on her poor little face, though her mouth was full of mud."

All agreed in saying that at least one hundred people were drowned below Nineveh.

Direful Incidents

The situation at Johnstown grows worse as fuller particulars are being received in Pittsburgh.

This morning it was reported that three thousand people were lost in the flood. In the afternoon this number was increased to six thousand, and at this writing dispatches place the number at ten thousand.

It is the most frightful destruction of life that has ever been known in the United States.

VAMPIRES AT HAND

It is stated that already a large gang of thieves and vampires have descended on and near the place. Their presumed purpose is to rob the dead and ransack the demolished buildings.

The Tenth regiment of the Pennsylvania National Guard has been ordered out to protect property.

A telegram from Bolivar says Lockport did not suffer much, but that sixty-five families were turned out of their homes. The school at that place is filled with mothers, fathers, daughters and children.

NOBLE ACTS OF HEROISM

Edward Dick, a young railroader living in the place, saw an old man floating down the river on a tree trunk whose agonized face and streaming gray hair excited his compassion. He plunged into the torrent, clothes and all, and brought the old man safely ashore. Scarcely had he done this when the upper story of a house floated by on which Mrs. Adams, of Cambria, and her two children were borne. He plunged in again, and while breaking through the tin roof of the house cut an artery in his left wrist, but, although weakened with loss of blood, succeeded in saving both mother and children.

George Shore, another Lockport swimmer, pulled out William Jones, of Cambria, who was almost exhausted and could not possibly have survived another twenty minutes in the water.

John Decker, who has some celebrity as a local pugilist [boxer], was also successful in saving a woman and boy, but was nearly killed in a third attempt to reach the middle of the river by being struck by a huge log. The most miraculous fact about the people who reached Bolivar alive was how they passed through the falls half way between Lockport and Bolivar. The seething waters rushed through that barrier of rock with a noise which drowned that of all the passing trains. Heavy trees were whirled high in the air out of the water, and houses which reached there whole were dashed to splinters against the rocks.

A Tale of Horror

On the floor of William Mancarro's house, groaning with pain and grief, lay Patrick Madden, a furnace man of the Cambria Iron Company. He told of his terrible experience in a voice broken with emotion. He said: "When the Cambria Iron Company's bridge gave way I was in the house of a neighbor, Edward Garvey. We were caught through our own neglect, like a great many others, and a few minutes before the houses were struck Garvey remarked that he was a good swimmer, and could get away no matter how high the water rose. Ten minutes later I saw him and his son-in-law drown.

"No human being could swim in that terrible torrent of debris. After the South Fork reservoir broke I was flung out of the building and saw, when I rose to the surface of the water, my wife hanging upon a piece of scantling. She let it go and was drowned almost within reach of my arm and I could not help or save her. I caught a log and floated with it five or six miles, but it was knocked from under me when I went over the dam. I then caught a bale of hay and was taken out by Mr. Morenrow.

A dispatch from Greensburg says the Day Express, which left Pittsburgh at eight o'clock on Friday morning was lying at Johnstown in the evening at the time the awful rush of waters came down the mountains. We have been informed by one who was there that the coach next to the baggage car was struck by the raging flood, and with its human freight cut loose from the rest of the train and carried down the stream. All on board, it is feared, perished. Of the passengers who were left on the track, fifteen or more who endeavored to flee to the mountains were caught, it is thought, by the flood, and likewise carried to destruction. Samuel Bell, of Latrobe, was conductor on the train, and he describes the scene as the most appalling and heart-rending he ever witnessed.

A special dispatch from Latrobe says: "The special train which left the Union Station, Pittsburgh, at half-past one arrived at Nineveh Station, nine miles from Johnstown, last evening at five o'clock. The train was composed of four coaches and locomotive, and carried, at the lowest calculation, over nine hundred persons, including the members of the press. The passengers were packed in like sardines and many were compelled to hang out upon the platform. A large proportion of the passengers were curiosity seekers, while there was a large sprinkling of suspicious looking characters, who had every appearance of being crooks and wreckers, such as visit all like disasters for the sole purpose of plundering and committing kindred depredations.

When the train reached Nineveh the report spread through it that a number of bodies had been fished out of the water and were awaiting identification at a neighboring planing mill. I stopped off to investigate the rumor, while the balance of the party journeyed on toward Sang Hollow, the nearest approach to Johnstown by rail. I visited Mumaker's planing mills and found that the report was true.

All day long the rescuers had been at work, and at this writing (six o'clock) they have taken out seventy-eight dead bodies, the majority of whom are women and children. The bodies are horribly mutilated and covered with mud and blood. Fifteen of them are those of men. Their terribly mutilated condition makes identification for the present almost impossible. One of the bodies found was that of a woman, apparently about thirty-five years of age.

Every conveyance that could be used has been pressed into service. Latrobe is all agog with excitement [extreme travail] over the great disaster. Almost every train takes out a load of roughs and thugs who are bent on mischief. They resemble the mob that came to Pittsburgh during the riots.

Measures of Relief

Pittsburgh is in a wild state of excitement [animation]. A large mass meeting was held yesterday afternoon and in a short space of time $1,000 was subscribed for the sufferers.

The Pennsylvania company has been running trains every hour to the scene of the disaster or as near it as they can get. Provisions and a large volunteer relief corps have been sent up. The physicians have had an enthusiastic meeting at which one and all freely offered their services.

The latest project is to have the wounded and the survivors who fled to the hillsides from the angry rush of waters brought to Pittsburgh. The Exposition Society has offered the use of its splendid new building as a temporary hospital. All the hospitals in the city have also offered to care for the sufferers free of charge to the full limit of their capacity.

Word has been received at Allegheny Junction, twenty-two miles above Pittsburgh, from Leechburg that a woman and two children were seen floating past there at five o'clock yesterday morning on top of some wreckage. They were alive, and their pitiful cries for help drew the attention of the people on the shore. Some men got a boat and endeavored to reach the sufferers.

As they rowed out in the stream the woman could be heard calling to them to save the children first.

The men made a gallant effort. It was all without avail, as the strong current and floating masses of debris prevented them from reaching the victims, and the latter floated on down the stream until their despairing cries could no longer be heard.

Mrs. Chambers, of Apollo, was swept away when her house was wrecked during the night. She had gone to bed when the flood came and she had not time to dress. Fortunately, she managed to secure a hold on some wreckage which was being carried past her. She kept her hold until her cries were heard by some men a short distance above Leechburg. They got out a boat and succeeded in reaching her, and took her to a house near the bank of the river. When they got her there it was found that she was badly bruised and all her clothing had been torn off by the debris with which she had come in contact, leaving her entirely naked. She was also rescued at Natrona.

A LUCKY CHANGE OF RESIDENCE

Mr. F. J. Moore, of the Western Union office in this city, is giving thanks today for the fortunate escape of his wife and two children from the devastated city. As if by some foreknowledge of the impending disaster, Mr. Moore had arranged to have his family move yesterday from Johnstown and join him in this city. Their household goods were shipped on Thursday, and yesterday just in time to save themselves, the little party departed in the single train which made the trip between Johnstown and Pittsburgh. I called on Mrs. Moore at her husband's apartments, No. 4 Webster Avenue, and found her completely prostrated by the news of the final catastrophe, coupled with the dangerous experience through which she and her little ones had passed.

"Oh, it was terrible," she said. "The reservoir had broken, and before we got out of the house the water filled the cellar, and on the way to the depot it was up to the carriage bed. Our train left at a quarter to two P. M., and at that hour the flood had commenced to rise with terrible rapidity. Houses and sheds were carried away, and two men were drowned almost under our very eyes. People gathered on the roofs to take refuge from the water which poured into the lower rooms of their dwellings, and many families took fright and became scattered beyond hope of being reunited.

Just as the train pulled out I saw a woman crying bitterly. Her house had been flooded and she had escaped, leaving her husband behind, and her fears for his safety made her almost crazy. Our house was in the lower part of the town, and it makes me shudder to think what would have happened had we remained in it an hour longer. So far as I know we were the only passengers from Johnstown on the train, and therefore I suppose we are the only persons who got away in time to escape the culminating disaster."

Mrs. Moore's little son told me how he had seen the rats driven out of their holes by the flood and running along the tops of the fences. Mr. Moore endeavored to get to Johnstown yesterday, but was prevented by the suspension of traffic and says he is very glad of it.

What the Eye Hath Seen

The scenes at Heanemyer's planing mill at Nineveh, where the dead bodies are lying, are never to be forgotten. The torn, bruised and mutilated bodies of the victims are lying in a row on the floor of the planing mill which looks more like the field of Bull Run after that disastrous battle than a work shop. The majority of the bodies are nude, their clothing having been torn off. All along the river bits of clothing, a tiny shoe, a baby dress, a mother's evening wrapper, a father's coat, and in fact every article of wearing apparel imaginable may be seen hanging to stumps of trees and scattered on the bank.

One of the most pitiful sights of this terrible disaster came to my notice this afternoon when the body of a young girl was taken out of the Conemaugh river. She was apparently quite young, though her features were terribly disfigured. Nearly all the clothing was torn off the body and she had no legs below her hips. The limp body, with matted hair had some holes in her head. Her eyes were knocked out and all bespattered with blood. It was a ghastly spectacle.

HAEL: ARRIVE COMPLETE

Forgive me for saying it like this, especially after the previous paragraph, but isn't it exciting to know that when you arrive in heaven, you arrive complete?

It is always a miraculous event for us angels to watch and experience. We are with you at death and if your body is mutilated, as happened so much in the Johnstown flood, when we reach out to you, to carry you to the Son, the body we hold is somehow complete. It is made whole so that we are not holding a mutilated body, but the whole, complete body that will inhabit heaven. Miraculous!

So, let me have one of the Guardian Angels tell you about Miss Cora.

Thank you Hael, I will call her Cora even though it is not her full name. It is close enough though. Her full name would be known by some of her family that still exist in the 21ˢᵗ century and they may not want me to tell this story of her family, of them. You see, Miss Cora was born with mere stubs for legs. The stubs did not reach even to where her knees would have been.

Her father and grandfather before him were liquor brewers from Tennessee that had moved to East Conemaugh ten years before she was born. After the flood they returned to Tennessee where they still make illegal liquor.

They chose East Conemaugh, which is situated just above Johnstown, for they saw the opportunity to build a whiskey still outside of town, which would accommodate the growing community of hard working and hard drinking men.

When Cora was born she was a great disappointment to her father. Her mother took her own life shortly after childbirth. Being drunk nearly the entire pregnancy she could not handle the pressure of giving birth to a deformed child.

Her father, we'll call him Herman although that is not his name, wanted to bury the baby alive, but instead chose to make Cora pay. So he made her six-year-old sister responsible for her. The child resented Cora and only cared for her when Herman was watching. As Cora grew she learned to get around using her arms only, for her sister would never carry her. Even as a child Cora would pull herself along the road, or a path and do the best she could to keep up with the other children who lived near them.

When the flood came, Cora, now 13 years old did her best to climb the steep mountainside to get away from the oncoming water. Her arms quickly gave out and her screams to her sister went unanswered. Just before the water and the preceding debris wave reached her, she remembered an old man who passed through East Conemaugh, riding a donkey with funny looking long ears, a full two years earlier.

He was a nice man, who treated her kindly and even let her ride his donkey as he ambled by their cabin on his way over the mountain. She had never known kindness and so his actions remained in her memory and returned to her now.

As the sound of the crashing of the debris got closer and closer to Cora, she was surprised that her memory was flooded with this kind man. And in that instant, she remembered a story he told her about a carpenter who lived a long time ago and died for her to be saved.

All she knew about this man from long ago was that He loved her, and she somehow knew that His love was real. Nearly not hearing the crashing that would be upon her in moments she smiled, and in that moment, I wrapped my wings around Cora, I had time to hum to her and then I carried her to this Man from long ago, she recognized something odd. Her legs were longer than they had been her whole life.

When I set her down before Jesus, she immediately knew He was the man who loved her. She was so excited she did not know whether to jump up and down on her new legs or hug Jesus. It would be the first time in her entire life that she hugged another human being.

With a smile on my face I can tell you that Cora jumped up and down, to the smiles of her Savior Jesus. And then she noticed a woman standing to the side of this man from long ago. This woman stared at Cora with wonder and awe for it was her mother. She had grown up a Christian, but fell far, far away from the Lord as she grew up.

As Cora hugged her mother she looked at Jesus and asked about the nice old man with the funny looking donkey. Jesus just smiled at her and turned to me. I knelt down in front of her and said, "Cora, I not only had the opportunity to carry you to heaven just now, but I met you two years ago, riding that crazy mule. Jesus knew that no one would take you to church, so He allowed me to tell you about Him.

As Cora and I hugged, her mother cried tears of joy that Jesus never did wipe away.

STORY OF THE FIRST FUGITIVES

The first survivors of the Johnstown wreck who arrived in the city last night were Joseph and Henry Lauffer and Lew Dalmeyer, three well known Pittsburghers. They endured considerable hardship and had several narrow escapes with their lives. Their story of the disaster can best be told in their own language. Joe, the youngest of the Lauffer brother said:

"My brother and I left on Thursday for Johnstown. The night we arrived there it rained continually, and on Friday morning it began to flood. I started for the Cambria store at a quarter past eight on Friday, and in fifteen minutes afterward I had to get out of the store in a wagon, the water was running so rapidly. We then arrived at the station and took the Day Express and went as far as Conemaugh, where we had to stop. The limited, however got through, and just as we were about to start, the bridge at South Fork gave way with a terrific crash, and we had to stay there. We then went to Johnstown. This was at a quarter to ten in the morning, when the flood was just beginning. The whole city of Johnstown was inundated and the people all moved up to the second floor.

Mountains of Water

"Now this is where the trouble occurred. These poor unfortunates did not know the reservoir would burst, and there are no skiffs in Johnstown to escape in. When the South Fork basin gave way mountains of water twenty feet high came rushing down the Conemaugh River, carrying before them death and destruction. I shall never forget the harrowing scene. Just think of it! Thousands of people, men, women and children, struggling and weeping and wailing as they were being carried suddenly away in the raging current. Houses were picked up as if they were but a feather, and their inmates were all carried away with them, while cries of, 'God help me!' 'Save me!' I am drowning!' 'My child!' and the like were heard on all sides. Those who were lucky enough to escape went to the mountains, and there they beheld the poor unfortunates being crushed among the debris to death without any chance of being rescued. Here and there a body was seen to make a wild leap into the air and then sink to the bottom.

"At the stone bridge of the Pennsylvania company people were dashed to death against the piers. When the fire started there, hundreds of bodies were burned. Many lookers-on up on the mountains, especially the women, fainted."

Mr. Lauffer's brother, Harry, then told his part of the tale, which was not less interesting. He said: "We had the most narrow escapes of anybody, and I tell you we don't want to be around when anything of that kind occurs again.

"The scenes at Johnstown have not in the least been exaggerated, and indeed the worst is to be heard. When we got to Conemaugh and just as we were about to start the bridge gave way. This left the Day Express, the accommodation, a special train and a freight train at the station. Above was the South Fork water basin, and all of the trains were well filled. We were discussing the situation when suddenly, without any warning, the whistles of every engine began to shriek, and in the noise, could be heard the warning of the first engineer, 'My God! Rush to the mountains, the reservoir has burst.' Then, with a thundering like peal came the mad rush of waters. No sooner had the cry been heard than those who could, with a wild leap rushed from the train and up the mountains. To tell this story takes some time, but the moments in which the horrible scene was enacted were few. Then came the tornado of water, leaping and rushing with tremendous force. The waves had angry crests of white and their roar was something deafening. In one terrible swath they caught the four trains and lifted three of them right off the track, as if they were only a cork. There they floated in the river. Think of it, three large locomotives and finely varnished Pullmans floating around, and above all the hundreds of poor unfortunates who were unable to escape from the car swiftly drifting toward death. Just as we were about to leap from the car I saw a mother with a smiling, blue eyed baby in her arms. I snatched it from her and leaped from the train just as it was lifted off of the track. The mother and child were saved, but if one more minute had elapsed we all would have perished.

HAEL: GOD'S TRANSFERABLE MERCY

I know that sounds like an unorthodox section title, "Transferable Mercy" but let me ask you, do you have a horse? The author who introduced me to the world does, and he has learned that your attitude transfers to the horse you are riding.

In that same way, the lady in the paragraph above experienced mercy from the Lord and passed it on to her "smiling blue-eyed baby in her arms." You see, she chose not to worry. It happened like this.

The mother had heard the tornado of water like everyone else, but she had learned something a long time ago that helped her through this incident. Growing up as a little girl in Altoona, Pennsylvania, Miss Luella lived with a mother that worried about everything. As a teenager her mother embarrassed her at church prayer meetings when she would pray, not trusting the Lord for His protection but nearly demanding that God tell her how He planned to help her troubles.

What Luella did not realize is that living under that kind of a mother caused her to worry just as much and maybe even more.

One day her pastor shared something that changed her mother forever and its impact affected Luella. He preacher said, "I found a verse this week that I had never seen before in this light. Psalm 103, verse 19 says "The Lord hath prepared His throne in the heavens and His kingdom ruleth over all." Explaining the verse he said, "This means that God's throne is above the heavens and He is sovereign over everything.

"Do you know what that means?" he asked. "It means that you do not have to worry, ever again."

Needless to say, this caught the attention of both Miss Luella and her mother.

The preacher went on to explain that when he learned what this meant, he seemed to stop worrying. "It has only been a few days," he acknowledged, "but there is a peace that completely transcends my understanding.[1] Reading through the gospels later that same day Matthew 6:34 had a different impact on me. I looked at the beginning of the passage where it says, 'Take therefore no thought for the morrow,' which of course is saying, do not worry about tomorrow.

"And do you know what I realized? I realized that worry is a sin. I had never considered that before."

Over time Luella and her mother stopped worrying, and then one day, while reading in the Epistles, Luella found a verse that had incredible consequences. It says in part, "Give thanks always for all things."[2]

As she and her mother meditated on these verses it became very clear to them, instead of their first reaction to difficulties being to bite their fingernails, so to speak, why not thank the Lord for the situation, good and bad. They made a game out of always trying to "thank the Lord" before the other one.

So it was, on May 31st, 1889, that Luella now Mrs. Luella Humphry grabbed her baby in her arms, and with the sound of hell breaking loose around her, cooed into her baby's face and said, "Chester, my son, we get to thank the Lord that we may get to see Him before your father."

BEYOND THE POWER OF WORDS

"During all of this time the waters kept rushing down the Conemaugh and through the beautiful town of Johnstown, picking up everything and sparing nothing.

The mountains by this time were black with people, and the moans and sighs from those below brought tears to the eyes of the most stony hearted. There in that terrible ramp age were brothers, sisters, wives and husbands, and from the mountain could be seen the panic-stricken marks in the faces of those who were struggling between life and death. I really am unable to do justice to the scene, and its details are almost beyond my power to

---

[1] Philippians 4:7
[2] Ephesians 5:20

relate. Then came the burning of the debris near the Pennsylvania Railroad bridge. The scene was too sickening to endure. We left the spot and journeyed across country and delivered many notes, letters, etc., that were entrusted to us.

We rode thirty-one miles in a buckboard, then walked six miles, reached Blairsville and journeyed again on foot to what is called the "Bow," and from thence we arrived home. On our way we met Mr. F. Thompson, a friend of ours, who resides in Nineveh, and he stated that rescuing parties were busy all day at Annom. One hundred and seventy-five bodies were recovered at that place. An old couple about sixty years of age were rescued from a tree, on which they came floating down the stream. They were clasped in each other's arms.

President Harrison's private secretary, Elijah Halford, and wife, were on the train which was swept away, but escaped and were in the mountains when I left.

Among the lost are Colonel John P. Linton and his wife and children. Colonel Linton was prominent in the Grand Army of the Republic and in the Knights of Pythias and other orders. He was formerly Auditor General of Pennsylvania.

CHAPTER IV
Multiplication of Terrors

The handsome brick High School Building is damaged to such an extent that it will have to be rebuilt. The water attained the height of the window sills of the second floor. Its upper stories formed a refuge for many persons. All Saturday afternoon two little girls could be seen at the windows frantically calling for aid. They had spent all night and the day in the building, cut off from all aid. Without food and drinking water their condition was lamentable. Late in the evening the children were removed to higher ground and properly cared for.

A number of persons had been taken from this building earlier in the day, but in the excitement the children were forgotten. Their names could not be obtained.

HAEL: PARENTLESS

My heart always hurts for children who find themselves parentless. That is what happened above, their parents were killed in the flood and they were left alone. Not on purpose, but just through the confusion of a great tragedy.

Interestingly, by what the Creator spoke, those 6000 or so years ago, we were created parentless. As it turns out, our relationship needs are different than yours. Our needs are not met by "parents" nor are they met completely by one another. As you would expect, our relationship needs are met by the Creator God Himself.

I can also tell you that we have a special relationship with the Holy Spirit and with Jesus that you will not be able to fathom until you get to heaven. It is kind of like ██ *. I hope the* auditors allow that explanation.

DEATH IN MANY FORMS

Morrell Institute, a beautiful building and the old homestead of the Morrell family, is totally ruined. The water has weakened the walls and foundations to such an extent that there is danger of its collapsing. Many families took refuge in this building and were saved. Now that the waters have receded there is danger from falling walls. All day long the crashing of walls could be heard across the river. Before daybreak this morning the sounds could not but make one shudder at the very thought of the horrible deaths that awaited many who had escaped the devastating flood.

Library Hall was another of the fine buildings of the many in the city that is destroyed. Of the Episcopal church not a vestige remains. Where it once stood, there is now a placid lake. The parsonage is swept away, and the rector of the church, Rev. Mr. Diller, was drowned.

BURIED UNDER FALLING BUILDINGS

The church was one of the first buildings to fall. It carried with it several of the surrounding houses. Many of them were occupied. The victims were swept into the comparatively still waters at the bridge, and there met death either by fire or water.

James M Walters, an attorney, spent the night in Alma Hall and relates a thrilling story. One of the most curious occurrences of the whole disaster was how Mr. Walters got to the hall. He has his office on the second floor. His home is at No. 135 Walnut street. He says he was in the house with his family when the waters struck it. All was carried away. Mr. Walter's family drifted on a roof in another direction. He passed down several streets and alleys until he came to the hall. His dwelling struck that edifice and he was thrown into his own office.

LONG DARK NIGHT OF TERROR

About two hundred persons had taken refuge in the hall, and were on the second, third and fourth stories. The men held a meeting and drew up some rules, which all were bound to respect. Mr. Walters was chosen president. Rev. Mr. Beale was put in charge of the first floor, A. M. Hart of the second floor, Doctor Matthews of the fourth floor. No lights were allowed, and the whole night was spent in darkness. The sick were cared for. The weaker women and children had the best accommodations that could be had, while the others had to wait. The scenes were most agonizing. Heartrending shrieks, sobs and moans pierced the gloomy darkness. The crying of children mingled with the suppressed sobs of the women. Under the guardianship of the men all took more hope. No one slept during all the long dark night. Many knelt for hours in prayer, their supplications mingling with the roar of the waters and the shrieks of the dying in the surrounding houses. In all this misery two women gave premature birth to children.

HAEL: A PRAY-ER PRAYS

Rev. Mr. Beale had been the pastor at the Presbyterian church long enough to be known as a pray-er who would open his sermons with a fifteen-minute prayer. The men and women on the first floor where he took responsibility were glad for his unending prayers. He prayed to the God of protection, to the sovereign God. He used the Word of God and his prayers brought comfort to all of those within earshot.

As is typical of a preacher who is also a man of prayer, he tried to teach, through his prayer to those who were on his floor. You may or may not know this, but your prayers are recorded in heaven[1] so I went to our ▮▮▮▮▮ machine and pulled out his prayer, and a few notes that we made. It follows here,[2] as we recorded it:

"I am concerned, my friends, that God is disciplining us.

"This flooding has challenged me to ask myself, have I had a proper perspective of prayer in general and of sin in particular in my life and in the church?

"1 Peter 4:17 says, it is time for judgment to begin in the church house.

"A famous man of prayer would say,

"The world doesn't need Jesus, the church needs Jesus."

"If we had revival we couldn't sustain it," because we're too busy with OTHER things.

"Paul says, I am the chief of sinners. . . well he was not, I am

"And I am convinced that until we can say this, like Paul, about ourselves, our prayers will be weak and amount to nothing. I trust that this prayer will challenge you.

"Father, thank You for the reminder of my lack of importunity.

"I have asked You to teach me to weep when I pray, and I trust that this is a part of that teaching, but beyond that, lead me, guide me, teach me to pray, Lord.

---

[1] Revelation 5:8

[2] Author's Note: This is actually my prayer from our modern era hurricanes and flooding on September 12, 2017, taken from my journal on that day. I merely adapted it to Dr. Rev. Beale, a real person and a mighty man of prayer: http://markmirza.com/hurricanes-harvey-irma-cause-pray/

"Lord, I pray a lot, but do I really bang on the doors of Heaven?

"When was the last time I prayed 'Lord hear my prayer, Let My Cry for Help come before You. Do not hide Your face from me in my day of trouble? Listen closely to me, answer me quickly when I call."[1]

"Father, when was the last time I came to You just begging You to Hear My Cry before I even shared my concern? Oh Lord, I am begging You, Hear My Cry this day.

"When was the last time I came to You with tears over this subject or any subject? Oh Lord, my Lord, forgive me, the idea of praying with importunity (or "being annoyingly persistent") is so outside of what I have practiced. Forgive Me Lord.

"God, Hear My Cry, pay attention to my prayer. I call to You from the ends of the Earth, my heart is without strength, lead me to a rock that is high above me, for You have been a refuge for me, a strong tower. . . I will live in Your tent forever and take refuge under the shelter of Your wings."[2]

At this point a heavy cry went up by the people who were his temporary congregation in that great hall. And he paused for a moment, allowing the people to experience God in their crying out. And then he continued:

"Be gracious to me God, be gracious to me for I take refuge in You. I will seek refuge in The Shadow of Your Wings until danger passes. I called to You, God most high, to God who fulfills His purpose in and for me. You reached down from heaven and saved me, challenging the one who tramples me. God, send Your faithful love and Your truth, for I am surrounded.[3]

"God, listen to my prayer and do not ignore my plea for help. Pay attention to me and answer me. I am restless and in turmoil with all of my troubles."[4]

Again, a great cry went up and the pastor said, "Yes, acknowledge your reliance upon Him." And after a few more minutes he went on:

"Hear my prayer, Lord, and listen to My Cry for Help. Do not to be silent at my tears for I am a foreigner residing with You, a temporary resident like all my fathers. Turn Your angry gaze from me so that I may be cheered up. . . [5]

---

[1] Psalm 102:1-2
[2] Psalm 61:1-4
[3] Psalm 57:1-4
[4] Psalm 55:1-2
[5] Psalm 39:12-13

"I called to the Lord in my distress and I cried to my God for help from His Temple. He heard my voice and my cry to Him reached His ears. [1]

"Lord, do not punish me in Your anger or discipline me in Your Wrath for Your arrows have sunk into me. And Your hand has pressed down on me. There is no health in my body because of Your indignation. There is no strength in my bones because of my sin, for my sins have flooded over my head, they are a burden too heavy for me to bear. My wounds are foul and festering because of my foolishness, Lord, I am bent over and brought low all-day long. I go around in mourning, I am filled with burning pain and there is no health in my body. I am faint and severely crushed. I groan because of the anguish of my heart." [2]

As another cry went up Dr. Beale merely continued, praying louder.

"And Father, I ask for forgiveness because I have not let sin impact me like this. I have not been sorrowful over sin in my past like I am today. And Lord, I acknowledge that it is all out of my own foolishness. [3] *There is no one else that I can blame for my sin. I am asking You for Mercy, Lord."*

Here he paused. He had been looking up into heaven as he prayed but now he looked downwards to all of those who were sitting or lying on the floor and asked them, "What sins do you need to confess before God? Do it now.

"Are there any wrong thoughts or attitudes you need to yield to God? (anger, lust, pride, fear, luke-warmness, jealousy, etc.)

"Are there sinful words that you need to yield? (lying, exaggerating, harshness, unclean or blasphemous speech, etc.)

"Do you have any wrong relationships that you need to address? (someone you need to forgive, or ask forgiveness of, family relationships: are you loving and nurturing your family, are you handling relationships selfishly)

"Are there things you need to stop doing, and things you need to do more faithfully?

"Are there any specific ways that you are ignoring or delaying to fully surrender to Christ's Lordship?" [4]

Rev. Mr. Beale then looked up to heaven again and continued: "Lord, my every desire is known to You. My sin is not hidden from You. My heart races, my strength leaves me and even the light of my eyes has faded. My loved ones and

---

[1] Psalm 18:6

[2] Psalm 38:1-8

[3] Psalm 38:5b

[4] These 5 sentences of questions come from Greg Frizzell "Praying God's Heart In Times Like These," page 36 (not exact quotes, but paraphrased quite closely.)

115

friends may be dead, and my relatives live at a distance away from me. And still, the evil one and those influenced by him, seek my life, set traps and those who want to harm me threaten to destroy me. They plot treachery all day long. I am like a deaf person, I do not hear. I am like a speechless person who does not open his mouth. I am like a man who does not hear and has no arguments in his mouth. I put my hope in You, Lord (another cry went up, but the pastor kept on) and I trust You to answer, Lord, my God. For I said, 'don't let them Rejoice over me, those who are arrogant toward me when I stumble, for I am about to fall, and my pain is constantly with me.' So I confess my guilt. I am anxious because of my sin but my enemies are vigorous and powerful. Many hate me for no reason. Those who repay me evil for good attacked me for pursuing good. Lord, do not abandon me, my God. Do not be far from me, hurry to help me, my Lord and my Savior.[1]

"Oh Lord, my Lord, I need You to be magnificent in my life. Father, forgive me for waiting until darkness has overtaken me to pray with this kind of emphasis. Forgive me for being a pastor and not regularly practicing this kind of Prayer. Forgive me for teaching this kind of prayer and not putting it into constant practice.

"God, listen to my prayer and do not ignore my plea for help. Pay attention to me and answer me. I am restless, and I am in turmoil with my troubles and with the turmoil in our land.[2]

"God, Hear My Cry, pay attention to my prayer. I call to You from the ends of the Earth, for my heart is without strength…[3]

"Lord, hear my prayer. Let My Cry for Help come before You. Do not hide Your face from me in my day of trouble. Listen closely to me, answer me quickly when I call.[4]

"For the Lord will not reject us forever. Even if and when You cause suffering, Father, You will show compassion according to Your abundant faithful love. You do not enjoy bringing Affliction or suffering on mankind."[5]

The great man now paused. I call him a great man for surely he must be to pray like this from memory of the Scriptures. His wailing to the Lord quieted and the people did too, and then he went on:

---

[1] Psalm 38:9-22
[2] Psalm 5:1-2
[3] Psalm 61:1-2a
[4] Psalm 102:1-2
[5] Lamentations 3:31-33

"Let us search out and examine our ways, Father. I have done that, I have searched and examined my ways and now I'm turning back to You. I lift up my heart and my hands to You, Father. I acknowledge that I have sinned and rebelled. If You have not already, please forgive me now. For You have gone so far as to cover Yourself in anger and pursue me, You have covered Yourself with a cloud so that none of my prayers passed through to You. Lord, I feel like You have made me as disgusting filth among the people.[1]

"Lord, I call upon Your name, Your name, Yahweh, from the depths of the pit where I am. I know that You hear my plea. Please do not ignore my cry for relief. I know that You come near when I call and when You do that You tell me to not be afraid. Oh Lord, my Lord, show me Your Majesty. Hear My Cry, hear it now.[2]

"Lord, do not rebuke me in Your anger. Do not discipline me in Your Wrath. Oh Father, be gracious to me. I am weak, I am stupid, and I am dumb. Heal Me Lord, for my bones shake. Lord rescue me, save me because of Your faithful love, for there is no remembrance of You when I am in Sheol, when I am dead. I can't thank You when I'm in the grave. Father, I am weary from my groaning. Lord, I acknowledge that with my tears I do not dampen my pillow. Oh, that I would drench my bed in my mourning and groaning, like I am now. My eyes are swollen from grief, they grow old because of all my enemies and Father, I am my worst enemy when I sin. Depart from me all evildoers and I know that includes my sin. Lord, You have heard the sound of my weeping. Oh Lord, You have heard my plea for help. Father, I have trusted You to accept my prayer. Lord, let the enemies of my heart be ashamed and shake with Terror, let them turn back and suddenly be disgraced. Father, I no longer want to sin anymore.[3]

"Now that I have prayed Lord, I simply close with, Praise be to You, the God of Heaven, the One who hears my prayers. Lord, I'm reminded of Jeremiah 1:12b, I pray to You, the One who hastens His word to perform it, Who hustles to do that which is His Word.

"And though I do not deserve any Mercy from You, I plead for it this day though, and I trust You for mercy, to honor Your name. And that is my expectation today, Father.

"I have come to You and laid these requests before You and now I wait in expectation."[4]

---

[1] Lamentations 3:40-45
[2] Lamentations 3:55-57
[3] Psalm 6
[4] Psalm 5:3

And from all over the first floor and even from some of the higher floors came "Amens" as Rev. Dr. Beale said amen. . . and in a few cases, people were glad that he was finally done.

HERE IS A HERO.

Dr. Matthews is a hero. Several of his ribs were crushed by a falling timber and his pains were most severe, yet through all he attended the sick. When two women in a house across the street shouted for help he with two other brave young men climbed across the drift and ministered to their wants. No one died during the night, but women and children surrendered their lives on the succeeding day as a result of terror and fatigue. Miss Rose Young, one of the young ladies in the hall, was frightfully cut and bruised Mrs. Young had a leg broken. All of Mr. Walter's family were saved.

While the loss of property about Brookville, the lumber center of Pennsylvania, by the great flood has been enormous, variously estimated at from $250,000 to $500,000, not a single life has been lost. At least there have been none reported so far, and I have traveled over the line from Red Bank, on the Valley road, to Dubois, on the low-grade division. Every creek is swollen to many times its natural size. A great deal of the low-lying farm lands and roads in places have water enough over them to float an ordinary steamboat.

Leaving Pittsburgh Saturday morning on the valley road, we ran past millions and millions of feet of lumber. From the city to the junction opposite Freeport the river was almost choked with debris of broken and shattered houses. In places the river was fairly black with floating masses of lath, shingles, roofs, floors and other lumber that had formerly been houses. The sight was appalling and spoke louder than any pen can describe.

At Red Bank the river was filled with a different kind of lumber, including huge saw logs ready for cutting. From the estimates of an old lumber man who was on the train I was told that between the stations named we passed at least ten million feet of lumber, which means a loss of fully $100,000 to the owner. A big portion of this came out of the Clarion river, the estimated money lost from that section alone being anywhere from $500,000 to $750,000.

All along the Allegheny river were gathered people trying to catch the logs, risking their lives, for the logs swept down the river in a current that was

118

running fully ten miles an hour. The work was very hazardous. The catchers are allowed by law six and a quarter cent for each log captured, and the river was almost lined with people trying to save the property.

At Red Bank, which we left at noon, there were at least six feet of water expected from Oil City, and with it, according to the reports from up the river, was an immense amount of lumber. Leaving the valley road at Red Bank we went up the low-grade division to Bryant, where immense sawmills, the largest in the vicinity are located. The current was rushing along at a rate anywhere from twelve to fifteen miles an hour, tossing the huge logs around like so many toothpicks and carrying everything before them. So great was the current and mass of logs that the big iron bridge at Reynoldsville, sixteen miles above Brookville, was swept away, as were two wagon bridges and several small foot bridges.

HUNDREDS HOMELESS AND SUFFERING.

Many houses here and there along Red Bank Creek were turned upside down, some of them floating clear away, while the more secure ones were flooded with water clear into the second floors. Many of the smaller cottages and shanties were covered, leaving only the peaks of the roofs sticking out to show the spots that families had but a few hours before called home. All along the railroad track was piled the few household effects, furniture, bedding, tables and clothes which the poor owners had saved before they were forced out on the high ground. These same people had gone to bed last evening thinking themselves safe from the high water, only to be wakened about midnight by the noise of the rushing floods and the huge saw logs bumping against their homes. The very narrow escapes that some of them made while getting their families into places of safety would fill many pages of this book.

FLOATING TO SAFETY ON SAW LOGS

One man had to mount the different members of his family on logs. The mother and children alike sat astride of them, and then, with the father on the other end, were poled across to the high ground.

Another man, whose house was in a worse place, swam ashore and, throwing a rope back to the mother, who was surrounded on the porch of the house by the children, yelled for her to tie one end to the little ones so he could pull them over the fast running water. This operation was continued until the entire family was rescued.

Willing workers from the neighborhood were not long in getting huge bonfires started, and with the aid of these and dry clothing brought in haste by people whose homes stood on higher ground the family were soon warmed.

The same willing hands hastily constructed sheds, and with immense bonfires the people were kept warm till daylight. Others, more fortunate, were able to save enough from their houses to make themselves comfortable for a short season of camping. One poor family I noticed had saved enough carpet to make a tent out of, and under this temporary shelter the mother was doing her best to prepare a meal and attend to her other household duties.

HAEL: YOUR INDOMITABLE SPIRIT

This will be the first time, but not the last time I refer to this spirit that you have. When a disaster strikes, you, as a people rise up, and regardless of ethnicity you "rise to the occasion." That is being seen even now, in Houston TX and the outlying areas, as I write this manuscript. Here in heaven we are watching you.

This indomitable spirit is much more prevalent than the notion of selfish men and women who will not help someone who looks or talks differently than them. Did you know that Jesus spoke to this issue? On his last night with His disciples, the evening He was betrayed, during His High Priestly prayer He said, that through unity, men and women would know that He came from the Father.[1]

In light of that, may I ask how connected you are to others in your town that perhaps pray differently than you, baptize differently than you, and heaven forbid, vote differently than you? Just a quick question that I consider relevant.

SHELTERED BY FRIENDLY NEIGHBORS

In Brookville, a great many houses were submerged, but no lives were lost. While the people were driven from their homes, they were more fortunate than the people of Bryants, because they could at once find shelter under the roofs of the neighbors' houses.

All of the saw mills, the chief industry of the town, were closed down. Some because the water was over the first floor, and others because their

---

[1] John 17:21

entire working force were on the creek trying to construct temporary booms, by which they expected to save at least a portion of the property from being swept away. One man rigged a boom with the aid of a cable 1,600 feet long and thick enough to hold the heaviest steamer. About fifty logs were chained together for further protection. This arrangement for a time checked the mass of logs, but just when everybody was thinking it would stop the output a small dam gave way, bringing down with it another half million feet of lumber. When this struck the temporary boom it parted, as if the huge cable was a piece of thread, and the logs shot past.

Just at Bryants, however, a gorge formed shortly after two o'clock Friday afternoon, and within a remarkably short time there was a pile of logs wedged in that stretched back fully a quarter of a mile and the top of which was more than ten feet high. This of course changed the course of the stream a little, but the natural gorge had saved enough logs to amount to more than $100,000 in money.

The following comments by one of our journals sum up the situation after receiving the dreadful news of the three preceding days:

THE GREAT CALAMITY

The appalling catastrophe which has spread such awful havoc through the teeming valley of the Conemaugh almost surpasses belief and fairly staggers imagination. Without yet measuring its dire extent, enough is known to rank it as the greatest calamity of the natural elements which this country has ever witnessed. Nothing in our history short of the deadly blight of battle has approached this frightful cataclysm, and no battle, though destroying more life, has ever left such a ghastly trail of horror and devastation. It seems more like one of those terrible convulsions of nature from which we have hitherto been happily spared, but which at rare intervals have swallowed up whole communities in remote South American or oriental lands.

Ingenious and masterful as the human intellect is in guiding and controlling the ordinary forces of nature, how impotent and insignificant it appears in the presence of such a transcendent disaster! It is well-nigh inconceivable that a great section throbbing with populous towns, and resonant with the hum of industry, should be wiped out in the twinkling of an eye by a mighty, raging torrent, more consuming than fire and more violent than the earthquake. The suddenness of the blow and the impossibility of communicating with the scene add to the terror of the event. The sickening spectacle of ruin and death which will be revealed when the veil of darkness is lifted is left to conjecture. The imagination can scarcely picture the dread realities, and it would be difficult to overdraw the awful features of a calamity which has every element of horror.

HAEL: ARROGANCE

As this 1889 author laments a very real issue, namely, the uncontrollable power of natural disasters, I am reminded of your towns, your cities, which are building bridges, "that are earthquake proof."

Am I missing something?

THE RIVER AND LAKE

Nature is so framed at the fated point for such a disaster that man was called upon for unceasing vigilance. The Conemaugh makes its channel through a narrow valley between high ranges. Numerous streams drain the surrounding mountains into its current. Along its course swarm frequent hamlets busy with the wealth dug from the seams of the earth. The chief of these towns, the seat of an immense industry, lies in a little basin where the gap broadens to take in a converging stream and then immediately narrows again, no outlet save the constricted waterway. High above stands a great lake which is held in check only by an artificial barrier, and which, if once unchained, must pour its resistless torrent through this narrow gorge like a besom of destruction overwhelming everything before it. There were all the elements of an unparalleled disaster. Years of immunity had given a feeling of security for all time without some extraordinary and unexpected occasion. But the occasion appeared when in unforeseen force the rains descended and the floods came, and today desolation reigns.

HAEL: WHAT REIGNS

The above paragraph says that, "desolation reigns" and in light of this incredible tragedy I will agree. Yes, desolation reigns. "But God." What great words that we find all over Scripture, "But God." You see, there is nothing that occurs on earth that does not run through His fingers first. While desolation is ruling, His throne is still fixed above the heavens and He still reigns and rules over all.[1]

And that is where your hope comes from, not focusing on the troubles around you. Paul said, "There are troubles without, there are fears within."[2] And then he goes on, "But God. . ." Amen? Amen!

But God comforts the humble,[3] and you have the opportunity to demonstrate humility before the Lord in the midst of tragedies when you say like Job, "The Lord takes away."[4] Or you may say like Eli, "He is the Lord. He will do what He thinks is good."[5]

A DIREFUL CALAMITY

It is impossible yet to measure the extent of the calamity. But the destruction of life and property must be something that it is appalling to think of, and the sorrow and suffering to follow are incalculable. A solemn obligation devolves upon the people of the whole country. We cannot remedy the past but we can alleviate the present and the future. Thousands of families are homeless and destitute; thousands are without means of support; perchance, thousands are bereft of the strong arms upon which they have relied. There is an instant, earnest demand for help. Let there be immediate, energetic, generous action. Let us do our part to relieve the anguish and mitigate the suffering of a community upon whom has fallen the most terrible visitation in all our history.

AN HISTORIC CATASTROPHE

When an American Charles Reade wishes in the future to weave into the woof of his novel the account of some great public calamity he will portray the misfortune which overwhelmed the towns and villages lying in the valley of the Conemaugh River. The bursting of a reservoir, and the ensuing scenes of death and destruction, which are so vividly described in "Put Yourself in His Place," were not the creatures of Mr. Reade's imagination, but actual occurrences. The novelist obtained facts and incidents for one of the most striking chapters in all of his works from the

---

[1] Psalm 103:19
[2] 2 Corinthians 7:5
[3] 2 Corinthians 7:6
[4] Job 1:21m
[5] 1 Samuel 3:18b

events which followed the breaking of the Dale Dyke embankment at Sheffield, England, in March 1864, when 238 lives were lost, and property valued at millions was destroyed.

It will need even more vivid and vigorous descriptive powers than Mr. Reade possessed to adequately delineate the scene of destruction and death now presented in Johnstown and the adjacent villages. The Sheffield calamity, disastrous as it proved to be, was a small affair when compared with this latest reservoir accident. The Mill River reservoir disaster of May 1874, with its 200 lives lost and $1,500,000 of property destroyed, almost sinks into insignificance beside it. The only recorded calamity of the kind which anywhere approaches it occurred in Estrecho de Rientes, in Spain, in April, 1802, when a dam burst and drowned 600 persons and swept $7,000,000 worth of property away. But above all these calamities in sad preeminence will stand the Conemaugh disaster.

But dark as the picture is, it will doubtless be relieved by many acts of heroism. The world will wait to learn if there was not present at Conemaugh some Myron Day, whose ride on his bareback steed before the advancing wall of water that burst from Mill River Dam in 1874, shouting to the unsuspecting people as he rode: "The reservoir is breaking! The flood is coming! Fly! Fly for your lives," was the one mitigating circumstance in that scene of woe and destruction. When the full story of the Conemaugh calamity is told it will, doubtless, be found that there were many deeds of heroism performed, many noble sacrifices made and many an act as brave as any performed on the field of battle. Already we are told of husbands and mothers who preferred to share a watery grave with their wives and children sooner than accept safety alone.

Such a calamity, while it makes the heart sick with its story of death and suffering, always serves to bring out the better and higher qualities in men and women, and to illustrate how closely all mankind are bound together by ties of sympathy and compassion. This fact will be made evident now by the open-handed liberality which will quickly flow in to relieve the suffering, and, as far as possible, to repair the loss caused by this historic calamity.

HAEL: THE AFTERMATH OF NOAH'S DELUGE

I so agree with the 1889 writer here. There were so many men and women that came together and helped one another through this calamity. Remember that his book was published a few months after the event, so there were many, many more acts of comfort that people gave that he did not see until later.

But I need to contrast this aftermath, in 1889, with Noah's flood. With Noah's flood there was a much different aftermath, there was no great joy as men and women were found alive for none but Noah and his family remained alive. There was no joining together with those different from themselves, for there were no others.

After Noah's flood, only water moved upon the face of the earth. All living beings outside the ark that had the breath of life were dead.[1] I will never forget that great and awesome deluge. We all sat there in heaven and for 150 days observed the waters surge upon the face of the earth.[2] We were amazed and trusted the Lord, knowing that He had a plan. The demons by contrast wondered if this would be when they were sent to the abyss.[3]

May I just remind you that a day like unto Noah's is coming to the earth again. It will not be in the form of a world-wide flood. There will be no warning as the people of Johnstown experienced. There will be no radar as the victims of Hurricanes Harvey and Irma had. No, this day will come as a thief in the night. Two men will be in the field: one will be taken and one left. Two women will be grinding at the mill: one will be taken and one left. So my friends, please be alert, since you don't know what day your Lord is coming. But know this: If the homeowner had known what time the thief was coming, he would have stayed alert and not let his house be broken into. This is why you also must be ready, because the Son of Man is coming at an hour you do not expect.[4]

And we will welcome you into heaven and the demons will be sent to their final home.

---

[1] Genesis 7:22
[2] Genesis 7:24
[3] Compare Luke 8:31 and Revelation 20:3
[4] Matthew 24:40-44

CHAPTER V
The Awful Work of Death

The record of June 3rd continues as follows: The horror of the situation does not lessen. The latest estimate of the number of dead is an official one by Adjutant General Hastings, and it places the number between 12,000 and 15,000.

The uncovering of hundreds of bodies by the recession of the waters has already filled the air with pestilential odors. The worst is feared for the surviving population, who must breathe this poisoned atmosphere. Sharp measures prompted by sheer necessity have resulted in an almost complete subsidence of cowardly efforts to profit by the results of the disaster. Thieves have slunk into places of darkness and are no longer to be seen at their unholy work.

All thoughts are now fixed upon the hideous revelation that awaits the light of day, when the waters shall have entirely quitted the ruins that now lie beneath them, and shall have exposed the thousands upon thousands of corpses that are massed there.

A sad and gloomy sky, almost as sad and gloomy as the human faces under it, shrouded Johnstown today. Rain fell all day and added to the miseries of the wretched people. The great plain where the best part of Johnstown used to stand was half covered with water. The few sidewalks in the part that escaped the flood were inches thick with black, sticky mud, through which tramped a steady procession of poor women who are left utterly destitute. The tents where the people are housed who cannot find other shelter were cold and cheerless.

HAEL: DEATH TOLL AND THE WEATHER

Again, I would remind you that the official death count was 2,209, far less than was early-on expected. But even that "official" number of 2,209 souls is low, and low by ███████ souls.

Weather was an act of mercy from the Lord, keeping the pestilence potential at a minimum.

A Great Tomb

The town seemed like a great tomb. The people of Johnstown have supped so full of horrors [drunk in so much horror] that they go about in a sort of a daze and only half conscious of their griefs. Every hour, as one goes through the streets, he hears neighbors greeting each other and then inquiring without show of feeling how many each had lost in his family. Today I heard a gray-haired man hail another across the street with this question, "I lost five; all are gone but Mary and I," was the reply.

"I am worse off than that," said the first old gentleman. "I have only my grandson left. Seven of us gone."

And so they passed on without apparent excitement. They and everyone else had heard so much of these melancholy conversations that somehow the calamity had lost its significance to them. They treat it exactly as if the dead persons had gone away and were coming back in a week.

The Ghastly Search

The melancholy task of searching the ruins for more bodies went on today in the soaking rain. There were little crowds of morbid curiosity hunters around each knot of workingmen, but they were not residents of Johnstown. All their curiosity in that direction was satiated long ago. Even those who come in from neighboring towns with the idea of a day's strange and ghastly experiences did not care to be near after they had seen one body exhumed. There were hundreds and thousands of these visitors from the country today. The effect of the dreadful things they saw and heard was to drive most of them to drink. By noon the streets were beginning to be full of boisterous and noisy countrymen, who were trying to counteract the strain on their nerves with unnatural excitement. Then the chief of police, foreseeing the unseemly sights that were likely to disgrace the streets, drove out and kept out all the visitors who had not some good reason for their presence. After that and far into the evening all the country roads were filled with drunken stragglers, who were trying to forget what they had seen.

One thing that makes the work of searching for the bodies very slow is the strange way that great masses of objects were rolled into intricate masses of rubbish.

HORRIBLE MASSES

As the flood came down the valley of the South Fork it obliterated the suburb of Woodvale, where not a house was left, nor a trace of one. The material they had contained rolled on down the valley, over and over, grinding it up to pulp and finally leaving it against an unusually firm foundation or in the bed of an eddy. The masses contain human bodies, but it is slow work to pick them to pieces. In the side of one of them I saw the remnants of a carriage, the body of a harnessed horse, a baby cradle and a doll, a tress of woman's hair, a rocking horse, and a piece of beefsteak still hanging on a hook.

The city is now very much better patrolled than it has been at any time since the flood occurred. Many members of the police force of Pittsburgh came in and offered their services. One of them showed his spirit during the first hour by striking a man, whom he saw opening a trunk among the rubbish, a tremendous blow over the head which knocked him senseless. Several big trunks and safes lie in full sight on the desolate plain in the lower part of the town, but no one dared to touch them after that.

The German Catholic Church at Cambria City, a short distance west of Johnstown, is almost a complete wreck. Rather a singular coincidence in connection with the destruction of the above is that the Immaculate Conception, that stood in the northwest corner of the lecture rooms, stands just as it was when last seen. The figure, which is wax, was not even scratched, and the clothes, which are made of white silk and deep duchess lace, were spotless. This seems strange, when the raging water destroyed everything else in the building. Hundreds of persons visited the place during the day.

HAEL: THE FOG OF WAR

As you see in the midst of tragedy, there are decisions that people would prefer to do over again if they could, but alas they cannot.

Here's my concern for what I see in your 21ˢᵗ century litigious society. You want someone "to pay" for every mistake. And forgive me, but I am reminded of Christ on the cross, not responding to those reviling Him, insulting Him.[1]

---

[1] 1 Peter 2:23

I see many of you touting, "What Would Jesus Do?" bracelets. But I wonder if you are more interested in what you would do, rather than what Jesus would do, especially if what He would do contradicts what you want to do, I'm just sayin'.

TEN BODIES AN HOUR

Bodies are now being brought in at lower Cambria at the rate of ten per hour.

A man named Dougherty tells a thrilling story of a ride down the river on a log. When the waters struck the roof of the house on which he had taken shelter he jumped astride a telegraph pole, riding a distance of some twenty-three miles, from Johnstown to Bolivar, before he was rescued.

Many inquiries have been made as to why the militia did not respond when ordered out by Adjutant General Hastings. "In the first place it is beyond the General's authority to order troops to a scene of this kind unless the Governor first issues a proclamation, then it becomes his duty to issue orders." The General said he was notified that the Pittsburgh troops, consisting of the Fourteenth and Eighteenth regiments, had tendered their services, and no doubt would have been of great service. The General consulted with the Chief Burgess of Johnstown and Sheriff of Cambria county in regard to calling the troops to the scene, but both officials strenuously objected, as they claimed the people would object to anything of this kind. As a proof of this not a breach of peace was committed last night in Johnstown and vicinity.

It has not been generally believed that the district in the neighborhood of Kernville would be so extremely prolific of corpses as it has proven to be. I visited that part of the town where both the river and Stony Creek have done their worst. I found that within the past twenty-four hours almost one thousand bodies had been recovered or were in sight. The place is one great repository of the dead.

THE TOTAL MAY NEVER BE KNOWN

The developments of every hour make it more and more apparent that the exact number of lives lost in the Johnstown horror will never be known. All estimates made to this time are conservative, and when all is known will doubtless be found to have been too small. Over one thousand bodies have been found since sunrise today, and the most skeptical concede that the remains of thousands more rest beneath the debris above the Johnstown bridge. The population of Johnstown, the surrounding towns and the portion of the valley affected by the flood is, or was, from 50,000 to 55,000. Numerous leading citizens of Johnstown, who survived the flood, have been interviewed, and the consensus of opinion was that fully thirty per cent. of the residents of Johnstown and Cambria had been victims of the continued disasters of fire and water. If this be true, the total loss of life in the entire valley cannot be less than seven or eight thousand and possibly much greater. Of the thousands who were devoured by the flames and whose ashes rest beneath the smoking debris is above Johnstown bridge, no definite information can ever be obtained.

HUNDREDS CARRIED MILES AWAY

As little will be learned of hundreds that sank beneath the current and were borne swiftly down the Conemaugh only to be deposited hundreds of miles below on the banks and in the driftwood of the raging Ohio. Probably one-third of the dead will never be recovered, and it will take a list of the missing weeks hence to enable even a close estimate to be made of the number of lives that were lost. That this estimate can never be accurate will be understood when it is remembered that in many instances whole families and their relatives were swept away, and found a common grave beneath the wild waste of waters. The total destruction of the city leaves no data to even demonstrate that the names of these unfortunates ever found place on the pages of eternity's history.

"All indications point to the fact that the death list will reach over five thousand names, and in my opinion the missing will reach eight thousand in number," declared General D. H. Hastings tonight.

At present there are said to have been twenty-two hundred bodies recovered. The great difficulties experienced in getting a correct list is the great number of morgues. There is no central bureau of information, and to communicate with the different dead houses is the work of hours. The journey from the Pennsylvania Railroad morgue to the one in the Fourth ward school house in Johnstown occupies at least one hour. This renders it impossible to reach all of them in one day, particularly as some of the morgues are situated at points inaccessible from Johnstown. At six o'clock in the evening the 630th body had been recovered at the Cambria depository for corpses.

None Left to Care for the Dead

Kernville is in a deplorable condition. The living are unable to take care of the dead. The majority of the inhabitants of the town were drowned. A lean-to of boards has been erected on the only street remaining in the town. This is the headquarters for the committee that controls the dead. As quickly as the dead are brought to this point they are placed in boxes and then taken to the cemetery and buried.

A supply store has opened in the town. A milkman who was overcharging for milk narrowly escaped lynching. The infuriated men appropriated all his milk and distributed it among the poor and then drove him out of the town.

There is but one street left in the town. About one hundred and fifty-five houses are standing where once there stood a thousand. None of the large buildings in what was once a thriving little borough have escaped. One thousand people is a low estimate of the number of lives lost from this town, but few of the bodies have been recovered. It is directly above the ruins and the bodies have floated down into them, where they burned. A walk through the town revealed a desolate sight. Only about twenty-five able-bodied men have survived and are able to render any assistance. Men and women can be seen with black eyes, bruised faces and cut heads.

Useless Calls for Help

The appearance of some of the ladies is heart-rending. They were injured in the flood, and since that have not slept. Their faces have turned a sickly yellow and dark rings surround the eyes. Many have succumbed to nervous prostration. For two days but little assistance could be rendered them. The wounded remained uncared for in some of the houses cut off by the water, and died from their injuries alone. Some were alive on Sunday, and their shouts could be heard by the people on the shore.

A man is now in a temporary jail in what is left of the town. He was caught stealing a gold watch. A shot was fired at him but he was not wounded. The only thing that saved him from lynching was the smallness of the crowd. His sentence will be the heaviest that can be given him.

Services in the chapel from which the bodies were buried consisted merely of a prayer by one of the servers. No minister was present. Each coffin had a descriptive card on it, and on the graves a similar card was placed, so that bodies can be removed later by friends.

There are about thirty Catholic priests and nuns here. The sisters are devoting themselves to the cure of the sick and injured in the hospitals, while the priests are doing anything and everything and making themselves generally useful. Bishop Phelan, who reached here on Sunday evening, returned to Pittsburgh on the three o'clock train yesterday afternoon. He has organized the Catholic forces in this neighborhood, and all are devoting themselves to hard work assiduously.

Mr. Derlin, who heeded the warning as to the danger of the dam, had hurried his wife and two children to the hills, but returned himself to save some things from his house. While in the building the flood struck it and swept it away, jamming it among a lot of other houses and hurling them all around with a regular churning motion. Mr. Derlin was in a fix, but went to his top story, clambered to the roof and escaped from there to solid structures and then to the ground. His property was entirely ruined, but he thinks himself fortunate in saving his family.

Where Woodvale once stood there is now a sea of mud, broken but rarely by a pile of wreckage. I waded through mud and water up the valley today over the site of the former village. As has been often stated, nothing is standing but the old woolen mills. The place is swept bare of all other buildings but the ruins of the Gautier wire mill. The boilers of this great works were carried one hundred yards from their foundations. Pieces of engines, rolls and other machinery were swept far away from where they once stood. The wreck of a fire hose carriage is sticking up out of the mud. It belonged to the crack company of Johnstown. The engine house is swept away, and the cellar is filled with mud, so that the site is obliterated.

A German watchman was on guard at the mill when the waters came. He ran for the hillside and succeeded in escaping. He tells a graphic story of the appearance of the water as it swept down the valley. He declares that the first wave was as high as the third story of a house.

The place is deserted. No effort is being made to clean off the streets. The mire has formed the grave for many a poor victim. Arms and legs are protruding from the mud and it makes the most sickening of pictures.

GENERAL HASTINGS' REPORT

In answer to questions from Governor Beaver, Adjutant General Hastings has telegraphed the following:

"Good order prevailed throughout the city and vicinity last night. Police arrangements are excellent. Not one arrest made. No need of sending troops. The Mayor of Johnstown and the Sheriff of Cambria county, with whom I am in constant communication; request that no troops be sent. I concur in their judgment. There is a great outside clamor for troops. Do not send tents. Have nine hundred here, which are sufficient. I advise you to make a call on the general public for money and other assistance.

"About two thousand bodies have been rescued and the work of embalming and burying the dead is going on with regularity. There is plenty of medical assistance. We have a bountiful supply of food and clothing today, and the fullest telegraphic facilities are afforded and all inquiries are promptly answered.

"Have you any instructions or inquiries? The most conservative estimates here place the number of lives lost at fully 5,000. The prevailing impression is that the loss will reach from 8,000 to 10,000. There are many widows and orphans and a great many wounded-impossible to give an estimate. Property destroyed will reach $25,000,000. The popular estimate will reach $40,000,000 to $50,000,000."

FROM THE GOVERNOR

"I will issue a proclamation tonight to the people of the country and to all who sympathize with suffering to give aid to our deeply afflicted people. Tell them to be of good cheer, that the sympathies of all our people, irrespective of section, are with them, and wherever the news of their calamity has been carried responses of sympathy and aid are coming in. A single subscription from England just received is for $1,000."

Grand View Cemetery has three hundred buried in it. All met death in the flood. They have thirty-five men digging graves. Seven hundred dead bodies in the hospital on Bedford street, Conneaut. One hundred dead bodies in the schoolhouse hospital, Adam street, Conneaut. Three hundred bodies found today in the sand banks along Stony Creek, vicinity of the Baltimore and Ohio [railroad tracks]; 182 bodies at Nineveh.

HAEL: THE HORROR LINGERS ONWARD

You are only partially through this book and it will not get easier as you read on. I just want to remind you to not be discouraged. Remember, there is a reason God has allowed me to write about these back stories. I have been given permission to share them and trust me, you will find them a great blessing.

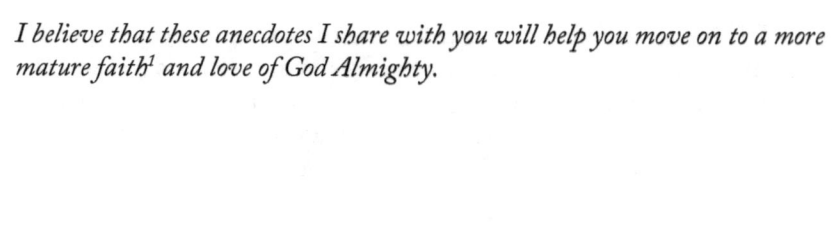

I believe that these anecdotes I share with you will help you move on to a more mature faith[1] and love of God Almighty.

---

[1] Hebrews 6:1m

CHAPTER VI
Shadows of Despair

Another graphic account of the fearful calamity is furnished by an eyewitness. The dark disaster of the day with its attendant terrors thrilled the world and drew two continents closer together in the bonds of sympathy that bind humanity to man. The midnight terrors of Ashtabula and Chatsworth evoked tears of pity from every fireside in Christendom, but the true story of Johnstown, when all is known, will stand solitary and alone as the acme of man's affliction by the potent forces to which humanity is ever subject.

The menacing clouds still hover darkly over the valley of death, and the muttering thunder that ever and anon reverberates faintly in the distance seems the sardonic chuckle of the demon of destruction as he pursues his way to other lands and other homes.

THE WATERS RECEDING

But the modern deluge has done its worst for Johnstown. The waters are rapidly subsiding, but the angry torrents still eddy around Ararat and the winged messenger of peace has not yet appeared to tell the pathetic tale of those who escaped the devastation.

It is not a hackneyed utterance to say that no pen can adequately depict the horrors of this twin disaster: holocaust and deluge. The deep emotions that well from the heart of every spectator find most eloquent expression in silence, the silence that bespeaks recognition of man's subservience to the elements and impotence to avert catastrophe. The insignificance of human life is only fully realized by those who witness such scenes as Johnstown, Chatsworth and Ashtabula, and to those whose memory retains the picture of horror the dread experience cannot fail to be a fitting lesson.

A DREARY MORNING.

This morning opened dark and dreary. Great drops of rain fell occasionally, and another storm seems imminent. Everyone feels thankful though that the weather still remains cold, and that the gradual putrefaction of the hundreds of bodies that still line the streams and lie hidden under the miles of driftwood and debris is not unduly hastened.

The peculiar stench of decaying human flesh is plainly perceptible to the senses as one ascends the bank of Stony Creek for a half mile along the smouldering ruins of the wreck, and the most skeptical now conceive the worst and realize that hundreds, aye, perhaps thousands of bodies lie charred and blackened beneath this great funeral pyre. Searchers wander wearily over this smoking mass, and as occasionally a sudden shout comes over the waters, the patient watchers on the hill realize that another ghastly discovery has been added to that long list of revelations that chill every heart and draw tears to the eyes of pessimists.

From the banks many charred remains of victims of flames and flood are plainly visible to the naked eye, as the retreating waters reluctantly give up their dead. Beneath almost every log or blackened beam a glistening skull or the blanched remnants of ribs or limbs mark all that remains of life's hopes and dreams.

Since ten o'clock last night the fire engines have been busy. Water has been constantly playing on the burning ruins. At times the fire seems almost extinguished, but fitful flames suddenly break out afresh in some new quarter, and again the water and flames wage fierce combat.

The Count is Still Lacking

As yet there is no telling how many lives have been lost. Adjutant General Hastings, who has charge of everything, stated this morning that he supposed there were at least two thousand people under the burning debris, but the only way to find out how many lives were lost was to take a census of the people now living and subtract that from the census before the flood. Said he, "In my opinion there are any way from twelve thousand to fifteen thousand lost."

Up to this morning people living here who lost whole families or parts of families hardly seemed to realize what a dreadful calamity had befallen them. Today, however, they are beginning to understand the situation. Agony is stamped on the faces of everyone, and it is truly a city of mourning.

The point of observation is on the hillside, midway between the woolen mills of Woodvale and Johnstown proper, which I reached today after a journey through the portions of the city from which the waters, receding fast, are revealing scenes of unparalleled horror. From the point on the hillside referred to an excellent view of the site of the town can be obtained. Here it can be seen that from the line of the Pennsylvania Railroad, which winds along the base of Prospect Hill, to a point at which St. John's Catholic Church formerly stood, and from the stone bridge to Conemaugh, on the Conemaugh River, but twelve houses by actual count remain, and they are in such a condition as to be practically useless. To anyone familiar with the geography of the iron city of Cambria county this will convey a vivid idea of a swarth averaging one-half mile in width and three miles in length. In all the length and breadth of the most peaceful and costly portion of Johnstown not a shingle remains except those adhering to the buildings mentioned.

HOUSES UPSIDE DOWN

But do not think for an instant that this comprehends in full the awfulness of the scene. What has just been mentioned is a large waste of territory swept as clean as if by a gigantic broom. In the other direction, some few of the houses still remain, but they are upside down, piled on top of each other, and in many ways so torn asunder that not a single one of them is available for any purpose whatever. It is in this district that the loss of life has been heartrending. Bodies are being dug up in every direction.

On the main street, from which the waters have receded sufficiently to render access and work possible, bodies are being exhumed. They are as thick as potatoes in a field. Those in charge seem to have the utmost difficulty in securing the removal of bodies after they have been found.

The bodies are lying among the mass of wrecked buildings as thick as flies. The fire in the drift above the bridge is under control and is being rapidly smothered by the Pittsburgh firemen in charge of the work. About seven o'clock this morning a crowd of Battery B boys discovered a family of five people in the smoking and burned ruins above the bridge. They took out father, mother and three children, all terribly burned and mutilated. The little girl had an arm torn off.

HAEL: A CATASTROPHE LIKE NOAH

As you read these descriptions, try to compare this to what was left after Noah's flood.

The land tore itself apart. The water deluged the entire earth standing a full 18 cubits (approximately 27 feet) above the highest land mass. And because this was a worldwide event, the "catastrophic processes continued on into post-flood times."[1]

---

[1] https://answersingenesis.org/geology/catastrophism/continuing-catastrophes/

My point here is very simple, imagine how much damage was done in Johnstown, now try and wrap your mind around what happened here on the earth some 4,500 years ago remembering that what occurred in Johnstown was very localized and lasted one hour, but what occurred in Noah's day encompassed the entire earth and lasted forty days and forty nights.

FINDING THE DEAD

The work of rescuing the bodies from the mud and debris has only fairly begun, and yet each move in that direction reveals more fully the horrible extent of the calamity. It is estimated that already 1,800 corpses have been found in all parts of the valley and given some little attention. Many of them were so mangled as to be beyond identification.

A regularly organized force of men has been at work most of the day upon the mass of debris about the stone bridge. Early in the forenoon ten bodies were found close together. There was nothing to identify them, as they were burnt almost to a crisp. Several of them must have belonged to one household, as they were taken from under the blackened timbers of a single roof.

Soon after a man, woman and child were taken from the ruins. The child was clasped in the arms of the woman, and the trio were evidently husband, wife and child. It is a most distressing sight to see the relatives of people supposed to be lost standing around and watching every body as it is pulled out, and acting more like maniacs than sensible people.

As the work progressed the number of the ghastly finds increased. The various parties of workmen turned out from ten to fifteen bodies and fragments of bodies an hour all day long.

Many of the corpses found had valuables still clasped in their hands. One woman taken from the mill this morning had several diamond rings and earrings, a roll of government bonds and some money clasped in her hands. She was a widow, and was very wealthy.

Her body has been embalmed and is at the house of relatives.

HAEL: GOD'S PREPARATION

As you read these ghastly descriptions - No - as I read these descriptions I want to weep! I have seen this kind of carnage for too long on your earth. This is not

140

what He planned when He created you on the 6th day. He planned immortality that now has to await His chosen ones passing from this life into the next.

Even hell He did not make for the unsaved around you.[1] Look, you humans always get the chronology wrong, so let me help you.

We angels are created beings, so we did not exist with Him before the six days of creation. We were created during the six days, specifically on the ████ day.

God created the abode for the demons when deceit showed itself in sataN and he drew 1/3 of the angels out of heaven.[2] This hell-hole he made ████ days after creation so that he could keep in there some of the fallen angels that refused to obey God and the remainder who would be thrown in at the end of days.

You realize that the demons obey God, don't you? It always amazes me that you can believe that sataN has some "special authority" on earth. No! If that were true than God would be a liar when He said, "I do whatever I want!"[3]

Look, you live in a fallen world that is ghastly and ugly, but you have promises that far exceed what even we angels get to experience.

Let me share with you a short uplifting prayer regarding the hurricanes that came from the modern-day author, the one who introduced me to the world in his first novel (The Pray-ers).

"Lord, You tell us that when we need comfort, You will comfort us, and You go on to say that this is so that we can in turn comfort others in the self-same way.[4] As I think of the recent tragedies, hurricanes, earthquakes, and shootings, I find solace only in Your Word:

"Lord, under Your protection, the protection of the Most High, we get to dwell in Your shadow, the shadow of the Almighty.

"You LORD, are my refuge and my fortress. You are my God, the One in whom I trust.

"Lord, You cover us with Your feathers; we take refuge under Your wings. You faithfully protect us with Your shield so that we do not fear the terror of the night.[5]

---

[1] Matthew 25:41
[2] Revelation 12:4
[3] Psalm 103:19, 115:3, 135:6, and numerous other passages
[4] 2 Corinthians 1:4
[5] Psalm 91:1-2, 4-5a

"And then Lord, because of who You are, we come together and shout out praises to You. We shout joyfully and triumphantly to You, our Rock and our Salvation. We enter Your presence with thanksgiving.

"In spite of all that goes on, You are a great God, greater than all other gods.

"You hold the earth, the mountain peaks and the seas in Your hand.

"Father, we ask that others too will bow down and worship You, kneeling to You, our Creator, for we are as sheep in Your pasture.

"Oh Lord, we ask that the recent events not cause us to harden our hearts towards You.[1]

"But rather Lord, we ask that we on the earth rejoice, and those on the coasts and islands in the midst of the hurricanes find their ways to be glad, for You are our Majestic King.[2]

"Lord, we know that our adversary prowls around like a roaring lion and he devours many.[3] But he does not have any power over the saved, for Christ defeated him and his minions on Calvary.[4] When Ephesians 6:12 reminds me that my struggle is not with flesh and blood, what is implicit in that verse is the reality that Jesus already won the battle over the evil one. Yes, I am to put on the armor, every piece of the armor. And every piece of the armor is a facet of who Jesus already is in my life.

Father, thank You that the New Testament tells me that Jesus is my peace.

Friends, this is Hael again and I am getting worked up here, recounting his prayer so I need to relax. Let me just say this: When you do spiritual warfare you are not trying to attain victory, you are battling from victory.

When you find yourself in the tragedies of these days you live in Jesus is your peace in the tragedy.

When you realize that you already possess this peace, you do not have to even consider suicide, as you will read in the next section.

---

[1] Psalm 95:1-8
[2] Psalm 97:1
[3] 1 Peter 5:8
[4] Colossians 2:15

SUICIDE BROUGHT RELIEF

From under the large brick schoolhouse 124 bodies were taken last night and today, and in every corner and place the bodies are being found and buried as fast as possible. The necessity for speedy burial is becoming manifest, and the stench is sickening. A number of bodies have been found with a bullet hole in them, showing conclusively that in their maddening fright suicide was resorted to by many.

Work was commenced during the day on the south side of the town. It is supposed that five hundred or six hundred bodies will be found in that locality.

About twelve o'clock ten bodies were taken out of the wreck near the Cambria Library. On account of the bruised and mangled condition, some having faces crushed in, it was impossible to identify them. It is supposed they were guests at the Hurlbert House, which is completely demolished.

Eight bodies were recovered near the Methodist Church at eleven o'clock. It is said that fully one hundred and fifty bodies were found last evening in a sort of pocket below the Pennsylvania Railroad signal tower at Sang Hollow, where it was expected there would be a big find.

KERNVILLE ONE VAST MORGUE

Over one thousand bodies have been taken from the river, dragged from the sluggish pools of mud or dug out of the sand about Kernville during the day. Three hundred of them were spread out upon the dry sand along the river's bank at one time this afternoon. The sight is one that cannot be described, and is one of the most distressing ever witnessed. A crowd of at least five hundred were gathered around, endeavoring to find the bodies of some friends or relatives. There were no coffins there at the time and the bodies had to be laid on the ground. However, five hundred coffins are on the way here, and the undertakers have sent for five hundred additional ones. Kernville from now on will be the place where most of the bodies will be found. The water has fallen so much that it is possible to get at the bodies. However, all the bodies have to be dug out of the sand, and it causes no end of work.

It is thought that most of the bodies that will be found at Kernville are under a large pile of debris, about an acre in length. This is where most of the buildings drifted, and it is natural to suppose that the bodies floated with them. A rain is now falling, but this does not interfere with the work.

143

Most of the rescuing party have been up for two days, yet they work with a determination that is wonderful.

NINEVEH, THE CITY OF THE DEAD.

Nineveh is literally a city of the dead. The entire place is filled with corpses. At the depot eighty-seven coffins were piled up and boxed. On the streets coffin boxes covered the sidewalks. Improvised undertaking shops have embalmed and placed in their shrouds 198 persons. The dead were strewn about the town in all conceivable places where their bodies would be protected from the thoughtless feet of the living.

Most of the bodies embalmed last night had been taken out of the river in the morning by the people at Nineveh, who worked incessantly night and day searching the river. The bodies when found were placed in a four-horse wagon, frequently twelve at a time, and driven away. Of the bodies taken out near Moorhead fully three-fourths are women and the rest children. But few men are found there. In one row at the planing mill today were eighteen children's bodies awaiting embalming. Next to them was a woman whose head had been crushed in so as to destroy her features. On her hand were three diamond rings.

Dr. Graff. of the State Board of Health, stationed at Nineveh, states that up till ten o'clock this morning they had embalmed about two hundred bodies, and by noon today would about double that number, as they were fishing bodies out of the river at this point at the rate of one every five minutes. In the driftwood and debris bodies are being exhumed, and an additional force of undertakers has been dispatched to this place.

HAEL: NINEVEH REVISTED

Nineveh of Biblical fame received the very great benefit of God putting off judgment of them, and it was for one reason only. Do you remember the reason? Basically, they chose to reverence God, to awe Him. I'm not making any judgment upon Johnstown, don't get me wrong. I am merely using their situation as a talking point, relative to God bringing judgment, and in the case of Nineveh, putting off judgment, for very specific reasons.

Do you remember why Moses was not allowed to enter the Promised Land? He tells us in Deuteronomy chapter three. He is standing in front of the Israelites eloquently telling them that because of them he does not get to enter. And to his defense, even the Psalmist says that the Israelites provoked him. But Moses still paid the consequences of his own actions, not awing God in front of the Israelites.

Here's the whole reason for this thought and concern. Who are you not awing God in front of? And then what blessings are you not receiving, or what judgment is God bringing upon you, since you have not awed Him before others? It's a sobering thought and one that we need to consider.

In your 21st century world you seem to think that God does not "bring" difficulties into one's life. You will argue that He allows things, but He does not bring them. And forgive me but that thinking implies that He is not sovereign.

Do you really believe that, that He is really not sovereign I mean? I recognize that you do not always know why He handles things in your life the way He does. But my friend He is sovereign, so trust Him to do what is best.

The writer who is recording my words right now found this wonderful old prayer book, written by John Frederick Stark from the late 18th century. He argues for God's sovereignty, just as I have above and then concludes with this, that "the sufferer's troubles were sent, not by an enemy who hates, but by a friend who loves him." . . . And that friend "who imposes the burden, will help to carry it."

In a Charnel House

At the public schoolhouse, the scene beggars description [defies description it is so solemn]. Boards have been laid from desk to desk, and as fast as the hands of a large body of men and women can put the remains in recognizable shape they are laid out for possible identification and removed as quickly as possible. Seventy-five still remain, although many have been taken away, and they are being brought in every moment. It is something horrifying to see one portion of the huge school taken up by corpses, each with a clean white sheet covering it, and on the other side of the room a promiscuous heap of bodies in all sorts of shapes and conditions, looking for all the world like decaying tree trunks. Among the number identified are two beautiful young ladies named respectively Mrs. Richardson, who was a teacher in the kindergarten school, and Miss Lottie Yost, whose sister I afterwards noticed at one of the corners nearby, weeping as if her very heart was broken. Not a single acquaintance did she count in all of the great throng who passed her by, although many tendered sincere sympathy, which was accentuated by their own losses.

Lost and Found

At the station of Johnstown proper this morning the following names were added to the list of bodies found and identified: Charles Marshall, one of the engineers Cambria Company. A touching incident in connection with his death is that he had been married but a short time and his widow is heartbroken.

Order at any Cost

Ex-Sheriff C. L. Dick, who was at one-time Burgess of Johnstown, has charge of a large number of special deputies guarding the river at various points. He and a posse of his men caught people robbing dead bodies. He says he has made up his mind to stand no more nonsense with this class of persons, and he has given orders to his men to drown, shoot or hang any man caught stealing from the dead.

Sheriff Dick, or "Chall" as he is familiarly called, is a tall, slim man, and is well known in Pittsburgh, principally to sportsmen. He is a first class wing shot; and during the past year he has won several live bird matches. He is slow to anger, but when forced into a fight his courage is unfailing.

Shooting Looters on the Wing

Dick wears corduroy breeches, a large hat, a cartridge belt, and is armed with a Winchester rifle. He is a crack shot and has taken charge of the deputies in the wrecked portion of the city. Yesterday afternoon he discovered two men and a woman cutting the finger from a dead woman to get her rings. The Winchester rifle cracked twice in quick succession, and the right arm of each man dropped, helplessly shattered by a bullet. The woman was not harmed, but she was so badly frightened that she will not rob corpses again. Some five robbers altogether were shot during the afternoon, and two of them were killed.

Treasure Lying Loose

Notwithstanding this, and the way that the town is most thoroughly under martial law, the pilfering still goes on. The wreck is a gold mine for pilferers. A jewel box containing several rings and a gold watch were found. In one house in Johnstown there is $1,700 in money, but it is impossible to get at it.

Pickets Set, Strangers Excluded

Up till noon today General Hastings has had his headquarters on the east side of the river, but this morning he came over to the burning debris, followed by about one hundred and twenty-five men carrying coffins. He started to work immediately, and has ordered men from Philadelphia, Harrisburg, and all eastern towns to do laboring work.

The Citizen's Committee are making desperate efforts to preserve peace, and there are thirteen Hungarians at Cambria City who are being kept in their houses by men with clubs, who will not permit them or their families to go outside. There seems be considerable race prejudice at Cambria City, and trouble may follow, as both the English and Hungarians are getting worked up to a considerable extent.

The Sheriff has taken charge of Johnstown and armed men are this morning patrolling the city. The people who have been properly in the limits are permitted to enter the city if they are known, but otherwise it is impossible to get into the town. The regulation seems harsh, but it is a necessity.

Troops Sent Home

Battery B, of Pittsburgh, arrived in the city this morning under command of Lieutenant Sheppard, who went to the quarters of Adjutant General Hastings in the railroad watch tower. The General had just got up, and as the officer approached the General said:

"Who sent you here?"

"I was sent here by the Chamber of Commerce," replied the Lieutenant.

"Well, I want to state that there are only four people who can order you out, viz.: The Governor, Adjutant General, Major General and the Commander of the Second Brigade. You have committed a serious breach of discipline, and my advice to you is to get back to Pittsburgh as soon as possible, or you may be mustered out of service. I am surprised that you should attempt such an act without any authority whatever."

This seemed to settle the matter, and the battery started back to Pittsburgh. In justice to Lieutenant Sheppard it might be stated that he was told that an order was issued by the Governor. General Hastings stated afterwards that the sending down of the soldiers was like waving a red flag, and it would only tend to create trouble. He said everything was quiet here, and it was an insult to the citizens of Johnstown to send soldiers here at present.

EXTORTIONERS HELD IN CHECK.

A riot was almost caused by the exorbitant prices that were charged for food. One storekeeper in Millville borough was charging $5 a sack for flour and seventy-five cents for sandwiches on Sunday. This caused considerable complaint and the citizens grew desperate. They promptly took by force all the contents of the store. As a result, this morning all the stores have been put under charge of the police. An inventory was taken and the proprietor was paid the market price for his stock

A strong guard is kept at the office of the Cambria Iron Company. Saturday was pay day at the works, and $80,000 is in the safe. This became known, and the officials are afraid that an attempt would be made to rob the place.

MEN HARD AT WORK

Order is slowly arising out of chaos. The survivors are slowly realizing what is the best course to pursue. The great cry is for men. Men who will work and not stand idly by and do nothing but gaze at the ruins. The following order was posted on a telegraph pole in Johnstown today:

> NOTICE-During the day men who have been idle have been begged to aid us in clearing the town, and many have not refused to work. We are now so organized that employment can be found for every man who wants to work, and men offered work who refuse to take the same and who are able to work must leave Johnstown for the present. We cannot afford to feed men who will not work. All work will be paid for. Strangers and idlers who refuse to work will be ejected from Johnstown.
>
> By order of Citizens' Committee

TURNING AWAY THE IDLERS

Officers were stationed at every avenue and railroad that enters the town. All suspicious looking characters are stopped. But one question is asked. It is, "Will you work?" If an affirmative answer is given a man escorts him to the employment bureau, where he is put to work. If not, he is turned back. The committee has driven one or two men out of the town. There are a lot of idle vagabonds in Johnstown who will not work. It is likely that a committee will escort them out of town.

It is a fact, although a disagreeable one to say, that not a few of the relief committees who came to this city, came only out of curiosity and positively refused to do any work, but would hang around the cars eating food. The leaders of the committee then had to do all the work. They deserve much credit.

BEGGING FOR HELP

An old man sat on a chair placed on a box at the intersection of two streets in Johnstown and begged for men. "For God's sake," he said, "can we not find men. Will not some of you men help? Look at these men who have not slept for three days and are dropping with fatigue. We will pay well. For God's sake help us." Tears rolled down his cheeks as he spoke. Then he would threaten the group of idlers standing by and again plead with them. Every man it seems wants to be a policeman.

CHAPTER VII
Burial of the Victims

Hundreds have been laid away in shallow trenches without forms, ceremonies or mourners. All day long the work of burial has been going on. There was no time for religious ceremonies or mourning and many a mangled form was coffined with no sign of mourning save the honest sympathy of the brave men who handled them. As fast as the wagons that are gathering up the corpses along the stream arrive with their ghastly loads they are emptied and return again to the banks of the merciless Conemaugh to find other victims among the driftwood in the underbrush, or half buried in the mud. The coffins are now beginning to arrive, and on many streets on the hillside they are stacked as high as the second and third story windows.

At Kernville the people are not so fortunate. It would seem that every man is his own coffin maker, and many a man can be seen here and there claiming the boards of what remains of his house in which perhaps he has found the remains of a loved one, and busily patching them together with nails and hoops or any available thing to hold the body.

When the corpses are found they are taken to the nearest dead house [morgue] and are carefully washed. They are then laid out in rows to await identification. Cards are pinned to their breasts as soon as they are identified, and their names will be marked on the headboards at the graves.

WHOLESALE FUNERALS

There were many rude funerals in the upper part of the town. The coffins were conveyed to the cemeteries in wagons, each one carrying two, three or more.

At Long View Cemetery and at one or two other points long trenches have been dug to receive the coffins. The trenches are only about three feet deep, it being thought unnecessary to bury deeper, as almost all the bodies will be removed by friends. Nearly three hundred bodies were buried thus today.

There will be no public ceremony, or funeral dirge, and but few weeping mourners. The people are too much impressed with the necessity of immediate and constant work to think of personal grief.

The twenty-six bodies taken to the hose house in Minersville were buried shortly after ten o'clock yesterday morning. Of the twenty-six, thirteen were identified. Eight women, a baby and four men were buried without having been identified.

All day yesterday men were engaged in burying the dead. They ran short of coffins, and in order to dispose of the rapidly decomposing bodies they built rough boxes out of the floating lumber that was caught. In this way they buried temporarily over fifty bodies in the Cemetery just above the town.

Putrefaction of dead bodies threatens the health of the whole region. Now that the waters are fast shrinking back from the horrid work of their own doing and are uncovering thousands of putrid and ill-smelling corpses the fearful danger of pestilence is espied, stalking in the wake of more violent destruction.

The air is already reeking with infectious filth, and the alarm is widespread among the desolated and overwrought population.

CREMATION BEST

Incident to this phase of the situation the chief sensation of the morning was the united remonstrance of the physicians against the extinguishment of the burning wreck of the demolished town which is piled up against the bridge. They maintain, with a philosophy that to anxious searchers seems heartless, that hundreds, if not thousands, of lifeless and decaying bodies lie beneath this mass of burning ruins.

"It would be better," they say, "to permit Nature's greatest scavenger-the flames-to pursue his work unmolested than to expose to further decay the horde of putrefying bodies that lie beneath this debris. There can be but one result. Days will elapse before the rubbish can be sufficiently removed to permit the recovery of these bodies, and long before that every corpse will be a putrid mass, giving forth those frightful emanations of decaying human flesh that in a crowded community like this can have but one result-the dreadful typhus. Every battlefield has demonstrated the necessity of the hasty interment of decaying bodies, and the stench that already arises is a forerunner of impending danger. Burn the wreck, burn the wreck."

Sorrow Rejects Safety

A loud cry of indignation arose from the lips of the vast multitude and the warnings of science were lost in the eager demands of those that sought the remains of the near and dear. The hose was again turned upon the hissing mass, and rapidly the flames yielded to the supremacy of water.

It is almost impossible to conceive the extent of these smoking ruins. An area of eight or ten acres above the dam is covered to a depth of forty feet with shattered houses, borne from the resident center of Johnstown. In each of these houses, it is estimated, there were from one to twenty or twenty-five people. This is accepted as data upon which to estimate the number that perished on this spot, and if the data be correct the bodies that lie beneath these ruins must run well up into the thousands.

Members of the State Board of Health arrived in Nineveh this morning and determined to proceed at once to dredge the river, to clean it of the dead and prevent the spreading of disease. To this end they have wired the State Department to furnish them with the proper appliances.

Drinking Poisoned Water

From other points in this and connecting valleys the same fear of pestilence is expressed. The cities of Pittsburgh and Allegheny, which have a population of three hundred and fifty thousand and drink the waters of the Allegheny River, down which corpses and debris from Johnstown must flow unless stopped above, are in danger of an epidemic. The water is today thick with mud, and bodies have been found as far south of here as Beaver, a distance of thirty miles below Pittsburgh. To go this distance the bodies followed the Conemaugh from Johnstown to the Kiskiminetas, at Blairsville, joining the Allegheny at Freeport, and the Ohio here, the entire distance from this point being about one hundred and fifty miles.

"This is a very serious matter," said a prominent Pittsburgh physician who is here and to me today said, "and one that demands the immediate attention of the Board of Health officials. The flood of water that swept through Johnstown has cleaned out hundreds of cesspools. These and the barnyards' manure and the dirt from henneries and swamps that were swept by the waters have all been carried down into the Alle-gheny River. In addition to this there are the bodies of persons drowned. Some of these will, in all likelihood, be secreted among the debris and never be found. Hundreds of carcasses of animals of various kinds are also in the river.

TYPHUS DREADED

"These will decay, throwing out an animal poison. This filth and poisonous matter is being carried into the Allegheny, and will be pumped up into the reservoir and distributed throughout the city. The result is a cause for serious apprehension. Take, for example, the town of Hazleton Pa. There the filth from some outhouse was carried into the reservoir and distributed through the town. The result was a typhoid fever epidemic and hundreds of people lost their lives. The water that we are drinking today is something fearful to behold."

The municipal authorities of Pittsburgh have issued a notice embodying the above facts.

SANITARY WORK

A message was received by the Relief Committee this morning confirming the report that for the health of the cities of Pittsburgh and Allegheny it is absolutely necessary that steps be taken immediately to remove the bodies and drift from the river, and begging the committee to take early action. The contract for clearing the river was awarded to Captain Jutte, and he will start up the Allegheny this afternoon as far as Freeport, and then work down. His instructions are to clear the river thoroughly of anything that might in any way affect the water supply.

HELPING HANDS

The work of relief at the scene of the great disaster is going on rapidly. The Alliance (Ohio) Relief Committee arrived here this morning on a special train with five carloads of provisions. The party is composed of the most prominent iron and steel merchants of Alliance.

They have just returned from a tour of the ruined town They have been up to Stony Creek, a distance of five miles and up the Conemaugh River toward South Fork, a distance of two miles.

In describing their trip, one of their number said: "I tell you the half has never been told. It is impossible to tell the terrible tale. I thought I had seen horrible sights, and I served five years in the War of the Rebellion, but in all my life it has never been my lot to look upon such ghastly sights as I have witnessed today.

"While making the circuit of the ruined places we saw 103 bodies taken out of the debris along the bank of the river and Stony Creek. Of this number, we identified six of the victims as our friends."

HAEL: A SOLEMN ASSEMBLY

Later that night Amos Farrelley, the one who had the discussion with our 1889 author in the previous section, continued to be moved by what he had seen earlier that day. Three of his co-relief workers attend the same church as him and while they did their devotions sitting in their small tents, Amos became so aroused by Psalm 91 that he read it again and again.

> *[1]He that dwelleth in the secret place of the Most High shall abide under the shadow of the Almighty.*
>
> *[2]I will say of the Lord, He is my refuge and my fortress: my God; in Him will I trust.*
>
> *[3]Surely, He shall deliver thee from the snare of the fowler, and from the noisome pestilence.*
>
> *[4]He shall cover thee with His feathers, and under His wings shalt thou trust: His truth shall be thy shield and buckler.*
>
> *[5]Thou shalt not be afraid for the terror by night; nor for the arrow that flieth by day;*
>
> *[6]Nor for the pestilence that walketh in darkness; nor for the destruction that wasteth at noonday.*
>
> *[7]A thousand shall fall at thy side, and ten thousand at thy right hand; but it shall not come nigh thee.*
>
> *[8]Only with thine eyes shalt thou behold and see the reward of the wicked.*
>
> *[9]Because thou hast made the Lord, which is my refuge, even the Most High, thy habitation;*
>
> *[10]There shall no evil befall thee, neither shall any plague come nigh thy dwelling.*
>
> *[11]For He shall give His angels charge over thee, to keep thee in all thy ways.*
>
> *[12]They shall bear thee up in their hands, lest thou dash thy foot against a stone.*

[13]Thou shalt tread upon the lion and adder: the young lion and the dragon shalt thou trample under feet.

[14]Because he hath set His love upon Me, therefore will I deliver him: I will set him on high, because he hath known My name.

[15]He shall call upon Me, and I will answer him: I will be with him in trouble; I will deliver him, and honour him.

[16]With long life will I satisfy him, and shew him My salvation.

As Amos went through this passage for a third time a demon shouted into his inner ear such that if it had been audible his eardrum would have pierced, "See Amos, you cannot trust your God, can you?"

And with that Amos fell from his knees and lay prostrate before his God. "Why Lord, oh why did these people have to endure this?"

His crying out to the Lord became louder and louder so that his two companions ran over to his tent. Looking in and seeing his anguish they pulled him out into the rain. Seeing that Amos agonized so much, they decided to stay with him until he calmed. The only building they could go to and be out of the rain was the workers eating hall that at night became desolate.

As they began to take him out of the rain to the hall, Amos motioned for them to grasp his Bible. Expectantly they too grabbed their Bibles.

Nearly carrying Amos between them, for he could not stand on his own yet, others in the sparsely crowded hall got up and ran over to see what was the matter.

After a few moments, the weakened Amos stood shakily to his feet and cried out as if preaching, "Men, the good book says. . .

"We shall be protected by the Most High if we abide under His shadow.[1]

"Men, how many of you say to the Lord, "You are my refuge and my fortress: my God; in You I trust?[2]

"Would you have expected God to deliver you, unlike these poor people we have seen today?[3]

---

[1] Psalm 91:1
[2] Psalm 91:2
[3] Psalm 91:3

"How many of you expect Him to cover thee with His feathers, and under His wings shalt thou trust: His truth shall be thy shield and buckler. Is this not true, men?"[1]

Amos lowered his head in exhaustion and then he whispered, "I have spent the afternoon going on and on, over and over this Psalm, chapter 91 and then this evening I remembered, the good book also says that He, our God Most High, is also a consuming fire.[2]

"Men, I am compelled by God Almighty to walk us through areas of sinfulness in our lives. May I do that with you, dear friends?"

Some of the men rolled their eyes, lit new cigarettes and walked out, but the majority of the men stayed, and Bro. Amos, being all the more invigorated, took them through a modified solemn assembly using the Lord's Prayer:

"Our Father who art in heaven. Men, can you say with assurance that you are His child, that if you died you would go to heaven?" and with that men started to groan all over the hall. But Amos did not ask them to get their hearts right yet.

He went on. "Hallowed be Your Name, Father. Oh Lord, forgive us for knowing about You, but not knowing You. For we cannot hallow Your name if we are only playing with Christianity."

And with that the volume of the groans increased, as men were moved by the Holy Spirit.

"Your kingdom will come to us whether we are ready or not." And building in intensity he went on, "Lord, cause us to be submissive to Your will being done here on earth."

There were more groans by men in the hall and Amos' two companions started to pray for Amos and his words rang out. They were his Aaron and Hur, holding up his heavy arms as he delivered the Word of God to these men.

"We trust You for our daily bread and those remaining alive here in Johnstown trust You for their bread and water, Father." A few "Amens" were now heard.

"And forgive us our trespasses, Lord." And here Amos stopped and lowered his head to talk to the men.

"Men," he continued, "isn't it time that you asked the Lord to forgive you? Come here to me and my companions that we may serve you this night, bringing you to the throne room of God."

---

[1] Psalm 91:4
[2] Exodus 24:17, Deuteronomy 4:24, Hebrews 12:29

And thus began a regular evening affair that Amos and his friends hosted as often as they could.

Many men and their families are in heaven today because Amos did not kick away the burden the Holy Spirit laid upon his heart that night in Johnstown.[1]

---

[1] This anecdote is partially based upon a 92-year-old friend of mine named George. I often say that "he is an old-guy who takes care of old people." And he is! He is constantly driving them to stores and to doctor's offices so that he can share the gospel with everyone he comes into contact with.

CHAPTER VIII
View of the Wreck

Each visitor to the scene of the great disaster witnessed sights and received impressions different from all others. The following graphic account will thrill [stimulate] every reader:

It is almost an impossibility to gain access to the region, and it was accomplished only after much difficulty in crossing the swiftly running stream.

Standing at a point in this abode of thousands of dead the work of the great flood can be more adequately measured than from any one place in the devastated region. Here I first realized the appalling loss of life and the terrible destruction of property.

It was about ten o'clock when the waters of Stony Creek rose, overflowed their banks and what is known as the "flats," which includes the entire business portion of the city of Johnstown. The Little Conemaugh was running high at the same time, and it had also overreached the limit of its banks. The water of both streams soon submerged the lower portion of the town. Up to this time there was no intimation that a terrible disaster was imminent. The water poured into the cellars of the houses in the lower districts and rose several inches in the streets, but as that had occurred before the people took no alarm.

Shortly after twelve o'clock the first drowning occurred. This was not because of the deluge, it was simply the carelessness of the victim, who was a driver for the Cambria Iron Company, in stepping into a cellar which had been filled with water. The water continued to rise, and at twelve o'clock had reached that part of the city about a block from the point between Stony Creek and the Little Conemaugh.

TOPOGRAPHY OF THE PLACE

The topography of Johnstown is almost precisely like that of Pittsburgh, only in a diminished degree. Stony Creek comes in from the mountains on the northeast, and the Little Conemaugh comes in from the northwest, forming the Conemaugh at Johnstown, precisely as the Allegheny and Monongahela form the Ohio at Pittsburgh. On the west side of Stony Creek are mountains rising to a great height, and almost perpendicularly from the water. On the north side of the Conemaugh River mountains equally as high as those on Stony Creek confine that river to its course.

159

The hills in Johnstown start nearly a half mile from the business section of the city. This leaves a territory between the two rivers of about four hundred acres. This was covered by costly buildings, factories and other important manufactories.

When the waters of South Fork and Little Conemaugh broke over their banks into that portion of the city known as the "flats," the business community turned its attention to putting endangered merchandise in a place of safety.

First Alarm

In the homes of the people the women began gathering household articles of any kind that may have been in the cellar. Little attention was paid to the water beyond this.

Looking from the "flats" at Johnstown toward and following the Pennsylvania Railroad tracks, which wind along the Little Conemaugh, the village of Woodville stands, or did stand, within sight of the "flats," and is really a continuation of the city at this point.

The mountains on the south side of the Little Conemaugh rise here and form a narrow valley where

Woodville was located. Next joining this, without any perceptible break in the houses, was the town of East Conemaugh. The extreme eastern limit of East Conemaugh is about a mile and a half from Johnstown "flats."

A Narrow Chasm

The valley narrows as it reaches eastward, and in a narrow chasm three miles from Johnstown "flats" is the little settlement of Mineral Point. A few of the houses have found a place on the mountain side out of harm's way, and so they still stand.

At East Conemaugh there is located a roundhouse of the Pennsylvania Railroad, for the housing of locomotives used to assist trains over the mountains. The inhabitants of this place were all employees of the Pennsylvania and the Gautier Steel Works, of the Cambria Iron Company. The inhabitants numbered about 1,500 people. Like East Conemaugh, 2,000 or 2,500 people, who lived at Woodville, were employees of the same corporation and the woolen mills located there. Just below Woodville the mountains upon the south bank of the Conemaugh disappear and form the commencement of the Johnstown "flats." The Gautier Steel Works of the Cambria Iron Company are located at this point, on the south bank. The Pennsylvania Railroad traverses the opposite bank, and makes a long curve from this point up to East Conemaugh.

Timely Warning to Escape

At what is known as the point where Stony Creek and the Little Conemaugh form the Conemaugh the mountains followed by Stony Creek take an abrupt turn northward, and the waters of the Little Conemaugh flow into the Conemaugh at right angles with these mountains.

A few hundred feet below this point the Pennsylvania Railroad bridge crosses the Conemaugh River. The bridge is a massive stone structure. From the east end of the bridge there is a heavy fill of from thirty to forty feet high to Johnstown Station, a distance of a quarter of a mile.

Within a few feet of the station a wagon bridge crosses the Little Conemaugh, five hundred feet above the point connecting the "flats" and the country upon the north side of the river.

The Cambria Iron Company's Bessemer department lies along the north bank of the Conemaugh, commencing at the fill, and extends for over two miles down the Conemaugh River upon its northern bank.

Below the Cambria Iron Company's property is Millville Borough, and on the hill back of Millville Borough is Minersville properly, the Second ward of Millville Borough.

The First ward of Millville was washed away completely.

While the damage from a pecuniary sense was large, the loss of life was quite small, inasmuch as the people had timely warning to escape.

Below the Pennsylvania Railroad Bridge at Johnstown, upon the south bank of the Conemaugh, was the large settlement of Cambria. It had a population of some five thousand people. At Cambria the mountain retreats for several hundred feet, leaving a level of two or three hundred acres in extent. Just below the bridge the Conemaugh River makes a wide curve around this level. About eight or nine hundred houses stood upon this level.

BELOW CAMBRIA STANDS MORRELLVILLE, A PLACE
ABOUT EQUAL IN SIZE TO CAMBRIA.

From this description of the location of Johnstown and neighboring
settlements the course of the waters may be better understood when
described. It was about ten minutes to three o'clock Friday afternoon when
Mr. West, of the local office of the Pennsylvania Railroad at Johnstown,
received a dispatch from the South Fork station, advising him to notify the
inhabitants that the big dam in the South Fork, above the city, was about
to break. He at once dispatched couriers to various parts of the city, and a
small section was notified of the impending danger. The messenger was
answered with:

"We will wait until we see the water."

Others called "Chestnuts!" and not one in fifty of the people who received
the warning gave heed to it.

THE DEBRIS OF THREE TOWNS

With the waters standing several inches deep in the streets of the "flats" of
the city the deluge from South Fork Lake, burst the dam and rushed full
upon Johnstown shortly after four o'clock on Friday afternoon the last day
of May.

First it swept the houses from Mineral Point down into East Conemaugh.
When the flood reached East Conemaugh the town was wiped out. This
mass of debris was borne on to Johnstown, reinforced by the material of
three towns.

The Gautier steel department of the Cambria Iron Company was the first
property attacked in the city proper. Huge rolls, furnaces and all the
machinery in the great mills, costing $6,000,000, were swept away in a
moment, and today there is not the slightest evidence that the mill ever
stood there.

SWEPT FROM THE ROOFS

Westward from this point the flood swept over the flats. The houses, as
soon as the water reached them, were lifted from their foundation and
hurled against their neighbors'. The people who at the first crash of their
property managed to reach the roof or some other floating material were
carried on until their frail support was driven against the next obstruction,
when they went down in the crash together.

The portion of the "flats" submerged is bounded by Clinton street to the Little Conemaugh River, to the point at Stony Creek, then back to Clinton street by way of Bedford.

This region has an area of one mile square, shaped like a heart, and in this district there are not more than a dozen buildings that are not total wrecks.

Ten per cent of this district is so covered with mud, stones, rocks and other material, where costly buildings once stood, that it will require excavating from eight to twenty feet to reach the streets of the city.

HAEL: WHERE YOUR TREASURE IS

"No, no, no, Mr. Superintendent. No, no, no, Mr. Tired Laborer," the demon overlord jolN would say. "No, you worked so hard all week, don't worry about getting up early for church today. Save your strength and go to church next week."

This adversary, like all of them, know the right buttons to push to weaken men and women's spiritual life. This particular demon, jolN (pronounce all three sounds in one syllable jo-l-n, remembering "o" as in go), made famous, or should I say, infamous when the writer of "The Pray-ers" introduced him to the world in his first novel, "Troubles." He has been over the territory of North America for a few hundred years.

The last few decades jolN has been encamped here in Western Pennsylvania breeding an attitude of greed and gain, and then just recently, he has taken the greed and gain attitude to another level by introducing an attitude of pride in their "costly buildings [that] once stood."

"Worry not," jolN would lie to them. "There is plenty of time for you to participate in church and save your soul. Now is the time for you to work hard, and build that large house so that you can bless people by your hospitality (when you have time for it).

Jesus said something when He inhabited space and time that is of great importance in this backstory. Jesus said that the road is difficult and the gate of entrance to heaven is narrow, and that only a few find it.[1] Many of these men who jolN has influenced have made their focus, "where costly buildings once stood."

---

[1] Matthew 7:13-14

Did you notice the rest of the quote? It says, "where costly buildings once stood". . . those spots now eight to twenty feet of mud, stones, rocks and other materials. Don't get me wrong, I am not saying anything about having lots of money. Money isn't the root of evil, "loving money" is the root of all kinds of evil.

My comments are merely a query to you. Where are you laying up your treasure?

REMNANTS OF THE CITY

Of the houses standing there is the Methodist church, the club house, James McMillen's residence, the Morrell mansion, Dr. Lohman's house and the First ward school building.

The Fourth ward school house and the Cambria Iron Works' general office building are the only buildings standing on the north side of the river from the Pennsylvania Railroad bridge to the limits of the "fiats." The Pennsylvania Railroad, from its station in Johnstown City nearly to Wilmore, a distance of seven miles, had a magnificent road bed of solid rock. From East Conemaugh to the point in Johnstown opposite the Gautier Steel Works, this road bed, ballast and all are gone. Only a few rails may occasionally be seen in the river below.

FREAKS OF THE FLOOD

When the crash came in Johnstown the houses were crushed as easily by the huge mass as so many buildings of sand, making much the same sound as if a pencil were drawn over the slats of a shutter. Houses were torn from their foundations and torn to pieces before their occupants realized their danger. Hundreds of these people were crushed to death, while others were rescued by heroic men; but the lives of the majority were prolonged a few minutes, when they met a more horrible death further down the stream.

There is a narrow strip extending from the club house to the point which, in some singular manner, escaped the mass of filling that was distributed on the flats. This strip is about 200 feet wide, 300 long and from 3 to 20 feet deep. What an odd turn the flood took to thus spare this section, when the surrounding territory was covered with mud, stones and other material, is a mystery. It is, however, one of the remarkable turns of the flood.

The German Catholic Church is standing, but is in an exceedingly shaky condition and may fall at any minute. This and Dr. Lohman's residence are the only buildings on the plot standing between Main street, Clinton street, Railroad street and the Little Conemaugh.

The destruction of life in this district was too awful to contemplate. It is estimated that not more than one thousand people escaped with their lives, and it is believed that there were fully five thousand persons remaining in the district when the flood came down. The flood wiped out the "flat" with the exception of the buildings noted. The water was twenty feet high here and hurled acres upon acres of houses against the Pennsylvania Railroad bridge which held it and dammed the water up until it was forty feet high. The mass accumulated until the weight became so great that it broke through the fill east of the bridge and the debris started out of the temporary reservoir with an awful rush.

It was something near five o'clock when the fill broke. The water rushed across the Cambria flats and swept every house away with the exception of a portion of a brewery. There is nothing else standing in this district which resembles a house.

The Johnstown Post Office Building, with all the office money and stamps, was carried away in the flood. The Postmaster himself escaped with great difficulty.

The dam broke in the center at three o'clock [3:15 actually] on Friday afternoon, and at four o'clock it was dry. That great body of water passed out in [less than] one hour. Park & Van Buren, who are building a new draining system at the lake, tried to avert the disaster by digging a sluiceway on one side to ease the pressure on the dam. They had about forty men at work and did all they could, but without avail. The water passed over the dam about a foot above its top, beginning at about half-past two. Whatever happened in the way of a cloud burst took place during the night. There had been but little rain up to dark. When the workmen woke in the morning the lake was very full and was rising at the rate of a foot an hour. It kept on rising until at two o'clock it first began breaking over the dam and undermining it. Men were sent three or four times during the day to warn people below of their danger.

THE BREAK TWO HUNDRED FEET WIDE

When the final break came, at three o'clock, there was a sound like tremendous and continued peals of thunder; rocks, trees and earth were shot up into mid-air in great columns, and then the wave started down the ravine. A farmer, who escaped, said that the water did not come down like a wave, but jumped on his house and beat it to fragments in an instant. He was safe upon the hillside, but his wife and two children were killed. At the present time, the lake looks like a cross between the crater of a volcano and a huge mud puddle with stumps of trees and rocks scattered over it. There is a small stream of muddy water running through the center of the lake site. The dam was seventy feet high and the break is about two hundred feet wide, and there is but a small portion of the dam left on either side. No damage was done to any of the buildings belonging to the club. The whole south fork is swept, with not a tree standing. There are but one or two small streams showing here and then in the lake. A great many of the workmen carried off baskets full of fish caught in the mud [when the lake emptied].

THREE MILLIONS INDEMNITY

It is reported that the Sportsman's Association, which owned the South Fork dam, was required to file an indemnity bond of $3,000,000 before their charter was issued. When the bill granting them these privileges was before the Legislature the representatives from Cambria and Blair counties vigorously opposed its passage and only gave way, it is said, upon condition that such an indemnifying bond was filed. This bond was to be filed with the prothonotary of Cambria county.

Father Boyle, of Ebensburg, said the records at the county seat had no trace of such a bond. He found the record of the charter, but nothing about the bond. As the association is known to be composed of very wealthy people, there is much talk here of their being compelled to pay at least a part of the damages.

HAEL: SPORTSMAN'S ASSOCIATION

This author published his work within a few months of the tragedy, so he would have no way knowing that the Sportsman's Association never paid anything for their part in the destruction below their dam. Of the two lawsuits brought against the Sportsman's Association, one was dropped and the other was won by the Association.

It should be noted however, that many, if not all of the members contributed much to the aid of the cities below their retreat area when the dam broke.

The Rain Did It

It begins to dawn on us that the catastrophe was brought about not merely by the bursting of the dam of the old canal reservoir, but by a rainfall exceeding in depth and area all previously recorded phenomena of the kind. The whole drainage basin of the Kiskiminetas, and more particularly that of the Conemaugh, was affected. An area of probably more than 600 square miles poured its precipitation through the narrow valley in which Johnstown and associate villages are located. It is easy to see how, with a rainfall similar to that which caused the Butcher Run disaster of a few years ago, fully from thirty to fifty times as much water became destructive. The whole of the water of the lake would pass Suspension Bridge at Pittsburgh inside of from seven to ten minutes, while the gorge at Johnstown, narrowed by the activity of mines for generations past, was clearly insufficient to allow a free course for Stony Creek alone, which is a stream heading away up in Somerset county, twenty-five or thirty miles south of Johnstown. That the rainfall of the entire Allegheny Mountain system was unprecedented is clearly demonstrated to anyone who has watched the Allegheny and Monongahela rivers for the past three days, and this view may serve to correct the impression in the public mind that would localize the causes of the widespread disaster to the bursting of any single dam.

Danger Was Anticipated

Charles Parke, of Philadelphia, the civil engineer in the employ of the South Fork Fishing Club, in company with George C. Wilson, ex-United States District Attorney, and several other members of the club, reached Johnstown and brought with them the first batch of authoritative news from Conemaugh Lake, the bursting of which, it is universally conceded, caused the disaster.

Mr. Parke was at first averse to talking, and seemed more interested in informing his friends in the Quaker City that he was still in the land of the living. On being pressed he denied most emphatically that the dam had burst, and proceeded to explain that he first commenced to anticipate danger on Friday morning, when the water in the lake commenced to rise at a rapid rate. Immediately he turned his force of twenty-five men to opening an extra waste sluiceway in addition to the one that had always answered before. The five members of the club on hand all worked like horses, but their efforts were in vain, and at three o'clock the supporting wall gave way with a sound that seemed like distant thunder and the work was done.

167

HAEL: DRAINAGE PIPES

Again, what no one would know until later, much later is about the drainage pipes.

These pipes make up the underwater low-level outlets which are used to allow the water out of a filling dam any time of the year. In other words, while the side spillway only lets water out of the dam where it exceeds the height of the spillway, the low-level outlets which are made up of these pipes allow the dam to be drained all the way down to these pipes which are always located low in the dam wall.

These pipes had been taken out a few years earlier and the metal sold as scrap, so there was no way to let extra water out of the dam had anyone wanted to.

Another hazard was the piping that let water out of the top of the sluice seemed to allow too many fish out of the lake so cross slats were put up. The problem was the debris that filled the lake could not be cleaned away once it had fastened itself to the drainage sluice. The water backed up all the more causing the eventual disaster.

THE GOVERNOR'S APPEAL

Harrisburg, Pa., June 3, 1889.-The Governor issued the following:

{COMMONWEALTH OF PENNSYLVANIA}

EXECUTIVE CHAMBER
HARRISBURG, PA., JUNE 3, 1889.

To the People of the United States:

"The Executive of the Commonwealth of Pennsylvania has refrained hitherto from making any appeal to the people for their benefactions, in order that he might receive definite and reliable information from the centers of disaster during the late floods, which have been unprecedented in the history of the State or nation. Communication by wire has been established with Johnstown today… Newspaper reports as to the loss of life and property have not been exaggerated…"

CHAPTER IX
Thrilling Experiences

Johnstown, Pa., June 3, 1889.

Innumerable tales of thrilling individual experiences, each one more horrible than the others, are told.

Frank McDonald, a conductor on the Somerset branch of the Baltimore and Ohio, was at the Pennsylvania Railroad depot in this place when the flood came. He says that when he first saw the flood it was thirty feet high and gradually rose to a least forty feet. "There is no doubt that the South Fork Dam was the cause of the disaster," said Mr. McDonald. "Fifteen minutes before the flood came Decker, the Pennsylvania Railroad agent read me a telegram that he had just received saying that the South Fork Dam had broken. As soon as he heard this the people in station, numbering six hundred, made a rush for a hill. I certainly think I saw one thousand bodies go over the bridge. The first house that came down struck the bridge and at once took fire, and as fast as the others came down they were consumed.

SAW A THOUSAND PERSONS BURN

"I believe I am safe in saying that 1 saw one thousand bodies burn. It reminded me of a lot of flies on fly paper struggling to get away, with no hope and no chance to save them.

"I have no idea that had the bridge been blown up the loss of life would have been any less. They would have floated a little further with the same certain death. Then, again, it was impossible for anyone to have reached the bridge in order to blow it out, for the waters came so fast that no one could have done it.

"I saw fifteen to eighteen bodies go over the bridge at the same time.

"I offered a man $20 to row me across the river, but could get no one to go, and finally had to build a boat and get across that way."

It required some exercise of acrobatic agility to get into or out of the town. A slide, a series of frightful tosses from side to side, a run and you had crossed the narrow rope bridge which spanned the chasm dug by the waters between the stone bridge and Johnstown. Crossing the bridge was an exciting task. Yet many women accomplished it rather than remain in Johnstown. The bridge pitched like a ship in a storm. Within two inches of your feet rushed the muddy waters of the Conemaugh. There were no ropes to guide one and creeping was more convenient than walking.

One had to cross the Conemaugh at a second point in order to reach Johnstown proper. This was accomplished by a skiff ferry. The ferryman clung to a rope and pulled the load over.

CONFUSION WORSE CONFOUNDED

It is impossible to describe the appearance of Main street. Whole houses have been swept down this one street and become lodged. The wreck is piled as high as the second story windows. The reporter could step from the wreck into the auditorium of the Opera House. The ruins consist of parts of houses, trees, saw logs, reels from the wire factory. Many houses have their side walls and roofs torn up, and you can walk directly into what had been second story bedrooms, or go in by way of the top. Further up town a raft of logs lodged in the street and did great damage.

The best way to get an idea of the wreck is to take a number of children's blocks, place them closely together and draw your hand through them.

At the commencement of the wreckage, which is at the opening of the valley of the Conemaugh, one can look up the valley for miles and not see a house. Nothing stands but an old woolen mill.

AS SEEN BY AN EYE-WITNESS

Charles Luther is the name of the boy who stood on an adjacent elevation and saw the whole flood. He said he heard a grinding noise far up the valley, and looking up he could see a dark line moving slowly toward him. He saw that it was made up of houses. On they came like the hand of a giant clearing off his tables. High in the air would be tossed a log or beam, which fell back with a crash. Down the valley it moved sedately and across the little mountain city. For ten minutes nothing but moving houses were seen, and then the waters came with a roar and a rush. This lasted for two hours, and then it began to flow more steadily.

HAEL: WHERE WAS THE SPIRITUAL BATTLE HERE

Charles Luther stood next to his Sunday School teacher, Dr. Emmett Lockyear watching the current and the rushing waters. Charles would become a local expert on Spiritual Warfare over time. But lately he found himself defending

170

men and women's beliefs that the spiritual warfare they faced was in men and women's heads, not out yonder.

As they watched the torrent, Charles saw Dr. Emmett begin to pray and so he followed suit, bowing his head. There seemed to be a time of silence and Charles picked up the praying.

"Oh Lord, our Lord, we need Your Majesty to shine forth in this time of need. The enemy, the avenger has not won here, Lord. Even the children know that when they see Your handiwork: the heavens, the moon, and the stars. Lord, You ordained them. We know that we are but dust, and yet You are still mindful of us, even visiting us. And Lord, we so need that right now. We do not feel crowned with any glory, or any honour. We do not feel like we have any dominion over the works of Your hands. Look at this Lord, we are at Your mercy. And yet, we know in our deepest recesses of our hearts, that You are excellent, and that You are majestic, in all of the earth, including here in Johnstown.[1]

As he concluded Dr. Emmett agreed with a solemn, "Amen."

After a few moments Dr. Emmett asked Charles, "I know that you have been very helpful to our Sunday School class these last few months as you have studied Spiritual Warfare. But Charles, I can just hear my friends who believe in Spiritism and they would argue that their prayers need to be registered towards the prevailing evil, namely the flood waters. Some would even rebuke the flood waters." Turning to look at Charles, Dr. Emmett had a genuine desire in his eyes. He continued, "Charles, it seems more zealous to point the subject of my prayers to the waters. And isn't it the fervency in my rebuking that the Lord responds to?"

Charles thoughtfully and carefully weighed his words, and then said, "My friend, I would love nothing more than to call out from the depths of my being, "waters, BE STILL! But the battle isn't out there. Here's how Paul made that plain to us. In Colossian two and fifteen the apostle made it clear that at the cross Jesus won the battle against the evil one."

"Then why did he say in Ephesians that our struggle is with the evil one," Dr. Emmett retorted a bit more strongly than he meant to.

Understandingly, Charles slowly responded. "I understand your question. It makes sense until we look at the whole counsel of God:

---

[1] Psalm 8

1. "Where did Paul tell us the battle was? In the mind, yes? Remember 2 Corinthians 10:5. We often get focused on verses three and four and miss verse five.

2. "What did Jesus say about the role the evil one plays here on earth? He said that sataN is a liar, and a murderer in John 8:44. The only thing he can do is perpetrate deception upon us.

3. "You mention verse twelve of Ephesians six, where Paul talks about our battle being against the principalities and the rulers and the authorities, but look at verse eleven where he defines the battle. He tells us that the warfare is against the devil's schemes. What schemes I ask you? Not to do physical harm, for God is the One who directs what he can do in that regard. Go back to Job chapters one and two.

"My friend," Charles began to wind down, "you told me about a European sport that was played at Rutgers the last time you were there in 1869. I think they called it Rugby. Did you know that during this decade they started to change the rules a bit? There is something they do now, in this game which explains Spiritual Warfare perfectly.

"Ephesians six talks a lot about the fact that we are "to stand" as a part of the Spiritual Warfare we do with our adversary. In this new football game, which is what they are calling it now, they do something called a "goal-line stand" where the defense stands and holds their position."

Charles paused to let the scene form in Dr. Emmett's mind, and watched as a smile started to form across his face.

"I get it," he said to Charles. "Just like the football team is to hold their position, we too are to hold our position or positions of truth that are found in God's Word."

"Exactly," Charles responded. "What are some truths we can take away as we watch this tragedy? As I think about them Doctor I can think of a few:

1. "Romans 8:28 is still true, He is working all things out for the better, regardless of what I see.

2. "Psalm 103:19 is still true, His throne is above the heavens and He is still sovereign over all.

3. "He knows the plans He has for me,[1] even though I define "hope" a little differently than He is today."

---

[1] Jeremiah 29:11

"Alright Charles," Dr. Emmett responded rather quickly. "I know that verse. It says something about God knowing His plans for us, thoughts of peace and not of evil. Well, how do you reconcile God saying that about His plans for us? I want to agree with you Charles, but you just brought up the verse that destroys your whole argument!"

"I know this exasperates you my friend," said Charles as kindly and as patiently as he could. "And I'm sorry, but there is an easy answer. Easy to say, but not easy to accept."

They looked at each other expectantly and Charles continued. "This is not our home, my friend. We are merely sojourners here.[1] God's provision is not perfected here on this fallen world. It is perfected in heaven our real home, and will be perfected here when we have the New Heaven and the New Earth.[2]

After a long silence the wind and the rain began to pick up again and Dr. Emmett turned to Charles, "Thank you for your patience, Charles. I would rather just yell at the elements and pretend, like my Spiritualist friend, that I can command the elements to do what I want them to do."

A few more moments elapsed, and Charles said, "I know. Believe me, I know. We declare His goodness. We declare who He is. We declare His majesty, and we accept that His sovereignty means He doesn't have to fit into my view of God, although right now I want Him to."

This is Hael again. Before I leave this anecdote, I need to tell you, those of you in the 21ˢᵗ century, you have got a bigger problem in this area than you realize. This is why when book two of The Pray-ers comes out you will enjoy it so much. The author is writing on Spiritual Warfare and he is rather ingeniously beginning the book with a scene in hell that actually occurred on the second day of the death and burial of Jesus. On that second day sataN got his demons together and he was livid with them, for they were acting like ignorant demons thinking that with Jesus in the grave they had won. But sataN knew better and made them realize the truth, namely that they were now defeated angels capable only of deception, which they would have to perfect.

A famous old preacher of yours, who is in heaven now, used to say, "You will be in heaven 5 minutes and wish you had prayed differently."[3]

---

[1] Hebrews 13:14 and 1 Peter 2:11
[2] Revelation 21:1-3 and Isaiah 65:17-21
[3] Leonard Ravenhill would say this both in print and in his preaching

An Improvised Morgue

The school house has been converted into a morgue, and the dead are being buried from this place. A hospital has been opened nearby and is full of patients. One of the victims was removed from a piece of wreckage in which he had been imprisoned three days. His leg was broken and his face badly bruised. He was delirious when rescued.

In some places it is said the railroad tracks were scooped out to a depth of twenty feet. A train of cars, all loaded, were run on the Conemaugh bridge. They with the bridge, now lie in the wreckage at this point. The Pennsylvania Railroad loses thirty-five engines and many cars.

Fire Still Raging

The cling-cling-clang of the engines has a homelike sound. The fire has spread steadily all day and the upper part of the drift is burning tonight. The fire engine is stationed on the river bank and a line of hose laid far up the track to the coal mine. The flames tonight are higher than ever before, and by its light long lines of the curious can be seen along the banks.

The natural gas has been shut off, owing to the many leaks in Johnstown. No fire is allowed in the city. The walls of many houses are falling. Their crash can be heard across the river, where the newspaper men are located. In the walk through the town today the word "danger" could be noticed, painted by the rescuers on the walls.

Cremated.

One of the Catholic churches in the town was burned on Saturday. A house drifted down against it and set it on fire. A funeral was being held at the church at the time of the flood. The congregation deserted the church and the body was burned with the building. Two large trees passed entirely through a brick Catholic church located near the center of the town. The building still stands, but is a total wreck.

Colonel Norman M. Smith, of Pittsburgh, while returning from Johnstown after a visit to Adjutant General Hastings, was knocked from the temporary bridge into the river and carried downstream a couple of hundred yards before he was able to swim ashore. He was not hurt.

A LUCKY ESCAPE

O. J. Palmer, travelling salesman for a Pittsburgh meat house, was on the ill-fated Day Express, one car of which was washed away. He narrowly escaped drowning, and tells a horrible tale of his experience on that occasion. The engineer, the fireman and himself, when they saw the flood coming, got upon the top of the car, and when the coach was carried away they caught the driftwood, and fortunately it was carried near the shore and they escaped to the hills. Mr. Palmer walked a distance of twenty miles around the flooded district to a nearby railroad station on this side.

FREAKS OF THE DISASTER

A novel scene was witnessed yesterday near Johnstown borough. Some women who managed to escape from the town proper had to wear men's clothes, as their own had been torn off by the flood.

The force of the flood can be estimated by the fact that it carried three cars a mile and a half and the tender of an engine weighing twelve tons was carried fourteen miles down the river. A team of horses which was standing on Main street just before the flood was found a mile and a quarter below the town yesterday.

The damage to the Cambria Iron Works was not so great as at first reported. The ends of the blooming mill and open-hearth furnace buildings were crushed in by the force of the flood. The water rushed through the mill and tore a great pile of machinery from its fastenings and caused other damage. The Bessemer steel mill is almost a ruin. The rolling and wire mills and the six blast furnaces were not much damaged. This morning the company put a large force of men at work and are making strenuous efforts to have at least a portion of the plant in operation within a few weeks. This has given encouragement to the stricken people of Johnstown, and they now seem to have some hope, although so many of their loved ones have met their death. The mill yard, with its numerous railroad tracks, is nothing but a waste. Large piles of pig metal were scattered in every direction. All the loose debris is being gathered into heaps and burned.

HAEL: SOME TRUST IN...

I'd like to contrast the 1889 author with the current author, the one who introduced me to the world in his first novel. I've heard him speak in churches and he says something interesting that, I admit, at first, I thought a little imprudent.

The name of his sermon, "When We Call God A Liar" seemed a bit harsh. But consider his words in the light of where men and women mentioned above, put their trust after the flood. Did you notice? When the major employer said they would be opening soon, THEN everyone had confidence. Nine days after the flood the churches had a large prayer meeting, but only when the Cambria Mill foreman stood up and said they would be paying people did the city breathe a sigh of relief.

Now let me speak out of the other side of my mouth. I am not saying anything against working hard and getting paid for your work. Remember, our Creator put you in the Garden and on the day He put you there gave you the responsibility of working it. He is all about you working and working hard.

Let me get back to your modern-day author who thinks that you sometimes call God a liar.

He says, "The way we pray, pleading and pleading with God, often belies our heart's real trust." He goes on to say, "unless we can see HOW God will 'fix' things, we pray as if He has no plans on fixing them."

And then Mark, the author, usually reads these verses:

"Instruct those who are rich in the present age not to be arrogant or to set their hope on the uncertainty of wealth but on God, Who richly provides us with all things to enjoy. (1 Timothy 6:17)

"Anyone trusting in his riches will fall, but the righteous will flourish like foliage. (Proverbs 11:28)

"Some take pride in chariots, and others in horses, but we take pride in the name of Yahweh our God. (Psalm 20:7)

"But seek first the kingdom of God and His righteousness, and all these things will be provided for you. (Matthew 6:33)"

Mark then continues. "And what are 'all these things' from Matthew 6:33? Just look back at verse 31, where it says, 'what you will eat, what you will drink and what you will wear.' The problem my friends is that in our lack of trust, of what He has clearly spoken, we call God a liar by our attitude in prayer."

I admit, the first time I heard him talk like this I cringed. But he is right, unless you see HOW God intends to fix the problem you do not trust that He WILL fix the problem.

Let me simply remind you of the passage that defines faith, "Now faith is the reality of what is hoped for, the proof of what is not seen."[1] Which means that if you have to see it before you believe it, you're not demonstrating faith.

HURLED TO A PLACE OF SAFETY

A pitiful sight was that of an old, gray haired man named Norn. He was walking around among the mass of debris, looking for his family. He had just sat down to eat his supper when the crash came, and the whole family, consisting of wife and eight children, were buried beneath the collapsed house. He was carried down the river to the railroad bridge on a plank. Just at the bridge a cross-tie struck him with such force that he was shot clear upon the pier and was safe. But he is a mass of bruises and cuts from head to foot. He refused to go to the hospital until he found the bodies of his loved ones.

HEROISM IN BRIGHT RELIEF

A Paul Revere lies somewhere among the dead. Who he is, is now known, and his ride will be famous in history. Mounted on a grand, big bay horse, he came riding down the pike which passes through Conemaugh to Johnstown, like some angel of wrath of old, shouting his warning: "Run for your lives to the hills! Run to the hills!"

A CLOUD OF RUIN

The people crowded out of their houses along the thickly settled streets awestruck and wondering. No one knew the man, and some thought he was a maniac and laughed. On and on, at a deadly pace, he rode, and shrilly rang out his awful cry. In a few moments, however, there came a cloud of ruin down the broad streets, down the narrow alleys, grinding, twisting, hurling, overturning, crashing, and annihilating the weak and the strong. It was the charge of the flood, wearing its coronet of ruin and devastation, which grew at every instant of its progress. Forty feet high, some say, thirty according to others, was this sea, and it travelled with a swiftness like that which lay in the heels of Mercury.

On and on raced the rider, on and on rushed the wave. Dozens of people took heed of the warning and ran up to the hills.

---

[1] Hebrews 11:1

Poor, faithful rider, it was an unequal contest. Just as he turned to cross the railroad bridge the mighty wall fell upon him, and horse, rider and bridge all went out into chaos together.

A few feet further on several cars of the Pennsylvania Railroad train from Pittsburgh were caught up and hurried into the caldron, and the heart of the town was reached.

The hero had turned neither to right nor left for himself, but rode on to death for his townsmen. He was overwhelmed by the current at the bridge and drowned. A party of searchers found the body of this man and his horse. He was still in the saddle. In a short time, the man was identified as Daniel Periton, son of a merchant of Johnstown, a young man of remarkable courage. He is no longer the unknown hero, for the name of Daniel Periton will live in fame as long as the history of this calamity is remembered by the people of this country.

HAEL: TO YOUR SHAME

I don't know how to say this any nicer, but a famous comedy line for years after this tragedy would be: "Run for the hills, the dam is busted."[1]

I don't know what to say to that, in light of what the 1889 writer correctly stated about Daniel Periton. The truth is he would be remembered, but this would not have been how he expected the "Paul Revere" of Johnstown to be remembered, for he is remembered as a line in a comedic joke.

A DEVOTED OPERATOR

Mrs. Ogle, the manager of the Western Union, who died at her post, will go down in history as a heroine of the highest order. Notwithstanding the repeated notifications which she received to get out of reach of the approaching danger, she stood by the instruments with unflinching loyalty and undaunted courage, sending words of warning to those in danger in the valley below. When every station in the path of the coming torrent had been warned she wired her companion at South Fork, "This is my last message," and as such it shall always be remembered as her last words on

---

[1] Johnstown Flood By David McCullough, page 266, Simon & Schuster, 1968

earth, for at that very moment the torrent engulfed her and bore her from her post on earth to her post of honor in the great beyond.

HAEL: DECEPTION

As usual, seeing only the side of this disaster from your vantage point misses a great deal of the "action," as you may want to call it.

Mrs. Hettie Ogle had been on the job with Western Union for nearly thirty years. She had lost her husband in the Civil War and had a tough outer skin that caused her to take her job more seriously than one would expect. She also took responsibility for her daughter Minnie, but both would perish as they did not expect the flood would do the damage that it did.

Remember that the evil one's deception is best told by Jesus who said he is here to steal, to kill and to destroy.[1] This is only half the verse though, for in the other half Jesus tells you that He has come that you might have an abundant life.[2]

The demon hoadtiE (pronounced like HŌD-tī, with a long "O" and a long "I") had been called in from Eastern Europe where he had spent the last 2000 years. It became obvious to us that the evil one had him, an upper echelon demon in the Western Union office to cause more deception and distraction.

Mid-morning on this rainy and dreary day hoadtiE had continued to speak into the ear of 52-year-old Hettie Ogle that, "this would not be a difficult day, very wet, and the creek will rise a bit. But Hettie, you do not have to take these fears you keep hearing seriously."

To her credit, she took the warnings coming to her very seriously and continued to keep her end of the messages flowing as long as she could. She always ate lunch early and so at 11:00 a.m., when her 32-year-old daughter Minnie brought her lunch she asked her to stay. "After all Minnie, the water in the streets is rising. Stay with me and we will walk home together after this rain subsides and the water level reduces."

Thinking that he had won, hoadtiE let out a cackle that we were all forced to hear.

Our role in these types of situations is to encourage the believer, even comforting them if necessary. We found ourselves doing that on behalf of Minnie. Hettie, too busy sending dispatches to fret, was also too busy to calm Minnie. When she

---

[1] John 10:10a
[2] John 10:10b

would worry, hoadtiE would cackle but one of us would wrap our wings round about her and then hum to her which always gave her comfort.

At 1:00 p.m. the water rose so much that they both went to the second floor. But Hettie, a brilliant worker, kept the Tribune editor Mr. Swank updated, as he kept a running diary of the day. She also kept Mr. Deckert, the Pennsylvania Railroad Freight Station agent updated.

Hettie would not know this but Mr. Swank had just noted that the Stoney Creek had just carried a live cow down by him.

Still thinking that that water would soon quit rising and all would be well, Hettie and Minnie Ogle could not hear hoadtiE scream his joy when at 3:15 Hettie called The Tribune to say that the South Fork Reservoir above her continued to worsen.

The dam had already burst and by this time was already headed towards them.

Cackling his approval of the certain death to come, hoadtiE watched from above while two of us encircled Hettie and Minnie.

From their second story perch, really, the second story of the telegraph tower, the sound of the debris being pushed by the mountain of water reached their ears first. The noise of scraping and bumping and grinding came from all around them. The sound began as a low rumble. It then began to vibrate their second story overlook.

Hettie looked up in bewilderment and saw a dark brown haze. She immediately pushed Minnie into a corner.

When Minnie saw her mother's eyes widen she started to scream and immediately heard her mother recite the 23rd Psalm.

As we wrapped our wings around them their fearful shaking eased, and hoadtiE watched the wave of debris reach their tower and squealed with delight. The power of the rolling turbulent debris crushed the tower into the already soft and wet ground.

Neither Hettie nor Minnie's bodies would ever be identified,[1] but as they breathed their last here on earth we carried them into heaven where Jesus stood, welcoming them into Paradise. Standing next to Jesus was Hettie's husband, smiling and awaiting their arrival.

---

[1] Some of Hael's story comes from Johnstown Flood By David McCullough, pages 97, 98, 283 Simon & Schuster, 1968

Another Hero

A telegraph operator at the railroad station above Mineral Point, which is just in the gorge a short distance below the dam, and the last telegraph station above Conemaugh, had seen the waters rising, and had heard of the first break in the dam. Two hours before the final break came he sent a message to his wife at Mineral Point to prepare for the flood. It read: "Dress the three children in their best Sunday clothes. Gather together what valuables you can easily carry and leave the house.   Go to the stable on the hillside. Stay there until the water reaches it; then run to the mountain. The dam is breaking. The flood is coming. Lose no time."

His wife showed the message to her friends, but they laughed at her. They even persuaded her to not heed her husband's command. The wife went home and about her work. Meanwhile the telegraph operator was busy with his ticker. Down to Conemaugh he wired the warning.   He also sent it on to Johnstown, then he ticked on, giving each minute bulletins of the break. As the water came down he sent message after message, telling its progress. Finally came the flood. He saw houses and bodies swept past him. His last message was: "The water is all around me; I cannot stay longer, and, for God's sake, all fly." Then he jumped out of his tower window and ran up the mountain just in time to save himself. A whole town came past as he turned and looked. Great masses of houses plunged up. He saw people on roofs yelling and crying, and then saw collisions of houses, which caused the buildings to crush and crumble like paper.

Racing with Death

All the time he felt that his family were safe. But it was not so with them. When the roar of approaching water came the people of Mineral Point thought of their warning. The wife gathered her children and started to run. As she went she forgot her husband's advice to go to the mountain and fled down the street to the lowlands. Suddenly she remembered she had left the key of her home in the door. She took the children and ran back. As she neared the house the water came and forced them up between the two houses. The only outlet was toward the mountain, and she ran that way with her children. The water chased her, but she and the children managed to clamber up far enough to escape. Thus, it was that an accident saved their lives. Only three houses and a school-house were saved at Mineral Point.

There is a "perversion" of scripture, endemic in your 21ˢᵗ century, but it is not unique to it. Look at what happened in the story above. Seriously consider it if you would.

Instead of respecting her husband's wishes and pleas, she ignored him and laughed at him. There is an Old Testament passage that says, basically, that divisiveness is as the sin of witchcraft.[1] Have you ever considered that something you may do in your own home is equal to witchcraft?

Please don't think that I am just picking on women, because believe me, I will speak truth to men just as easily. So ladies, take this and learn from it. It nearly cost this family their lives and why? Because some wife listened to her mocking friends rather than her husband.

A DANGEROUS VENTURE

One of the most thrilling incidents of the disaster was the performance of A. J. Leonard, whose family reside in Morrellville. He was at work and hearing that his house had been swept away determined at all hazards to ascertain the fate of his family. The bridges having been carried away he constructed a temporary raft, and clinging to it as close as a cat to the side of a fence, he pushed his frail craft out into the raging torrent and started on a chase which, to all who were watching, seemed to mean an embrace in death.

Heedless of cries "For God's sake go back, you will be drowned." "Don't attempt it," he persevered. As the raft struck the current he pulled off his coat and in his shirt sleeves braved the stream.   Down plunged the boards and down went Leonard, but as it arose he was seen still clinging. A mighty shout arose from the throats of the hundreds on the banks, who were now deeply interested, earnestly hoping he would successfully ford the stream.

Down again went his bark, but nothing, it seemed, could shake Leonard off. The craft shot up in the air apparently ten or twelve feet, and Leonard stuck to it tenaciously. Slowly but surely, he worked his boat to the other side of the stream, and after what seemed an awful suspense he finally landed amid ringing cheers of men, women and children.

---

[1] 1 Samuel 15:23

The last seen of him he was making his way down a mountain road in the direction of the spot where his house had lately stood. His family consisted of his wife and three children.

A Thrilling Escape.

Henry D. Thomas, a well-known dry goods merchant, tells the following story: "I was caught right between a plank and a stone wall and was held in that position for a long time. The water came rushing down and forced the plank against my chest. I felt as if it were going through me, when suddenly the plank gave way, and I fell into the water. I grabbed the plank quickly and in some unaccountable way managed to get the forepart of my body on it, and in that way I was carried down the stream. All around me were people struggling and drowning, while bodies floated like corks on the water. Some were crying for help, others were praying aloud for mercy and a few were singing as if to keep up their courage.

"A large raft which went by bore a whole family, and they were singing, 'Nearer my God to Thee.' In the midst of their song the raft struck a large tree and went to splinters. There were one or two wild cries and then silence. The horror of that time is with me day and night. It would have driven a weak-minded person crazy.

"The true condition of things that night can never be adequately described in words. The water came down through a narrow gorge, which in places was hardly two hundred feet wide. The broken dam was at an elevation of about five hundred feet above Johnstown. The railroad bridge across the Conemaugh River is at the lower side of Johnstown, and the river is joined there by another mountain stream from the northeast. It was here that the debris collected and caught fire, and I doubt if it will ever be known how many perished there. The water came down with the speed of a locomotive. The people there are absolutely paralyzed; So much so that they speak of their losses in a most indifferent way. I heard two men in conversation. One said: 'Well, I lost a wife and three children.' 'That's nothing,' said the other; 'I lost a wife and six children.'

HAEL: WILD CRIES

There have been numerous section titles where I am giving you a balanced description. I need to use a story above in the same way. Do not miss the author's accurate assessment that the family were heard singing, "Nearer my God to Thee.'. . . There were one or two wild cries and then silence."

Please do not think that because we are with you there should be no "wild cries." And please, do not think another unfit for Christendom simply because they may be scared.

Do not ever forget . . . We are there with you. When you pass from this world to the next, we are carrying you to glory. You are never left alone. You are never forsaken. We are there, and my friend, your cries do not scare us away.

As Hael recorded the above paragraph he thought of this terrible time of tragedy and a tear slipped from his eye.

Hael continued, "We take our job seriously, and we are here to serve you as we serve our Creator."

THE SUDDEN BREAK

A man named Maguire was met on his way from South Fork to Johnstown. He said he was standing on the edge of the lake when the walls burst. The waters were rising all day and were on a level with a pile of dirt which he said was above the walls of the dam. All of a sudden it burst with a report like a cannon and the water started down the mountain side, sweeping before it the trees as if they were chips. Boulders were rolled down as if they were marbles. The roar was deafening. The lake was emptied in an hour.

At the time there were about forty men at work up there, building a new draining system at the lake for Messrs. Parke and Van Buren. They did all they could to try and avert the disaster by digging a sluice-way on one side to ease the pressure on the dam, but their efforts were fruitless.

"It was about half-past two o'clock when the water reached the top of the dam. At first it was just a narrow white stream trickling down the face of the dam, soon its proportions began to grow with alarming rapidity, and in an extremely short space of time a volume of water a foot in thickness was passing over the top of the dam.

"There had been little rain up to dark. Whatever happened in the way of a cloud burst took place during the night. When the workmen woke in the morning the lake was very full and was rising at the rate of a foot an hour.

"When at two o'clock the water began to flow over the dam, the work of undermining began. Men were sent three or four times during the day . . .

184

To Warn the People

. . . below of their danger. At three o'clock there was a sound like tremendous and continued peals of thunder. The earth seemed to shake and vibrate beneath our feet.

"There was a rush of wind, the trees swayed to and fro, the air was full of fine spray or mist: then looking down just in front of the dam we saw trees, rocks and earth shot up into mid-air in great columns. It seemed as though some great unseen force was at work wantonly destroying everything; then the great wave, foaming, boiling and hissing, dashing clouds of spray hundreds of feet in height as it came against some obstruction in the way of its mad rush, clearing everything away before it, started on its terrible death-dealing mission down the fatal valley."

Engineer Henry's Awful Race

Engineer Henry, of the second section of the express train, No. 8, which was caught at Conemaugh tells a thrilling story. His train was caught in the midst of the wave and were the only cars that were not destroyed. "It was an awful sight," he said. "I have often seen pictures of flood scenes, and I thought they were exaggerations, but what I witnessed last Friday changes my former belief. To see that immense volume of water, fully fifty feet high, rushing madly down the valley, sweeping everything before it, was a thrilling sight. It is engraved indelibly on my memory. Even now I can see that mad torrent carrying death and destruction before it.

"The second section of No. 8, on which I was, was due at Johnstown about 10:15 in the morning. We arrived there safely, and were told to follow the first section. When we arrived at Conemaugh the first section and the mail were there. Washouts further up the mountain prevented our going, so we could do nothing but sit around and discuss the situation. The creek at Conemaugh was swollen. high, almost overflowing. The heavens were pouring rain, but this did not prevent nearly all the inhabitants of the town from gathering along its banks. They watched . . .

The Waters Go Dashing

. . . by and wondered whether the creek could get much higher. But a few inches more and it would overflow its banks. There seemed to be a feeling of uneasiness among the people. They seemed to fear that something awful was going to happen. Their suspicions were strengthened by the fact that warning had come down the valley for the people to be on the lookout.

The rains had swelled everything to the bursting point. The day passed slowly, however.

"Noon came and went, and still nothing happened. We could not proceed, nor could we go back, as the tracks about a mile below Conemaugh had been washed away, so there was nothing for us to do but to wait and see what would come next.

"Sometime after 3 o'clock Friday afternoon I went into the train despatcher's office to learn the latest news. I had not been there long when I heard a fierce whistling from an engine away up the mountain. Rushing out I found dozens of men standing around. Fear had blanched every cheek. The loud and continued whistling had made everyone feel that something serious was going to happen. In a few moments I could hear a train rattling down the mountain. About five hundred yards above Conemaugh the tracks make a slight curve and we could not see beyond this. The suspense was something awful. We did not know what was coming, but no one could get rid of the thought that something was wrong at the dam.

"Our suspense was not very long, however. Nearer and nearer the train came, the thundering sound still accompanying it. There seemed to be something behind the tram, as there was a dull, rumbling sound which I knew did not come from the train. Nearer and nearer it came; a moment more and it would reach the curve. The next instant there burst upon our eyes a sight that made every heart stand still. Rushing around the curve, snorting and tearing, came an engine and several gravel cars. The train appeared to be putting forth every effort to go faster. Nearer it came, belching forth smoke and whistling long and loud. But . . .

THE MOST TERRIBLE SIGHT

. . . was to follow. Twenty feet behind came surging along a mad rush of water fully fifty feet high. Like the train, it seemed to be putting forth every effort to push along faster. Such an awful race we never before witnessed. For an instant the people seemed paralyzed with horror. They knew not what to do, but in a moment, they realized that a second's delay meant death to them. With one accord they rushed to the high lands a few hundred feet away. Most of them succeeded in reaching that place and were safe.

"I thought of the passengers in my train. The second section of No. 8 had three sleepers. In these three cars were about thirty people, who rushed through the train crying to the others 'Save yourselves!' Then came a scene of the wildest confusion. Ladies and children shrieked, and the men seemed terror-stricken. I succeeded in helping some ladies and children off the train and up to the highlands. Running back, I caught up two children and ran for my life to a higher place. Thank God, I was quicker than the flood! I deposited my load in safety on the high land just as it swept past us.

"For nearly an hour we stood watching the mad flood go rushing by. The water was full of debris. When the flood caught Conemaugh it dashed against the little town with a mighty crash. The water did not lift the houses up and carry them off, but crushed them one against the other and broke them up like so many egg shells. Before the flood came there was a pretty little town. When the waters passed on there was nothing but a . . .

FEW BROKEN BOARDS

. . . to mark the central portion of the city. It was swept as clean as a newly brushed floor. When the flood passed onward down the valley I went over to my train. It had been moved back about twenty yards, but it was not damaged. About fifty persons had remained in the train and they were safe. Of the three trains ours was the luckiest. The engines of both the others had been swept off the track and one or two cars in each train had met the same fate.

"What saved our train was the fact that just at the curve which I mentioned the valley spread out. The valley is six or seven hundred yards broad where our train was standing. This, of course, let the floods pass out. It was only twenty feet high when it struck our train, which was about in the middle of the valley. This fact, together with the elevation of the track, was all that saved us. We stayed that night in the houses in Conemaugh that had not been destroyed. The next morning, I started down the valley and by 4 o'clock in the afternoon had reached Conemaugh furnace, eight miles west of Johnstown. Then I got a team and came home.

"In my tramp down the valley I saw some awful sights. On the tree branches hung shreds of clothing torn from the unfortunates as they were whirled along in the terrible rush of the torrent. Dead bodies were lying by scores along the banks of the creeks. One woman I helped drag from the mud had tightly clutched in her hand a paper. We tore it out of her hand and found it to be a badly water-soaked photograph. It was probably a picture of the drowned woman."

A Ghastly Scene

At the present moment, away down in its terrible depths, this mass of torn and twisted timbers and dead humanity is slowly burning, and the light curling smoke that rises as high almost as the mountain, and the sickening smell that comes from the center of this fearful funeral pile tell that the unseen fire is feeding on other fuel than the rafters and roofs that once sheltered the population of Johnstown.

The mind is filled with horror at the supreme desolation that pervades the whole scene. It is small wonder that the pen cannot in the hands of the most skillful even pretend to convey one-hundredth part of what is seen and heard every hour in the day in this fearful place. At the present moment firemen and others are out on that ghastly aggregation of wood, work and human kind jammed against the unyielding mass of arched masonry.

Round them curls the white smoke from the smoldering interior of the heaped-up houses of Johnstown. Every now and then the gleam of an axe and a group of stooping forms tell that another ghastly find has been made, and a whisper goes round among the hundreds of watchers that other bodies are being brought to light.

How many hundreds or thousands there are who found death by fire at this awful spot will never be known, and the people are already giving up hopes of ever reaching the knowledge of how their loved and lost ones met their doom, whether in the fierce, angry embrace of the waters of Conemaugh, or in the deadly grip of the fire fiend, who claimed the homes of Johnstown for his own above the fatal bridge.

Every hour it becomes more and more apparent that the exact number of lives lost will never be known. Up to the present time the disposition has been to under rather than overestimate the number of lives sacrificed.

HAEL: ESCORTS

With the descriptions given above by our 1889 author, I want to salve your fears by reminding you of something we have already mentioned, but it bears repeating, namely, that death has lost its sting, which the Holy Spirit clearly said through Paul in 1 Corinthians 15:55. So let me give you a different visual to contemplate.

As you have already read above, and will read below, we are honored to carry[1] you to heaven. Here is the picture I want you to see though. It is the saved, the bride, those who have trusted Christ as their Savior that we carry, right?

Here's my question to you. If we meet and carry that person at death to take them to heaven, what meets the dying person who is not going to heaven?

Your God and Father, our Creator, has so engineered relationships that He is concerned for you and wants you to experience death as "well" as you can. That is part of the meaning behind the Psalmist saying that "death of His faithful servants is precious to Him.[2]

A MOTHER RESCUED BY HER DAUGHTER

A daughter of John Duncan, superintendent of the Johnstown Street Car Company, had an awful struggle in rescuing her mother and baby sister. Mrs. Duncan and family had taken refuge on a roof, when a large log came floating down the river, striking the house with immense force, knocking Mrs. Duncan and daughter into the fast running river. Seeing what had happened, Alvania, her fifteen-year-old daughter, leaped into the water, and after a hard struggle landed both on the roof of the house.

The members of the Cambria Club tell of their battle for life in the following manner: They were about to sit down to dinner when they heard the crash, and knowing what had occurred they started for the attic just as the flood was upon them. When the members were assured of their safety they at once commenced saving others by grasping them as they floated by on tree tops, houses, etc. In this manner they saved seventy persons from death.

THE CLOCK STOPPED AT 5:20

One of the oddest sights in the center of the town is a three-story brick residence standing with one wall, the others having disappeared completely, leaving the floors supported by the partitions. In one of the upper rooms can be seen a mantel with a lambrequin on it and a clock stopped at twenty minutes after five. In front of the clock is a lady's fan, though from the marks on the wall-paper the water has been over all these things.

---

[1] Luke 16:22
[2] Psalm 116:15

In the upper part of the town, where the back water from the flood went into the valley with diminished force, there are many strange scenes. There the houses were toppled over one after another in a row, and left where they lay. One of them was turned completely over and stands with its roof on the foundations of another house and its base in the air. The owner came back, and getting into his house through the windows walked about on his ceiling. Out of this house a woman and her two children escaped safely and were but little hurt, although they were stood on their heads in the whirl. Every house has its own story. From one a woman shut up in her garret escaped by chopping a hole in the roof. From another a Hungarian named Grevins leaped to the shore as it went whirling past and fell twenty-five feet upon a pile of metal and escaped with a broken leg. Another is said to have come all the way from very near the start of the flood and to have circled around with the back water and finally landed on the flats at the city site, where it is still pointed out.

CHAPTER X
New Tales of Horror

The accounts contained in the foregoing chapters bring this appalling story of death down to June 4th. We continue the narrative as given from day to day by eye-witnesses, as this is the only method by which a full and accurate description of Johnstown's unspeakable horror can be obtained.

On the morning of June 5th one of the leading journals contained the following announcements, printed in large type, and preceding its vivid account of the terrible situation at Johnstown:

- Death, Ruin, Plague!
- Threatened Outbreak of Disease in the Fate Stricken Valley.
- Awful Effluvia [Odor] from Corpses!
- Swift and Decisive Means Must be Taken to Clear Away the Masses of Putrefying Matter that Underlie the Wreck of What was Once a Town.
- Proposed Use of Explosives.
- Crowds of Refugees are Already Attacked by Pneumonia and the Germs of Typhus Pervade Both Air and Water.
- Victims Yet Unnumbered.
- Dreadful Discoveries Hourly Made!
- Heaps of the Drowned, the Mangled and the Burned are Found in Pockets Between Rocks and Under Packed Accumulations of Sand!
- Pennsylvania Regiments Ordered to the Scene to Keep Ward Over an Afflicted and Heart-Broken People.
- Blame Where it Belongs.
- The Ears of the Inhabitants were Dulled to Fear by Warnings Many Times Repeated.
- Forty-two years ago the Dam Broke.
- Vivid Stories of Witnesses of the Great Tragedy.
- The Owners of the Lake Must Bear a Gigantic Burden of Remorse.
- Sufferings of Survivors!

These were the terrible headings in a single issue of a newspaper.

A registry of the living who were residents of Johnstown prior to the flood was begun today. Out of a total population of 39,400 the names of only 10,600 have been recorded. This may give an approximate idea of the number of those who lost their lives.

GAUNT MENACE OF PESTILENCE

The most important near fact of today is the increasing danger of pestilence.

As the work of disengaging the bodies of the dead progresses the horrible peril becomes more and more apparent. There is need of the speediest possible measures to offset the gravity of the sanitary situation.

From every part of the stricken valley the same cry of alarm arises, for at every point where the dead are being discovered, as the waters continue to abate, the same peril exists.

The use of explosives, especially dynamite, has been discussed. There is some opposition to it, but it may yet be resorted to. The great mass of ruins at the Pennsylvania Railroad bridge, which is still smoking and smoldering, is a ghastly mine of human flesh and bones in all sorts of hideous shapes, and unless desperate means are employed, cannot be cleared away in weeks to come.

Still, vigorous work in that direction is being performed, and explosives will be used in a limited degree to further it. This great work may be divided into two parts, the clearing away of the mass of debris lodged against the Pennsylvania Railroad bridge, and the examination and removal of the many wrecked buildings which mark the site of Johnstown.

HAEL: PESTILENCE

God is speaking, ". . . if I [meaning, when I] send pestilence on My people."[1]
Since this clearly tells you that God can send pestilence upon His people. I want
to also say that not every pestilence is sent by God.

---

[1] 2 Chronicles 7:13e

May I share a severe frustration I have with many of you? I get so upset when you want to have answers, explanations, reasons, and conclusions when bad things happen.

Look, the laws of nature that will happen, pestilences occur, difficulties happen, and God interjects Himself into your circumstances, but please, please, quit trying to figure-it-out and say, "this God caused," or "this God allowed." At best, you are guessing.

How do I know this? Well, forget that I'm an angel and so I see things in the heavenlies that you do not. Look at what our Creator said through the Old Testament prophet. He said, "My ways are higher than your ways. And My thoughts are higher than your thoughts."[1]

Why am I making a big deal about this? Because you are missing that the evil one is deceiving you into focusing on the wrong issue. You are spending every day of your life trying to figure out "why did this happen and why did that happen" when God is wanting you to accept that He is sovereign, and because He is sovereign, He is trustworthy.

Let me give you just a few passages that express this:

A man's heart plans his way, but the Lord determines his steps.[2]

And He said to me, "It is done! I am the Alpha and the Omega, the Beginning and the End. I will give water as a gift to the thirsty from the spring of life.[3]

[15] As for man, his days are like grass—he blooms like a flower of the field; [16] when the wind passes over it, it vanishes, and its place is no longer known. [17] But from eternity to eternity the Lord's faithful love is toward those who fear Him, and His righteousness toward the grandchildren [18] of those who keep His covenant, who remember to observe His precepts. [19] The Lord has established His throne in heaven, and His kingdom rules over all.[4]

One of the great strengths of human-kind is your ability to analyze a matter and figure it out. God has gifted you in this area. But that wonderful strength is also a magnificent weakness when you believe that you need to analyze and figure out everything. Sometimes you just need to trust God and accept the situation.

Otherwise you put God in a little box that YOU can understand, which completely hampers your ability to trust Him to do "God-sized" miracles.

---

[1] Isaiah 55:8-9
[2] Proverbs 16:9
[3] Revelation 21:6
[4] Psalm 103:15-19

Order Begins to Appear

Slowly something like order is beginning to appear in the chaos of destruction. Enough militia came today to put the town under strict martial law. Four hundred men of the Fourteenth regiment, of Pittsburgh, are here. There will be no more tramping over the ruins by ungoverned mobs. There will be no more fears of rioting.

The supplies of food are constantly growing. The much-needed money is beginning to come in, though not at all needless relief committees are beginning to go out. Better quarters for the sufferers are being provided. Better arrangements for systematic relief are made. Something of the deep gloom has been dispelled, though Johnstown is still the saddest spot on earth.

The systematic attempt to clear up the ruins at the gorge and get out the bodies imprisoned there began today. The expectations of ghastly discoveries were more than realized. Scores of burned and mangled bodies were removed.

Freaks of the Torrent

The great waste where the city stood looked a little different today. Some attempt was made to clear up the rubbish, and fires were burning in a dozen places to get rid of it. Tents for the soldiers and some of the sufferers were put up in the smooth stretch of sand where a great, five story hardware store used to stand. The dead animals that were here and there in the debris were removed, to the benefit of the townspeople's health.

Curious things come to light where the rubbish was cleared away. The solid cobblestone pavement had been scooped up by the force of the water and in some places swept so far away that there was not a sign of it. Behind a house that was resting on one corner was found a wickerwork baby carriage full of mud, but not injured or scratched in the least nor yet buried in the mud, but looking as if it had been rolled there and left. Very close to it was a piece of railroad iron that must have been carried half a mile, bent as if it were but common wire. Exactly on the site of a large grocery store was a box of soap and a bundle of clothespins, while of all the brick and stone, of which the store was built, and all the heavy furniture it contained there was not the slightest trace.

Many articles of wearing apparel were found here, but no bodies could be discovered in the whole stretch of the plain, from which it is inferred that most of the deaths occurred at the gorge or else the flood swept them far away.

REMINDERS OF A BROKEN HOME

One of the few buildings that are left in this part of town is the fine house of Mr. Geranheiser, of the Cambria Iron Company. It presents an odd spectacle that is common here but has not often been seen before. The flood reached almost to the second floor and was strong enough to cut away about half the house, leaving the rest standing. The whole interior of the place can be seen just as the frightened inmates left it. The carpets are torn up from the first floor, but the pictures are still hanging on the walls and an open piano stands against the wall full of mud; a Brussels carpet being half way out of the second story on the side where the wreck was and showing exactly how high the water came. There was a center table in the room and an open book on it. Chairs stood about the room and the pictures were on the walls, and half of the room was gone miles away.

SEVEN ACRES OF WRECKAGE

Just below the bare plain where the business block of Johnstown stood, and above the stone arch bridge on which the Pennsylvania Railroad crossed the river, are seven acres of the wreckage of the flood. The horrors that have been enacted in that spot, the horrors that are seen there every hour, who can attempt to describe? Under and amid that mass of conglomerate rubbish are the remains of at least one thousand persons who died the most frightful of deaths.

This is the place where the fire broke out within twenty minutes after the flood. It has burned ever since. The stone arch bridge acted as a dam to the flood, and five towns were crushing each other against it. A thousand houses came down on the great wave of water, and were held there a solid mass in the jaws of a Cyclopean vise.

A kitchen stove upset. The mass took fire. A thousand people were imprisoned in these houses. A thousand more were on the roofs. For most of them there was no escape. The fire swept on from house to house. The prisoners saw it coming and shrieked and screamed with terror, and ran up and down their narrow quarters in an agony of fear.

SIGHTS TO FREEZE THEIR BLOOD

Thousands of people stood upon the river bank and saw and heard it all and still were powerless to help. They saw people kneeling in the flames and praying. They saw families gathered together with their arms around each other and waiting for death. They saw people going mad and tearing their hair and laughing. They saw men plunge into the narrow crevices between the houses and seek death in the water rather than wait its coming in the flames. Some saw their friends and some their wives and children perishing before them, and some in the awful agony of the hour went mad themselves and ran shrieking to the hillsides, and stronger men laid down on the ground and wept.

All that night and all the next day, and far into the morning of Monday, these dreadful shrieks resounded from that place of doom. The fire burned on, aided by the fire underneath, added to by fresh fuel coming down the river. All that time the people stood helpless on the bank and heard those heartrending sounds. What could they do? They could not fight the fire. Every fire engine in the town lay in that mass of rubbish smashed to bits. For hours had to wait until they could get telegraph word to surrounding towns and hours more until the fire engines arrived at noon on Monday.

HAEL: ONGOING COMFORT

I have been given permission to share the following with you. An ongoing angelic project has its roots in each disaster. This disaster is no exception. It is the project of comforting you in your sleep and each of us are charged with this unique opportunity. You will remember that when the Lord Jesus engaged heartrending, agonizing prayer in the Garden of Gethsemane, one of our company came to strengthen and comfort Him. We are given the same charge to each of you.

Let me take you into the life of a rather lonely family. They were lonely, not taking the time to reach out to those around them. Charles and Victoria Phillips who considered themselves sensible, but in reality, lacked any desire to love others, thought others were "below-them" spiritually. During the flood they lost all seven of their children in the most tormenting way possible. Here is their angel's account:

Charles and Victoria, strict Christian parents who knew the need to daily meet at the family altar, took advantage of the rain outside and kept the children inside doing chores and memorizing Scripture. As the water rose to the top step and then over the porch and entered the sitting rooms on the lower level, Charles immediately summoned both John and David, ages 14 and 12 to pull up the carpet, taking it upstairs along with the furniture. The smaller boys and girls carried the smaller items and before long everything was safely on the second level.

About this time Victoria heard the sound of the horseman, later described as the Johnstown Paul Revere who road by saying, "Run for the hills, the dam is busted."

Looking pleadingly to Charles she stopped and wanted to grab the children and run.

"No," Charles stated emphatically, "The water cannot reach this high. By the time it makes its way to us, spreads out to our part of the town the water will raise only a few feet. We will remain and take care of our belongings."

In a frightful state she submitted to her husband's orders and made her way back upstairs with her children. She held back tears, having her own dam of water that wanted to break its boundaries and flood her eyes.

It seemed like hours to her, fearful and trying to steady herself, but less than 30 minutes later the incredible sound of logs being tossed in the air, breaking upon one another and the slapping of houses hitting one another, crashing upon one another and in a few cases being lifted up right off of their foundations, crashed into her already frantic world.

And then amazingly, the Phillip's house lifted upon the tops of nearby houses and fairly floated. While their trip was rocky, she counted all of her children and knew they were safe in their upstairs room together. As they slipped and slid from one side of the room to the other, their house obviously careening off of other debris, the house made an abrupt stop and the back half of the wall where Victoria sat disappeared.

As soon as it did she fell into the water and Charles, a rugged and athletic thirty-nine years old dove in after her. Grabbing her almost instantly he started to return to the room with the children. Just moments before they reached the outstretched arms of John and David, another huge portion of the house disappeared and this time the children went with it. As Victoria's eyes widened she tried to scream but just then the wall of water following the wall of debris scooped up her and her husband and threw them against the side of the mountain.

Charles again grabbed Victoria, pulled her to her feet and ran as quickly as they could up the hill, all the while watching the room where the children were still concealed churning in the water. They had just stopped, and Charles pointed out to the now crying Victoria, that he saw the children and would get them when the unthinkable occurred.

Another home on the other side of the children had just come to an abrupt stop. The children and the remains of the room rammed into the home stopped in front of them. There was a popping sound, and then an explosion and a fire began. Horrified, Charles and the now screaming Victoria watched their children enter into the fire. Over the torrential sounds of the water they could hear the screams of their children.

Two years later Charles and Victoria still could not sleep without nightmares. As you could imagine, their relationship suffered, their health suffered, and their trust in the sovereign God suffered, for He chose to save them rather than their children.

Victoria no longer trusted or respected her husband and Charles's love for Victoria waned. They may have lived in the same home, but they did not live in the same universe. They rarely talked to one another and they lived completely separate lives. Charles provided, and Victoria existed. He would never consider divorce and she longed for suicide but would never consider the act.

As the Holy Spirit became backed into a smaller and smaller corner of their individual lives, a curious thing began to occur. Victoria began to sing phrases of the hymns she grew up with. Her singing began as humming, and it grew into mumbling a few bars. For the next six months she intermittently hummed and mumbled, and often experienced some relief from her pain, until she would blame her husband, focus upon her children's screams, be angry toward God, then silence, and then, no more humming of hymns.

A now broken and humbled Charles saw this and remaining quiet as he watched her, found himself longing to serve his desperate wife. During the previous two and a half years he had apologized over and over again and realized that it made no difference. On November 8th, 1891 he decided to go to the church around the corner from him. Neither he nor Victoria had been to church since the Johnstown Flood.

As Charles sat down in the back of the church he sat by himself. He didn't bring a Bible for he had none. The pastor opened his message saying, "We take sin too lightly!" And then opened his Bible to Psalm 38 and Psalm 39 where he spoke on, "Crying Out to God for Mercy," because of sin in one's life.

He explained that, of course, when the sin is confessed, the Lord forgives that sin and forgets the sin as far as the east is from the west, but while the pastor spoke, *the Holy Spirit prompted a calloused memory inside of Charles: his arrogance and pride.*

Returning home, with the Bible he borrowed from church Charles read the two chapters over and over. The more he read them, the more they awakened a feeling of despair in him. He started to silently cry out to God because of the death of his children, but almost instantly he could tell that was not the reason for his discomfort.

As Charles sat pensively in the small sitting room he began to weep. "Where is this coming from?" he asked between sobs. With his eyes closed he asked, "Have I too taken sin lightly, Lord?" Wiping his eyes he got off of the settee and knelt on the floor, burying his head in his hands.

Grabbing his borrowed Bible, he opened it to Psalm 38 and read, "Lord, do not punish me in Your anger."

"But what have I done, Lord?"

Skipping down he read, "sins have flooded over my head." And he asked, "What sins, Lord?"

Reading verse eight he saw, "I am faint, crushed and in anguish."

"Yes, Lord, yes. That I do admit to You."

Proceeding to verse nine Charles read only the first half of the verse and stopped. Rereading it, "My every desire is known to You." He asked, "Why is this the problem, Lord? What are You trying to say to me?"

After a few more moments he began to sob. His shoulders heaved, and he realized what he had not seen in his life before. He was an arrogant, prideful man. Being broken was not enough. Owning his sin, first before God, and then before Victoria was necessary.

Slowly making his way to Victoria's room he entered. She noticed something was different. After they talked for a while she saw the difference. Charles was not merely broken, but also repentant.

Their lives remained tender toward one another for the rest of their time here on earth. They never had any more children, but loved each other as if they were the only two people upon the earth. When they died, one month apart at the ripe ages of 81 and 83, their children were standing next to Jesus welcoming them into eternity.

I don't have the opportunity to tell you of the lives they comforted, because God comforted them,[1] but I can tell you that they had a long, long line of people next to their children who wanted to welcome them into heaven. They were those they had comforted in their time of need, something they could never have done had they not been so broken in their own lives.

WRECKS OF FIVE IRON BRIDGES

The shrieks ceased early in the morning. Men had begun to search the ruins and had taken out the few that still lived. The fire engines began to play on the still smoldering fire. Other workmen began to remove the bodies. The fire had swept over the whole mass from shore to shore and burned it to the water. A great field of crushed and charred timbers was all that was left. The flood had gorged this in so tightly that it made a solid bridge above the water. A tremendous, irresistible force had ground and churned and macerated the debris until it was a confused, solid, almost welded, conglomerate, stretching from shore to shore, jammed high up against the stone bridge and extending up the river a quarter of a mile, perhaps half as wide. In this tangled heap and crush of matter were the twisted wrecks of five iron bridges, smashed locomotives, splintered dwellings and all their contents; human beings and domestic animals, hay and factory machinery; the rich contents of stores and brick walls ground to powder, all the products of human industry, all the elements of human interests, twisted, turned, broken in a mighty mill and all thrown together.

A SICKENING SPECTACLE

I walked over this extraordinary mass this morning and saw the fragments of thousands of articles. In one place the roofs of forty frame houses were packed in together just as you would place forty bended cards one on top of another. The iron rods of a bridge were twisted into a perfect spiral six times around one of the girders. Just beneath it was a woman's trunk, broken up and half filled with sand, with silk dresses and a veil streaming out of it. From under the trunk men were lifting the body of its owner, perhaps, so burned, so horribly mutilated, so torn from limb to limb, that even the workmen, who have seen so many of these frightful sights that they have begun to get used to them, turned away sick at heart.

---

[1] 2 Corinthians 1:4

I saw in one place a wrecked grocery store, bins of coffee and tea, flour, spices and nuts, parts of the counter and safe mingled together. Near it was the pantry of the house, still partly intact, the plates and saucers regularly piled up, a waiter and a teapot, but not a sign of the woodwork, not a recognizable outline of a house. In another place a halter, with a part of a horse's head tied to a bit of a manger, and a mass of hay and straw about, but no other signs of the stable in which the horse was burned. Two cindered towels, a cake of soap in a dish, and a bit of carpet were taken to indicate the location of a hotel. I saw a child's skull in a bed of ashes, but no sign of a body.

RECOGNIZED BY FRAGMENTS

In another place was a human foot and crumbling indications of a boot, but no signs of a body. A hay rick, half ashes, stood near the center of the gorge. Workmen who dug about it to-day found a chicken coop, and in it two chickens, not only alive but clucking happily when they were released. A woman's hat, half burned, a reticule (a woman's small decorative handbag), with a part of a hand still clinging to it, two shoes and part of a dress told the story of one unfortunate's death. Close at hand a commercial traveler had perished. There was his broken valise, still full of samples, fragments of his shoes and some pieces of his clothing.

Scenes like these were occurring all over the charred field where men were working with pick and axe and lifting out the poor, shattered remains of human beings, nearly always past recognition or identification, except by guesswork, or the locality where they were found. Articles of domestic use scattered through the rubbish helped to tell who some of the bodies were. Part of a set of dinner plates told one man where in the intangible mass his house was. In one place was a photograph album with one picture recognizable. From this the body of a child nearby was identified. A man who had spent a day and all night looking for the body of his wife, was directed to her remains by part of a trunk lid.

DEAD BODIES CARESSED

Poor old John Jordan, of Conemaugh! Many a tear ran over swarthy cheeks for him today. All his family, his wife and children, had been swept from his sight in the flood. He wandered over the gorge yesterday looking for them, and last night the police would not bring him away. At daylight he found his wife's sewing machine and called the workmen to help him. First, they found a little boy's jacket that he recognized and then they came upon the rest of them all buried together, the mother's burned arms still clinging to the little children. Then the white headed old man sat down in the ashes and caressed the dead bodies and talked to them just as if they were alive until someone came and led him quietly away. Without a protest he went to the shore and sat down on a rock and talked to himself, and then got up and disappeared on the hills.

HAEL: THE RESIDUE OF TENDERNESS

Reaching the small treehouse he had made for his little boy, Mr. Jordan sat there without moving. He couldn't believe that they were all gone. He sat there in shock until he finally fell asleep.

He awakened to the screams of his wife and children. Sitting up quickly, looking around for them, he realized he had just dreamt it. They were still gone and nothing would bring them back.

Sitting there unable to move, he didn't hear the angel walk up to his son's treehouse. The angel, a friend of mine named Tephillah[1], was dressed as a man and said softly, "Mr. Jordan, Mr. Jordan."

Mr. Jordan slowly came to life and turned to look down at the angel. "Who are you?" he asked with great sorrow in his voice.

"I'm with the relief committee." And with that he offered Mr. Jordan something to eat.

For the next few days Mr. Jordan shuffled around his home like a dead man walking. He rarely entered the house. Even though it had been built high enough on the hill to still be intact, he rarely went in. All he could do was to remember the opportunities he had with his son, hunting on Saturdays and Sundays, or the garden work he did with his girls and wife. Sundays were the easiest day to do this, so they spent many a Sunday, in their garden and around the house. A perfect life that he realized would never again be his.

A number of families had moved into his home, as they were homeless, which was fine with him. He told himself that it gave him an excuse to not go into the house. Periodically he would see one of the family's wives wearing a dress that his wife had worn before. He didn't react neither good nor bad. He just looked on with a nearly uncomprehending look. And the kids would run around the yard wearing clothes that his children had worn, but this too didn't faze him.

---

[1] pronounced tef-EE-luh, "e" as in end, "EE" as in seen, "uh" as in up

The relief worker kept coming back every couple of days with food, making Mr. Jordan eat. Reluctantly he did and regained his strength. After a few more visits, the angel as our relief committee worker, returned with food and a Bible, told him about Jesus, and Mr. Jordan told him to leave and never return, nearly hitting the poor relief worker.

After a month of wandering aimlessly in and around Johnstown, Mr. Jordan left, abandoning his home and made his way to Pittsburgh, Pennsylvania. There he lived on whiskey and cigarettes, sleeping at a Salvation Army when he was sober.

He lived like this for seven years, eating at the Salvation Army and listening through boring sermons, but he did it for the food.

On Sunday May 31st, 1896 Mr. Jordan was particularly hungry, and reasonably sober. He had been in jail for the previous three days, which was becoming a regular habit with him. So when he showed up for breakfast he knew clearly, and without the effects of his usual inebriation, that this would be a long day of messages.

He hadn't realized what the day was, and even when the speaker who looked familiar stood up, Mr. Jordan had not connected the speaker with the date. But when he started to speak, and told of that great flood seven years earlier, "seven years to that very day," Mr. Jordan started to get sick, but not in his stomach, in his heart.

Sitting next to him, a kindly, crippled old man looked up to Mr. Jordan and said with a squeaky voice, "You don't look well, sonny."

The hardened Mr. Jordan, without looking at the old man, stared at the speaker and angrily, but quietly responded, "I thought I had drunk that memory out of my mind."

The two were silent for a time when Mr. Jordan said, to no one in particular, "This is going to be a long day."

Ninety minutes later they had a break and the old man, limping along, now came up to Mr. Jordan who had his coffee and was heading outside for a smoke. "What do you remember about that tragic day in Johnstown?" he asked.

"All of it," came the rigid answer. "I lost my entire family, every single one."

"Well, listening to this preacher, it would seem they are in a better place, would it not?" The old squeaky voice had a touch of an Irish accent that Mr. Jordan hadn't noticed before.

"Who are you?" Mr. Jordan asked the old man.

"Oh, just a friend, my boy, just a friend."

Mr. Jordan retorted, "I don't have any friends, you old shriveled up man, and I don't want any."

"Aye, but you might. And when you do, I'll be there," said the old man a bit too cheerfully. Mr. Jordan stubbed out his cigarette and returned to the Salvation Army Hall.

Three hours later another break allowed for a fresh cigarette, but Mr. Jordan had been angry at the speaker and wanted to speak to him privately.

"You can't sell me on that carpenter Jesus. I was a carpenter. A Mason even, a good man, and your God took my family from me up there in Johnstown."

His voice started to crack but he regained his composer and continued. "Your carpenter had no regard for his fellow Masons."

At this the speaker cut in, "Mister, I don't know who you are, but I know who Jesus is, and He has never sanctioned a group who accepts all kinds of gods as equal with Him. But as for His kindness to you, personally, you are still alive, aren't you?"

And at that, Mr. Jordan lunged at the speaker who was expecting it. He side-stepped and Mr. Jordan fell onto his face.

Dazed, Mr. Jordan remained on his face for a moment. When a Salvation Army worker moved to help him, the speaker waved him off. They just stood there watching Mr. Jordan, who by this time was shaking his head, slightly bewildered.

After a few more moments the speaker knelt down and spoke softly to Mr. Jordan, "Friend, I don't know why God took our families from us on that fateful day. I do not know and will probably never know until I get to heaven. And even then, I fear that I may have some strong words for Him."

And with that he helped Mr. Jordan up and asked him to sit down with him. They both sat, facing one another. He had a round, dark face, and when he looked at Mr. Jordan, his closely set eyes seemed to hold the smallest hint of compassion. Mr. Jordan, still a bit dazed, looked quizzically at the speaker.

"What did you mean when you said, 'our families?'" asked Mr. Jordan angrily.

"Just what I said, can't you hear?" the speaker responded rather curtly. "I lost my family too. You're not the only one. There are many of us."

And with that Mr. Jordan started to soften ever so slightly. They exchanged stories over the next few minutes and when the speaker rose to begin again, Mr. Jordan went back to his seat next to the little old man.

He and the old man sat listening to the speaker, but Mr. Jordan now listened differently, more intently than he had throughout the morning. Even the old man seemed to follow the speaker closely, saying a few "amens" and periodically poking Mr. Jordan as if to say, "Now that's preaching."

"I don't know why I hate his question though?" said a thoughtful Mr. Jordan.

"What question?" asked the old man, who already knew the answer.

"The one he keeps asking: 'What are you going to do about Jesus?' If we've heard it once we've heard it ten times today."

The old man did not respond but just sat there hunched over and smiling.

At the end of the night the old man asked Mr. Jordan, who had opened up to him over the day, where he would sleep that night. When they both agreed that they would be sleeping outside, he pulled Mr. Jordan aside. "Come with me. I have some extra newspapers."

The next few days they scavenged together, slipped into the Salvation Army for a meal periodically and spoke about various things, always coming back to the question asked by the speaker numerous times on that day: "What are you going to do about Jesus?"

It was a particularly hot summer that year in Pittsburgh and one evening, some months along, the old man started to cough and would not stop. Mr. Jordan didn't know what to do and tried to sit him up.

"Thank you, boy." The old man wheezed and then slowly continued. "I'm dying."

They both sat in silence and the little old man asked Mr. Jordan, "What are you going to do about Him?"

"What?" asked a tearful Mr. Jordan.

"Jesus, boy. What are you going to do about Jesus?" The old man could barely get the words out.

The old man began to cough again and didn't stop until his lifeless body lay there in Mr. Jordan's arms.

The next day, a bewildered and lonely Mr. Jordan returned to the Salvation Army with some questions. The speaker from back in May happened to be there again and sat with Mr. Jordan as he answered his questions about death and heaven and hell.

As they talked about the death of the old man the speaker said gruffly, "Many drunks die without anyone before they are carried to hell by the demons of hell-fire."

Not really speaking to him, Mr. Jordan said to himself, "No, something was different about this man. Something was different."

Mr. Jordan volunteered to help other men, and over time came to a saving knowledge of Jesus Christ. Never quite able to quit drinking, Mr. Jordan died of a destroyed liver. The angel Tephillah carried him to heaven where he saw Jesus standing, reaching out a nail-scarred hand and welcoming him to His side.

"Well done, my brother, well done." Jesus said to Mr. Jordan, who was now somehow robed in white.

As Mr. Jordan said hello to many of the men he recognized from the Salvation Army, he noticed Tephillah walking with him. Looking closely at Tephillah he recognized some features he hadn't noticed before.

"You and I have met, haven't we? Mr. Jordan asked.

And with a smile Tephillah took the form of the relief committee man who would bring him food those first few days after the flood. Jesus was there too as Mr. Jordan now noticed. Looking closely at the angel, Mr. Jordan remembered how he treated the relief committee man and then said sorrowfully, "I treated you badly, didn't I?" And without waiting for an answer said, "I'm sorry."

"I know, my friend, I know." responded the angel.

Noticing that he was looking around, Jesus asked Mr. Jordan, "Who are you looking for, John?"

"Well, Sir, my family and a friend I knew in Pittsburgh," replied Mr. John Jordan still looking around.

Jesus put His arm around Mr. Jordan and said lovingly and with deep compassion, "You never gave any importance to Christianity before your children John. And while they were given opportunities by Me to accept Me, for they were old enough on their own to choose Me, they never did."

With the understanding that his selfishness on Sundays had cost his family the opportunity of salvation, time seemed to stand still in heaven. The thought of spending eternity without them began to bombard him, "How can I live all of eternity without them? Why had I been so selfish? What can be done now?" And knowing the answer to that question, he bowed his head and cried for what seemed like hours.

When he looked up, Jesus was gone, but an old man stood next to him and put his arm around a sobbing Mr. Jordan. After a time his sobbing slowed and he looked up to see the old man. They hugged and then Mr. John Jordan said, "but you are not an old man, are you? You're an angel. You're Tephillah."

To Blow Up the Gorge

Was this the only such scene the day saw? There were scores like it. People worked in ruins all day to find their relatives and then went home with horrible uncertainty. People found what they were looking for and fainted at the sight. People looked and cried aloud and came and stood on the banks all day, afraid to look and still afraid to go away. The burned bodies are not the only ones in the gorge. Under the timbers and held down in the water there must be hundreds that escaped the fire, but were drowned. To get at these the gorge is to be blown up with dynamite. The sanitary reasons for such a step are becoming hourly more apparent. It is the belief of the physicians that a pestilence will be added to the other horrors of the place if such a thing is not done. All day the bodies have been brought to shore. Those that were not recognized were carried on stretchers to the Morgue. One hundred and twenty of the identified bodies were carried over the bridge in one procession.

Relief work for the suffering goes on at the headquarters of the Relief Committee on that little, muddy, rubbish-filled street which escaped destruction at the edge of the flood.

The building is a wretched shanty, and a long line of miserable women stretches out in front of it all day waiting for relief. They are the unfortunate who have lost everything in the flood.

Quarters for five thousand of these people are provided in tents on the hillside. For provisions they are dependent on the charity of the country. Bread and meat are served out to them on the committee's order.

They are the most mournful and pitiable sight. There was not one in the line who had not lost some one dear to her. Most of them were the wives of merchants or laborers who went down in the disaster. They were the sole survivors of their families. Very few had any more clothes than they wore when their houses were washed away. They stood there for hours in the rain yesterday without any protection, soaked with the drizzle, squalid and utterly forlorn, a sight to move a heart of stone.

Silent Sufferers

They did not talk to one another as women generally do even when they are not acquainted. They got no words of sympathy from any one, and they gave none. Not a word was spoken along the whole line. They simply stood and waited. In truth, there is nothing about the survivors of the disaster that strikes one so forcibly as their evident inability to comprehend their misfortune and the absence of sympathetic expressions among them. It is not because they are naturally stolid, but the whole thing is so vast and bears upon them so heavily they cannot grasp it.

People in California know much more about the disaster than any resident of Johnstown knows; more information about it can be gotten from towns-people forty miles away than from those who saw it. The people here are not at all lacking in sympathy or kindliness of heart, but what words of sympathy would have any meaning in such a tremendous catastrophe? Every person of Johnstown has lost a relative or a friend, and so has every other resident he meets. They seem to see instinctively that condolence would be meaningless.

Famine Happily Averted

On the west side of the lower town one or two little streets are left from the flood. They are crowded all the time with the survivors. As I have gone among them I have heard nothing but such conversations as this, which is literally reproduced:

"Hello, Will! Where's Jim?" "He's lost."

"Is that so! Goodbye."

Another was:

"Good morning, Mr. Holden; did you save Mrs. Holden?"

"No, she went with the house. You lost your two boys, didn't you?"

"Yes. Good morning."

Two women met on the narrow rope bridge which spans the creek. As they passed one said:

"How about Aunt Mary?"

"Oh, she's lost; so is Cousin Hattie."

It gives an outside listener a strange sensation to hear people talk thus with about as little emotion as they would talk about the weather. But the people of Johnstown had so much to do with death that they think about nothing else. I will undertake to say that half the people have not the slightest idea what day of the week or month this is.

A Rope Bridge of Sighs

To get from one part of the town to another it is necessary to cross the river or creek which is now flowing over the sites of business blocks. Of course, every vestige of a bridge was swept far away, and to take their places two ropes have been hung from high timbers built upon the sandy island that was the city's site. On these ropes narrow boards are tied. The whole structure is not more than four feet wide, and it hangs trembling over the water in a way that makes nervous people shudder. Over this frail thing hundreds of people crowd every hour, and why there has not been another disaster is something no one can understand.

The river is rising steadily, and all the afternoon the middle of the bridge sagged down into the water, but the people kept on struggling across. Many of them carried coffins containing bodies from the Morgue. There are no express wagons, no hearses, scarcely any vehicles of any kind in the town. And all the coffins have to be carried on the shoulders of the men.

Coffins are a dreadfully common sight. It is impossible to move a dozen steps in any direction without meeting one or very likely a procession of them. One hundred of them were piled up in front of the Morgue this morning. Twice as many more were on the platform of the Pennsylvania station. Carloads of coffins were being unloaded from freight cars below town and carried along the roads. Almost every house has a coffin in it. Every boat that crosses the river carries one, and rows of them stood by the bank to receive the bodies.

Merely a Mud Plain.

There is a narrow fringe of houses on each side of the empty plain, which escaped because they were built on higher ground. fine brick blocks and paved streets filled the business part of the town, which was about a mile long and half a mile wide. Where these blocks stood mud is in some places six feet deep. Over and through it all is scattered an extraordinary collection of rubbish, boilers, car wheels, fragments of locomotives, household furniture, dead animals, clothing, sewing machines, goods from stores, safes, passenger and street cars, some half buried in the sand, some all exposed, helter-skelter.

It is simply impossible to realize the tremendous force exercised by the flood, though the imagination is assisted by the presence of heavy iron beams twisted and bent, railroad locomotives swept miles away, rails torn up, the rocks and banks slashed away, and brick walls carried away, leaving no traces of their foundations. The few stone houses that resisted the shock were completely stripped of all their contents and filled four feet deep with sand and powdered debris,

---

HAEL: 40 DAYS AND 40 NIGHTS

Just a quick comparison, okay? All of this occurred in the course of approximately one hour of flooding. Compare this to 40 days and 40 nights of nonstop flooding, plus earthquakes, mountains bulging up and folding over and back down, land rolling atop itself. Just think, if you can, of all the ravages that occurred during Noah's flood. Look at the devastation in one hour. Can you imagine the devastation due to the Flood of Noah's time?

A GLIMPSE FROM A WINDOW.

As I write this, seated within a curious circular affair, which was once a mould for sewer pipe, are two operators busy with clicking instruments. The floor is a foot deep with clay. There are no doors. There are no windows which boast of glass or covering of any kind. The lookout embraces the bulk of the devastated districts. Just below the windows are the steep river banks, covered with a miscellaneous mass thrown up by the flood. The big stone bridge is crowded with freight cars loaded with material for repairing the structure and with people who are eager to see something horrible.

HAEL: SEE SOMETHING HORRIBLE

May I just bring a bit of perspective to those in the above paragraph? They were there for the sole purpose of wanting to "see something horrible."

Many of you will want to judge them, but in your 21st century, I need to remind you, or at least ask you, to consider the movies that you watch. Consider Friday The 13th, Halloween, etc.

I'm just sayin'.

That Funeral Pyre

The further half of the bridge which was swept away has been replaced by a trembling wooden affair, wide enough only for two persons to walk abreast. To the left of the bridge and across the river are the great brick mills of the Cambria Iron and Steel Company, crushed and torn out of a semblance to workshops. Just in front of the office is what has been called the "funeral pyre," and which threatens to become a veritable breeding spot of pestilence.

Just before me a group of red-capped firemen are directing a stream of water upon such portions of the mass as can be reached from the shore.

HAEL: First Responders

You have always had respect for first responders. I have not been given permission to properly describe these particular red-capped firemen's experiences, but you must know that standing there, that close to the "funeral pyre" and smelling the burning flesh was terrible and very difficult for these men to handle.

We angels do not react like you to those things, but we are told that when you smell burning flesh, you never get it out of your nostrils. These men remembered this event for a very long time, and it affected their decisions for time and eternity, and not all for the good.

Where Death Was Busiest

Over to the right, at the edge of a muddy lagoon which marks the limit of the levelling rush of the mad torrent, there are dozens and dozens of buildings leaning against each other in the oddest sort of jumble. The spectacle would be ludicrous if it were not so awfully suggestive of the tragic fate of the inmates. Behind this border land are the regions where death was woefully busy. In some streets a mile from any railroad track locomotives and cars are scattered among the smoldering ruins. In the river the rescuers are busy.

Men take odd souvenirs away sometimes. One came up the bank a short time ago with a skull and two leg bones, all blackened and burned by the fire.

There is, of course, no business done, and those who have been spared have little to do save watch for a new phase of the greatest tragedy of the kind in modern history. On Prospect Hill is a town of tents where the homeless are housed and fed, and where also a formidable city of the dead has been just prepared. Such are some of the scenes visible from the window.

THE SKELETON OF ITS FORMER SELF

The water has receded in the night almost as rapidly as it came, and behind it remains the sorriest sight imaginable. The dove that has come has no green leaf of promise, for its wings are draped with the hue of mourning and desolation. There now lies the great skeleton of dead Johnstown. The great ribs of rocky sand stretch across the chest scarred and covered with abrasions. Acres of mud, acres of wreckage, acres of unsteady, tottering buildings, acres of unknown dead, of ghastly objects which have been eagerly sought for since Friday; acres of smoky, streaming ruin, of sorrow for somebody, lie out there in the sunshine.

LIKE UNTO ARCADIA AFTER THE FIRE

The awful desolation of the scene has been described often enough already to render a repetition of the attempt here unnecessary. These descriptions have been as truthful and graphic as it is possible for man to make them; but none have been adequate, none could be. Where once stood solid unbroken blocks for squares and squares, with basements and sub-cellars, there is now a level plain as free from obstruction or excavation as the fair fields of Arcadia after they had been swept by the British flames. The major and prettier portion of the beautiful city has literally been blotted from the face of the earth.

DISEASE SUCCEEDS TO CALAMITY

Up the ragged surface of Prospect Hill, whither hundreds of terrified people fled for safety Friday night, I scrambled this afternoon. I came upon a pneumonia scourge which bids fair to do for a number of the escaped victims what the flood could not. Death has pursued them to their highest places, and terror will not die. Every little house on the hill, and there are a hundred or two of them, had thrown its doors open to receive the bruised, half-clad fugitives on the dark day of the deluge, and everyone was now a crude hospital. Half the women who had scaled the height were so overcome with fright that they have been bedridden ever since. There had been pneumonia on the hill, but only a few cases. Today, however, several fresh cases developed among the flood fugitives, and a local physician said the prospects for a scourge are all too promising. The enfeebled condition of the patients, the unhealthy atmosphere pervading the valley and the necessarily close quarters in which the people are crowded render the spread of the disease almost certain.

HAEL: GOD'S ATTITUDE REGARDING AFFLICTION

God is the One who does not enjoy bringing affliction or suffering to men and women.[1] I bring this issue up because many of you do not accept that He even does BRING affliction, and the rest of you will wonder WHY God brings affliction in the first place.

Let me answer these concerns with a few quotes

- *God . . . makes adversity beneficial. (Donald MacLeod)*
- *I have never met with a single instance of adversity that I have not in the end seen was for my good. (Alexander M. Proudfit)*
- *Afflictions are in the covenant; and therefore, they are not meant for hurt, but are intended for our good. (Matthew Henry)*
- *The Lord gets His best soldiers out of the highlands of affliction. (Charles Spurgeon)*
- *God causes everything to work together for the good of those who love God and are called according to his purpose for them. (Romans 8:28)*

THE MILITARY CALLED OUT

At the request of the Sheriff, Adjutant General Hastings called out the Fourteenth regiment of Pittsburgh, who are to be stationed at Johnstown proper, to guard the buildings and against emergencies. Other reasons are known to exist for this precaution. Bodies were recovered today that have been robbed by the ghouls. It is known that one lady had several hundred dollars in her possession just before the disaster, but when the body was recovered there was not a cent in her pocket.

Some attacked a supply wagon between Morrellville and Cambria City today. The drivers of the wagon repulsed them, but they again returned. A

---

[1] Lamentations 3:33

second fight ensued, but after lively scrambling they were again driven away. After that drivers and guards of supply wagons were permitted to go armed.

General Hastings was seen later in the day, and when asked what caused him to order the militia said: "There is no need of troops to quell another disturbance, but now there are at least two thousand men at work in Johnstown clearing up the debris, and I think that it will not hurt to have the Fourteenth regiment here, as they can guard the banks and all valuables. The Sheriff consulted me in the matter. He stated that his men were about worn out, and he thought that we had better have some soldiers. So, I ordered them."

Indignant Battery B

A number of the members of Battery B and the Washington infantry, who were ordered back from Johnstown, are very indignant at Adjutant General Hastings, who gave the order. They claim that General Hastings not only acted without a particle of judgment, but when they offered to act as picket, do police duty or anything else that might be required of them, they state that they were treated like dogs.

They also insist that their services are badly needed for the reason that the hills surrounding Johnstown, are swarming with tramps, who are availing themselves of every opportunity to secure plunder from the numerous wrecks or dead bodies.

They told the General that they came more as private citizens than as soldiers, and were willing to do what they could. The General abruptly ordered them back to Pittsburgh. Lieutenant Gammel, who had charge of the men, said, "We would like to have stayed but we had to obey orders and we took the first train for home. Even the short time we were there the fifty-five men had pulled out thirty-five bodies."

Members of the battery said, "This is a fine Governor we have, and as for Hastings, the least said about his actions the better."

The Adjutant General's order calling out the Fourteenth regiment and ordering them to this place is not looked upon as being altogether a wise move by many citizens.

JOHNSTOWN SUCCORED

There will be no more charity except for the helpless. The lengthening of the death roll has fearfully shortened the list to be provided for. There is now an abundance of food and clothing to satisfy the present necessities of all who are in need. Beginning tomorrow morning, June 5th, aid will not be extended to any who are able to work except in payment for work. All the destitute who are able and willing will be put to work clearing up the wreck in the river and the wastes where the streets stood. They will be paid $2.50 and $3.00 per day for ordinary laboring work, and thus obtain money with which to buy provisions, which will be sold to them at reduced prices.

Those who will not work will be driven off. The money collected will be paid out in wages, in defraying funeral expenses and in relieving those whose bread providers have been taken away.

DAINTIES NOT WANTED

The supplies of food and clothing are far in excess of the demand today. The mistake of sending large quantities of dainties has been made by some of the relief committees. Bishop Phelan has been on the ground all day in company with a number of Catholic priests from Pittsburgh.

He has ordered provisions for all the sufferers who have taken shelter in the buildings over which he has placed the Little Sisters of the Poor. There are several hundred people now being cared for by the relief corps, and as the work of rescue goes on the number increases.

BENT ON CHARITY

Mrs. Campbell, president of the Allegheny Woman's Christian Temperance Union, arrived this morning, and with Miss Kate Foster, of Johnstown. organized a temporary home for destitute children on Bedford street. On the same train came a delegation from the Smithfield Methodist Episcopal Church. They began relieving the wants of the suffering Methodists.

Committees from the Masonic and Odd Fellows from Pittsburgh are looking after their brethren.

Mr. Moxham, the iron manufacturer, is Mayor pro tem of Johnstown today. He is probably the busiest man in the United States; although for days without sleep, he still sticks nobly to his task. Hundreds of others are like him. Men fall to the earth from sheer fatigue. There are many who have not closed an eye in sleep since they awoke on Friday morning; they are hollow-eyed and pitiful looking creatures. Many have lost near relatives and all friends.

HAEL: FATIGUE FACTOR SOMETIMES

The demon jolN[1] is more self-absorbed than most. He has been working here in North America for a few hundred years and something that he has learned to exploit, perhaps better than most, is the fatigue that leads to drunkenness. He has even heralded it amongst the survivors of the proud noble people who inhabited this land some years after Noah's flood.

This focus of his has caused not merely drunkenness, but laziness, anger and insensitivity in these people you call Indians, and also in the New Americans that have found themselves pitted against these noble people. So I want one of our angelic team members to share a backstory here regarding a "fatigued worker."

Hael has asked me to tell you about Long-tailed Puma (called Puma for short), a Seneca Indian. On paper he was actually from the Erie Tribe. He became a laborer in Johnstown on day two after the flood, and unlike the others, great fatigue motivated him to work all the harder. He felt compelled, even driven, for he had completely different issues to deal with, of which the pulverized people of Johnstown had no clue.

He came from the far Western portion of Pennsylvania, where he had had the opportunity to learn to read and speak English as well or better than most. But he had come to Johnstown months earlier, during the bitter winter, with a nefarious goal. He intended to kill their big chief named Life Master, as soon as he was found.

Two hundred years earlier this tribe inhabited the land from Lake Erie to the Allegheny River. Puma's ancestors were farmers, cultivating the land, but when they needed to defend themselves against the Iroquois they did so with bravery and warlike necessities, such as bows and poisoned arrows. But they could not sustain themselves against the muskets, the sheer numbers of the Iroquois, and their leader, Life Master. All this combined to lead to their eventual defeat.

But like many proud people, a remnant remained. And Puma's great-grandmother was the last of this remnant except for her Puma. On her deathbed,

---

[1] pronounce as three sounds in one syllable jo-l-n, remembering "o" as in go

just three years earlier, she called her twenty-two-year-old great-grandson to her side and told him about "The Master of Life" whom she had heard about from her great-grandmother.

"Never forget this Puma," she whispered to her great-grandson, "This big Chief makes the clouds his horse and rides on the wings of the wind."[1]

Pausing to catch her breath she continued, even more quietly now so that Puma had to lean his ear toward her mouth to hear her last words. They would be the most important and he knew he must hear them and never forget them.

She continued, "My son, my only remaining son, this Big Chief sounds fearsome, He does not become weary, He knows everything,[2] and somehow he lives from generation to generation,[3] but you must find him and destroy him, just like he destroyed our people."

Puma was brought up a warrior under the influence of the Seneca Indians and so out of his defiance towards any chief but his own, he responded to his great-grandmother, "We will not follow this so called 'Master of our lives.' I acknowledge nothing and no one but my arms and my hatchets." She then breathed her last and Puma had his "marching orders."

And so for three years Puma had been searching for Life Master.

I don't have time to tell you about the three years Puma spent living off the land and looking for this enemy combatant "The Life Master," except to tell you that he found an arrogant man, who called himself "The Rev" and claimed to know Puma's mortal enemy.

Puma had met The Rev in February of 1889. The Rev came across Puma quite accidentally. The Rev, also known as Michael Mann, had become disoriented in a heavy blizzard, and when his horse could not handle the snow, The Rev had started to pass out. The snow that day was sub-zero and he was nearly dead from weakness.

Puma had carved out an ice hut in the trees well above Lake Conemaugh. The Rev, who had become turned around in the snow fell off his horse, a mere two miles from his home, but heading in the wrong direction. Puma of course did not know this, but heard the grunting of a man and the weak plodding of a dying horse.

When Puma reached The Rev he carried him to his ice-hut where they remained for a few days until The Rev could ride again. Taking him back to his cabin

---

[1] Psalm 104:3
[2] Isaiah 40:28
[3] Psalm 102:12

where The Rev lived alone, Puma nursed him back to health over the following weeks and a bond developed between the two men.

At one point, while still in the ice hut, The Rev asked, "Puma, what are you doing out here? Didn't you say that your tribe is beyond the great lake?"

"Yes," responded Puma carefully, for he did not want to give away his mission to kill "The Life Master." But I am looking for someone called "The Life Master."

"Hmm, what did you say his name is, Puma?" asked The Rev.

"He is called The Life Master," repeated Puma.

"The Life Master, the Life Master. . . Puma, I think I know someone whose name is similar to that. Have you ever heard of "The Master of Life?"

"Yes," an excited Puma responded, "that is one of the names my great-grandmother used."

"Oh, wonderful, Puma! I can introduce you to Him." The Rev stated with a confidence that nearly caused Puma to scream out a war-cry right then and there.

Puma knew his success would be rooted in his friendship with The Rev. And so not wanting to give away his ultimate plan, Puma changed the subject. "You must get stronger. You get stronger, then we can go to the Life Master."

"You are right, Puma. I am tired," said The Rev as he closed his eyes.

The next morning Michael Mann started to tell Puma of a great Spirit that sees everyone and everything. "He is called El Roi, Puma. And he sees you wherever you are, and saw you here in your ice hut while I rode my horse away from my home. El Roi means "the God who sees." He was so named by a woman who was in the desert, near death, and was saved by this great Spirit.

Puma was in rapt attention listening to the words of Michael Mann and nearly forgot about his marching orders to find and kill the Life Master. Over the next few days Puma heard about Elohim, the strong Creator, El Elyon, the God most high, El Shaddai, God Almighty, and El Kanna, the jealous God. But The Rev never mentioned his arch enemy, Life Master, again.

As the snow began to thaw, Puma became an important asset to Michael Mann. While Puma joined him in the iron works during the week, The Rev was a self-styled, itinerant preacher on the weekends, who now had a helper in Puma. Puma not only accompanied him as he rode his circuit but also did many of the chores around the cabin that The Rev had neglected.

218

As Puma kept his eyes open for any sign of when Life Master would arrive, something began to happen in Puma's heart. He felt a discomfort that made him want to cry. He could not understand these feelings, but he knew that they had something to do with his life that he had lived, and his desire to kill Life Master.

One Sunday, May 26th, 1889, five days before the great flood, as they were heading home from a small country church up in the Alleghanies, Puma said, "I have listened to you speak to your different tribes about sin, and I agree that I need your big Chief to forgive me, but which One do I chose to follow?"

Apologizing profusely, The Rev said, "Oh Puma, I am so sorry, I didn't realize that I had misled you." And then he explained that his God, his big Chief, had many names and that these names were characteristics of who He is.

The Rev continued, "When we first met, and you mentioned one of His names, I assumed you recognized that, my friend. The big Chief you are looking for, the Giver and Sustainer of life, is this God. He is the creator and the One whom I serve. Even His Son has many names.

Puma sat back confused, but an important puzzle piece had just fallen into place. Puma sat on his horse and contemplated what he had just learned, and The Rev let him do so without interrupting.

All that week, Puma's hunger and thirst arose for the Word of this new Chief he had learned about. Suddenly what nature had been trying to tell him, Puma heard. Even in the rocks by day and the stars by night, Puma began to understand the eternal power and divine nature of this, the only true God. Puma knew that he was now without excuse,[1] and he needed to submit himself to The Master of Life.

On Saturday morning, May 31st, the two men awoke, a bit groggy for they had experienced an entire night of storms that left the hills around them awash with water. Michael Mann's cabin sat just a few hundred yards below the dam that was now rising so rapidly.

They had coffee as usual on this Saturday. Puma was up early, had the coffee ready and opened the Bible to the questions he would have for The Rev. Puma noticed, but never called attention to the fact, that many times his Saturday questions were the things that The Rev would preach on the next day.

Today Puma had a series of questions about a "road-in-Romans" that The Rev had been telling Puma about since his recent understanding of sin in his life. Puma understood that he needed to deal with this sin. Finally, Puma felt like he understood his need for forgiveness and walked with The Rev from Romans

---

[1] Romans 1:20

*1:20 and 21 to Romans 3:23, 5:8, 6:23, 10:9-10 and then finished with
Romans 10:13. There Puma explained, "I recognize that none of my tribe's
rituals will save me. The only thing that will save me is calling upon the Name
of the Lord, even if one of His names is "The Master of Life."*

*Later that afternoon, Michael Mann, better known as The Rev, was the first
known casualty of the dam break.[1] When the dam breached, Puma had been up
on the mountain top checking his traps which needed a review after the strong
night of storms.*

*Not realizing what the loud sound meant, he took his time returning to the
cabin. When he arrived it was gone. Not only was it gone, but seventy-five feet
up the steep incline above the Conemaugh River all vegetation and outbuildings
were stripped completely clean in the exact path that had been taken by the water
as it leapt out of the dam.*

*The Rev would never be found, and while Puma, near exhaustion like all the
other men working, labored in Johnstown, he thought of another people that
needed him. Puma would become a teacher to the Indian tribes that would listen
to him, just like The Rev, had been to him.*

*Many years later Puma was carried across Jordan where he saw Jesus welcoming
him into heaven. Standing next to Jesus was his longtime friend Michael Mann,
and the many people of the various tribes he had witnessed to since The Rev's
death. And while none of Puma's ancestors were present in heaven, a burden he
knew he was not to carry but a burden nevertheless, there was a young man
whom Puma did not know. It was the leader of the Iroquois who two hundred
years earlier had followed The Master of Life.*

SHYLOCKS

Men and horses are what are most needed today. Some of the unfortunates
who could not go to the relief trains endeavored to obtain flour from the
wrecked stores in Johnstown. One dealer was charging $5 a sack for flour,
and was getting it in one or two cases. Suddenly the crowd heard of the
occurrence. Several desperate men went to the store and doled the flour
gratuitously to the homeless and stricken. Another dealer was selling flour
at $1.50 a sack. He refused to give any away, but would sell it to anyone
who had the money. Otherwise he would not allow anyone to go near it,
guarding his store with a shot-gun.

---

[1] The Johnstown Flood, David McCullough, Simon & Schuster, 1968

MASONS ON THE FIELD

The special train of the Masonic Relief Association which left Pittsburgh at one o'clock yesterday afternoon on the Baltimore and Ohio Railroad did not reach here until just before midnight, at which time it was impossible to do anything. Under the circumstances, the party concluded to pass the night in the cars, making themselves as comfortable as possible with packing boxes for beds and candle boxes for pillows.

They spent the morning distributing the food and clothing among the Masonic sufferers. In addition to a large quantity of cooked food, sandwiches, etc., as well as flour and provisions of every description, the Relief Committee brought up 100 outfits of clothing for women and a similar number for girls, and a miscellaneous lot for men and boys. The women's outfits are complete, and include underwear, stockings, shoes, dresses, wraps and hats. They are most acceptable in the present crisis, and much suffering has already been relieved by them.

The Knights of Pythias have received a large donation of money from Pittsburgh lodges.

HAEL: HE DRESSES THE LILIES OF THE FIELD

Our Creator and Maker uses a variety of different sources to dress the lilies of the field. In this case, He is using the "good will" offered by others. But realize that He is blessing both those who receive the "good will" and those extending it.

There is a 21st century preacher who tells the story of an opposite kind of giver from what you see above. Dr. David Jeremiah speaks of being overseas in a missionary's home when the missionary received a care package from the USA. They were so excited when they opened it. In the care package were a bunch of used tea bags with a note. It said, "We were drinking our tea one day and realized that you might be able to get some use out of them. God Bless You."

Now to the missionary's credit, they were appreciative. But Dr. Jeremiah was strongly moved. He ended his story with, and I am paraphrasing: "I learned an important lesson on that mission trip. I learned that if and when I send things to missionaries it will ALWAYS be brand new. If I would buy it new for my family, then I will buy it new for our missionaries."

Appeal to President Harrison

Adjutant General Hastings yesterday afternoon telegraphed to President Harrison requesting that government pontoons be furnished to enable a safe passageway to be made across the field of charred ruins above Johnstown Bridge for the purpose of prosecuting search for the dead. Late last night an answer was received from the President stating that the pontoons would be at once forwarded by the Secretary of War.

A dispatch of sympathy has been received by Adjutant General Hastings from the Mayor of Kansas City, who states that the little giant of the West will do her duty in this time of need.

Fraternities Uniting

The various fraternities, whose work has been referred to in various dispatches, have established headquarters and called meetings of surviving local members. These meetings are held in Alma Hall, belonging to the Odd Fellows, which, owing to its solid construction, withstood the pressure of the flood. From the headquarters at Alma Hall most of the committees representing the various secret societies are distributing relief.

The first hopeful view of the situation taken by the Odd Fellows' Committee has been clouded by the dis- mal result of further investigations. At last night's meeting at the old schoolhouse on Prospect Hill definite tidings were received from but thirty members out of a total of 501.

Cambria Lodge, with a membership of eighty-five, mostly Germans, seems to have been entirely wiped out, not a single survivor having yet reported.

Call for Workers

Last night Robert Bridgard, a letter carrier of Johnstown, marched at the head of three hundred men to the corner of Morrell avenue and Columbia street, where he mounted a wagon and made a speech on the needs of the hour. Chiefest of these, he considered, was good workmen to clear away the debris and extract the bodies from the wreckage.

He closed with a bitter attack on those who refused to aid in the work of relief and yet are begging and even stealing the provisions that are sent here to feed the sufferers. The crowd numbered nearly one thousand, and greeted Bridgard's words with cheers.

Another resident of the city then mounted a barrel and made a ringing speech condemning the slothful, who have proven themselves a menace to the valley and its inhabitants. The feelings of the crowd were aroused to such an alarming extent that it was feared it would culminate in an attack on these people talked about.

The following resolution was adopted with a wild shout of approval, and the meeting adjourned:

"Resolved, That we, the citizens of Johnstown, in public meeting assembled, do most earnestly beg the Relief Corps of the Johnstown sufferers to furnish no further provisions except in payment of services rendered for the relief of unfortunate neighbors.

"Resolved, Further, that in case of their refusal to render such service they be driven from the doors of the relief trains and warned to vacate the premises."

HOSPITALS AND MORGUES

Those who doubt that many thousands lost their lives in this disaster have not visited the morgues. There are three of these dreadful places crowded so full of the unidentified dead that there is scarcely room to move between the bodies. To the largest morgue, which I visited this morning, one hundred and sixty bodies have been brought for identification. When it is remembered that most of the bodies were swept below the limits of Johnstown, that many more found here have been identified at once by their friends and that it is certain that many bodies were consumed entirely in the fire at the gorge, the fact gives some idea of the extent of the calamity.

The largest morgue is at the Fourth ward schoolhouse, a two-story brick building which stands just at the edge of the high mark of the flood. The bodies were laid across the school children's desks until they got to be so numerous that there was not room for them, excepting on the floor. Soldiers with crossed bayonets keep out the crowd of curious people who have morbid appetites to gratify. None of these people are of Johnstown. People of Johnstown do not have time to come to look for friends, and they give the morgue a wide berth. Those who do come have that dazed, miserable look that has fallen to all the residents of the unhappy town. They walk through slowly and look at the bodies and go away looking no sadder nor any less perplexed than when they came in. One of the doctors in charge at the morgue told me that many of these people had come in and looked at the bodies of their own fathers and brothers and gone away without recognizing them, though not at all disfigured.

"THAT'S JIM"

In some instances, it had been necessary for other persons, who knew the people, to point out the dead to the living and assure them positively of the identification before they could be aroused. I saw a railroad laborer who had come in to look for a friend. He walked up and down the aisles like a man in a trance. He looked at the bodies, and took no apparent interest in any of them. At last he stopped before one of them which he had passed twice before, muttered, "That's Jim," and went out just as he had come in. Two other identifications I saw during the hour I was there were just like this. There was no shedding of tears nor other showing of emotion. They gazed upon the features of their dead as if they were totally unable to comprehend it all, and reported their identification to the attendants and watched the body as it was put into a coffin and went away. Many came to look for their loved ones, but I did not see one show more grief or realization of the dreadful character of their errand than this. Arrangements with the morgues are complete and efficient. The bodies are properly prepared and embalmed and a description of the clothing is placed upon each.

HOSPITAL ARRANGEMENTS

The same praise cannot be given the hospital arrangements. The only hospital is a small wooden church, in which apartments have been roughly improvised, with blankets for partitions. Only twenty patients can be cared for here, and the list of wounded is more than two hundred. The rest have been taken to the private houses that were not overcrowded with the homeless survivors, to farmers in the country and to outlying towns. Two have died. It did not occur to any one until lately to get any nurses from other places to take care of the patients, and even now most of the nurses are Johnstown people who have lost relatives and have their own cares. These persons sought out the hospital and volunteered for the work.

A PROCESSION OF COFFINS

A sight most painful to behold was presented to view about noon today, when a procession of fifty unidentified coffined bodies started up the hill above the railroad to be buried in the improvised cemetery there. Not a relation, not a mourner was present. In fact, it is doubtful if these dead have any surviving relatives.

The different graveyards are now so crowded that it will take several days to bury all the bodies that have been deposited in them. This was the day appointed by the Citizens' Committee for burying all the unidentified dead that have been laying in the different morgues since Sunday morning, and about three hundred bodies were taken to the cemeteries today.

It was not an unusual sight to see two or three coffins going along, one after another. It is impossible to secure wagons or conveyances of any kind, consequently all funeral processions are on foot.

Several yellow flags were noticed sticking up from the black wreckage above the stone bridge. This was a new plan adopted by the sanitary corps to indicate at what points bodies had been located. As it grows dark the flags are still up, and another day will dawn upon the imprisoned remains. People who had lost friends, and supposed they had drifted into this fatal place, peered down into the charred mass in a vain endeavor to recognize beloved features.

HAEL: INCOMPREHENSIBLE

In the 21ˢᵗ century you are used to a hearse with a long line of mourners in cars. Imagine a long line of coffins, with no mourners.

UNRECOGNIZABLE VICTIMS OF FIRE

There are now nearly two thousand men employed in different parts of the valley clearing up the ruins and prosecuting diligent search for the undiscovered dead, and bodies are discovered with undiminished frequency. It becomes hourly more and more apparent that not a single vestige will ever be recognized of hundreds that were roasted in the flames above the bridge.

A party of searchers have just unearthed a charred and unsightly mass from the smoldering debris. The leader of the gang pronounced the remains to be a blackened leg, and it required the authoritative verdict of a physician to demonstrate that the ghastly discovery was the charred remains of a human being. Only the trunk remained, and that was roasted beyond all semblance to flesh. Five minutes' search revealed fragments of a skull that at once disintegrated of its own weight when exposed to air, no single piece being larger than a half dollar, and the whole resembling the remnants of shattered charcoal.

Within the last hour a half dozen discoveries in no way less horrifying than this ghastly find have been made by searchers as they rake with sticks and hooks in the smoldering ruins. So difficult is it at times to determine whether the remains are those of human beings that it is apparent that hundreds must be burned to ashes. The number that have found a last resting place beneath these ruins can at the best never be more than approximated.

A VAST CHARNEL HOUSE

Every moment now the body of some poor victim is taken from the debris, and the town, or rather the remnants of it, is one vast charnel house. The scenes at the extemporized morgue are beyond powers of description in their ghastliness, while the moans and groans of the suffering survivors, tossing in agony, with bruised and mangled bodies, or screaming in a delirium of fever as they issue from the numerous temporary hospitals, make even the stoutest hearted quail with terror. Nearly two thousand bodies have already been recovered, and as the work of examining the wreckage progresses the conviction grows that the magnitude of the calamity has not yet been approximated.

HAEL: WARS AND RUMORS OF WAR

The above passage is of course from Matthew 24:6 where Jesus told you about the end times. Forgive me, for I want to be nice about the way I say this, but I am not sure that I will be. You realize of course that many of you who read this book and especially the last few sections are reading about something that you cannot imagine. Unless you have seen the degradations of war, or have lived in third world countries, you know nothing of this kind of moroseness."

I don't write this because I want you to have to experience this. I write this to you because I fear that too many of you have lived such pristine, sterile lives that these descriptions do not move you to tears for the unsaved!

How many died and were not carried to heaven? How many will spend eternity away from the ones they hoped were in heaven?

When you read this, is your heart hurting for the unsaved? And if not, why not?

The Pile of Debris Still Burning

The debris wedged against the big Pennsylvania Railroad stone bridge is still burning, and the efforts of the firemen to quench or stay the progress of the flames are as futile as were those of Gulliver's Lilliputian firemen. The mass, which unquestionably forms a funeral pyre for thousands of victims who lie buried beneath it, is likely to burn for weeks to come. The flames are not active, but burn away in a sullen, determined fashion.

There are twenty-six firemen here now, all level-headed fellows who keep their unwieldy and almost exhausted forces under masterful control.

Although they were scattered all over the waste places today, the heavy work was done in the Point district, where a couple hundred mansions lie in solid heaps of brick, stone and timbers.

One Corpse Every Five Minutes

Here the labors of the searchers were rewarded by the discovery of a corpse about every five minutes. As a general thing the bodies were mangled and unrecognizable unless by marks or letters on their persons. In every case decomposition has set in and the work of the searchers is becoming one that will test their stomachs as well as their hearts. Wherever one turns Pittsburghers of prominence are encountered. They are busy, determined men, rendering valuable service.

Chief Evans, of the Pittsburgh Fire Department, was hustling around with a force of twenty-four more firemen, just brought up to relieve those who have been working so heroically since Saturday. Morris M. Mead, superintendent of the Bureau of Electricity, headed a force of sixteen sanitary inspectors from Pittsburgh, who are doing great work among the dead.

HAEL: JOHNSTOWN BORN AND JOHNSTOWN RETURNED

Jefferson Wallace was one of the first Pittsburgh Firemen to arrive in Johnstown. He was from Johnstown, and his hometown needed him.

When the word of the flood reached Pittsburgh, Jefferson had just arrived for the night shift. Upon hearing of the disaster, he contacted his wife, who understood his need to go to Johnstown as swiftly as he could. And so with that, he was off.

Taking the train for the first leg of the trip, Jefferson sat back remembering Johnstown. He was in an orphanage there, well taken care for until age nine was adopted. The Wallace's in Pittsburgh cherished and loved him as their only son.

But the circumstances were not to be the same for his best friend, Grover Dixon. Grover stayed at the orphanage until he escaped for the last time at age sixteen. Once he turned sixteen the orphanage did not have to take him back and they were glad to be rid of him.

Immediately Grover started working for the Cambria Iron Works, putting money in his pocket for the first time in his life. Grover was large for his age, and he tended toward a mean streak, which made him a hard worker for five days a week but an angry, scary drunk all weekend long.

The last time Jefferson saw Grover was six years ago when he returned for a weekend trip to show his wife and young son where he lived the first nine years of his life. Jefferson and his family were at the Opera House when a loud disturbance occurred in the bar. The local police were called, and Grover Dixon was hauled out by the Johnstown Constable.

The next day a slightly scared but trusting wife, a son looking for adventure, and an embarrassed Jefferson Wallace walked over to the jail to see if they could speak to Grover.

The Constable looked shocked, "Grover spends the night here often on the weekends but this is the first time he's ever had a visitor."

Jefferson's wife squeezed his hand in silent encouragement.

Now, as the train slowly made its way along the track, Jefferson continued in his unceasing prayer. "What would he be like now, Father? How can I serve Grover, Lord?" The two hour trip took two days, and still Jefferson prayed.

The town was not even a shadow of its former self. When he got into town he could not tell where a street would have ended and another started. "Where is Grover, Lord," was all he could utter.

By the middle of that first day, because of his experience as a fireman, he was leading a group of men who tried to enter crumpled up houses. They were looking for survivors, but none were to be found. What they did find would haunt their dreams for a long time, for everywhere they turned up people, their faces were crumpled and smashed.

Every day and every night it was the same thing: faces, faces and more faces. And they would not go away. Jefferson did not want to close his eyes, for fear of their returning.

228

When on the fourth morning he pulled back a piece of siding. He was staring into a man's face which whispered of the young boy this man had once been. His wide-open eyes were frozen in the terror of the moment of his death. The bottom half of his face and the top of his chest were crushed flat. It seemed as if he had watched as the log headed straight for him. It tried to go down his throat but instead it flattened him in instant death. But those eyes still showed the unimaginable fear he experienced. As Jefferson got up from where he had slumped over looking at the corpse, he lifted the body into a fireman's carry and took him to the closest morgue. When he laid him down on the slab the coroner asked if there was any identification on him.

"No need," Jefferson replied. "His name is Grover Dixon. He was my friend."

A long silence ensued and then the fireman went back to work.

Fourteen years later Jefferson Wallace died when a roof he was walking on collapsed as he carried an injured firefighter to safety.

Grover Dixon was not waiting in heaven at Jesus' side to welcome him.

HOW BODIES ARE TREATED

There are six improvised morgues now in Johnstown. They are in churches and schoolhouses, the largest one being in the Fourth Ward schoolhouse, where planks have been laid over the tops of desks, on which the remains are placed. A corpse is dug from the bank. It is covered with mud. It is taken to the anteroom of the school, where it is placed under a hydrant and the muck and slime washed off. With the slash of a knife the clothes are ripped open and an attendant searches the pockets for valuables or papers that would lead to identification. Four men lift the corpse on a rude table, and there it is thoroughly washed and an embalming fluid injected in the arm. With other grim bodies the corpse lies in a larger room until it is identified or becomes offensive. In the latter case it is hurried to the large grave, a grave that will hereafter have a monument over it bearing the inscription "Unknown Dead."

The number of the latter is growing hourly, because pestilence stalks in Johnstown, and the bloated. disfigured masses of flesh cannot be held much longer.

LEVELLED BY DEATH

Bodies of stalwart workmen lie beside the remains of refined ladies, many of whom are still decked with costly earrings and have jewels glittering on the fingers. Rich and poor throng these quarters and gaze with awe-struck faces at the masses of mutilations in the hope of recognizing a missing one, so as to accord the body a decent burial.

FROM DEATH'S GAPING JAWS

We give here the awful narrative of George Irwin's experience. Irwin is a resident of Hillside, Westmoreland county, and was discovered in a dying condition in a clump of bushes just above the tracks of the Pennsylvania Railroad, about a mile below Johnstown. When stretched upon two railroad ties near the track his tongue protruded from his mouth and he gasped as if death was at hand. With the assistance of brandy and other stimulants he was in a degree revived. He then told the following story:

"I was visiting friends in Johnstown on Friday when the flood came up. We were submerged without a moment's warning. I was taken from the window of the house in which I was then a prisoner by Mr, Hay, the druggist at Johnstown, but lost my footing and was not rescued. I clung to a saw log until I struck the works of the Cambria Iron Company, when I caught on the roof of the building. I remained there for nearly an hour, when I was knocked again from my position by a piece of a raft. I floated on top of this until I got down here and I stuck in an apple tree.

PREFERRED DEATH TO SUCH SIGHTS

"I saw and heard a number of other unfortunate victims when swept by me appealing for someone to save them. One woman and two children were floating along in apparent safety, then they struck the corner of a building and all went down together.

"I would rather have died than have been compelled to witness that sight.

"I have not had a bit to eat since Friday night, but I don't feel hungry. I am afraid my stomach is gone and I am about done for."

He was taken to a hospital by several soldiers and railroad men who rescued him.

A Young Lady's Experiences

Miss Sue Caddick, of Indiana, who was stopping at the Brunswick Hotel, on Washington street, and was rescued late Friday evening, returned home today. She said she had a premonition of danger all day and had tried to get Mrs. Murphy to take her children and leave the house, but the lady had laughed at her fears and partially dissipated them.

Miss Caddick was standing at the head of the second flight of stairs when the flood burst upon the house. She screamed to the Murphys, father, mother and seven children to save themselves. She ran upstairs and got into a higher room, in which the little children, the oldest of whom was fourteen years, also ran. The mother and father were caught and whirled into the flood and drowned in an instant.

The waters came up and the children clung to the young lady, who saw that she must save herself, and she was compelled to push the little ones aside and cling to pieces of the building, which by this time had collapsed and was disintegrating. All of the children were drowned save the oldest boy, who caught a tree and was taken out almost unhurt near Blairsville. Miss Caddick clung to her fraction of the building, which was pushed into the water out of the swirl, and in an hour she was taken out safe. She said her agony in having to cut away from the children was greater than her fear after she got into the water.

Hael: Instantaneous Decisions

Can you imagine the pictures in the mind of Miss Caddick? Can you imagine the thoughts in the minds of those children going through their last moments on earth with a woman pushing them away from herself?

I need to share with you the backstory that you did not read. Whether or not Miss Caddick was right or wrong in what she did, I will make no judgment.

But know this. The God of the universe has given her the grace to destroy those arguments in her mind, and the self-loathing that says something else should have or could have been done. But she had to take every thought captive[1] that pushed her into those thoughts that are not from God.

---

[1] 2 Corinthians 10:5

And the immediate shock for the children was offset by us, for we carried them to heaven, and they were waiting for Miss Caddick with smiles and hugs when, many years later, she joined them across Jordan.

AN OLD LADY'S GREAT PERIL

Mrs. Ramsey, mother of William Ramsey and aunt of Lawyer Cassidy, of Pittsburgh, was alone in her house when the flood came. She ran to the third story, and although the house was twisted off its foundation, it remained intact, and the old lady was rescued after being tossed about for twenty-four hours.

James Hines, Jr., of Indiana, one of the survivors, today said that he and twelve of the other guests took refuge on the top of the Merchants' Hotel. They were swept off and were carried a mile down the stream, then thrown on the shore. One of the party, James Ziegler, he said, was drowned while trying to get to the top of the building.

One hundred and seventy-five of the corpses brought to Nineveh by the flood were buried this afternoon and tonight on the crest of a hill behind the town. Three trenches were dug two hundred feet long, seven feet wide and four feet deep. The coffins were packed in very much as grocers' boxes are stored in a warehouse. Of the two hundred bodies picked up in the fields after the waters subsided 117 were unidentified and were buried marked "Unknown." Twenty-five were shipped to relatives at outside points. In many cases friends of those who were recognized were unable to do anything to prevent their consignment to the trenches. Altogether twenty-seven were identified today. The bodies as fast as they were found were taken to the storehouse of Theodore F. Nimawaker, the station agent here, and laid out on boards. It was impossible on account of their condition to keep them any longer. The County Commissioners bought an acre of ground for $100, out of which they made a cemetery.

BY LOCOMOTIVE HEADLIGHTS

It was sad to see the coffins going up the steep hill on farm wagons, two or three on each wagon. No tender mourners followed the mud-covered hearses. Enough laborers sat on each load to handle it when it reached its destination. The Commissioners of Cumberland county have certainly behaved very handsomely. The coffins ordered were of the best. Some economical citizens suggested that they buy an acre of marsh land by the river, which could be had for a few dollars, but they declared that the remains should be placed in dry ground. The lifeless clay reposes now far out of the reach of the deadly waters which go suddenly down the Conemaugh Valley. It is a pretty spot, this cemetery, and one that a poet would choose for a resting place. Mountains well wooded are on every hand, no black factory smoke defaces the sky line.

Two locomotive headlights shed their rays over the cemetery tonight and gave enough light for the men to work by. They rapidly shoveled in the dirt. No priests were there to consecrate the ground or say a prayer over the cold limbs of the unknown. Upon the coffins 1 noticed such inscriptions as these:

"No. 61, unknown girl, aged eight years, supposed to be Sarah Windser."

"No. 72, unknown man, black hair, aged about thirty-five years, smooth face."

Some of the bodies were more specifically described as "fat," "lean," and to one I saw the term "lusty" applied.

HAEL: CHRIST'S SECOND COMING

After reading this author's morose and accurate account of the burial scene I find it necessary to remind you that none of these pathetic graves is lost to our Creator. He says that He knows the starry hosts and has given them specific names.[1] This is especially noteworthy when you, in the 21st century realize that your scientists have just found ten times more galaxies than they thought existed.

And hasn't He said that He knows the number of hairs upon your head?[2] Of course He has! So do not fret, those of you who wonder about your friends and family in unmarked or unidentified graves. Your Father in Heaven is aware of everything and when Jesus returns (before the tribulation, during the tribulation or after the tribulation, for we don't know yet either), He will make sure that those who died in Him will rise first, and ever meet Him in the air.[3]

---

[1] Isaiah 40:26
[2] Matthew 10:30
[3] 1 Thessalonians 4:16-17

CHAPTER XI
Pathetic Scenes

Some of the really pathetic scenes of the flood are just coming to the public ear. John Henderson, his wife, his three children, and the mother of Mrs. Henderson remained in their house until they were carried out by the flood, when they succeeded in getting upon some drift. Mr. Henderson took the babe from his wife, but the little thing soon succumbed to the cold and the child died in its father's arms. He clung to it until it grew cold and stiff and then, kissing it, let it drop into the water. His mother-in-law, an aged lady, was almost as fragile as the babe, and in a few minutes Mr. Henderson, who had managed to get near to the board upon which she was floating saw that she, too, was dying. He did what little he could to help her, but the cold and the shock combined were too much. Assuring himself that the old lady was dead, Mr. Henderson turned his attention to his own safety and allowed the body to float down the stream.

In the meantime, Mrs. Henderson, who had become separated from her husband, had continued to keep her other two children for some time, but finally a great wave dashed them from her arms and out of her sight. They were clinging to some driftwood, however, and providentially were driven into the very arms of their father, who was some distance down the stream quite unconscious of the proximity of his loved ones. Another whirl of the flood and all were driven over into some eddying water in Stony Creek and carried by backing water to Kernville, where all were rescued. Mrs. Henderson had nearly the same experience.

Dr. Holland's Awful Plunge

Dr. Holland, a physician who lived on Vine street, saw both of his children drown before his eyes, but they were not washed out of the building. He took both of them in his arms and bore them to the roof, caring nothing for the moment for the rising water. Finally composing himself, he kissed them both and watched them float away. His father arrived here today to assist his son and take home with him the bodies of the children, which have been recovered. Dr. Holland, after the death of his children, was carried out into the flood and finally to a building, in the window of which a man was standing. The doctor held up his hands; the man seized them and dextrously slipping a valuable ring from the finger of one hand, brutally threw him out into the current again. The physician was saved, however, and has been looking for the thief and would-be murderer ever since.

HAEL: GOD'S GRACE, GOD'S MERCY AND A SCOUNDREL

"There is another one," screamed jolN into the inner ear of Lucius Clay.

"Yes," he responded to no one as he looked around and saw that he was by himself. "A few more like this and I shall be very wealthy."

"Besides," said jolN, "they won't live in that torrent. Steal the ring and toss him back into the flood waters." Lucius immediately did so.

But Dr. Holland did not die. Dr. Holland was very much alive, as Lucius noted the next night. He was making his way by one of the morgues to see if there was any jewelry within easy stealing distance. Immediately upon rounding the corner of the morgue, heading to the front door, out walked Dr. Holland. Scared stiff, Lucius stopped and turned his body around slowly, while his head disappeared from the line of site of Dr. Holland instantly.

Lucius learned something that evening. He learned, or at least the foundation was set for him to learn, a life and death lesson, maybe. For as Dr. Holland left the morgue with the Constable, he heard him say, "then I will pray for him. May his thievery not cost him his life."

As they turned to walk towards where Lucius stood, he listened as the Dr. explained his meaning to the questioning Constable. "I looked into his eyes, Constable, when I was in the water. This man is not free. He is under the influence of the evil one and will face a life of torment in hell if he is not freed from those evil clutches."

Years later Lucius was a prominent underworld businessman in Altoona, Pennsylvania. He had made his money from unsavory means and continued to grow his fortune in the same way. One evening while dining in his favorite restaurant, Lucius was approached by an old, bent over lady with a long, hooked nose.

He was used to being badgered by poor people for he was one of the few that would give them money. Call it sentimental, or maybe guilt, Lucius himself couldn't tell you. He just knew that every day he kept a wad of singles in his pants pocket to give to street urchins that would come his way.

As he reached for his wad the hook-nosed woman said in a scraggly voice, "I don't want your money Lucius. I want your heart."

This scared him so he pushed her away and she left quietly.

Two weeks later in the same restaurant and at the same time, the same thing happened again. This went on for two months when finally he pulled up a chair for her and got to the bottom of her request.

"What do you mean?" croaked a very angry and slightly scared Lucius to the old woman.

Over the next few weeks Lucius met with this woman weekly and learned about something called Spiritualism. It wasn't very long before he began to sense what she really wanted of him, not merely his soul to follow this religion, but money, lots of money, to build a building. At this Lucius started to pull away from the old woman's teaching, and one day she showed up in the restaurant again. But this time he pushed her away and told her to never approach him again.

As she left the woman yelled over her shoulder to him, "You selfish old man, Lucius. I will pray to my powers, and my prayer for you is that you would be put into bondage until you are dead."

It was just then that he remembered the words of Dr. Holland from many years earlier. The very opposite words that he had said about Lucius. He said that he would see me, "out of bondage and given life?"

When Lucius finally crossed over the Jordan into heaven, standing next to Jesus was Dr. Holland. The two men smiled at one another and then Lucius broke into a huge grin.

"My friend," Dr. Holland then said. "I need to ask your forgiveness."

To which Lucius said, "No sir, it is I who owe you an apology."

"No son," Dr. Holland said putting up his hands as if to ward off a swarm of bees. "No son, had you not stolen my ring, I would have never prayed for you. Once I started praying for you I knew that I needed to pray for your salvation. And Lucius, I fear that I would never have prayed for your salvation had you not hurt me like that.

Thanking Dr. Holland for his honesty, Lucius turned to Jesus Who was awaiting his questioning look. "I don't understand, why does Dr. Holland's explanation satisfy me, my Lord?"

"Because," Jesus answered, "saving you took time. I had been calling you for years, but it was years before your heart was ready.

Dr. Holland's wife had created that ring you stole, and had given it to him on their anniversary only days before the flood. I know Dr. Holland well and knew his pain of losing that ring would solidify his memory of if you tried to drown

237

him. *"All of these things, Lucius, I had to weave into your life. Even the old woman who would eventually be contrasted with Dr. Holland.*

"The thing is, Lucius, for the last 6000 of your earth years I have used humankind as a way to break up the fallow ground of men's hearts."

"I don't understand, Jesus," a bewildered Lucius said.

"I have them praying fervently for other people. And Dr. Holland prayed for you the remainder of his life, trusting that I was already in the process of working out the details for your salvation.

"And in your case, Lucius," Jesus went on, "there were a lot of details to take care of!"

They all smiled, and then Jesus was gone, leaving Dr. Holland and Lucius to talk with one another.

Okay, so this is Hael again. I need to have a short "come to Jesus meeting" with you. Is that okay?

How do you pray for the unsaved? Do you just "throw up a hope and a prayer," or do you pray for salvation with confidence that God is already in the process of working out the details for their salvation?

I'm setting you up here! You know that, right?

You often pray for your grown son, "Oh Lord, I know you can save my son, Jimmy. . ." But, isn't it interesting that when you are praying for a newborn, you "trust God" that He is already in the process of working out that baby's salvation.

Why do you pray that way for the baby? Simple! The Word says that He is not willing that any should perish.[1]

So, what's the difference? Why don't you pray that way for your son, Jimmy? There is only one reason, and that is, "what you see with your eyeballs." You are letting what you see with your eyeballs have more importance, and carry more weight than the promises in the Word of God.

Some might say that this is akin to calling God a liar. I'm just sayin'.

You see, in one instance you trust God, and in the other your attitude of pleading, and pleading is more like, "I don't trust you God! Show me that You are working!"

He really wants you to simply trust Him.

---

[1] 1 Timothy 2:4, 2 Peter 3:9

CRUSHED IN HIS OWN HOUSE

David Dixon, an engineer in the employ of the Cambria Iron Works, was with his family in his house on Cinder Street, when the flood struck the city. The shock overturned his house against that of his neighbor, Evans, and he, with his infant daughter, Edith, was pinned between the houses as a result of the upturning Both houses were carried down against the viaduct of the Pennsylvania Railroad and there, in sight of his wife and children, excepting a 15-year-old lad, he was drowned, the water rising and smothering him because of his inability to get from between the buildings. His wife was badly crushed and it is thought will be an invalid the remainder of her days. The children, including the babe in its father's arms, were all saved, and the other boy, Joe, one of the brightest, bravest, handsomest little fellows in the world, was in his newsstand near the Pennsylvania passenger station, and was rescued with difficulty by Edward Decker, another boy, just as the driftwood struck the little store and lifted it high off its foundation.

BABIES WHO DIED TOGETHER

This morning two little children apparently not over three and four years old, were taken from the water clasped in each other's arms so tightly that they could not be separated, and they were coffined and buried together.

A bright girl, in a gingham sun bonnet and a faded calico dress came out of the ruins of a fine old brick house next to the Catholic church on Jackson street this afternoon. She had a big platter under her arm and announced to a bevy of other girls that the china was all right in the cupboard, but there was so much water in there that she didn't dare go in. She chatted away quite volubly about the fire in the Catholic church, which also destroyed the house of her own mother, Mrs. Foster. "I know the church took fire after the flood," she said," for mother looked out of the window and said: 'My God! Not only flood, but fire!'" It was a burning house from Conemaugh that struck the house the other side of the church and set it on fire.

AUNT TABBY'S TRUNK

"I didn't think last Tuesday I'd be begging today, Emma," interrupted a young man from across the stream of water which ran down the center of Main Street. "I'm sitting on your aunt Tabby's trunk." The girl gave a cry, half of pained remembrance, half of pleasure. "Oh, my dear Aunt Tabby!" she cried, and, rushing across the rivulet, she threw herself across the battered leather trunk, sole surviving relic of Aunt Tabby, but Aunt Tabby and the finding thereof was a light among other shadows of the day.

HAEL: THE DESTITUTE

I may get into trouble by ███████ for saying this. He is our Administrator of ████████████████. But many members of your churches are unwilling to take care of the poor around you. They seem to think that God will not honor their generosity, so rather than generously helping the poor, they ignore them.

And I don't know any other way to say this so let me simply be blunt, it is the churches responsibility to take care of the poor,[1] not your government's responsibility!

NOTHING BUT A BABY

Gruesome incidents came oftener than pathetic ones or seriocomic. General Axline, the Adjutant General of Ohio, was walking down the station platform this afternoon, when a boy came sauntering up from the viaduct with a bundle in a handkerchief. The handkerchief dripped water. "What have you there, my boy?" asked the General. The boy cowered a minute, though the General's tone was kindly, for the boy, like everyone else in Johnstown, was prepared for a gruff accostal every five minutes from some official, from Adjutant General to constable. Finally, he answered: "Nothing but a baby, sir," and began to open his bundle in proof of the truth of his statement. But the big soldier did not put him to the proof He turned away sick at heart. He did not even ask the boy if he knew whose baby it was.

HOW THE COFFINS WERE CARRIED

A strangely utilitarian device was that of a Pittsburgh sergeant of Battery B. With one train from the West came several hundred of the morbidly curious, bent upon all the horrors which they could stomach. A crowd of them crossed the viaduct and stopped to gaze round-eyed upon a pile of

---

[1] Deuteronomy 15:7, Matthew 25:35-36 Luke 3:11, James 2:15-16, 1 John 3:17, and numerous other verses

empty coffins meant for the bodies of the identified dead found up and across the river in the ruins of Johnstown proper. As they gazed the Sergeant, seeking transportation for the coffins, came along. A somewhat malicious inspiration of military genius lighted his eye. With the best imitation possible of a regular army man, he shouted to the idlers, "Each of you men take a coffin." The idlers eyed him.

"What for? "one asked.

"You want to go into town, don't you?" replied the Sergeant "Well, not one of you goes unless he takes a coffin with him."

In ten minutes time way was made at the ticklish rope bridge for a file of sixteen coffins, each borne by two of the sergeant's unwilling conscripts, while the Sergeant closed up the rear.

Some of the scenes witnessed here were near trending in the extreme. In one case a beautiful girl came down on the roof of a building which was swung in near the tower. She screamed to the operator to save her and one big, brave fellow walked as far into the river as he could and shouted to her to try to guide herself into the shore with a bit of plank. She was a plucky girl, full of nerve and energy, and stood upon her frail support in evident obedience to the command of the operator. She made two or three bold strokes and actually stopped the course of the raft for an instant.

Then it swerved and went out from under her. She tried to swim ashore, but in a few seconds, she was lost. Something hit her, for she lay quietly on her back, with face pallid and expressionless. Men and women in dozens, in pairs and singly, children, boys, big and little, and wee babies were there in among the awful confusion of water, drowning, gasping, struggling and fighting desperately for life.

HAEL: HIS MERCIES NEVER END

It pains me to bring this up again, but I must. The beautiful girl was hit and knocked unconscious. Did it occur to you that this could have been another instance of God's mercy, saving her from experiencing her own death by drowning?

Two Men

Two men on a tiny raft shot into the swiftest part of the current. They crouched stolidly, looking at the shores, while between them, dressed in white and kneeling with her face turned heavenward was a girl, seven years old. She seemed stricken with paralysis until she came opposite the tower and then she turned her face to the operator. She was so close they could see big tears on her cheeks and her pallor was as death. The helpless men on shore shouted to her to keep up courage, and she resumed her devout attitude and disappeared under the trees of a projection a short distance below. "We could not see her come out again," said the operator; "and that was all of it."

"Do you see that fringe of trees?" said the operator, pointing to the place where the little girl had gone out of sight.

"Well, we saw scores of children swept in there. I believe that when the time comes they will find almost a hundred bodies of children in there among those bushes."

HAEL: JUDGING SPECTATORS

As you read this you may be tempted to judge many of these folks who watched others go to their death. You may be asking why they did not help more than it appears that they did?

Let me record for you what a modern-day report says about the flow of water from this flood. "When the wave of water reached Johnstown, it was moving at a speed of 37 miles/hour."[1]

Have any of you stood near Niagara Falls? Now let me put that into context for you. The upper rapids above Niagara Falls can reach speeds for 41 miles/hour and the speed of the rapids below the falls is about 22 miles/hour.

Do you know what the biggest, most haunting issue for many of these survivors was? For the remainder of their lives, the evil one would suggest that they could have saved people, but they did not even try.

And after time, their memory faded a bit and they do not remember the swirling, troubling waters. No, what they remembered were the many faces of the people that passed by them, while they could do nothing to save them.

---

[1] http://large.stanford.edu/courses/2012/ph240/fairbanks2/

Truly, the evil one comes as a roaring lion seeking whom he may devour.[1] And he will devour you any way he can.

FLOATED TO THEIR DEATH

A bit of heroism is related by one of the telegraph operators at Bolivar. He says: "I was standing on the river bank about 7:30 last evening when a raft swept into view. It must have been the floor of a dismantled house. Upon it were grouped two women and a man. They were evidently his mother and sister, for both clung to him as though stupefied with fear as they were whirled under the bridge here. The man could save himself if he had wished by simply reaching up his hand and catching the timber of the structure. He apparently saw this himself, and the temptation must have been strong for him to do so, but in one second more he was seen to resolutely shake his head and clasp the women tighter around the waist.

On they sped. Ropes were thrown out from the tree tops, but they were unable to catch them, though they grasped for the lines eagerly enough. Then a tree caught in their raft and dragged after them. In this way they swept out of view."

Still finding bodies by scores in the burning debris, still burying the dead and caring for the wounded, still feeding the famishing and housing the homeless, and this on the fourth day following the one on which Johnstown was swept away. The situation of horror has not changed; there are hundreds, and it is feared thousands, still buried beneath the scattered ruins that disfigure the V-shaped valley in which Johnstown stood. A perfect stream of wagons bearing the dead as fast as they are discovered is constantly filing to the improvised morgues, where the bodies are taken for identification. Hundreds of people are constantly crowding to these temporary houses, one of which is located in each of the suburban boroughs that surround Johnstown. Men armed with muskets, uniformed sentinels, constituting the force that guard the city while it is practically under martial law, stand at the doors and admit the crowd by tens.

IN THE CENTRAL DEAD HOUSE

In the Central dead house in Johnstown proper, as early as 9 o'clock today there lay two rows of ghastly dead. To the right were twenty bodies that had been identified. They were mostly women and children and they were

---

[1] 1 Peter 5:8

entirely covered with white sheets, and a piece of paper bearing the name was pinned at the feet. To the left were eighteen bodies of the unknown dead. As the people passed they were hurried along by an attendant and gazed at the uncovered faces seeking to identify them. All applicants for admission if it is thought they are prompted by idle curiosity, are not allowed to enter. The central morgue was formerly a school-house, and the desks are used as biers for the dead bodies. Three of the former pupils yesterday lay on the desks dead, with white pieces of paper pinned on to the white sheets that covered them, giving their names.

LOOKING FOR THEIR LOVED ONES

But what touching scenes are enacted every hour about this mournful building. Outside the sharp voices of the sentinels are constantly shouting: "Move on." Inside, weeping women and sad-faced, hollow-eyed men are bending over loved and familiar faces. Back on the steep grassy hill which rises abruptly on the other side of the street are crowds of curious people who come in from the country round about to look at the wreckage strewn around where Johnstown was. "Oh, Mr. Jones," a pale-faced woman asks, walking up, sobbing, "can't you tell me where we can get a coffin to bury Johnnie's body?"

"Do you know," asks a tottering old man, as the pale-faced woman turns away, "whether they have found Jennie and the children?"

"Jennie's body has just been found at the bridge," is the answer, "but the children can't be found." Jennie is the old man's married daughter, and she was drowned, with her two children, while her husband was at work over at the Cambria Mills.

THEY RAN FOR THEIR LIVES

Miss Jennie Paulson, who was on the Chicago Day Express, is dead. She was seen to go back with a companion into the doomed section of the Day Express in the Conemaugh Valley, and is swept away in the flood.

Last evening, after the evening train had just left Johnstown for Pittsburgh, it was learned that quite a number of the survivors of the wrecked train, who have been at Altoona since last Saturday, were on board. After a short search they were located, and quite an interesting talk was the result. Probably the most interesting interview, at least to Pittsburghers, was that had with Mrs. Montgomery Wilcox, of Philadelphia, who was on one of the Pullman sleepers attached to the lost express train. She tells a most exciting [appalling] tale and confirms beyond the shadow of a doubt the story of Miss Jennie Paulson's tragic death.

A Fatal Pair of Rubbers

She says: "We had been making but slow progress all the day. Our train laid at Johnstown nearly the whole day of Friday. We then proceeded as far as Conemaugh, and had stopped for some cause or other, probably on account of the flood. Miss Paulson and a Miss Bryan were seated in front of me. Miss Paulson had on a plaid dress with shirred waist of red cloth goods. Her companion was dressed in black. Both had lovely corsage bouquets of roses. I had heard that they had been attending a wedding before they left Pittsburgh. The Pittsburgh lady was reading a novel. Miss Bryan was looking out of the window. When the alarm came we all sprang toward the door, leaving everything behind us. I had just reached the door when poor Miss Paulson and her friend, who were behind me, decided to return for their rubbers, which they did.

Chased as by a Serpent

"I sprang from the car into a ditch next the hillside in which the water was already a foot and a half deep and with the others climbed up the mountain side for our very lives. We had to do so as the water glided up after us like a huge serpent. Any one ten feet behind us would have been lost beyond a doubt. I glanced back at the train when I had reached a place of safety, but the water already covered it and the Pullman car in which the ladies were, was already rolling down the valley in the grasp of the angry waters. Quite a number of us reached the house of a Mr. Swenzel, or some such name, one of the railroad men, whom we afterward learned had lost two daughters at Johnstown. We made ourselves as comfortable as possible until the next day, when we proceeded by conveyances as far as Altoona, having no doubt but what we could certainly proceed east from that point. We found the middle division of the Pennsylvania Railroad was, if anything, in a worse condition than the western, so we determined to go as far as Ebensburg by train, whence we reached Johnstown today by wagon."

Mrs. G. W. Child's Escape

Mrs. George W. Childs, of Philadelphia, was also a member of the party. She was on her way West, and reached Altoona on Friday, after untold difficulties. She is almost prostrated by the severe ordeal through which she and many others have passed, and therefore had but little to say, only averring that Mrs. Wilcox and her friends, who were on the lost train, had passed through perils beside which her own sank into insignificance.

Assistant Superintendent Crump telegraphs from Blairsville Junction that the Day Express, eastbound from Chicago to New York, and the mail train from Pittsburgh bound east, were put on the back tracks in the yard at Conemaugh when the flooded condition of the main tracks made it apparently unsafe to proceed further. When the continued rise of the water made their danger apparent, the frightened passengers fled from the two trains to the hills nearby. Many in their wild excitement threw themselves into the raging current and were drowned. It is supposed that about fifteen persons lost their lives in this way.

After the people had deserted the cars, the railroad officials state, the two Pullman cars attached to the Day Express were set on fire and entirely consumed. A car of lime was standing near the train. When the water reached the lime, it set fire to the car and the flames reaching the sleepers they were entirely consumed.

HAEL: THE PRAY-ER MEETS JESUS

The above Day Express train left Chicago. Alfred James Terrey, famed pastor of downtown Chicago's Wesleyan Metropolitan Tabernacle, just a few blocks away from Moody Church, had arrived just in time for this train. He couldn't miss this train, for barring any delays it would put him in New York City the night before his two-week prayer conference.

Reverend Terrey had prepared for this for the better part of nine months. The conference would be a combination of teaching, praying, and field trips. "There is rich prayer history all over New York City that I have been visiting, mining, if you will, for several years. And now it is time that we explore it as a group of men and women longing to see revival return to our land, like we saw in 1856 when Jeremiah Lanphier and six others started a prayer movement, right there in New York City at the Dutch Reformed church in Lower Manhattan. That prayer revival stretched across the entire land of America, which is why we are having our conference there. At that very church."

"What do you mean we have to stop here?" Reverend Terrey was doing his best to stay calm when the porter told him that they would be delayed there in the Alleghanies, above a little town called Johnstown.

The reverend's forehead started to bead with sweat when the porter leaned over and said in his ear, "Brotha Alfred, I have been watching you for a few years. In fact, when I am home in Chicago me and the Mrs. attend Chicago's Wesleyan Metropolitan Tabernacle."

Reverend Terrey looked up with a start, searching the negro porter's face for any recognition. He loved the fact that his church was a multi-ethnic church, but he did not recognize the porter.

Sensing his lack of recognition, the porter continued, "Brotha Alfred, me and my wife are not at church but once or so per month because I's workin' here most weekends.

"But pastor, I want to remind you somethin' you always tell us, 'when you're in the prayer business you don't has to worry.' And with that, I's got to get back to the otha's."

Before he could leave, Reverend Terrey stood up and gave the porter a heartfelt hug. It was Friday, May 30ᵗʰ.

Saturday morning there was no change. They were stuck on the tracks. The second day grew into more and more hours of waiting, and the people in the Day Express car became more and more friendly. Finding out that the Reverend was a man of prayer, a few of the men who had been drinking tried coaxing him into praying for God to lift the rain like He did for Elijah.

The reverend, not without a sense of humor, went to the front of the train and lifted his eyes to heaven. He laid his hands on the two men and said, "Oh dear God, we pray that You will lift this rain, just like You did for Elijah." Then he paused for a long moment and squeezed the men's shoulders a bit stronger than they expected so that they let out a bit of a yelp and added, "but if You prefer to treat us like the wicked men and women of Noah's day, I pray that these two men do not forsake the Ark, Your Son, Jesus Christ, before eternity takes them away."

Everyone chuckled, except the two men who were a bit nervous for his words had bit deep, even if they were meant for humor.

Three hours later their Day Express coach was lifted above the debris wave that ran across the tracks with such force that all would perish. As Reverend Alfred James Terrey crossed over Jordan and came to stand at the right hand of Jesus nearly everyone from the Day Express coach was there at Jesus' side.

One of the two drinking men said, "Reverend, when that great wall of debris lifted our car all I could do was remember your words. And I knew without saying a word, for I couldn't, I needed an Ark, and I knew that the only Ark, even in this tragedy would be Jesus. I yelled out His name, knowing I needed Him. Thank you, Reverend."

And with that, many others gave the same type of story.

As "Brotha Alfred" reached the porter they smiled at one another, hugged, and he said to him, "I never did get your name on the train."

"My name's Alfred also, pastor," the porter responded.

The two men hugged again and Reverend Alfred James Terrey simply said, "I look forward to getting to know you, my friend."

EXHUMING THE DEAD

Three hundred bodies were exhumed today. In one spot at Main and Market streets the workmen came upon thirty, among whom were nine members of the Fitzparis family, the father, mother, seven children and the grandfather. Only one child, a little girl of nine years, is left out of a family of ten. She is now being cared for by the citizens' committee. The body of a beautiful young girl was found at the office of the Cambria Iron Company. When the corpse was conveyed to the morgue a man entered in search of some relatives. The first body he came to he exclaimed: "That's my wife," and a few feet further off he recognized in the young girl found at the Cambria Iron Company's office his daughter, Theresa Downs. Both bodies had been found within a hundred yards of each other.

A dozen instances have occurred where people have claimed bodies and were mistaken. This is due to the over-zeal of people to get their relatives and bury them. Nine children walked into one of the relief stations this morning, led by a girl of sixteen years. They said that their father, mother and two other children had been swallowed up by the flood, the family having originally comprised thirteen persons in all. Their story was investigated by Officer Fowler, of Pittsburgh, and it was found to be true. Near Main street the body of a woman was taken out with three children lying on her. She was about to become a mother.

NURSING THEIR SORROWS

The afflicted people quietly bear their crosses. The calamity has been so general that the sufferers feel that everybody has been treated alike. Grouped together, the sorrows of each other assist in keeping up the strength and courage of all. In the excitement and hurry of the present, loss of friends is forgotten, but the time will come when it is all over and the world gradually drifts back to business, forgetful that such a town as Johnstown ever existed.

Then it is that sufferers will realize what they have lost. Hearts will then be full of grief and despair and the time for sympathy will be at hand. Michael Martin was one of those on the hillside when the water was rushing through the town. The spectacle was appalling. Women on the hills were shrieking and wringing their hands, in fact, people beyond reach of the flood made more noise than those unfortunate creatures struggling in the water. The latter in trying to save themselves hadn't time to shriek.

Michael Martin said: "I was on the hillside and watched the flood. You ask me what it looked like. I can't tell. I never saw such a scene before and never expect to again. On one of the first houses that struck the bridge there was standing a woman wearing a white shawl. When the house struck the bridge, she threw up her hands and fell back into the water. A little boy and girl came floating down on a raft from South Fork. The water turned the raft toward the Kernville hill and as soon as it struck the bank he jumped on the hill, dragging his little sister with him. Both were saved.

"I saw three men and three women on the roof of a house. When they were passing the Cambria Iron Works the men jumped off and the women were lost. Mr. Overbeck left his family in McM row and swam to the club house, then he tried to swim to Morrell's residence and was drowned. His family was saved.

"At the corner of the company's store a man called for help for two days, but no one could reach him. The voice finally ceased and I suppose he died."

HAEL: AN UNEXPECTED SAVE

As I read this account I want to give you the full story of the man who called out for two days. I won't give you his name for his family still lives to this day and would be embarrassed to know the full story he never told but which I feel duty bound to share.

I have entitled this section as I have because the man who was saved had a foul mouth and said the most disgusting things as he yelled for two days. No one would consider him a devout and pious man, yet he was well known, for he was one of the town drunks.

The truth was, he had scampered over to the company store when the floods rose, looking to steal some items. As he greedily filled his pockets, the water outside rose so that he could never leave the company store.

Our role as angels is to do the bidding of our Creator, your Lord and God. And we do this without questioning, ever! After all, we have seen these 6000 years that the Lord God Almighty is always right in His choices and decisions.

And yet, I humbly admit to you that sometimes I do not understand His decisions. But every time I wonder why God is moving the way He is, I am surprised and can humbly say, "I never saw that coming." And oh my friends, it is always a beautiful result.

I think the Lord smiles when He sees me finally understanding what He is doing. And even now as I write that sentence I know I need to offer this explanatory sentence or the editors will redact my comment entirely. Here is the amplification, you live on Terra Firma. You are only seeing things as through a glass darkly.[1] So do NOT think that you will ALWAYS understand what the Lord is doing in your life or in another's. The truth is, many things you need to take on faith that the Lord is truly sovereign and working all things out for the better for those who love Him and are called according to His purposes.[2]

Let me tell you the full story of Mr. Smith (not his real name). In a major tragedy like this there are a number of angels who are called in to help who are not focused full time in this region like myself. I had been watching and listening to this man in disgust for nearly two days when the Lord told me to rescue Mr. Smith.

Of course I did not hesitate, and I went into the water upriver from this vile man. Since the stars were hidden by an overcast sky I mounted a log in the darkness and pointed to Mr. Smith. I rammed the log into the company store, off-balancing him and causing him to fall headlong into the rushing water.

As he cursed and screamed thinking his life lost, I glided or rather jostled the log to him, grabbed his skinny body and fairly threw my "scared to death" companion to a sand bar that had been made over the last two days.

Throwing him out of the water, he landed on the beach, continuing to curse. I returned to my station and never had a cause to look into this man's life, why the Creator had me save him when so many godly and truly pious people were perishing.

Imagine my surprise when heading to ██████████████████ ████████ here in heaven and looking into Mr. Smith's life history I found that he died two months later in a bar fight. What surprised me though was when I researched his life and I found what happened the next day.

---

[1] 1 Corinthians 13:12
[2] Romans 8:28

Instead of leaving that night like so many others, Mr. Smith remained in Johnstown, for he thought he could make some money deceiving visitors who did not know him. Stealing a ring from the hand of a woman he found in the bushes, Mr. Smith arose to run when he heard the bushes behind the woman shuffle to life. A young urchin of a child huddled under the leaves to stay warm asked, "Are you helping my mommy?"

Mr. Smith poised to run, felt like his legs were leaden, and couldn't move. As he looked into this young boy's face his big, scared, round blue eyes pierced Mr. Smith and he asked the boy's name.

The boy told Mr. Smith his name and what had happened: that his mother had saved him and then lain here for the previous few days. Mr. Smith asked, "Are you hungry, son?"

"Yes, sir," came the boy's reply, as if he were being reminded he needed to eat.

"Come with me," replied Mr. Smith. "I know where we can eat."

"But what about. . ." started the boy.

"Don't worry. I will have someone return and take good care of her," he said to the boy.

For the next few days Mr. Smith and the boy searched the morgues for the lad's father and three sisters, but none were ever identified. Finally, Mr. Smith explained to the boy that he would have to let the town council supply his needs.

When the boy said he wanted to stay with him, Mr. Smith wiped back a tear and lied to the boy saying that since he didn't have a wife, it would not be appropriate for him to take care of the boy. When Mr. Smith came to the location of the Town Council with the boy, holding his hand, he walked with him into the office. In front of the shocked office workers who recognized the town drunk, Mr. Smith knelt down facing the boy.

Holding the boy's hand, he uncharacteristically kissed the boy's forehead, gave him a hug and told him, "These fine ladies will take care of you."

Though sin played havoc with Mr. Smith's life, his life might have been a blessing and benediction to mankind.[1] Instead, he influenced a life that did accomplish this blessing and benediction.

You see, for the rest of this lad's life, he remembered a kind man who helped him in his time of need. This lad went on to be a pastor who championed the efforts to improve the conditions of orphanages in the USA. And while he spent his life telling the story of this wonderful man, he would never know of the old man's

---

[1] From, Thine Is The Kingdom, James H Hunter, Zondervan, page 142

death. He would never know that the man actually had stolen from his mother and died two months later in a bar fight. He would never know that the man was a drunk.

As far as this lad knew, this unknown man would be in heaven awaiting the boy when he died, and they would greet each other as old friends.

Many years later when the lad died at a ripe old age, standing next to Jesus was his mother, his father and his three sisters. Walking up to Jesus, the lad had tears in his eyes and Jesus lovingly wiped them away, gently saying, "Mr. Smith never trusted Me for salvation."

A Brave Girl

"Rose Clark was fastened in the debris at the bridge. Her coolness was remarkable and she was more calm than the people trying to get her out. She begged the men to cut her leg off. One man worked six hours before she was released. She had an arm and leg broken. I saw three men strike the bridge and go down. William Walter was saved. He was anchored on Main street and he saw about two hundred people in the water. He believes two-thirds of them were drowned. A frightened woman clung to a bush near him and her long hair stood straight out. About twenty people were holding to those in the neighborhood, but most of them were lost.

"John Reese, a policeman, got out on the roof of his house. In a second afterward the building fell in on his wife and drowned her. She waved a kiss to her husband and then died. Two servant girls were burned in the Catholic priest's house. The church was also consumed.

Along the Valley of Death

Fifteen miles by raft and on foot along the banks of the raging Conemaugh and in the refugee trains between Johnstown and Pittsburgh. Such was the trip, fraught with great danger, but prolific of results, which the writer has just completed. All along the line events of thrilling interest mingled with those of heartrending sadness transpired, demonstrating more than ever the magnitude of the horrible tragedy of last Friday.

Just as the day was dawning I left the desolate city of Johnstown, and, wending my way along the shore of the winding Conemaugh to Sheridan, I succeeded in persuading a number of brave and stout-hearted men, who had constructed a raft and were about to start on an extended search for the lost who are known to be strewn all along this fated stream, to take me with them.

The river is still very high, and while the current is not remarkably swift, the still flowing debris made the expedition one of peril. Between the starting point and Nineveh several bodies were recovered. They were mostly imbedded in the sand close to the shore, which had to be hugged for safety all the way. Indeed, the greater part of the trip was made on foot, the raft being towed along from the water's edge by the tireless rescuers.

Just above Sang Hollow the party stopped to assist a little knot of men who were engaged in searching amid the ruins of a hut which lay wedged between a mass of trees on the higher ground. A man's hat and coat were fished out, but there was no trace of the human being to whom they once belonged. Perhaps he is alive, perhaps his remains are among the hundreds of unidentified dead, and perhaps he sleeps beneath the waters between here and the gulf. Who can tell?

DIED IN HARNESS

A little farther down we came across two horses and a wagon lying in the middle of the river. The animals had literally died in harness. Of their driver nothing is known. At this point an old wooden rocker was fished out of the water and taken on shore. Here three women were working in the ruins of what had once been their happy home. When one of them spied the chair, it brought back to her a wealth of memory and for the first time, probably, since the flood occurred she gave way to a flood of tears, tears as welcome as sunshine from heaven, for they opened up her whole soul and allowed pent-up grief within to flow freely out and away.

ONE TOUCH OF NATURE

"Where in the name of God," she sobbed, "did you get that chair? It was mine. . . no, I don't want it. Keep it and find for me, if you can, my album; in it are the faces of my dead husband and little girl." When the rough men who have worked days in the valley of death turned away from this scene there was not a dry eye in the crowd. One touch of nature, and the thought of little ones at home, welded them in heart and sympathy to this Niobe of the valley.

At Sang Hollow we came up with a train-load of refugees en route for Pittsburgh. As I entered the car I was struck by two things. The first was an old man, whose silvered locks betokened his four-score years, and the second was a little clump of children, three in number, playing on a seat in the upper end of the coach.

JUDGE POTTS' ESCAPE

The white-haired patriarch was Judge James Potts, aged 80, one of the best known residents of Johnstown, who escaped the flood's ravages in a most remarkable manner. Beside him was his daughter, while opposite sat his son. There was one missing to complete the family party, Jennie, the youngest daughter, who went down with the tide and whose remains have not yet been found. The thrilling yet pathetic story of the escape of the old Judge is best told in his own language. Said he:

"You ask me how I was saved. I answer, God alone knows. With my little family I lived on Walnut street, next door to the residence of President McMillan, of the Cambria Iron Company. When the waters surrounded us we made our way to the third floor, and huddled together in one room, determined, if die we must, to perish together.

ENCIRCLED BY WATER

"Higher and higher rose the flood, while our house was almost knocked from its foundations by the ever-increasing mountain of debris floating along. At last the bridge at Woodvale, which had given way a short time before, struck the house and split it asunder, as a knife might have split a piece of paper.

"The force of the shock carried us out upon the debris, and we floated around upon it for hours, finally landing near the bridge. When we looked about for Jennie (here the old man broke down and sobbed bitterly) she was nowhere to be seen. She had obeyed the Master's summons."

HAEL: THE MASTER'S SUMMONS

We know not when the Master's summons comes. And the pain may not be eliminated, whether the summons is for a child or a mature adult. But know this, our job is comforting and strengthening[1] you in the midst of the summons.

Of that you have our promise and the Lord's demonstration, which I think these anecdotal stories and these backstories make clear.

---

[1] Hebrews 1:14

A Miraculous Escape

The three little girls, to whom I have referred, were the children of Austin Lountz, a plasterer, living back of Water street. They were as happy as happy could be and cut up in childish fashion all the way down. Their good spirits were easily accounted for when it was learned that father, mother, children and all had a miraculous escape, when it looked as if all would be lost. The entire family floated about for hours on the roof of a house, finally landing high upon the hillside.

Elmer G. Speck, traveling salesman of Pittsburgh, was at the Merchants' Hotel when the flood occurred, having left the Hurlburt House but a few hours before. He said:

"With a number of others, I got from the hotel to the hill in a wagon. The sight from our eminence was one that I shall never forget, that I can never fully describe. The whole world appeared to be topsy-turvy and at the mercy of an angry and destroying demon of the elements. People were floating about on house- tops and in wagons, and hundreds were clinging to tree-trunks, logs and furniture of every imaginable description.

"My sister, Miss Nina, together with my stepbrother and his wife, whom she was visiting, drifted with the tide on the roof of a house a distance of two blocks, where they were rescued. With a number of others, I built a raft and in a short time had pulled eleven persons from the very jaws of death." Continuing, Mr. Speck related how a number of folks from Woodvale had all come down upon their house-tops. Mr. Curtis Williams and his family picked their way from house to house, finally being pulled in the Catholic church window by ropes.

Three of a Family Drowned

William Hinchman, with his wife and two children, reached the stone bridge in safety. Here one of the babies was swept away through the arches. The others were also swept with the current, and when they came out on the other side the remaining child was missing, while below Mrs. Hinchman disappeared. leaving her husband, the sole survivor of a family of four.

"Did your folks all escape alive? " I asked of George W. Hamilton, late assistant superintendent of the Cambria Iron Company, whom I met on the road near New Florence.

"Oh, no," was his reply. "Out of a family of sixteen seven are lost. My brother, his wife, two children, my sister, her husband and one child, all are gone; that tells the tale. I escaped with my wife by jumping from a second story window onto the moving debris. We landed back of the Morrell Institute safe and sound."

HAIRBREADTH ESCAPES

The stories of hairbreadth escapes and the annihilation of families continue to be told. Here is one of them. J. Paul Kirchmann, a young man, boarded with George Schroeder's family in the heart of the town, and when the flood came the house toppled over and went rushing away in the swirling current. There were seven in all in the party and Kirchmann found himself wedged in between two houses, with his head under water. He dived down, and when he again came to the surface succeeded in getting on the roof of one of them. The others had preceded him there, and the house floated to the cemetery, over a mile and a half away, where all of them were rescued. Kirchmann, however, had fainted, and for seven or eight hours was supposed to be dead. He recovered, and is now assisting to get at the bodies buried in the ruins.

Saloon-keeper Fitzharris and his family of six had the lives crushed out of them when their house collapsed, and early this morning all of them, the father, mother and five children were taken from the wreck, and are now at the morgue. Emil Young, a jeweler, lived with mother, wife, three sons and daughter over his store on Clinton street, near Main. They were all in the house when the wild rush of water surrounded their home, lifted it from its foundation and carried it away. Young and his daughter were drowned, and it was then that his mother and wife showed their heroism and saved the life of the other members of the family.

The mother is 80 years of age, but her orders were so promptly given and so ably executed by the younger Mrs. Young that when the house floated near another in which was a family of nine all were taken off and eventually saved. Even after this trying ordeal the younger woman washed the bodies of her husband and nineteen others and prepared them for burial.

THE WHOLE FAMILY ESCAPED

Another remarkable escape of a whole family was that of William H. Rosensteel, a tanner, of Woodvale, a suburb of Johnstown. His house was in the track of the storm, and, with his two daughters, Tillie and Mamie, his granddaughter and a dog, he was carried down on the kitchen roof. They floated into the Bon Ton Clothing House, a mile and a half away, on Main street. Here they remained all night, but were taken off by Mrs. Emil Young and went to Pittsburgh.

Jacob I. Horner and his family of eight had their house in Hornerstown thrown down by the water and took refuge in a tree. After a while they returned to their overturned house, but again got into the tree, from which they were rescued after an enforced stay of a number of hours.

Charles Barnes, a real estate dealer on Main street, was worth $10,000 last Friday and had around him a family of four. Today all his loved ones are dead, and he has only $6 in his pockets.

The family of John Higson, consisting of himself, wife, and young son, lived at 123 Walnut street. Miss Sarah Thomas, of Cumberland, was a visitor, and a hired man, a Swede, also lived in the house. The water had backed up to the rear second-story windows before the great wave came, and about 5 o'clock they heard the screeching of a number of whistles on the Conemaugh. Rushing to the windows they saw what they thought to be a big cloud approaching them. Before they could reach a place of safety the building was lifted up and carried up Stony creek for about one-quarter of a mile. As the water rushed they turned into the river and were carried about three-quarters of a mile further on. All the people were in the attic and as the house was hurled with terrific force against the wreckage piled up against the Pennsylvania Railroad bridge Higson called to them to jump. They failed to do so, but at the second command Miss Thomas leaped through the window, the others followed, and after a dangerous walk over fifty yards of broken houses safely reached the shore.

CHAPTER XII
Digging for the Dead

The corps of workmen who were searching the ruins near the Methodist Church late this evening were horrified by unearthing one hundred additional bodies. The great number at this spot shows what may be expected when all have been recovered.

When the mass which blazed several days was extinguished it was simple to recover the bodies on the surface. It is now a question, however, of delving into the almost impenetrable collection to get at those lodged within. The grinding tree trunks doubtless crushed those beneath into mere unrecognizable masses of flesh. Those on the surface were nearly all so much burned as to resemble nothing human.

Meanwhile the searchers after bodies, armed with spikes, hooks and crowbars, pry up the debris and unearth what they can. Bodies, or rather fractions of them, are found in abundance near the surface.

TRACING BODIES BY THE SMELL

I was here when the gang came across one of the upper stories of a house. It was merely a pile of boards apparently, but small pieces of a bureau and a bed spring from which the clothes had been burned showed the nature of the find. A faint odor of burned flesh prevailed exactly at this spot. "Dig here," said the physician to the men. "There is one body at least quite close to the surface." The men started in with a will. A large pile of underclothes and household linen was brought up first. It was of fine quality and evidently such as would be stored in the bedroom of a house occupied by people quite well to do. Shovels full of jumbled rubbish were thrown up, and the odor of flesh became more pronounced. Presently one of the men exposed a charred lump of flesh and lifted it up on the end of a pitchfork. It was all that remained of some poor creature who had met an awful death between water and fire.

The trunk was put on a cloth, the ends were looped up making a bag of it, and the thing was taken to the river bank. It weighed probably thirty pounds. A stake was driven in the ground to which a tag was attached giving a description of the remains. This is done in many cases to the burned bodies, and they lay covered with cloths upon the bank until men came with coffins to remove them. Then the tag was take n from the stakes and tacked on the coffin lid, which was immediately closed up, as identification was of course out of the question. There is a stack of coffins by the railroad bridge. Sometimes a coffin is carried to the spot on the charred debris where the find is made.

PRODDING CORPSES WITH CANES

The searchers by thrusting down a stick or fork are pretty sure to find a corpse. I saw a man run a cane in the debris down to the hilt and it came up with human flesh sticking to it. Another ran a stick into the thoroughly cooked skull of a little boy two feet below the surface. There are bodies probably as far down as seventy feet in some cases, and it does not seem plain now how they are to be recovered. One plan would be to take away the top layers of wood with derricks, and of course the mass beneath will rise closer to the surface. The weather is cold to-day, and the offensive smell that was so troublesome on the warm days is not noticeable at a distance.

SAVED FROM DISFIGURATION

The workers began on the wreck on Main street just opposite the First National Bank, one of the busiest parts of the city. A large number of people were lost here, the houses being crushed on one side of the street and being almost untouched on the other, a most remarkable thing considering the terrific force of the flood. Twenty-one bodies were taken out in the early morning and removed to the morgue. They were not very much injured, considering the weight of lumber above them. In many instances they were wedged in crevices. They were all in a good state of preservation, and when they were embalmed they looked almost lifelike. In this central part of the city examination is sure to result in the unearthing of bodies in every corner. Cottages which are still standing are banked up with lumber and driftwood, and it is like mining to make any kind of a clear space. I have seen relations of people who are missing, and who are supposed to be in the ruins of their homes, waiting patiently by the hour for men to come and take away the debris.

When bodies are found, the location of which was known, there are frequently two or three friends on the spot to see them dug up. Four and five of the same family have been taken from a space of ten feet square. In one part of the river gorge this afternoon were found the bodies of a woman and a child. They were close together and they were probably mother and infant. Not far away was the corpse of a man looking like a gnarled and misshapen section of a root of a tree. The bodies from the fire often seem to have been twisted up, as if the victims died in great agony.

RAPIDLY BURYING THE DEAD.

The order that was issued last night that all unidentified dead be buried today is being rapidly carried out. The Rev. Mr. Beall, who has charge of the morgue at the Fourth ward school-house, which is the chief place, says that a large force of men has been put at work digging graves, and at the close of the afternoon the remains will be laid away as rapidly as it can be done.

In the midst of this scene of death and desolation, a relenting Providence seems to be exerting a subduing influence. Six days have elapsed since the great disaster, and the temperature still remains low and chilly in the Conemaugh Valley. When it is remembered that in the ordinary June weather of this locality from two to three days are sufficient to bring an unattended body to a state of decay and putrefaction that would render it almost impossible to prevent the spread of disease throughout the valley, the inestimable benefits of this cool weather are almost beyond appreciation.

The emanations from the half mile of debris above the bridge are but little more offensive than yesterday, and should this cool weather continue a few days longer it is possible hundreds of bodies may yet be recovered from the wreck in such a state of preservation as to render identification possible. Many hundreds of victims, however, will be roasted and charred into such shapeless masses as to preclude a hope of recognition by their nearest relative.

HAEL: PROVIDENTIAL WEATHER

It is always interesting to us, as we have spent 6000 years with you, to see that Providence is thanked and recognized when good things happen, like the unusually cool temperatures, but is complained about for His absence when bad things happen.

Now don't get me wrong, I am not giving you a license to decide to blame God when bad things happen, for often the issues occur as a result of a sin-cursed world.

Here's my query for you, don't you think that God is big enough to use every situation, especially bad situations, for the better for those who love Him and are

261

called according to His purposes?[1] *Of course He is, and I have just given you the Scriptural reason why you can believe that.*

But my point is more basic than that. Let me explain it this way. In heaven we trust God completely. We don't second guess Him. We may not understand everything He is doing but we know that He is trustworthy. But we don't see that in you.

If you'll permit me, here is what we see and hear. Now we know that you would never say this as directly as I will, but by your attitude this is what we see you saying when a difficulty comes your way.

We find that you look up into the heavens and say, "Yeah, yeah, yeah, God, I know. You spoke the words and the worlds leapt into existence. I know all that, but would You please explain to me how You are going to fix this?"

Forgive me, but why aren't you able to say, when difficulties arise, "it is God's providence" and be thankful?[2] *After all, you do this when good things come your way.*

One of the editors, the one named ▮▮▮▮ *just arrived at my writing desk. I think I need to get over this subject, after all I feel like I am going around in circles. Look, we watch you. We just want to hear you say, when bad things come your way, "it is God's providence and thank You Lord," but I fear you are more like the Israelites from the book of Judges than you realize.*

I'm getting "the eye" from ▮▮▮▮ *, I need to move on.*

GETTING DOWN TO SYSTEMATIC WORK

The work of clearing up the wreck and recovering the bodies is now being done most systematically. Over six thousand men are at work in the various portions of the valley, and each little gang of twenty men is directed by a foreman, who is under orders from the general headquarters. As the rubbish is gone over and the bodies and scattered articles of value are recovered, the debris is piled up in one high mass and the torch applied. In this way the valley is assuming a less devastated condition. In twenty-four hours more, every mass of rubbish will probably have been searched, and the investigations will be confined to the smoking wreck above Johnstown bridge.

---

[1] Romans 8:28
[2] Ephesians 5:20

The Westmoreland Relief Committee complained of the Indiana county authorities for not having a committee to search the shores on that side for bodies. They say that all that is being done is by parties who are hunting for anything valuable they can find.

Up to two o'clock this afternoon only eight bodies had been taken out of the drift above the bridge. None of them was recognized. The work of pulling it out goes on very slowly. It has been suggested that a stationary engine should be planted on the east side of the pile and a rope and pulley worked on it.

The Keystone Hotel, a huge frame structure, was rapidly being pulled to pieces this morning, and when this had been done the work of taking out the bodies will be begun at this point.

The immense wreck will most undoubtedly yield up many bodies. The bodies of a woman and three children were taken from the debris in front of the First National Bank at ten o'clock this morning. The woman was the mother of the three children, ranging in age from one to five years, and she had them ail clasped in her arms.

Booth & Flinn, the Pittsburgh contractors, have just put to work another large force of men. They have divided the town into districts, and the work is being conducted in a systematic manner. Main street is being rapidly opened up, and scores of bodies have been taken out this morning from under the Hurlburt House.

ONLY FOUND ONE OF HER FAMILY

The first body taken from the ruins was that of a boy named Davis, who was found in the debris near the bridge. He was badly bruised and burned. The remains were taken to the undertaking rooms at the Pennsylvania Railroad station, where they were identified as those of William Davis. The boy's mother has been making a tour of the different morgues for the past few days, and was just going through the undertaking rooms when she saw the remains of her boy being brought in. She ran up to the remains and demanded the child. She seemed to have lost her mind, and caused quite a scene by her actions. She stated that she had lost her husband and six children in the flood, and that this was the first one of the family that had been recovered. At the First Presbyterian Church, which is being used as a morgue, seventeen bodies taken from the debris and river have been brought in.

The relief corps from Altoona found a body near Stony Bridge this morning. On his person was found a gold watch and chain, and $250 in money, which was turned over to the proper authorities. This corps took out some thirty-two bodies or more from the ruins yesterday.

A. J. Hayes, whose wife's body was taken out of the river last night, had the body taken up into the mountains where he dug her grave and said, "I buried all that is dear to me. As for myself I don't care how soon death overtakes me."

At quarter past one this afternoon, fifty bodies had been taken from the debris in front of the Catholic Church in Johnstown borough. About forty of the bodies were those of women. They were immediately removed to the morgue for identification.

Dr. Beall, who has the supervision of the morgues in Johnstown, said that so far 2,300 bodies had been recovered in Johnstown proper, most of which had been identified and buried.

HAEL: CHURCH WORSHIPPERS

I must relate a story now that is as old as religion. And it is I am embarrassed to say, the worshipping OF THE church rather than IN THE church.

You see, the Reverend Dr. Beall was the Presbyterian minister in Johnstown, and quite properly he opened up the church, one of the few standing structures in Johnstown, to be used as a temporary morgue.

From all that you have read by our 1889 author, can you not see that this act of generosity, one might say "Christian charity" was a needed thing to have been done? Of course, it was.

However, within a few months after the flood there arose a controversy. Apparently, some of the deacons were disgruntled over their pastor opening up the church as a temporary morgue. And as is typical, instead of backing their pastor, they chose to not back down from their silly controversy and argumentation. They chose to run this selfless servant off the job.[1]

These kinds of examples continue to prove to us in heaven how some people are more interested in worshipping the church as God, rather than worshipping God in the church.

---

[1] 5th Paragraph, https://www.nps.gov/jofl/learn/historyculture/reverend-dr-david-j-beale-dd.htm

DYNAMITE AND DERRICKS USED

At one o'clock this afternoon the use of dynamite was resumed to burst the logs so that the debris in the dam at the bridge can be loosened and floated down the river. The dynamite is placed in holes bored into the massive timbers. When the log has been broken a chain is attached to its parts and it is then hoisted by a machine on the bridge and dropped into the current of the river. Contractor Kirk has abandoned the idea of constructing a dam to overflow the mass of ruins at the bridge. The water has fallen and cannot be raised to a serviceable height. A powerful windlass [winch] has been constructed at a point about one hundred feet below the bridge, and a rope attached to it is fastened to logs at the edge of the debris. In this way the course between one of the six spans of the railroad bridge has been cleared out. Where dynamite has been used to burst the logs another span has been freed of the debris, a space of about twenty by forty feet being cleared. The men are now well supplied with tools, but the force is not large enough to make rapid headway. It is believed that many more bodies will be found when the debris is loosened and started down the river.

DYNAMITE TEARS THE BODIES

Thirteen bodies were taken from the burning debris at the stone bridge at one time this afternoon. None of the bodies were recognizable, and they were put in coffins and buried immediately. They were so badly decomposed that it was impossible to keep them until they could be identified. During a blast at the bridge this afternoon two bodies were almost blown to pieces. The blasting has had the effect of opening the channel under the central portion of the bridge.

A MUDDY DESERT

Streams were running through the principal streets of the city. In some parts all that was left of the thoroughfares were the cobble stones, by which it was possible to trace streets for a short distance, and the street railway tracks remaining in places for spaces of a hundred feet or so. There were some buildings outside of the track of the full force of the torrent, the roofs of which seemed not to have been reached. Others had been on fire and had lost parts of their walls. It was a dismal sight, this desolation, as shown up by the fitful camp fires. It was only after climbing over perilous places, crossing streams and narrowly escaping with our necks, that we came within sight of the car at two o'clock this morning. We passed by a school house used as a morgue. Several people were inside gazing by lamp light at the silent bodies in a hunt for lost ones. Piles of coffins, brown and white, were in the school playground, which resounded not many days ago with the shouts of children, some of whom lie there now. There are heaps of coffins everywhere throughout the city.

MISTAKEN IDENTIFICATION

At St. Columba's Catholic Church, the scenes were striking in their individual peculiarities. One woman came in and identified a body as that of Katie Frank. The undertakers labeled it accordingly, but in a few moments another woman entered the church, raised the lid of the coffin, scanned the face of the corpse, and then tore the label from the casket. The undertakers were then warned by the woman to be more careful in labelling coffins in the future. She then began to weep, and left the church in despair. She was Katie's mother, and Katie is yet among the wreck in the river below.

The lot of bodies held and coffined at Morrellville presented a different feature. The mud was six inches deep, and the drizzling rain added gloom to the scene. Here and there could be seen, kneeling in the mud, broken hearted wives and mothers who sobbed and prayed. The incidents here were heartrending.

At the Fourth ward schoolhouse morgue a woman from Erie, whose name could not be learned, went to the morgue in search of some one, but fainted on seeing the long line of coffins. At the Kernville morgue one little boy named Elrod, on finding his father and mother both dead, seized a hatchet, and for some time would let no one enter the place, claiming that the people were lying to him and wanted to rob him of his father and mother.

One sad incident was the sight of two coffins lying in the Gautier graveyard with nobody to bury them. A solitary woman was gazing at them in a dazed manner, while the rain beat on her unprotected head.

CHAPTER XIII
Hairbreadth Escapes

So vast is the field of destruction that to get an adequate idea from any point level with the town is simply impossible. It must be viewed from a height. From the top of Kernville Mountain just at the east of the town the whole strange panorama can be seen. Looking down from that height many strange things about the flood that appear inexplicable from below are perfectly plain. How so many houses happened to be so oddly twisted, for instance, as if the water had a whirling instead of a straight motion, was made perfectly clear.

The town was built in an almost equilateral triangle, with one angle pointed squarely up the Conemaugh Valley to the east, from which the flood came. At the northerly angle was the junction of the Conemaugh and Stony creeks. The Southern angle pointed up the Stony Creek Valley. Now about one-half of the triangle, formerly densely covered with buildings, is swept as clean as a platter, except for three or four big brick buildings that stand near the angle which points up the Conemaugh.

COURSE OF THE FLOOD

The course of the flood from the exact point where it issued from the Conemaugh Valley to where it disappeared below in a turn in the river and above by spreading itself over the flat district of five or six miles, is clearly defined. The whole body of water issued straight from the valley in a solid wave and tore across the village of Woodvale and so on to the business part of Johnstown at the lower part of the triangle. Here a cluster of solid brick blocks, aided by the conformation of the land, evidently divided the stream. The greater part turned to the north, swept up the brick block and then mixed with the ruins of the villages above down to the stone arch bridge. The other stream shot across the triangle, was turned southward by the bluffs and went up the valley of Stony Creek. The stone arch bridge in the meantime acted as a dam and turned part of the current back toward the south, where it finished the work of the triangle, turning again to the northward and back to the stone arch bridge. The stream that went up Stony Creek was turned back by the rising ground and then was reinforced by the back water from the bridge again and started south, where it reached a mile and a half and spent its force on a little settlement called Grubbtown.

WORK OF THE WATER.

The frequent turning of this stream, forced against the buildings and then the bluffs, gave it a regular whirling motion from right to left and made a tremendous eddy, whose centrifugal force twisted everything it touched. This accounts for the comparatively narrow path of the flood through the southern part of the town, where its course through the thickly clustered frame dwelling houses is as plain as a highway. The force of the stream diminished gradually as it went south, for at the place where the currents separated every building is ground to pieces and carried away, and at the end the houses were only turned a little on their foundations. In the middle of the course they are turned over on their sides or upside down. Further down they are not single, but great heaps of ground lumber that look like nothing so much as enormous pith balls.

To the north the work of the waters is of a different sort. It picked up everything except the big buildings that divided the current and piled the fragments down about the stone bridge or swept them over and soon down the river for miles. This left the great yellow, sandy and barren plain so often spoken of in the dispatches where stood the best buildings in Johnstown, the opera house, the big hotel, many wholesale warehouses, shops and the finest residences In this plain there are now only the Baltimore and Ohio Railroad train, a schoolhouse, the Morrell Company's stores and an adjoining warehouse and the few buildings at the point of the triangle. One big residence, badly shattered, is also standing.

HOUSES CHANGED BASE

These structures do not relieve the shocking picture of ruin spread out below the mountain, but by contrast making it more striking. That part of the town to the south where the flood tore the narrow path there used to be a separate village which was called Kernville. It is now known as the South Side. Some of the oddest sights of the wreck are there, though few persons have gone to see them. Many of the houses that are there, scattered helter-skelter, thrown on their sides and standing on their roofs, were never in that neighborhood nor anywhere near it before. They came down on the breast of the wave from as far up as Franklin, were carried safely by the factories and the bridges, by the big buildings at the dividing line, up and down on the flood and finally settled in their new resting places little injured. A row of them, packed closely together and everyone tipped over at about the same angle, is only one of the odd freaks the water played.

I got into one of these houses in my walk through the town today. The lower story had been filled with water, and everything in it had been torn out. The carpet had been split into strips on the floor by the sheer force of the rushing tide. Heaps of mud stood in the corners. There was not a vestige of furniture. The walls dripped with moisture. The ceiling was gone, the windows were out, and the cold rain blew in and the only thing that was left intact was one of those worked worsted mottoes that you always expect to find in the homes of working people. It still hung to the wall, and though much awry the glass and frame were unbroken. The motto looked grimly and sadly sarcastic. It was:

"There is no place like home."

A melancholy wreck of a home that motto looked down upon.

A TREE IN A HOUSE

I saw a wagon in the middle of a side street sticking tongue, and all, straight up into the air, resting on its tail-board, with the hind wheels almost completely buried in the mud. I saw a house standing exactly in the middle of Napoleon street, the side stove in by crashing against some other house and in the hole the coffin of its owner was placed. Some scholar's library had been strewn over the street in the last stage of the flood, for there was a trail of good books left half sticking in the mud and reaching for over a block. One house had been lifted over two others in some mysterious way and then had settled down between them and there it stuck, high up in the air, so its former occupants might have got into it again with ladders.

Down at the lower end of the course of the stream, where its force was greater, there was a house lying on one corner and held there by being fastened in the deep mud. Through its side the trunk of a tree had been driven like a lance, and there it stayed sticking out straight in the air. In the muck was the case and key board of a square piano, and far down the river, near the debris about the stone bridge, were its legs. An upright piano, with all its inside apparatus cleanly taken out, stood straight up a little way off. What was once a set of costly furniture was strewn all about it, and the house that contained it was nowhere.

The remarkable stories that have been told about people floating a mile up the river and then back two or three times are easily credible after seeing the evidences of the strange course the flood took in this part of the town. People who stood near the ruins of Poplar Bridge saw four women on a roof float up on the stream, turn a short distance above and come back and

269

go past again and once more return. Then they went far down on the current to the lower part of the town and were rescued as they passed the second story window of a school house. A man who was imprisoned in the attic of his house put his wife and two children on a roof that was eddying past and stayed behind to die alone. They floated up the stream and then back and got upon the roof of the very house they had left, and the whole family was saved.

At Grubbtown there is a house that came all the way from Woodvale. On it was a man who lived near Grubbtown, but was working at Woodvale when the flood came. He was carried right past his own house and coolly told the people at the bridge to bid his wife good-bye for him. The house passed the bridge three times, the man carrying on a conversation with the people on shore and giving directions for his burial if his body should be found. The third time the house went up it grounded at Grubbtown, and in an hour or two the man was safe at home.

Three girls who went by on a roof crawled into the branches of a tree and had to stay there all night before they could make any one understand where they were. At onetime scores of floating houses were wedged in together near the ruins of Poplar street bridge. Four brave men went out from the shore, and, stepping from house roof to house' roof, brought in twelve women and children.

Starvation Overcomes Modesty

Some women crawled from roofs into the attics of houses. In their struggles with the flood most of their clothes had been torn from them, and rather than appear on the streets they stayed where they were until hunger forced them to shout out of the windows for help. At this stage of the flood more persons were lost by being crushed to death than by drowning. As they floated by on roofs or doors the toppling houses fell over upon them and killed them.

Nineveh was Spared

The valley of death, twenty-three miles long, practically ends at Nineveh. It begins at Woodvale, where the dam broke, and for the entire distance to this point the mountains make a canyon, a water trap, from which escape was impossible. The first intimation this city had of the impending destruction was at noon on Friday, when Station Agent Nunamaker got this dispatch:

"We just received word from South Fork that water is coming over dam at Conemaugh Lake, and is liable to burst at any moment. Notify people to look out."

J. C. WAUKEMSHAW
"Despatcher at Conemaugh."

Nunamaker started on a dead run to the water front, along which most of the houses are situated, crying: "The dam is breaking. Run for your lives!"

Every spring, the station agent tells me, there have been a score of such alarms, and when the people heard Nunamaker they laughed and called him an old fogy for his pains. They had run too often to the mountains to escape some imaginary flood to be scared by anything less than the actual din of the torrent in their ears. Two hours and a half later a dispatch came saying that the dam had indeed broken.

Again, the station agent went on a trot to the residential part of the town. That same dispatch had gone thundering down the whole valley. Johnstown heard the news and so did Conemaugh. No one believed it. It was what they called "a chestnut." But the cry had put the people a little on the alert. One hour after the dispatch came the first warning note of the disaster. Mr. Nunamaker tells me that it took really more than that time for the head of the leaping cataract to travel the twenty-three miles. If that is so the people of Johnstown must have had half an hour's warning at least, for Johnstown is half way between here and the fatal dam.

Awful Scenes

Nineveh is very flat on the river side where the people live, though, fortunately, the main force of the current was not directed on this side of the stream. In a second the river rose two feet at a jump. It then reared up like a thing of life, then it steadily rose inches at a time, flooding the whole town. But the people had had warning and saved themselves. Pitiful cries were heard soon from the river. People were floating down on barrels, roofs, beds, anything that was handy. There were pitiful shrieks from despairing women. The people of Nineveh could do nothing. No boat could have stemmed the cataract. During the night there were shrieks heard from the flooded meadows. Next morning at nine o'clock the flood had fallen three feet. Bodies could be seen on the trees by the Nineveh people, who stayed up all night in the hope of being able to do some act of humanity.

271

THE LIVING AND THE DEAD

Only twenty-five were taken alive from the trees and drift on this side.
Across the stream a score were secured and forty-seven corpses taken out.
This, with the 200 corpses here, makes a total of 300 people who are
known to have come down to this point. There are perhaps a hundred
and fifty bodies within a mile. Only a few were actually taken from the
river bed. They sank in deep water. It is only when they have swollen by
the effect of the water that they rise to the surface. Most of those recovered
were found almost on dry land or buried in drift. There are tons of wood,
furniture, trees, trunks, and everything that is ever likely to float in a river,
that must be "dug over." It will be work of the hardest kind to get at the
remaining corpses. I went over the whole ground along the river bank
between here and Johnstown today.

THE FORCE OF THE FLOOD

The trees on the banks were levelled as if by battering rams, telegraph
poles were snapped off as a boy breaks a sugar stick, and parts of the
Pennsylvania Railroad track were wrenched, torn and destroyed.

Jerry McNeilly, of this place, says he was at the Johnstown station when
the flood came down, preceded by a sort of cloud or fog. He saw people
smoking at their windows up to the last moment, and even when the water
flooded their floors they laughed and seemed to think that the river had
risen a few feet and that was all. Jerry, however, ran to the hills and saved
himself while the water rose and did its awful work. Some houses were
bowled over like ninepins. Some floated to the surface and started with the
flood, others stood their ground and were submerged inch by inch, the
occupants climbing from story to story, from the top story to the roof, only
to be swept away from their foothold sooner or later.

HAEL: THE FLOOD CONTINUED 40 DAYS . . .

After reading the descriptions of the forces of water, reread the following:

*The flood continued for 40 days on the earth; the waters increased and lifted up
the ark so that it rose above the earth. The waters surged and increased greatly
on the earth, and the ark floated on the surface of the water. Then the waters
surged even higher on the earth, and all the high mountains under the whole sky
were covered. The mountains were covered as the waters surged above them
more than 20 feet. Every creature perished—those that crawl on the earth, birds,*

272

livestock, wildlife, and those that swarm on the earth, as well as all mankind. Everything with the breath of the spirit of life in its nostrils—everything on dry land died. He wiped out every living thing that was on the surface of the ground, from mankind to livestock, to creatures that crawl, to the birds of the sky, and they were wiped off the earth. Only Noah was left, and those that were with him in the ark. And the waters surged on the earth 150 days. (Genesis 7:17-24)

I would like to know that you now read this portion of Scripture more humbly. But I suspect some of you will say, "Well, they got what was coming to them!" May I just prod you a bit though? I would ask you to listen to the great 17th century theologian and martyr, John Bradford, and say with him, "there but by the grace of God go I."

The Dam's History

I asked a gathering of men here in what light they had been accustomed to look upon the dam. They say that from the time it was built, somewhere about 1831, by the Commonwealth of Pennsylvania to collect water for the canals, it has been the "bogie" of the district. Babies were frightened when naughty by being told the dam would break. Time and time again the people of Nineveh have risen from their beds in the night and perched upon the mountains through fear. A body of water seven miles or more, long from eighty to one hundred and twenty feet deep, and about a mile wide, was indeed something to be dreaded. This lake had a circumference of about eighteen miles, which gives some idea of the volume of water that menaced the population. The dam was thick enough for two carriages to drive abreast on its top, but the people always doubted the stability of that pile of masonry and earth.

Morrellville was for a few days in a state of starvation, but Sheridan, Sang Hollow and this town are in no distress.

Nineveh has lost no life, although wild rumors said it had. Though the damage to property is very great, robbers and marauders find nothing to tempt them.

What "Chal" Dick Saw

"I'll kill the first man that dares to cross the bridge."

"Chal" Dick, lawyer, burgess and deputy sheriff and sportsman, sat upon his horse with a Winchester rifle across his saddle and a thousand or two of fiends dancing a war dance in his eyes. Down in Johnstown proper they think "Chal" Dick is either drunk or crazy. Two newspaper men bunked with him last night and found he was not afflicted in either sense. He is the only recognized head in the borough of Kernville, where every man, woman and child know him as "Chal," and greet him as he passes by.

"Yes," he said to me last night, "I saw it all. My house was on Somerset street. On Thursday night it rained very hard. My wife woke me and called my attention to the way the water was coming down. I said nothing, but I got up about five o'clock and took a look around. In a little while Stony Creek had risen three feet. I then knew that we were going to have a flood, but I did not apprehend any danger. The water soon flooded the streets, and boards and logs began coming down.

SPORT BEFORE SORROW

"A lot of us turned in to have some sport. I gave my watch and what money I had to a neighbor and began riding logs down the stream. I had lots of company. Old men acted like boys, and shouted and shouted and splashed about in the water like mad. Finally, the water began to rise so rapidly that I became alarmed. I went home and told my wife that it was full time to get out. She was somewhat incredulous, but I made her get ready, and we took the children and we went to the house of Mr. Bergman, on Napoleon street, just on the rise of Kernville. I got wet from head to foot fooling in the water, and when I got to Bergman's I took a chill. I undressed and went to bed and fell asleep. The first thing I knew I was pulled out of bed on to the floor, by Mr. Bergman, who yelled, 'the dam has burst.' I got up, pulled on my pantaloons and rushed down stairs. I got my youngest child and told my wife to follow with the two others. This time the water was three feet in the house and rising rapidly. We waded up to our waists out through it, up the hill, far beyond the reach of danger.

A STUPENDOUS SIGHT

"From the time I left Bergman's till I stopped is a blank. I remember nothing. I turned and looked, and may my eyes never rest on another such sight. The water was above the houses from the direction of the railroad bridge. There came a wave that appeared to be about twelve feet high. It was perpendicular in its face and moved in a mist. I have heard them speak of the death mist, but I then first appreciated what the phrase meant. It came on up Stony Creek carrying on its surface house after house and moving along faster than any horse could go [generally, a horse can travel 25 – 30 miles per hour]. In the water there bobbed up and down and twisted and twirled the heads of people making ripples after the manner of shot dropped into the water. The wave struck houses not yet submerged and cut them down. The frames rose to the surface, but the bricks, of course, were lost to sight. When the force of the water spent itself, and began retracing its course, then the awfulness of the scene increased in intensity. I have a little nerve, but my heart broke at the sight. Houses, going and coming, crashed up against each other and began; grinding each other to pieces. The buildings creaked and groaned as they let go their fastenings and fairly melted.

"At the windows of the dwellings there appeared the faces of people equally as ill-fated as the rest. God forbid that I should ever again look upon such intensity of anguish. Oh, how white and horror-stricken those faces were, and such appeals for help that could not come. The woman wrung their hands in their despair and prayed aloud for deliverance, Down-stream went houses and people at the rate of twenty-five miles an hour and stopped, a conglomerate mass, at the stone abutment of the railroad bridge. The first buildings that struck the bridge took fire, and those that came after were swept into a sea of flame. I thought I had already witnessed the greatest possible climax of anguish, but the scene that followed exceeded in awfulness anything I had before looked upon. The flames grew, hundreds of people were wedged in the driftwood and imprisoned in the houses. Rapidly the fire approached them, and then they began to cry for aid, and hundreds of others stood on the bank, powerless to extend a single comfort.

JUDGMENT DAY

"As the fire licked up house after house and pile after pile, I could see men and women bid each other goodbye, and fathers and mothers kiss their children. The flames swallowed them up and hid them from my view, but I could hear their shrieks as they roasted alive. The shrieks mellowed into groans, and the groans into silence, only to be followed by more shrieks, more groans and more silence, as the fire caught up and destroyed its victims. Heavens! but I was glad when the end came. My only anxiety was to have it come quickly, and I prayed that it might come, oh! So quick! It was a splendid realization of the judgment day. It was a magnificent realization of the impotency of man in a battle with such a combination of fire and flood."

I am not allowed to speak of hell the way I want to. Hell will be the final resting place of the unsaved, and yet I am burdened to stop your reading and ask you to consider something that, by the grace of our Creator, I don't deal with. But I watch you every day, and so I know that you, the Body of Christ, deal with this issue.

In the book in which your author introduced me to the world, The Pray-ers,[1] much is made of the need for personal repentance. But where your author could have done a better job is in talking about the need for sorrow over your sin.

So consider this without focusing on hell. Consider how close you have been to hell, and then go to Psalm 38 and Psalm 39 and really cry out to the Lord for mercy, not to gain salvation, for you that are saved already have that, but to acknowledge the depravity of your sin.

There is another reason too. So many of you have looked at the recent hurricanes and said, "Well, God is telling us something!" But my friends, if He is speaking, you are not hearing.

Consider this point: How many of you pray 2 Chronicles 7:14 and forgive me, but usually your attitude is that those people "out yonder who need to change and humble themselves, right?" But, that is not what the verse is saying.

While God spoke this passage to the Israelites, it is absolutely appropriate to apply it to your life to humble yourself, not the other guy!

Since I wrote this, the author spoke in a church in Columbus, Georgia, surprisingly on this very subject. Since that it appears that he finally gets it, I have gone to our archive department and with their permission I am giving you an outline and brief description of his message. Surprisingly, for I know this guy well, he gives a decent challenge to this congregation.

Here is his sermon[2] and description, in a modified outline form:

His title was, "Taking Sin Lightly."

Mark began with Psalm 51:17, where David acknowledges that God wants a broken spirit on your part, "a broken and humbled heart."

After talking about "besetting-sins" he made an interesting comparison to then comedian Flip Wilson and 1 Corinthians 10:13 saying that you do not have to sin.

---

[1] www.ThePray-ers.com
[2] This particular sermon is on his website at MarkMirza.com/TakingSinLightly

He eventually got to his statement that he "is tired of sinning."

While it was well said, his impact came when he asked the congregation what goes on in their heart when they sin?

"Not when you are caught," he went on. "But when you are by yourself, does your heart hurt because you have sinned?"

It's a great question. Something that I think is way above him as a preacher. Clearly it came from the Holy Spirit.

He mentioned a number of verses that demonstrates sin's impact on your prayer life;[1] next he did something interesting.

He got onto his belly in front of the congregation, opened his Bible to Psalm 38 and just prayed those verses out loud, crying out to God.

He finished the service with Psalm 118:19, about the Lord opening the gates of righteousness for him and said, "You have to go through Psalm 51:17, brokenness and humility, to get to Psalm 118:19, specifically, thanking the Lord for righteousness."

I thought he did a nice job, in spite of all that I know about him.

SOME HAVE CAUSE FOR JOY

In the midst of the confusion of the disaster and the strain of excitement [anticipation] which followed it was but natural that everyone who could not readily be found was reported dead. Amid the throng of mourners now an occasional soul is made happy by finding that some loved one has escaped death. Today a few of the living had time to notify their friends throughout the country of their safety.

General Lew Wallace, now at West Point, telegraphed President Harrison, in response to an inquiry last night, that his wife was "coming out of the great calamity at Johnstown safe." Several reports have been sent out from Johnstown, one as late as last night, to the effect that Mrs. Wallace was believed to be among the victims of the disaster. Private Secretary Halford received a telegram this afternoon from his wife at Altoona, announcing that Mrs. Lew Wallace was with her and safe.

---

[1] Deuteronomy 3:26, Isaiah 1:15, 59:2, Lamentations 3:44 and Proverbs 28:9

Did Not Lose Their Presence of Mind

A dispatch from Carthage, Ill., says: "Mrs. M. J. Smith, a traveling saleslady for a book concern in New York City, was at Johnstown at the time of the flood and was swept away with others. Her brothers, Lieutenant P. and James McKee, received the following telegram at Carthage yesterday from Johnstown:

> "Escaped with my life on housetop; am all right.
>
> M. J. SMITH.
>
> "The lady is well known in this county."

Rich Made Poor

John Kelly, the prominent Odd Fellow of Conemaugh, who was supposed to be lost, escaped with his entire family, though his house and store were swept down the river.

John Rowley, who stands high among the Masons and Odd Fellows, tells me that out of $65,000 worth of property which he could call his own on Friday last, he found just two bricks on the site of his residence this morning. He counts himself wealthy, however, in the possession of his wife and children who were all saved. His wife, who was very ill, was dragged through the water in her nightclothes. She is now in a critical condition, but has the best of medical attendance and may pull through.

In a frame house which stood at No. 121 Union street, Johnstown, were Mrs. O. W. Byrose, her daughters Elsie, Bessie and Emma, and sons Samuel and Ray. When the flood struck the house, they ran to the attic. The house was washed from its foundation and carried with the rushing waters. Mrs. Byrose. and her children then clung to each other, expecting every minute to meet death. As the house was borne along the chimney fell and crashed through the floors, and the bricks were strewn along the course of the river. The house was caught in the jam and held about two hundred feet above the bridge and one hundred and fifty feet from the shore. The terrified inmates did not lose all presence of mind, and they made their escape to the hole made by the fallen chimney. They were seen by those on shore, and after much difficulty each was rescued. A few minutes later the house caught fire from the burning buildings, and was soon consumed.

It is hard to discern the size of this burning debris field at the bridge in Johnstown. But the paragraph above helps. Notice that before the Byrose family were in the debris field it's size approximated 200 feet by 150 feet. But then this debris field grew all night long.

SWEPT FROM HIS SIDE

At ten o'clock this morning an old gray bearded man stood amid the blackened logs and ashes through which the polluted water of the Conemaugh made its way, wringing his hands and moaning in a way that brought tears to the eyes of all about him. He was W. J. Gilmore, whose residence had stood at the corner of Conemaugh and Main streets. Being on low ground the house was flooded by the first rush of water and the family, consisting of Mr. Gilmore, his brother Abraham, his wife, four children and mother-in-law, ran to the second story, where they were joined by Frances, the little daughter of Samuel Fields, and Grandmother Maria Prosser. When the torrent from South Fork rushed through the town the side of the house was torn out and the water poured into the second floor. Mr. Gilmore scrambled upon some floating debris, and his brother attempted to pass the women and children out to him. Before he could do so, however, the building sank and Mr. Gilmore's family was swept from his side. His brother disappeared for a moment under the water, but came to the surface and was hauled upon the roof. The brothers then strove frantically to tear a hole in the roof of the house with their bare hands, but their efforts were, of course, unavailing, and they were soon struggling for their own lives in the wreck at the viaduct. Both finally reached the shore. The body of Mrs. Gilmore, when taken from the ruins this morning, was but little mutilated, although her body was bloated by the water. Two of the children had been almost burned to cinders, their arms and legs alone being something like their original shape.

HAEL: A VALUABLE DEATH

Please forgive me for the coarseness of the sound of this section title. But it is important for you to see death from God's view, and I know of few verses as pertinent to this concept as Psalm 116:15 where the Psalmist writes, "The death of His faithful ones is valuable in the Lord's sight."

May I just leave you to contemplate that view of the Christian's death from the Lord's vantage point? In a very real way you have to say, "Sweet. Death can have a sweet view when seen this way."

One closes his eyes in torment and opens them again in heaven.

STATUE OF THE VIRGIN

St. Mary's German Catholic Church, which is badly wrecked, was temporarily used as a morgue, but a singular circumstance connected with the wrecking having been noticed, the duty of becoming a receptacle for the dead is transferred to the Church of St. Columba. The windows of St. Mary's are all destroyed. The floor for one-third of its extent on St. Mary's side is torn up to the chancel rail in one piece by the water and raised toward the wall. One-half the chancel rail is gone, the mud is eighteen inches deep on the floor, St. Joseph's altar is displaced and the statue gone. The main altar, with its furniture for Easter, is covered with mud, and some fine potted flowers are destroyed. Nearly all the other ornaments are in place, even to the candlesticks. Strange to relate, the statue of the Virgin in her attire is unsoiled, the white vestments with silken embroidery are untarnished.   This discovery led to the change of morgue. The matter being bruited abroad the desolated women of Cambria and Johnstown, as well as those who had not been sufferers from the flood, visited the church, and with most affecting devoutness adored the shrine. Some men also were among the devout, and not one of those who offered their prayers but did it in tears. For several hours this continued to be the wonder of the parishioners of the Catholic churches.

The entire family of Mr. Howe, the wealthiest man in Cambria, with some visitors from Pittsburgh and Ohio, were hurried to death by the collapse of their residence on that fatal Friday night.

In the rubbish heaped high on the shore near the stone arch bridge is a flat freight car banged and shattered and with a hole stove in its side. One of the workmen who were examining the debris today got into the car and found a framed and glazed picture of the Saviour. It was resting against the side of the car, right side up. Neither frame nor glass were injured. When this incident got noised about among the workmen they dropped their pickaxes and ran to look at the wonderful sight with their hats off.

What do you imagine happen today, if the same two religious relics weathered a storm the way the above two did?

It's a rhetorical question. I don't want you to imagine the ugliness and sarcasm you would see today on social media. I just want to take you through some of Scripture with this thought in mind.

The attitude of today in the 21ˢᵗ century is not unique. Look at God's description of mankind before Noah's flood. He says that he saw man's wickedness, that it was widespread on the earth and that every scheme in his mind, and every one of his thoughts were nothing but evil, all the time. It says that the Lord even regretted that He had made man and put him on the earth. And then get this, it also says that He was grieved in His heart.[1]

Move forward to the ungrateful Israelites (whom we read about in Pentateuch). They were given so much from the Lord, from Abraham to the escape from Egypt, and yet they rebelled so much that the entire generation died and were not allowed into the promised land.

And then the book of Judges shows God's chosen people over and over again choosing unrighteousness.

Now before you throw stones at others, do you not see that the 21ˢᵗ century world has become the same thing? Look again above at the respectful attitude of 1889, and the attitudes of today, and see how quickly things have changed.

You can't even blog that you're praying for Houston without getting "prayer-shamed."

Here is the point I wanted to get to. Pride comes before destruction, and an arrogant spirit before a fall.[2] Now is not the time to point the finger out yonder, but rather, point it back toward yourself and ask yourself: Do I also look down my nose at people that believe differently than me?" And if you're honest enough to ask that, then answer this: "How can you look down your nose at them when many of them will be in heaven with you?"

SAVED HIS MOTHER AND SISTER

A man who came up from Lockport today told this: "On the roof of a house were a young man, his mother and a young girl apparently his sister.

---

[1] Paraphrase of Genesis 6:5-6
[2] Proverbs 16:18

As they passed the Lockport bridge, where the youth hung in an eddy for a moment, the men on the bridge threw them a rope. The young man on the house caught and tried to make it fast around his mother and then around his sister. They were afraid to use it or they were unwilling to leave him, for they would not take the rope. They tried to make him take it, but he threw it away and stayed on the roof with them. The house was swept onward and in another moment, was lodged against a tree. The youth seized his mother and sister and placed them in safety among the branches. The next instant the house started again. The young man's foot slipped. He fell into the water and was not seen again.

HAEL: DEATH POSTPONED FOR A MOMENT

A few pages earlier I reminded you of a precious view of death from God's perspective: namely that His faithful one's deaths are valuable to Him. [1]

In the above example of young Mordechai saving his mother and sister, I have been given permission to open up what went on behind the scenes where your eyes could not see.

Mordechai had just turned 16 years of age on May 31ˢᵗ, 1889, the day of his death. He lived at home with his mother, 34-year-old Abigale and his 13-year-old sister Cornelia. These were all that were left in the family after Harley, Abigale's husband, passed away 10 years earlier of Diphtheria. This disease killed many of the children and not a few adults in Johnstown. They said the epidemic began in Minnesota in 1877 and by 1879 had traveled to Western Pennsylvania.

From that day on Mordechai took over the household. He started working at the Cambria Mill, putting in long grueling hours, but when he had an occasional day off he worked in the feed store stacking grain bags to bring in extra income.

His sister Cornelia learned the trade of sewing and did a fair amount of work to supplement the household income while Abigale took in washing. Still a very beautiful woman she had many would-be suitors approach her, but rebuffing every one of them she remained true to her husband, her children and her faith.

And readers, here, with her faith is where the real story occurs. In heaven we have a special lounge, called the ███████████████████████, *where we often share with each other what is happening with our charges. Our minds have been designed by God that we do not forget what is shared with us,*

---

[1] Psalm 116:15

or what we see, so in reading the above story I was instantaneously reminded of the story I heard from Mordechai's Guardian Angel.

Growing up, Mordechai and his sister Cornelia watched the example of their father, Harley, reading the Bible every night, and then praying for each of them as well as their mother. Interestingly, every night Harley prayed two things for each person. First, he prayed that his wife Abigale would be given great joy and peace from the God of hope, simply because Abigale was a child of the King.[1] And sure enough, nearly every night Abigale overflowed with hope because of the power of the Holy Spirit living inside of her.

He would then pray for Cornelia, that because she was being brought up in the admonition of the Lord, that as she got older, she would not depart from her upbringing.[2]

Harley would then turn to his son and putting his hand on Mordechai's shoulder he would quote his namesake, who spoke to his niece Esther about her being placed in the situation she was, for such a time as this.[3] And Harley would pray, "Father God, You have burdened me since my son was born, that he was placed in our family for such a time as I know not when, but I trust You to make clear to him the time when it is appropriate."

Harley would then take the verses he had been reading and craft them into a prayer for his wife, himself and his son and daughter. Mordechai would never forget those times of learning Scripture and learning prayer from his father.

The day after Harley was buried, Abigale read Scripture and did her best to pray for the kids and herself the way Harley used to, but it wasn't the same.

On his 10th birthday, his father had been dead for 4 years. Mordechai asked for the Bible when they sat down to read, and he read beginning in Genesis until something struck his heart for his mother. Then he stopped and prayed for her. He also prayed Romans 15:13 for his mother just as his father had.

He then continued reading until he found something for his sister. And then he would pray that passage for her, as well as Proverbs 22:6, just as his father had done.

And this continued, every night for the next six years.

He usually already had a passage to pray for himself but felt like he needed to pray for his mother and sister first. So then he would simply pray for himself what he had found while reading and then always pray like his father had,

---

[1] Romans 15:13
[2] Proverbs 22:6
[3] Esther 4:14

"Father God, I know that you have placed me here for such a time as this, but if there is something else, give me the boldness to see when it comes and the grace to live out what You would have me do."

Mordechai grew up praying that prayer for himself using almost the exact words. On that fateful day, May 31st, 1889, his 16th birthday, when going by the Lockport Bridge he caught the rope, but could not get it around his mother and sister. He knew he could not save himself, even though they both told him to. He disengaged the rope and waited for a more opportune moment.

The more opportune moment came when the roof they were on tangled with the branches and he was able to put his mother and sister onto the branches in safety.

As he looked at them and gave a short satisfying smile the roof started to move again. Agile as he was, he bent down to jump to the trees and put his foot onto a moldy shingle. As he fell, I hummed just loud enough for him to hear and then enclosed him in my wings and carried him to Jesus where his father Harley waited, standing next to Jesus.

Seeing his Jesus and his father Mordechai broke out into tears of joy. Running to them, he heard Jesus say, "Welcome, Mordechai, well done my good and faithful servant. You were there for such a time as you knew not what, until it was necessary." Mordechai then knelt down at Jesus' feet and immediately stood up to hug his father. Looking into his eyes Harley said, "Mordechai, I am very proud of you, son."

Walking along the streets of gold a few minutes later, Harley introduced his son to two special people, Mordechai and Esther.

On earth Abigale wept for Mordechai, but not bitterly. She knew that there would be times when she would want to ask the Lord, "Why did You take my son, too." But then she would remember, that He had given her His Son, and she would submit herself to His will, accepting her cross and thanking Him for the time she had on earth with these two great men, Harley and Mordechai.

WHERE DEATH LAY IN WAIT

A great deal has been written and published about the terrible disaster, but in all the accounts nothing has been said about South Fork, where in proportion to its size as much damage has been done as at any other point.

For the purpose of ascertaining how the place looked which in the annals of history will always be referred to as the starting point of this great calamity, I came here from Johnstown. I left on Monday morning at half-past six, and being unable to secure a conveyance of any character was compelled to walk the entire distance. Thinking the people of Johnstown knew whereof they spoke, I started over the Edensburg turnpike and tramped, as a result, six more miles than was absolutely necessary. After I left Johnstown it began raining and continued until I reached South Fork.

Two miles out from Johnstown I passed the Altoona Relief Committee in carriages, with their supply train following, and from that until I reached Fair View, where I turned off toward the Conemaugh river, it was a continuous line of vehicles of all kinds, some containing supplies, other passengers, many of whom were ladies. I followed a cow-path along the mountain until I reached Mineral Point. Here is where the flood did its first bad work after leaving South Fork. There had been thirty-three dwelling houses, a store and a large sawmill in the village, and in less than one minute after the flood struck the head of the place there were twenty-nine of these buildings wiped out; and so sudden had been the coming of the water that but a few of the residents succeeded in getting away.

HAEL: WARNING

On that terrible day, the Holy Spirit moved in such a way that the residents of Mineral Point, many of who were saved, were clearly warned of the coming catastrophe. Even a rider was dispatched a number of times to warn those downriver from the potential disaster.

Far from telling you about "listening to God," I am burdened to focus on a different direction. You have already read from the 1889 author of so many instances where men and women heard the warnings and DID NOT take them seriously.

All of you, I am sure, have heard your pastor talk about Christ's Second Coming, and you have, forgive me, purchased your fire insurance. But how seriously have you taken this warning of His coming again? How seriously have you determined to tell others about Christ before it is everlastingly too late?

Look in the mirror, those of you that already have your fire insurance. When you get to heaven, will our Creator welcome you in saying, "well done my good and faithful servant,"[1] or will He show you rewards that you never came near to receiving? And actually if you look at the end of this parable (verse 30) it appears this servant was thrown into what we could call hell.

---

[1] Matthew 25:14-30

I am concerned for you. I know your ultimate destination and so do you, but who are you bringing with you?

Do you know that verse where God says he takes the trees that produce no fruit and does something with them? Do you remember what it is? That's right, He cuts them down and burns them.[1]

Again forgive me please. I am not trying to make a difficult book more difficult, but I believe that our God, your Savior, has burdened me to share these words this strongly. He is warning you! The end is coming! What are you doing with that warning?

As a Boy would Marbles.

Jacob Kohler, one of the residents of the place, said he had received a telegram stating that the flood was coming, but paid no attention to it as they did not understand its significance. "I saw it coming," he said, "with the water reaching a height of at least twenty-five feet, tearing trees up by the roots and dashing big rocks about as a boy would marbles. I hardly had time to grab a child and run for the hills when it was upon us, and in less time than it takes for me to tell it our village was entirely wiped out and the inhabitants were struggling in the water and were soon out of sight. I never want to see such a sight again."

From Mineral Point another cow-path was taken over the mountains. I came just below the viaduct within about one mile of South Fork, and here the work of destruction had been as complete as it was possible for it to be. The entire road-bed of the Pennsylvania Railroad had been washed away.

At this point a freight train had been caught and all the men on it perished, but the names could not be learned. The engine was turned completely upside down and the box cars were lifted off the track and carried two hundred feet to the side of the hill. Fifteen of them are there with the trucks, about one· hundred feet from the old road-bed, and turned completely upside down.

Another freight train just ahead of it was also swept away in the same manner, all excepting two cars and the engine. One of the cars was loaded with two heavy boilers from the works of James Witherow, Newcastle.

---

[1] Matthew 7:19

Rails Twisted Double

Coming in to South Fork the work of destruction on the railroad was found to be even greater, the rails being almost bent double. The large iron bridge over the river at this point is gone, as is also one of the piers. The lower portion of this place is completely wiped out, and two men were lost. This is all the loss of life here, excepting two who were working at the lake proper. The loss in individual property to the people of this place will reach $75,000, and at Mineral Point $50,000 [$1,250,000 in 2017 dollars].

For the purpose of seeing how the lake looked after all the water was out of it, a trip was taken to it, fully three miles distant. The driveway around it is fully thirty-five feet wide, and that was the width at the point of the dam where the break occurred.

Like a Thunderbolt

Imagine, if you can, a solid piece of ground, thirty- five feet wide and over one hundred feet high, and then, again, that a space of two hundred feet is cut out of it, through which is rushing over seven hundred acres of water, and you can have only a faint conception of the terrible force [which modern day geologists say flowed as rapidly as any river in the USA],[1] of the blow that came upon the people of this vicinity like a clap of thunder out of a clear sky. It was irresistible in its power and carried everything before it. After seeing the lake and the opening through the dam it can be readily understood how that outbreak came to be so destructive in its character.

The lake had been leaking, and a few men were at work just over the point where the break occurred, and in an instant, without warning, it gave way, and they were down in the whirling mass of water and were swept into eternity. The people of this place had been told by some of those who had been to the lake that it was leaking, but paid no attention any more than to send telegrams to Johnstown and Mineral Point.

---

[1] The peak discharge rate from the dam is estimated at 424,000 cfs. In comparison, the average discharge of the Mississippi River, the largest in the United States, is 593,000 cfs. The second largest river in the United States, the St. Lawrence River, has an average discharge of 348,000 cfs.
From: http://large.stanford.edu/courses/2012/ph240/fairbanks2/

THRILLING ESCAPES

A local freight train with a passenger coach attached, standing on the east side of the track was compelled to run into the rear end of the passenger train so as to get out of the way of the flood. A young man who was on the rear end of the train grabbed a young lady who was floating by and thus saved her life. The house of an old man, eighty-two years of age, was caught in the whirlpool, and he and his aged wife climbed on the roof for safety. They were floating down the railroad track to certain death, when their son-in-law, from the roof of the Pennsylvania Railroad station-house, pulled them off and saved their lives as the house was dashed to pieces.

Mr. Brown, a resident of this place, said: "I was just about opposite the mouth of the lake when it broke. When I first saw it, the water was dashing over the top of the road just where it broke about a foot high, and not eight or ten feet, as has been stated, and I told Mr. Fisher, who lived there, that he had better get his family out at once, which he did. going to the hillside, and it was lucky for him that he did, because in a half minute after it broke, and his home was wiped away."

HAEL: AGED PRAYER WARRIOR

Let me tell you the backstory of this aged man who was rescued by his son-in-law.

We'll call him Bro. Don, for I do not want to give away too much information as his progeny is still alive these many years later in greater Johnstown.

Bro. Don is an older prayer warrior who is now doing the real heavy lifting. I say it that way purposely because you face in the 21st century what they faced in the 19th century, namely the older you get, the LESS you have to offer society. But this Bro. Don and his prayer partner knew very well that this was not the case. The truth is that the older one gets, the more experiences one has, and the more one has witnessed the Lord laying burdens upon ones heart, and as such the MORE one has to offer society.

So Bro. Don's prayer partner, a younger man who would travel to the older man's home and pray with him all morning once a week, had spent the previous year praying to the Lord, 'Father, the desire of my heart[1] is to pray with my Bro. Don for the next twenty years. I trust you to honor that desire for me, or take it off of my heart."

---

[1] Psalm 37:4

Interestingly, Bro. Don was buried by his family on April 3rd, 1908, at the ripe old age of 102 years young. His prayer partner was there, now an older man himself, and had the great opportunity to share with the family how Bro. Don had prayed for them for the previous twenty years. He jokingly shared that he was very glad when Bro. Don's community installed a telephone exchange for then they could talk on the phone and pray without being in the same town. "Even though," the prayer partner added, "people in the community said we were "spending too much time on the telephone." A few people laughed, and then a few people lowered their head in shame.

I would like to leave this backstory here, but I cannot. I need to ask you; do you have a person that you pray with on a regular basis? If not, why not? Unlike these two men who had to travel to one another's side to pray together, you have the luxury of telephones. Are you using them?

Let me push just a tiny bit further. What do you think would happen if you turned off one television show per week and spent that time in prayer?

No Safety Outlet

Mr. Burnett, who was born and raised a mile from the lake, and is now a resident of Hazelwood, and who was at South Fork, said: "When the State owned this lake they had a tower over the portion that gave way and a number of pipes by which they were enabled to drive off the surplus water, and had the present owners had an arrangement of that kind this accident would not have occurred. The only outlet there was for the water was a small waterway around to the right of the lake, which is totally inadequate. The people of this valley have always been afraid of this thing, and now that it is here it shows that they had every reason for their fears."

In company with Mr. Burnett I walked all over the place, and am free to confess that it looks strong, but experience shows the contrary.

Mr. Moore, who has done nearly all the hauling for the people who lived at the lake in summer, said: "About eight years ago this dam broke, but there was not as much water in it as now, and when it broke they were working at it and hauled cart load after cart load of dirt, stone and logs, and finally about ten tons of hay, and by that means any further damage was prevented. That was the time when they should have put forth strenuous efforts to have that part strengthened where the break occurred. This lake is about three miles long and about a mile wide and fully ninety feet deep, and of course when an opening of any kind was forced it was impossible to stop it.

THIRSTING FOR VENGEANCE

"The indignation here against the people who owned that place is intense. I was afraid that if the people here were to hear that you were from Pittsburgh they would jump to the conclusion that you were connected with the association, and I was afraid they would pull you from the carriage and kill you. That is the feeling that predominates here, and we all believe justly."

Mr. Ferguson, of the firm of J. P. Stevenson & Co., said: "It is a terrible affair, and shows the absolute necessity of people not fooling with matters of that kind. We sent telegrams to Mineral Point, Johnstown and Conemaugh, notifying them that the lake was leaking and the water rising, and we were liable to have trouble, and two minutes before the flood reached here a telegram was sent to Mineral Point that the dam had broken. But you see for the past five years so many alarms of that kind have been sent that the people have not believed them."

SURVIVORS IN CAMP

There are two camps on the hillside to the north of Johnstown, and they are almost side by side. One is a camp for the living, for the most woebegone and unfortunate of the refugees from the Conemaugh Valley of the shadow of death, and the other is for the dead. The camp of the living is Camp Hastings and the ministering spirits are members of the Americus Republican Club of Pittsburgh. The camp for the dead is the new potters' field that was laid out on Monday for the bodies of unknown victims. The former is populous and stirring, but the latter has more mounds already than the other has living souls. The refugees are widely scattered; some are in the hospital, some are packed as closely as the logs and dead bodies at the stone bridge in the houses yet tenable, and the rest are at Camp Hastings.

In the despairing panic and confusion of Saturday the first thought that presented itself to those who were hurried in to give relief was to prepare shelter for the survivors. The camp has been in operation ever since, and will be for days and may be weeks to come.

It looked desolate enough today after the soaking downpour of last night, and groups of shivering mothers, with their little ones, stood around a smoky fire at either end of the streets. The members of the Americus Committee, for the time being cooks, waiters, grocery dealers and dry goods men, were in striking contrast to their usual appearance at home. Major W. Coffey, one of the refugees, who was washed seven miles down the Conemaugh, was acting as officer of the guard, and limped up and down on his wooden leg, which had been badly damaged by the flood.

Pale faced women looked out through the flaps of tents on the scene, and the only object that seemed to be taking things easy was a lean, black dog, asleep in front of one of the fires.

In one of the tents a baby was born last night. The mother, whose husband was lost in the flood, was herself rescued by being drawn up on the roof of the Union Schoolhouse. One of the doctors of the Altoona Relief Corps at the Cambria Hospital attended her, and mother and babe are doing better than thousands of the flood sufferers who are elsewhere. There are other babies in Camp Hastings, but none of them receive half of the attention from the people in the camp that is bestowed upon this little tot, whose life began just as so many lives were ended. The baby will probably be named Johnstown Camp O'Connor.

The refugees who are living along the road get their supplies from the camp. They pour into the wretched city of tents in a steady stream, bearing baskets and buckets of food.

HAEL: CALMLY, HUMBLY, BRAVELY SMILING

As the water crashed through the valley, picking up houses and throwing them in the air, the evil one assigned to young Kathryn, kept yelling in her ear. "Run, run fat cow. Run to save your life."

But Albert, her husband of 10 months, was level headed and as the Spirit spoke into his inner ear he calmed his very scared, very pregnant wife and helped her waddle up the stairs to the second story of their home.

They lived in Mineral Point, so they heard the sound of the rushing debris followed by the 25-foot wave of water for much longer than they saw it.

When they arrived on the second story landing they looked out the window and saw a brown debris pile coming straight for them. The wave of debris eclipsed the height of the houses on their block, theirs included.

"You're going to die." the demon said again.

And again, a shudder ran through Kathryn.

Though they had been married less than a year, Albert had become a good observer and read his wife's emotions well. As soon as he saw her fear, Albert gently held her hand as if there was not a worry in the world. With the noise so loud now, they could only hear the debris coming towards them.

Albert had just seated her on the upstairs settee when their home was struck and pushed over until it felt like it leaned back at a 45-degree angle. Immediately the home seemed to give way from its foundations and then rose rather than fall backwards and be crushed.

As Kathryn screamed, Albert braced his feet up against the wall behind him, doing the best he could to hold his pregnant wife on the settee and up against the wall in front of him. In all of the excitement, Albert had forgotten that the wall was not within reaching distance, but given permission from heaven one of our angels helped him hold Kathryn and the baby in her womb safe.

As the house floated and bobbed along, the torrent kept their journey from being far from a lazy summer raft trip. It seemed more like what a raft might experience on Niagara Falls, which is where they honeymooned. Albert saw the Niagara Falls in his mind's eye when he noticed that the water in the house was rising. Kathryn noticed it too and wanted to scream, but looking at her husband and knowing that he was thinking through the problem, she remained silent.

He jumped up and scrambled to the other side of the room when the topsy-turvy, unstable house nearly threw him back to where he started. He jumped up and grabbed the chain that held the attic door. Pulling it down he grabbed his wife and they made their way into the attic where Albert began to break through the ceiling. He put his wife atop the roof, then followed after her.

As they held on for dear life, a demon yelling into her inner ear, Kathryn saw that her Albert was singularly focused, not merely to protect her but to stay calm before his wife. She would never forget this sight of him, for it lasted 23 minutes, which seemed like hours. She was tempted to scream and wail, but her rock holding her, protecting their baby and smiling into her eyes calmly, humbly, and bravely kept her emotions in check.

As their house roof came around Woodvale into Johnstown it seemed to slow, and they experienced some relief, but it was only for a few moments for their home was in the middle of a body of water that had just gone as far in one direction as it could and now was headed back in a completely different direction. When the direction of the flood flow changed, so did their roof, for it started to twist in swift moving circles.

Albert had positioned Kathryn's foot on one side of the hole in the roof and motioned to her to push with her hands on the other side of the hole, thus giving her body the opportunity to fight against the centrifugal force of their spinning roof. Just as she realized what he was having her do the home spun in the other direction and Albert, not holding onto anything could only hold her with his calm, humble, brave eyes, which he did for such an ever short moment of time as he was thrown into the water, never to be found or identified.

A short distance away, the roof of the Union Schoolhouse was on a crash course directly for her. Moments later she was being rescued by being drawn up on the roof of the Union Schoolhouse.

Nearly a week later Kathryn had weathered the largest storm in her life, lost her only and truest love, and had given birth to Roberta, a healthy daughter. Their pastor, Dr. Mr. Beale of the Presbyterian church had just come by to see her. He was in charge of the morgue records and said he would keep searching, but by this time did not hold out much hope for finding Albert's body.

As she sniffled, too exhausted to cry much more than that, Dr. Beale started to pray for her.

"Father in heaven, You tell us that You are the God of Hope,[1] but we confess that it is hard for us to see You like that right now. And yet we can look at Roberta and trust You to fill her and Kathryn with great joy and great peace. . ."

His prayer faded into the distance for she felt like she would never know peace again. She remembered the pastor leaving but then quickly fell asleep. When she awoke in the middle of the night, it was to the screams of her husband, screaming and screaming to be saved. Awakened with a start, she realized she had dreamt and the only crying came from Roberta who wanted to be fed.

As she fed her daughter, a calm and serene picture of her husband entered her mind. It was the same picture of him she had seen every time she closed her eyes and thought of him. He was her rock, smiling gently into her eyes, even when the raging waters took him. It was his calm that allowed her and her daughter to be alive.

She never again feared, and when others would question her they saw a peace that completely transcended their ability to understand this brave, calm smile she

---

[1] Romans 15:13

portrayed. Once she was asked if it were fake peace. She simply smiled, waited a moment before she responded, and then simply said, "There are troubles without, there are fears within, but God comforts the humble."[1]

She paused for a moment before she continued, "My humble Albert taught me that, with his calm smile, in the midst of tragedy."

Many years later, Kathryn crossed over Jordan into heaven and Albert, standing next to Jesus, just smiled at her calmly, humbly, and bravely.

HE WANTED TOBACCO OR NOTHING

An old Irishman walked up to the tent early in the day. "Well, what can we do for you?" was asked.

"Have yez any tobaccy?"

"No, tobacco don't go here."

"I want tobaccy or nothin'. This is no relief to a mon at all, at all."

The aged refugee walked away in high dudgeon. Just down the row from the clothing tent are located two little girls, named Johnson, who lost both father and mother. They had a terrible experience in the flood, and were two of the forty-three people pulled in on the roof of the house of the late General Campbell and his two sons, James and Curt.

"How do you fare?" one of the little girls was asked.

"Oh, very well, sir, only we are afraid of catching the measles," she answered; and with a grimace she tossed her head toward a tent on the other side and further up. A baby in the tent indicated has a slight attack of the measles, but is getting better, and is next door to a tent in which is a young woman shaking with the ague [malaria].

A MULTITUDE TO BE FED

In the houses along the road above the camp are several hundreds of refugees. In one of them are thirty or forty people rendered homeless by the flood. These are all supplied with food from the camp. Some idea of the number of people who have to be fed can be gathered from the fact that 350 pounds of coffee have been given out since yesterday. In the hills back of Cambria there are many hundreds of survivors. Dr. Findley, of the

---

[1] 2 Corinthians 7:5-6

Altoona Relief Corps, went there today and found that they were without a physician. One from Baltimore had been there, but had gone away. He found many people needing medical care, and they will be looked after from day to day.

"Wherever we go," said one of the doctors yesterday, "we find that there is an alarming spread of pneumonia." Of the refugees at the Cambria Hospital but two have died.

BAYONETS IN CONTROL

The ruined city lies tonight within a girdle of steel, the bayonets of the 14th regiment. The militia has captured Johnstown and tonight over the desolate plain where the city proper stood, through the towering wrecks and by the river passes, marches the patrol, crying "Halt" and challenging vagabonds, vandals and ghouls, who cross their path. General Hastings, being the highest officer in rank, is in command, and, when the survivors of the flood awake tomorrow, when the weary pickets are relieved at sunrise a brigade headquarters will be firmly established on the slope of Prospect Hill overlooking the hundreds of white tents of the regiments that will lie down below by the German Catholic Church.

First this afternoon arrived Governor Beaver's staff, mostly by way of Harper's Ferry on the Baltimore and Ohio. All the officers in brilliant uniform and trappings reported to General Hastings.   They found their commander in a slouch hat, a rough-looking cutaway and rubber boots.

The 14th Regiment, reinforced this morning until it is now 600 strong, is still camped in freight cars beyond the depot, opposite the late city proper. Space is being rapidly cleared for its tents, however, over by the German Catholic Church, and near the ruins of the Irish Catholic Church, which was on fire when the deluge came.

Early this morning the 14th Regiment went into service, but it was a volunteer service of two young officers and three privates when at noon they dragged gently from the rushing Conemaugh the body of a beautiful young girl. She was tenderly borne through the lines by regimental headquarters to the church house morgue, while the sentinels stood aside with their bayonets and the corporal ordered "Halt!" Guards were placed at the Johnstown stations and all the morgues.

Marched out of Camp

During the day many people of questionable character, indeed all who were challenged and could not satisfactorily explain their business here, had a military escort to the city limits, where they were ordered not to return. Every now and then two of the National Guard could be seen marching along with a rough fellow between them to the post where such beings, are made exiles from the scene of desolation. Tonight the picket lines stretch from brigade headquarters down Prospect Hill past General Hastings' quarters even to the river. The patrol across the river is keeping sharp vigilance in town. At the eastern end of the Pennsylvania Railroad's stone bridge you must stop and give the countersign. If you don't no man can answer for your safety.

A Lieutenant's Disgrace

Down the Cambria Road, past which the dead of the River Conemaugh swept into Nineveh in awful numbers, was another scene today that of a young officer of the National Guard in full uniform and a poor deputy sheriff, who had lost home, wife, children and all, clinched like madmen and struggling for the farmer's revolver. If the officer of the Guard had won, there might have been a tragedy, for he was drunk. The homeless deputy sheriff with his wife and babies swept to death past the place where they struggled was sober and in the right.

The officer of the National Guard came with his regiment into this valley of distress to protect survivors from ruffianism and maintain the peace and dignity of the State. The man with whom he fought for the weapon was Peter Fitzpatrick, almost crazy in his own woe, but singularly cool and self-possessed regarding the safety of those left living.

Hael: Political Myopia

I cannot tell you how I wanted to delete the previous section. I wanted to delete it because in your 21st century political zeal (in whatever country you are reading this) your political myopia is a very real danger, and the story allows me the opportunity to remind you of something that is slipping away from all y'all. It does not matter what side of politics, religion, etc. you are on, you will read this story and be tempted to either say, "yes, these people in uniform cannot be trusted," or say, "allow the person in uniform the freedom to do his bidding."

May I just be extra personal with you for a moment? I've been here for some 6,000 of your earth years. Our Creator made us in the first week too. So I have watched you and you haven't changed, you're still the same. You have the same weaknesses, the same strengths, the same needs, etc.

So judge your own political motives. You will need to be your own judge. I cannot do it. Well I can, but it will have more meaning if you have an honest conversation with yourself. Let me remind you of three verses:

Woe to those who call evil good and good evil (Isaiah 5:20a). Have you drunk this kool-aid? Then stop if you see evil and call it for what it is.

The Lord's slave [servant] must not quarrel, but must be gentle to everyone, able to teach, and patient, instructing his opponents with gentleness. Perhaps God will grant them repentance leading them to the knowledge of the truth. (2 Timothy 2:24-25) Did you notice that the passage doesn't say, ". . . unless you are correct, for then you can beat up your opponent verbally." Too many Christians are desirous to win the argument for argument's sake. Get over yourself! Sorry.

Let me end this "soapbox-standing" with your Savior's words, "The way they will know that I came from the Father is if you have unity."[1] Now I can just hear you, "But Hael, you get over it, Big Guy. I have unity with my family of believers. It's not my fault if some out there are idiots!"

Let me say this, without putting my nine-foot-tall weight into this, okay? When you get here to heaven, there will be people here who baptized differently than you, there will be people here who prayed differently than you, there will be people here with different amounts of melanin in their skin, and there will be people here who voted differently than you.

You keep saying that you want Jesus to return, but you don't want it enough to be obedient to Him. If you did you would have unity. Let me say it differently and then I'll allow the 1889 author to finish his reporting of this officer.

When the unsaved see the way you argue with others, are they saying to themselves, "Yes, I want that person's Jesus?" Or are they saying, "If that is how your Jesus tells you to act, I don't want Him?"

I will remind you that the 2nd Timothy passage above admonishes you to "gently" correct. I will simply add if you cannot do it gently, then shut-up!

Our story of the drunken officer continues. Again, stop and reflect on your unity, or lack of unity, with others. Quit looking out yonder.

---

[1] John 17:21

A Man Who Had Suffered

It was one o'clock this afternoon when I noticed on the Cambria road the young officer with his long military coat cut open leaning heavily for support upon two privates of Company G, Hawthorn and Stewart (boys). He was crying in a maudlin way, "You just take me to a place and I'll drink soft stuff." They entreated him to return at once to the regimental quarters, even begged him, but he cast them aside and went staggering down the road to the line, where he met the grave-faced deputy face to face. The latter looked in the white of his eyes and said, "You can't pass here, sir."

"Can't pass here?" he cried, waving his arms. "You challenge an officer? Stand aside!"

"You can't pass here," this time quietly, but firmly, "not while you're drunk."

"Stand aside," yelled the Lieutenant. "Do you, you know who I am? You talk to an officer of the National Guard."

"Yes, and listen," said the man in front of him so impatiently that it hushed his antagonist's tirade, "I talk to an 'officer' of the National Guard, I, who have lost my wife, my children and all in this flood no man has yet described, we, who have seen our dead with their bodies mutilated are not afraid to talk for what is right, even to an officer of the National Guard."

A Big Man's Honest Rage

While he spoke another great, dark, stout man, who looked as if he had suffered, came up, and upon taking in the situation every vein in his forehead swelled purple with rage.

"You dirty cur," he cried to the officer, "you dirty, drunken cur, if it was not for the sake of peace I'd lay you out where you stand."

"Come on," yelled the Lieutenant, with an oath.

The big man sent out a terrible blow that would have left the Lieutenant senseless had not one of the privates dashed in between, receiving part of it and warding it off. The Lieutenant got out of his military coat. The privates seized the big man and with another, who ran to the scene, held him back. The Lieutenant put his hand to his pistol pocket, the deputy Fitzpatrick seized him and the struggle for the weapon began. For a moment it was fierce and desperate, then another private came to the deputy's assistance. The revolver was wrested from the drunken officer and he himself was pushed back panting to the ground.

THE VICTOR WAS MAGNANIMOUS

Deputy Fitzpatrick seized the military coat he had thrown on the ground, and with it and the weapon started to the regimental headquarters. Then the privates got around him and begged him, one of them with tears in his eyes, not to report their officer, saying that he was a good man when he was sober. He studied a long while, standing in the road, while the officer slunk away over the hill. Then he threw the disgraced uniform to them, and said, "Here, give them to him, and, mind you, if he does not go at once to his quarters, I'll take him there, dead or alive."

AT THE SCHOOLHOUSE MORGUE

Away from the devastation in the valley and the gloomy scenes along the river, on Prospect Hill, stands the schoolhouse, the morgue of the unidentified dead. People do not go there unless they are hunting for a friend or relative. They treat it as a pest house. They have seen enough white faces in the valley and the living feel like fleeing from the dead.

This afternoon at sunset every desk in every classroom supported a coffin. Each coffin was numbered, and each lid turned to show the face within. On the blackboard in one of the rooms, between the pretty drawing and neat writing of the school children, was scrawled the bulletin, "Hold No. '59' as long as possible, supposed to be Mrs. Paulson, of Pittsburgh." "But '59' wasn't Mrs. Paulson," said a little woman. "It is Miss Frances Wagner, of Market street, Johnstown." Her brother found her here. "Fifty-nine" has gone, one of the few identified today, and others had come to take its place.

Strongly appealing to the sympathies of even those looking for friends and relatives was the difference in the size of the coffins. There were some no larger than a violin case hidden below large boxes, telling of the unknown babies perished, and there were coffins of children of all years. On the blackboards were written such sentences as "Home sweet home," "Peace on earth, good will toward men." For all the people who looked at their young faces knew, they might have stood by the coffin of the child who helped to write them.

The bodies found each day are kept as long as possible and then are sent away for burial with their numbers, where their names should be, on rough boards, their only tombstones.

Just as a black storm-cloud was driving hard from the West over the slope of the hills yesterday the body of young Henry G. Rose, the district attorney of Cambria County, was lowered into a temporary grave beside unknown victims. Three people attended his burial, his father-in-law, James A. Lane, who saw him lost while he himself was struggling for life in their floating house, the Rev. Dr. H. L. Chapman, of the Methodist Episcopal Church, and the Rev. L. Maguire. Dr. Chapman read the funeral services, and while he prayed the thunder rumbled and the cloud darkened the scene. The coffins are taken there in wagonloads, lowered quickly and hidden from sight.

Miss Nina Speck, daughter of Rev. David Speck, pastor of the First United Brethren Church of Chambersburg, was in Johnstown visiting her brother last week and narrowly escaped death in the flood.

She arrived today clad in nondescript clothing, which had been furnished by an old negro washer-woman and told the following story of the flood:

"Our house was in Kernville, a part of Johnstown, through which Stony Creek ran. Although we were a square from the creek, the backwater from the stream had flooded the streets in the morning and was up to our front porch. At 4 o'clock on Friday afternoon we were sitting on the front porch watching the flood, when we heard a roar as of a tornado or mighty conflagration.

"We rushed upstairs and got out upon the bay window. There an awful sight met our eyes. Down the Conemaugh Valley was advancing a mighty wall of flame and mist with a terrible roar. Before it were rolling houses and buildings of all kinds, tossing over and over. We thought it was a cyclone, the roar sounding like a tempest among forest trees. At first, we could see no water at all, but back of the mist and flames came a mighty wall of water. We started downstairs and through the rear of the house to escape to the hillside nearby. But before we could get there the water was up to our necks and we could make no progress. We turned back and were literally dashed by the current into the house, which began to move off as soon as we were in it again. From the second story window 1 saw a young man drifting toward us. I broke the glass from the frames with my hands and helped him in, and in a few moments more I pulled in an old man, a neighbor, who had been sick.

MIRACULOUS ESCAPE

"Our house moved rapidly down the stream and fortunately lodged against a strong building. The water forced us out of the second story up into the attic. Then we heard a lot of people on our roof begging us for God's sake to let them in. I broke through the roof with a bed slat and pulled them in. Soon we had thirteen in all crouched in the attic.

"Our house was rocking, and every now and then a building would crash against us. Every moment we thought we would go down. The roofs of all the houses drifting by us were covered with people, nearly all praying and some singing hymns, and now and then a house would break apart and all would go down. On Saturday at noon we were rescued, making our way from one building to the next by crawling on narrow planks. I counted hundreds of bodies lying in the debris, most of them covered over with earth and showing only the outlines of the form."

A SAD HOSPITAL STORY

On a cot in the hospital on Prospect Hill there lies at present a man injured almost to death, but whose mental sufferings are far keener than his bodily pains. His name is Vering. He has lost in the flood his whole family, wife and five children. In an interview he said, "I was at home with my wife and children when the alarm came. We hurried from the house, leaving everything behind us. As we reached the door a gentleman friend was running by. He grasped the two smaller children, one under each arm, and hurried on ahead of us. I had my arm around my wife, supporting her. Behind us we could hear the flood rushing upon us. In one hurried glance, as I passed a corner, I could see the fearful crunching and hear the crackling of the houses in its fearful grasp. I then could see that there was no possibility of our escape, as we were too far away from the hill-side. In a few moments it was upon us. In a flash I saw the three dear children licked up by it and they disappeared from sight as I and my wife were thrown into the air by the vanguard of the rushing ruins. We found ourselves in a lot of drift, driving along with the speed of a racehorse. In a moment or two we were thrown with a crash against a frame building whose walls gave way before the flood as easily as if they were made of piecrust, and the timbers began to fall about us in all directions.

"Up to this time I had retained a firm hold upon my wife, but as I found myself pinned between two heavy timbers the agony caused my senses to leave me momentarily. I recovered instantly in time to see my wife's head just disappearing under the water. Like lightning I grasped her by the hair and as best I could, I pinioned as I was above the water by the timber, I raised her above it. The weight proved too much, and she sank again. Again, I pulled her to the surface and again she sank. This I did again and again with no avail. She drowned in my very grasp, and at last she dropped from my nerveless hands to leave my sight forever. As if I had not suffered enough, a few moments after I saw some objects whirling around in an eddy which circled around, until, reaching the current again, they floated past me. My God, man, would you believe me? it was three of my children, dead. Their dear little faces are before me now, distorted in a look of agony that, no matter what I do, haunts me. O, if I could only have released myself at that time I would have willingly died with them. I was rescued some time after, and have been here ever since. I have since learned that my friend who so bravely endeavored to save two of the children was lost with them."

HAEL: WHAT A FRIEND WE HAVE IN JESUS

As I read of Vering's anguish I am remined of a few lines from the novel that introduced me to the world in The Pray-ers, Book 1.[1] The author tells of itinerant preacher, Alexander Rich. Let me relate part of his story to you here. I did not ask for permission from the publishers, as they are not allowed to reach me here in heaven. I trust that there will be no legal issues.

Alexander now looked at verse four: Yea, though I walk through the valley of the shadow of death, I will fear no evil, for You are with me. Your rod and Your staff they comfort me.

As Brother Alex thought about this passage, meditating on it, turning its words over and over in his mind. He thought about the love and care that God had given him, not the love of a "young maiden" as Dwight had cajoled him about earlier in his letter.[2] And then Al remembered Joseph Scriven, a man who had truly known the comfort of the Lord. Alexander read back over the passage in his mind: Yea, though I walk through the valley of the shadow of death. . . and he remembered that this man, Scriven, had two fiancées die just before their weddings.

---

[1] The Pray-ers, Book 1 by Mark S Mirza, CTM Publishing, 2016, pages 228-230
[2] The itinerant preacher and Dwight L. Moody grew up together and so exchange letters, in the novel The Pray-ers

Alex went on, I will fear no evil for You are with me. And he marveled at Brother Joseph Scriven again, because he took a vow of poverty, helping others, after his second fiancée's death. Your rod and your staff they comfort me.

At this Alexander pulled his handkerchief out of his pocket to wipe the tears from his eyes, for he had read that this dear man had written *What a Friend We Have in Jesus* upon learning of his mother's illness back in Europe, and he did not have the funds to go help her. So he wrote her this poem, which would later be put to music by Charles Converse.

As all of these thoughts ran through his mind, he felt an incredible sense of gladness that he had the opportunity to share this poem and this story with his friend Dwight Moody. And through his friend Dwight this song had become a blessing to so many others.

And as these thoughts calmed him, he found himself singing this great hymn:

What a Friend we have in Jesus, all our sins and griefs to bear!
What a privilege to carry everything to God in prayer!
O what peace we often forfeit, O what needless pain we bear,
All because we do not carry, everything to God in prayer.

Have we trials and temptations? Is there trouble anywhere?
We should never be discouraged; take it to the Lord in prayer.
Can we find a friend so faithful, who will all our sorrows share?
Jesus knows our every weakness; take it to the Lord in prayer.

Are we weak and heavy laden, cumbered with a load of care?
Precious Savior, still our refuge, take it to the Lord in prayer.
Do your friends despise, forsake you? Take it to the Lord in prayer!
In His arms He'll take and shield you; you will find a solace there.

Blessed Savior, Thou hast promised Thou wilt all our burdens bear.
May we ever, Lord, be bringing all to Thee in earnest prayer.
Soon in glory bright unclouded there will be no need for prayer
Rapture, praise and endless worship will be our sweet portion there.

This is Hael again, as I take you to the next chapter, may I just ask a question? Why has that fourth verse of this wonderful hymn been deleted out of so many of your hymn books?

CHAPTER XIV
Terrible Pictures of Woe

The proportion of the living registered since the flood as against the previous number of inhabitants is even less than was reported yesterday. It was ascertained today that many of the names on the list were entered more than once and that the total number of persons registered is not more than 13,000 out of a former population of between 40,000 and 50,000.

A new and more exact method of determining the number of the lost was inaugurated this morning. Men are sent out by the Relief Committee, who will go to every abode and obtain the names of the survivors, and if possible those of the dead.

The lack of identification of hundreds of bodies strengthens the inference that the proportion of the dead to the living is appalling. It is argued that the friends who might identify these unclaimed bodies are themselves all gone.

Another significant fact is that so large a number of those whom one meets in the streets or where the streets used to be are non-residents, strangers who have come here out of humane or less creditable motives. The question that is heard very often is, "Where are the inhabitants?" The town does not appear to have at present a population of more than 10,000.

It is believed that many of the bodies of the dead have been borne down into the Ohio, and perhaps into the Mississippi as well, and hence may finally be deposited by the waters hundreds of miles apart, perhaps never to be recovered or seen by man again.

HAEL: DEATH COUNT

I would remind you that the official death count is 2,209. I am not at liberty to share with you the actual number. The editors here have not even allowed me to hint at the number, but I am allowed only to say 2,209 is incorrect.

THE GENERAL SITUATION

Under the blue haze of smoke that for a week has hung over this valley of the shadow of death the work which is to resurrect this stricken city has gone steadily forward. Here and there over the waste where Johnstown stood in its pride black smoke arises from the bonfires on which shattered house walls, rafters, doors, broken furniture and all the flotsam and jetsam of the great flood is cast.

Adjutant General Hastings, who believes in heroic measures, has been quietly trying to persuade the town council to allow him to burn up the wrecked houses wholesale without the tedious bother of pulling them down and handling the debris. The timorous committees would not countenance such an idea. Nothing but piecemeal tearing down of the wrecked houses tossed together by the mighty force of the water and destruction by never dying bonfires would satisfy them. Yet all of them must come down. Most of the buildings reached by the flood have been examined, found unsafe and condemned. Can the job be done safely and successfully wholesale or not? That is the real question for the powers that be to answer, and no sentiment should enter into it.

Four thousand workmen are busy today with ropes and axe, pick and shovel. But the task is vast, it is herculean, like unto the cleaning of the Augean stables.

"To clean up this town properly," said General Hastings today, "we shall need twenty thousand workmen for three months."

The force of the swollen river upturned the town in a half hour. These same timorous managers weakened today, after having the facts before their eyes brought home to their understanding by constant iteration. They have found out that they have, vulgarly speaking, bitten off more than they can chew. Poisons of the foulest kind pollute the water which flows down the turgid Conemaugh into the Allegheny River, whence is Pittsburgh's water-supply, and thence into the Ohio, the water-supply of many cities and towns. Fears of a pestilence are not to be pooh-poohed into the background. It is very serious, so long as the river flows through the clogged and matted mass of the bridge so long it will threaten the people along its course with pestilence. The committee confess their inability to do this needed work, and today voted to ask the Governors of the several States to cooperate in the establishment of a national relief committee to grapple with the situation. Action cannot and must not be delayed.

HOPE OUT OF DESPAIR

The fears of an outbreak of fever or other zymotic diseases appear to be based on the alleged presence of decomposed animal matter, human and of lower type, concealed amid the debris. The alleged odor of burnt flesh coming from the enormous mass of conglomerated timber and iron lodged in the cul-de-sac formed by the Pennsylvania Railroad bridge is extremely mythical. There is an unmistakable scent of burnt wood. It would not be strange if the carcasses of domestic animals, which must be hidden in the enormous mass, were finally to be realized by the olfactory organs of the bystanders.

BLASTING CONTINUES

All day long the blast of dynamite resounded among the hills. Cartridges were let off in the debris, and a cloud of dust and flying spray marked the result of the mining operation. The interlaced timbers in the cul-de-sac yielded very slowly even to the mighty force of dynamite. There were no finds of especial import. At the present rate of clearing, the cul-de-sac will not be free from the wreckage in two months.

There was a sad spectacle presented this morning when the laborers were engaged in pulling over a vast pile of timber and miscellaneous matter on Main street. A young woman and a little puny baby girl were found beneath the mass, which was as high as the second story windows of the houses nearby.

TOGETHER IN DEATH

The girl must have been handsome when in the flush of youth and health. She had seized the helpless infant and endeavored to find safety by flight. Her closely cut brown hair was filled with sand, and a piece of brass wire was wound around the head and neck. A loose cashmere house-gown was partially torn from her form, and one slipper, a little bead embroidered affair, covered a silk-stockinged foot. Each arm was tightly clasped around the baby. The rigidity of death should have passed away, but the arms were fixed in their position as if composed of an unbendable material instead of muscle and bone. The fingers were imbedded in the sides of the little baby as if its protector had made a final effort not to be separated and to save if possible the fragile life. The faces of both were scarred and disfigured from contact with floating debris. The single garment of the baby, a thin white slip, was rent and frayed. The body of the young woman was identified, but the babe remained unknown. Probably its father and mother were lost in the flood, and it will never be claimed by friendly hands.

A Strange Discovery

This is only one among the many pathetic incidents of the terrible disaster. There were only nine unidentified bodies at the Adams street morgue this afternoon, and three additions to the number were made after ten o'clock. Two hundred and eight bodies have been received by the embalmers in charge. The yard of the school house, which was converted into a temporary abode of death, contains large piles of coffins of the cheaper sort. They come from different cities within two or three hundred miles of Johnstown, and after being stacked up they are pulled out as needed. Coffins are to be seen everywhere about the valley, ready for use when a body is found. A trio of bodies was found near the Hurlburt House under peculiar circumstances. They were hidden beneath a pile of wreckage at least twenty-five feet in height. They were a father, a mother and son.

Around the waist of each a quarter inch rope was tied so that the three were bound together tightly. The hands of the boy were clasped by those of the mother, and the father's arms were extended as if to ward off danger. The father probably knotted the rope during the awful moments of suspense intervening between the coming of the flood and the final destruction of the house they occupied. The united strength of the three could not resist the mighty force of the inundation, and like so many straws they were swept on the boiling surge until life was crushed out.

Child and Doll in One Coffin

I beheld a touching spectacle when the corpse of a little girl was extricated and placed on a stretcher for transportation to the morgue. Clasped to her breast by her two waxen hands was a rag doll. It was a cheap affair, evidently of domestic manufacture. To the child of poverty, the rag baby was a favorite toy. The little mother held fast to her treasure and met her end without separating from it. The two, child and doll, were not parted when the white coffin received them, and they will moulder together.

I saw an old-fashioned cupboard dug out of a pile of rubbish. The top shelf contained a quantity of jelly of domestic manufacture. Not a glass jar was broken. Indeed, there have been some remarkable instances of the escape of fragile articles from destruction. In the debris near the railroad bridge you may come upon all manner of things. The water tanks of three locomotives which were borne from the roundhouse at Conemaugh, two miles away, are conspicuous. Amid the general wreck, beneath one of these heavy iron tanks, a looking glass, two feet by one foot in dimensions, was discovered intact, without even a scratch on the quicksilver.

Johnstown people surviving the destruction appear to bewail the death of the Fisher family. "Squire" Fisher was one of the old time public functionaries of the borough. He and his six children were swept away. One of the Fisher girls was at home under peculiar circumstances. She had been away at school, and returned home to be married to her betrothed. Then she was to return to school and take part in the graduating exercises. Her body has not yet been recovered.

Something to be Thankful For

There is much destitution felt by people whose pride prevents them from asking for supplies from the relief committees. I saw a sad little procession wending up the hill to the camp of the Americus Club. There was a father, an honest, simple German, who had been employed at the Cambria works during the past twenty-two years. Behind him trooped eight children, from a girl of nineteen to a babe in the arms of the mother, who brought up the rear. The woman and children were hatless, and possessed only the calico garments worn at the moment of flight. Forlorn and weary, they ranged in front of the relieving stand and implored succor.

"We lost one only, thank God!" exclaimed Lynn, the mother. "Our second, a son, Josh is gone." Her shoulders heaved heavily and she continued. "We had a comfortable house which we owned. It was paid for by our savings. Now all is gone." Then the unhappy woman sat down on the wet ground and sobbed hysterically. The children crowded around their mother and joined in her grief. You will behold many of these scenes of domestic distress about the ruins of Johnstown in these dolorous days.

HAEL: Josh, It's Okay To Go

There is an interesting backstory to this German family that their humbleness kept them from ever mentioning. When the torrent made its way to this family's home, they had escaped by the fast thinking father and nimble son, Josh, who handed the children to his father and mother, where they sat atop a wall, turned raft.

As he handed the last child to his father a log, tossed high into the air came down, missing the raft but hit the water near the family. There was a loud crash and some of the children screamed. When Lynn turned back to Josh she saw that the log had bounced and crashed into Josh's head and shoulders.

The father pulled Josh's unconscious body to the raft where he cradled his seventeen-year-old son until his mother could scoot over and help. They found themselves in a relatively peaceful flow, so Josh's father and mother switched positions, she cradled her son and the father gathered his brood to protect them.

Two hours later their makeshift raft glided to a high sandbar above Johnstown. Josh had been protected as best Lynn could do. Pulling Josh under a tree and trying to keep him warm she prayed again. She had been praying all the way down and back along the river. She at once prayed for her family and Josh, and then again she would pray for her family, lifting up Josh with tears.

"Lord, this is too much for us to bear."

The children would alternately cry for Josh, and pray for him. At one-point Josh's life seemed to be fleeing away, and then as quickly as ever his breathing would return to normal and the family would relax.

This continued for a number of hours under that tree. The family huddled around Josh and their mother. For a time her husband held Josh and she stood up. She looked out across the massive river which right now looked like a lake. As she stood and enfolded her children with her arms, she didn't look at them. She looked beyond them and thought of her life to that point.

She had married her husband thinking that he would be her excuse to get away from the home she grew up in. Her parents loved her, but they could not show it without favoritism for the other children. Favoritism over Lynn. Being the eldest child she felt more like a foreigner in her own home. She was not a loved and nurtured daughter even though she was a daughter who would do anything her parents needed. She swore she would never treat her children like she had been treated.

So when her suitor came along, she jumped at the chance to go, and even now, twenty-three years later she remembered how her choice to marry him was motivated by pride and selfishness rather than love and the leading of the Holy Spirit.

She turned to look back at Josh. Her children, seeing her look for Josh, were all huddled around her. They parted so that she could look down at him and caress him with her eyes. She asked herself, "Have I let Josh feel the same lack of love I felt growing up? Or any of my children? Have I done that to any of them?"

She now reached out to each of them, touching one's head, another's hand, rubbing one's face, and another's shoulder. And she looked at her husband. Their marriage was not easy. He was a hard man. "Could I have been nicer to him? Could I have treated him better?"

Resolved to resubmit herself to the Lord, whatever may come, she reached over and kissed the top of the closest head she found. She wasn't sure which of her children she kissed, she was on her way back to Josh. Her husband, whose shoulders shuddered slightly, not with cold but with concern for his son, looked up at her with tears. He moved over and they both held Josh when all of a sudden Josh's eyes began to flicker.

Everyone was still, for all saw the miracle occurring before them. Josh, whose eyes looked heavy, tried to focus on those before him. He smiled slightly and tried to acknowledge them when his attention left his family and went to something beyond them.

"They're calling my name," Josh whispered.

The children looked around, wondering who he was listening to calling his name.

And as Lynn and her husband looked at each other Josh continued, "I see the other shores."

As tears started to fall from her eyes she said, with as much bravery as she could muster, "It's okay, Josh. It's okay, son, you can go." [1]

A few moments later Josh entered those other shores.

Lynn immediately shut up her emotions, feeling she had to be strong for her family. It was two days later when something broke. When she saw the 1889 author and told him about her son being gone, the Holy Spirit broke her spirit, and she wept like she had not since she was a child.

SAW A FLOOD OF HELPLESS HUMANITY.

Mr. L. D. Woodruff, the editor and proprietor of the Johnstown Democrat, tells his experiences during the night of horrors. He was at the office of the paper, which is in the upper portion of the Baltimore and Ohio Railway station. This brick edifice stands almost in the center of the course of the flood, and its preservation from ruin is one of the remarkable features of the occasion. A pile of freight cars lodged at the corner of the building and the breakwater thus formed checked the onslaught of floating battering rams. Mr. Woodruff, with his two sons, remained in the building

---

[1] Author's Note: I hesitate to share much information about Josh's family, except to say that Josh's words are based on a real seventeen-year-old Josh, whose father is one of my prayer partners. The remainder of the story is all fiction, but the words between parent and Josh are not.

until the following day. The water came up to the floor of the second story. All night long he witnessed people floating past on the roofs of houses or on various kinds of wreckage. A number of persons were rescued through the windows.

A man and his wife with three children were pulled in. After a while the mother for the first time remembered that her baby of fifteen months was left behind. Her grief was violent, and her cries were mingled with the groans of her husband, who lay on the floor with a broken leg. The next day the baby was found, when the waters subsided, on a pile of debris outside and it was alive and uninjured.

During the first few hours Mr. Woodruff momentarily expected that the building would go. As the night wore away it became evident the water was going down. Not a vestige of Mr. Woodruff's dwelling has been found.

The newspapers of Johnstown came out of the flood fairly well. The Democrat lost only a job press, which was swept out of one corner of the building.

THE FLOOD'S AWFUL SPOIL

In the broad field of debris at the Pennsylvania Railroad viaduct, where the huge playthings of the flood were tossed only to be burned and beaten to a solid, intricate mass, are seen the peculiar metal works of two trains of cars. The wreck of the Day Express east, running in two sections that fatal Friday, lie there about thirty yards above the bridge. One mass of wreckage is unmistakably that of the Pullman car section, made up of two baggage cars and six Pullman coaches, and the other shows the irons of five-day coaches and one Pullman car. These trains were running in the same block at Johnstown and were struck by the flood two miles above, torn from their tracks and carried tumbling down the mighty torrents to their resting place in the big eddy.

RAILROAD MEN SUPPRESSING INFORMATION

The train crew, who saw the waters coming, warned the passengers, escaped, and went home on foot. Conductor Bell duly made his report, yet for some unknown reasons one of Superintendent Pitcairn's subordinates has been doing his best to give out and prove by witnesses, to whom he takes newspaper men, that only one car of that express was lost and with it "two or three ladies who went back for overshoes and a very few others not lively enough to escape after the warnings." That story went well until the smoke rolled away from the wreckage and the bones of the two sections of the Day Express east were disclosed. Another very singular feature was the apparent inability of the conductor of the express to tell how many passengers they had on board and just how many were saved. It had been learned that the first section of the train carried 180 passengers and the second 157. It may be stated as undoubtedly true that of the number fifty, at least, swell the horrible tale of the dead.

From the wreck where the trains burned there have been taken out fifty-eight charred bodies, the features being unrecognizable. Of these seven found together were the Gilmore family, whose house had floated there. The others, all adults, which, with two or three exceptions, swell the list of the unidentified dead, are undoubted corpses of the ill-fated passengers of the east express.

HAEL: A CONSTANT REVEALED

Below this anecdote is a story about a missionary that has a unique backstory and a most satisfying result. You will then read in the very next paragraph, that the 1889 author begins to speak of a conspiracy which we will not address, except to quote Solomon in Ecclesiastes, "There is nothing new under the sun."[1] What this author alludes to here, you have alluded to in all of your history, you and all other nations, and is going on even now in the politics of the USA, in Kenya's politics, and numerous other nations' politics.

But let me get back to this backstory. In spite of your conspiracy proclivity, there is the most satisfying story of Miss Anna Clara Chrisman's companion. While the two did not grow up in the faith together, their paths crossed at critical times in their lives. They matured together and would hopefully now share the gospel together.

Miss Anna's companion, Louise Lane Hitchens, was affectionately called Lula for short. She and Miss Anna formally met in their first year of college in a women's prayer class, although they had known of each other, being from the same town.

At university Miss Anna took the prayer class to learn more about prayer, while Lula took the class, "to see if the instructor knew what she was talking about," she later confessed to Miss Anna.

---

[1] Ecclesiastes 1:9e

Lula came from a church that taught prayer, lived prayer, and made sure everyone in her pastor's congregation could teach others how to pray. He took literally and personally the admonition of Jesus when He said, "My house, or temple, shall be called a house of prayer."[1]

"If your family does not look at you, the temple of God, and see you as a house of prayer," her pastor would preach, "then you need to forget every other Christian discipline, until this is exactly who you are, a temple and a house of prayer."

Under this environment she became a strong proponent of prayer, but also a bit of a legalist, arguing with anyone who did not pray the way she did, or prayed in ways she considered contrary to the Word of God.

"It is hard to argue with you, Lula," Miss Anna would say to her friend during their college years, "for you are so focused on winning the argument that you become mean."

Their first interaction came as school girls in a city-wide Christmas pageant. Both attending different churches, they had an informal relationship at best. And perhaps it was because they both attended different churches and had enough separation that their friendship remained.

When they graduated high school they had both agreed that the missionary life was for them. They so looked forward to it that missionary training for both of them was more fun than strenuous. And Lula, always disagreeing with someone's prayer life, continued asking theological questions that often turned into sparring matches. Others found it to be a fun sport to watch and listen to.

The trip on the Day Express, train 8, was no exception. No sooner had they sat down, some poor pastor sat near them who seemed to be a bit of a worry wart. From Pittsburgh to Johnstown, Lula sparred with Dr. Reverend Lyon.

"He's a liberal preacher and pray-er," Lula whispered to Miss Anna who frowned her disappointment to her friend.

"Be nice to him, Lula." Miss Anna quietly exclaimed.

"I will," Lula responded and rolled her eyes.

"So, Dr. Reverend Lyon, how do you teach your people to not worry?" Lula asked in her best respectful voice.

"Oh my dear, why would you try to teach someone to not worry?" he responded rather pompously.

Holding her temper, Lula said nicely, "Isn't it a sin Doctor?"

---

[1] Matthew 21:13a

"Well, I wouldn't call it a sin, Miss Lula." Dr. Reverend Lyon responded with some annoyance.

He didn't concern himself with this back and forth banter. It would be over soon, and this pesky "know-it-all" would be gone.

And then it happened. The train slowed where Dr. Reverend Lyon knew it should not. "Don't worry ladies," he said encouragingly to the two missionaries-to-be, "this kind of delay happens often."

"But not this early," he thought to himself.

Two hours later they realized they would be spending the night on the train, and not moving.

The next morning came, and while they were cold, they were well fed by the Railroad company.

After eating a late breakfast, and being periodically questioned (inquisition-ed, more like) the reverend felt like he was on more confident ground with his pesky "friend" so he asked, in hopes she would shut up, "Miss Lula, how would you pray about this situation we are in?"

Smiling back at him, with a slight concern she said, "I have been asking myself a similar question, and that is, 'did I pray the wrong prayer when we left Pittsburgh?' I don't think I did." She paused and then more confidently she continued, "What I prayed is disappointing, but I believe it is accurate."

"Pray, share with me what you uttered up to the Holy One," he said condescendingly.

*"Well, I prayed what I always do when I travel, Exodus 23:20. I shared with you yesterday that I do not ask for protection, I trust the Lord for protection,[1] because He has already promised to be my protector, but I confess that a part of the verse that I have never experienced, I suspect I am, forgive me, **we are** experiencing right now."*

"And what, my dear, is the part of the verse you are experiencing?" He didn't recall the verse so he fumbled for a way to get her to tell him the verse without admitting he did not know it.

"Well," Lula continued, "the verse says that He is alongside us, guarding us along the way so that we arrive at the place that He has prepared for us."

Lula paused and then looked curiously at the doctor and at Miss Anna and pointing her words to Miss Anna she said, "I have been so focused on my own

---

[1] Psalm 91:14-15

will that I have completely missed that God has prepared this place, right here, where we have currently ended up, Anna. Here," she continued, "here He has prepared for us, you Anna, you and I, Doctor, and what am I doing? I am sparring with you, sir, merely for pleasure and probably missing how the Lord can use me while we are here."

"For He has prepared this place for us," Miss Anna said with new interest in her voice.

"Ah, well then ladies. Let me not detain you. Work unto the Lord as you see fit." He then motioned with his hands dismissing them, glad that he was rid of them, especially Miss Lula.

The girls did not recognize his attitude but immediately got up and started ministering to the other people on the train. By the middle of the afternoon they had spent time with everyone on the train, encouraging them as best they could when they returned to their seats.

They were sitting next to each other when they heard the crashing sound of thunder. The girls looked at each other perplexed, and then up the track just as the reverend, who was now sitting across from them facing them, looked in the same direction.

They saw nothing on the tracks and then saw the top of the thirty-foot cloud of debris. It headed straight for them with such speed they knew they could not escape. The girls grabbed each other's hands and looked up at the Dr. Reverend Lyon who looked scared to death.

The girls heard our humming, but Dr. Lyon was completely oblivious.

It is an interesting sight for us too as angels. For just as we three began our humming and enclosed our wings around them, Miss Anna, Miss Lula and Dr. Lyons' emotions came through to us. It always does and we "feel it," much as a horse feels the confidence or the anxiety of a rider who is in the saddle.

As we entered heaven, the two girls were wide-eyed and excited, while their reverend friend was a bit bewildered and somewhat apprehensive for a time.

THE CHURCH LOSES A MISSIONARY

Today another corpse was found in the ruins of a Pullman car badly burned. It was fully identified as that of Miss Anna Clara Chrisman, of Beauregard, Miss., a well-developed [sophisticated] lady of about twenty-five years, who was on her way to New York to fill a mission station in Brazil. Between the leaves of her Greek testament was a telegram she had written, expecting to send it at the first stop, addressed to the Methodist Mission headquarters, No. 20 East Twelfth street, New York, saying that she would arrive on "train 8" of the Pennsylvania Railroad, the Day Express east. In her satchel were found photographs of friends and her Bible, and from her neck hung a $20 gold piece, carefully sewn in a bag.

Is it possible that the Pennsylvania Railroad is keeping back the knowledge in order simply to avoid a list of "passengers killed" in its annual report, solely to keep its record as little stained as possible? It can hardly be that they fear suits for damages, for the responsibility of the wreck does not rest on them.

Two hundred bodies were recovered from the ruins yesterday. Some were identified, but the great majority were not. This number includes all the morgues, the one at the Pennsylvania Railroad station, the Fourth ward school, Cambria city, Morrellvile, Kernville and the Presbyterian Church.

At the latter place a remarkable state of affairs exists. The first floor has been washed out completely and the second, while submerged, was badly damaged, but not ruined. The walls, floors and pews were drenched, and the mud has collected on the matting and carpets an inch deep. Walking is attended with much difficulty, and the undertakers and attendants, with arms bared, slide about the slippery surface at a tremendous rate. The chancel is filled with coffins, strips of muslin, boards, and all undertaking accessories. Lying across the tops of the pews are a dozen pine boxes, each containing a victim of the flood. Printed cards are tacked on each. Upon them the sex and full description of the enclosed body is written with the name. if known.

THE NAMELESS DEAD

The great number of bodies not identified seems incredulous and impossible. Some of these bodies have lain in the different morgues for four days. Thousands of people from different sections of the State have seen them, yet they remain unidentified.

At Nineveh they are burying all the unidentified dead, but in the morgues in this vicinity no bodies have been buried unless they were identified.

The First Presbyterian Church contains nine "unknown." Burials will have to be made tomorrow. This morning workmen found three members of Benjamin Hoffman's family, which occupied a large residence in the rear of Lincoln street. Benjamin Hoffman, the head of the family, was found seated on the edge of the bedstead. He was evidently preparing to retire when the flood struck the building. He had his socks in his pocket. His twenty-year-old daughter was found close by attired in a night-dress. The youngest member of the family, a three-year-old infant, was also found beside the bed.

WHERE THE DEAD ARE LAID

I made a tour of the cemeteries today to see how the dead were disposed in their last resting place. There are six burying grounds, two to the south of this place, one to the north, and three on Morrellsville to the west. The principal one is Grand View, on the summit of Kernville Hill.

But the most remarkable, through the damage done by the flood, is Sandy Vale Cemetery, at Hornersville, on Stony Creek, and about half a mile from the city of Johnstown. Its grounds are level, laid out in lots, and were quite picturesque.

SNATCHED FROM THE FLOOD

One of the most thrilling incidents of narrow escapes is that told by Miss Minnie Chambers. She had been to see a friend in the morning and was returning to her home on Main street when the suddenly rising waters caused her to quicken her steps. Before she could reach her home or seek shelter at any point, the water had risen so high and the current became so strong that she was swept from her feet and carried along in the flood. Fortunately, her skirts served to support her on the surface for a time, but at last as they became soaked she gave up all hope of being saved.

Just as she was going under a box car that had been torn from its tracks floated past her and she managed by a desperate effort to get hold of it and crawled inside the open doorway. Here she remained, expecting every moment her shelter would be dashed to pieces by the buildings and other obstructions that it struck. Through the door she could see the mass of angry, swirling waters, filled with all manner of things that could be well imagined.

AN ARK OF REFUGE

Men, women and children, many of them dead and dying, were being whirled along. Several of them tried to get refuge in the car with her, but were torn away by the rushing waters before they could secure an entrance. Finally, a man did make his way into the car. On went the strange boat, while all about it seemed to be a perfect pandemonium. Shrieks and cries from the thousands outside who were being driven to their death filled the air.

Miss Chamber, says it was a scene that will haunt her as long as she lives. Many who floated by her could be seen kneeling on the wreckage that bore them, with clasped hands and upturned faces as though in prayer. Others wore a look of awful despair on their faces. Suddenly, as the car was turned around, the stone bridge could be seen just ahead of them. The man that was in the car called to her to jump out in the flood or she would be dashed to pieces. She refused to go.

He seized a plank and sprang into the water. In an instant the eddying current had torn the plank from him, and as it twisted around struck him on the head, causing him to throw out his arms and sink beneath the water never to reappear again. Miss Chambers covered her face to avoid seeing any more of the horrible sight, when with an awful crash the car struck one of the stone piers. The entire side of it was knocked out. As the car lodged against the pier the water rushed through it and carried Miss Chambers away. Again, she gave herself up as lost, when she felt herself knocked against an obstruction, and instinctively threw out her hand and clutched it.

Here she remained until the water subsided, when she found that she was on the roof of one of the Cambria mills, and had been saved by holding on to a pipe that came through the roof.

HAEL: NOT THE REAL ARK

Forgive me, but I must interrupt the 1889 author's story of Miss Chamber. The section title this author gives caught my eye. Did it catch yours? And then as you read the four paragraphs, did the contrast from Noah's ark strike you?

Surely, there were many people "whirled along" in the water with many trying "to take refuge" with Noah and his family, but all too late.

And praise the Lord, no one tried to exit Noah's Ark before God said to. And one more thing. Never did any of Noah's family have to "hold on for dear life," thinking that they should give themselves "up as lost."

Have you successfully trusted in the Ark, Jesus Christ as your Savior? Or are you clutching onto anything and everything but Him?

319

A Night of Agony

All through that awful night Miss Chamber remained there, almost freezing to death, and enveloped in a dense mass of smoke from the burning drift on the other side of the bridge. The cries of those being roasted to death were heard plainly by her. On Saturday some men succeeded in getting her from the perilous position she occupied and took her to the house of friends on Prospect Hill. Strange to say that with the exception of a few bruises she escaped without any other injuries.

Another survivor who told a pathetic story was John C. Peterson. He is a small man, but he was wearing clothes large enough for a giant. He lost his own and secured those he had on from friends.

"I'm the only one left," he said in a voice trembling with emotion. "My poor old mother, my sister, Mrs. Ann Walker, and her son David, aged fourteen, of Bedford county, who were visiting us, were swept away before my eyes and I was powerless to aid them.

"The water had been rising all day, and along in the afternoon flooded the first story of our house, at the corner of Twenty-eighth and Walnut streets. I was employed by Charles Mun as a cigarmaker, and early on Friday afternoon went home to move furniture and carpets to the second story of the house.

"As near as I can tell it was about four o'clock when the whistle at the Gautier Steel Mill blew. About the same time the Catholic church bell rang. I knew what that meant, and I turned to mother and sister and said, 'My God, we are lost!'"

Here's A Hero

"I looked out of the window and saw the flood, a wall of water thirty feet high, strike the steel works, and it melted quicker than I tell it. The man who stopped to blow the warning whistle must have been crushed to death by the falling roof and chimneys. He might have saved himself, but stopped to give the warning. He died a hero. Four minutes after the whistle blew the water was in our second story.

"We started to carry mother to the attic, but the water rose faster than we could climb the stairs. There was no window in our attic, and, we were bidding each other good-by when a tall chimney on the house adjoining fell on our roof and broke a hole through it. We then climbed out on the roof, and in another moment our house floated away. It started down with the other stuff, crashing, twisting and quivering. I thought every minute it would go to pieces.

"Finally, it was shoved over into water less swift and near another house.

"I found that less drift was forced against it than against ours, and decided to get on it. I climbed up on the roof, and in looking up saw a big house coming down directly toward ours, I called to sister to be quick. She was lifting mother up to me. I could barely reach the tips of her fingers when her arms were raised up while I lay on my stomach reaching down. At that moment the house struck ours and my loved ones were carried away and crushed by the big house. It was useless for me to follow, for they sank out of sight. I floated down to the bridge, then back with the current and landed at Vine street.

"I saw hundreds of people crushed and drowned. It is my opinion that fully fifteen thousand people perished."

When the whistles of the Gautier Steel Mill of the Cambria Iron Company blew for the shutting down of the works at 10 o'clock last Friday morning nearly 1400 men walked out of the establishment and went to their homes, which were a few hours later wiped off the face of the earth. When the men today answered the notice that all should present themselves ready for work only 487 reported. That shows more clearly than anything else that has yet been known the terrible nature of the fatality of the Conemaugh. The mortality wrought among these men in a few hours is thus shown to have been greater than that in either of the armies that contended for three days at Gettysburg.

"Report at 9 o'clock tomorrow morning ready for work," the notice posted read. It did not say where, but everybody knew it was not at the great Gautier Mill that covered half a dozen acres, for the reason that no mill is there. By a natural impulse the survivors of the working force of the steel plant began to move from all directions, before the hour named, toward the general office of the company.

What the Superintendent Saw

This office is located in Johnstown proper and is the only building in that section of the town left standing uninjured. It is a large brick building, three stories high, with massive brick walls. L. L. Smith, the commercial agent of the company, arrived at eight o'clock to await the gathering of the men, pausing a minute in the doorway to look at two things. One was an enormous pile of debris, bricks, iron girders and timbers almost in front of

321

the office door which swarmed with 200 men engaged in clearing it away. This is the ruins of the Johnstown Free Library, presented to the town by the Cambria Iron Company, the late I. V. Williamson and others, and beneath it Mr. Smith knew many of his most intimate friends were buried. The other thing he looked at was his handsome residence partly in ruins, a few hundred yards away. When he entered the office he found that the men who had been shoveling the mud out of the office had finished their work and the floor was dark and sticky. A fire blazed in the open grate. A table was quickly rigged up and with three clerks to assist him, Mr. Smith prepared to make up the roster of the Gautier forces.

THE SURVIVOR'S ADVANCE CORPS

Soon they began to come like the first reformed platoon of an army after fleeing from disaster. The leader of the platoon was a small boy. His hat was pulled down over his eyes and he looked as if he were sorely afraid. After him came half a dozen men with shambling gait. One was an Irishman, two were English, one was a German and one a negro. Two of them carried pickaxes in their hands, which they had been using to clear away the wreckage across the street.

"Say, mister," stammered the abashed small boy, "is this the place?"

"Are you a Gautier man?" asked Mr. Smith kindly.

"Yes sir, me and me father, but he's gone."

"Give us your name, my boy, and report at the lower works at 4 o'clock. Now, my men, we want to get to work and pull each other out of the hole, this dreadful calamity has put us in. It's no use having vain regrets. It's all over and we must put a good face to the front. At first it was intended that we should go up to the former site of the Gautier Mill and clean up and get out all the steel we could. Mr. Stackhouse now wants us to get to work and clear the way from the lower mills right up the valley. We will rebuild the bridge back of the office here and push the railroad clear up to where it was before."

NOT ANXIOUS TO TURN IN

The men listened attentively, and then one of them asked: "But, Mr. Smith, if we don't feel just like turning in today we don't have to, do we?'

"Nobody will have to work at all," was the answer, "but we do want all the men to lend a hand to help us out as soon as they can."

While Mr. Smith was speaking several other workmen came in. They, too, were Gautier employees, and they had pickaxes on their shoulders. They heard the agent's last remark, and one of them, stepping forward, said: "A good many of us are working cleaning up the town. Do you want us to leave that?"

"It isn't necessary for you to work cleaning up the town," was the reply. "There are plenty of people from the outside to do that who came here for that purpose. Now, boys, just give your names so we can find out how many of our men are left, and all of you that can, go down and report at the lower office."

All the time the members of the decimated Gautier army were filing into the muddy-floored office. They came in twos and threes and dozens, and some bore out the idea of an army reforming after disaster, because they bore grievous wounds. One man had a deep cut in the back of his head, another limped along on a heavy stick, one had lost a finger and had an ugly bruise on his cheek. J. N. Short, who was the foreman of the cold-rolled steel shafting department, sat in the office, and many of the men who filed past had been under him in the works.

Mutual Congratulations

There were handshakes all the more hearty and congratulations all the more sincere because of what all had passed through. When the wall of water seventy-five feet high struck the mill and whipped it away like shot Mr. Short was safe on higher ground, but many of the men had feared he was lost.

"I tell you, Mr. Short," said J. T. Miller, "I'm glad to see you're safe. ·

"And how did you make out, old man?" "All right, thank God."

Then came another man bolder than all and apparently a general favorite. He rushed forward and shook Mr. Smith's hand. "Mr. Smith," he exclaimed, "good morning, good morning."

"So, you got out of it, did you, after all?" asked Mr. Smith.

"Indeed, I did, but Lord bless my soul, I thought the wife and babies were gone." The man gave his name and hurried away, brushing a tear from his eye.

Mr. Shellenberger, one of the foremen, brought up the rear of the next platoon to enter. He caught sight of Mr. Smith and shouted: "Oh, Mr. Smith, good for you. I'm glad to see you safe."

"Here to you, my hearty," was the answer. "Did you all get off?"

"Every blessed one of us," with a bright smile. "We were too high on the hill."

He was Tired of Johnstown

A little bit later another man came in. He looked as if he had been weeping. He hesitated in front of the desk, "I am a Gautier employee," he said, speaking slowly, "and I have reported according to orders."

"Well, give us your name and go to work down at the lower works," suggested Mr. Smith.

"No, sir, I think not," he muttered, after a pause. "I am not staying in this town any longer than I can help, I guess. I've lost two children and they will be buried today."

"All right, my man, but if you want work we have plenty of it for you."

The reporting of names and these quiet mutual congratulations of the men went on rapidly, but expected faces did not appear. This led Mr. Smith to ask, "How about George Thompson? Is he alive?"

"I do not know," answered the man addressed. "I do not think so."

"Who do you know are alive?" asked Mr. Smith, turning to another man. Mr. Smith never once asked who was dead.

"Well," answered the man speaking reflectively, "I'm pretty sure Frank Smith is alive. John Dagdale is alive. Tom Sweet is alive, and I don't know any more, for I've been away at Nineveh." The speaker had been at Nineveh looking for the body of his son. Not another word was said to him.

"Say, boys," exclaimed Mr. Smith suddenly, a few minutes after he had looked over the list, "Pullman hasn't reported yet."

"But Pullman's all right," said a man quickly, "I was up at his sister's house last night and he was there. That's more than I can say of the other men in Pullman's shift though," added the speaker in a low tone. Mr. Short took this man aside, "That is a fact," said he, "yesterday I knew of a family in which five out of six were lost. Today I find out there were twenty people in the house mostly our men and only three escaped."

Each Thought the Other Dead

Just then two men met at the door and fairly fell on each other's necks. One wore a Grand Army badge and the other was a young fellow of twenty-three or thereabouts. They had been fast friends in the same department, and each thought the other dead. They knew no better till they met at the office door. "Well, I heard your body had been found at Nineveh," said the old man.

"And I was told you had been burned to death at the bridge," answered the other. Then the two men solemnly shook hands and walked away together.

A pale-faced woman with a shawl over her shoulders entered and stood at the table. "My husband cannot report," she said simply, in almost a whisper.

"He worked for the Gautier Mill?" she was asked. She nodded, bent forward and murmured something. The man at the desk said: "Make a note of that; so-and-so's wife reports him as gone, and his wages due are to be paid to her."

The work of recording the men went on until nearly one o'clock. Then, after waiting for a long time, Mr. Smith said, "Out of 1400 men we now have 487. It may be there are 200 who either did not see the notice or who are too busy to come. Anyway, I hope so, my God, I hope so." All afternoon the greater part of the 487 men were swinging pickaxes and shovels, clearing the way for the railroad leading up to the Gautier Steel Works of the future.

Remembering the Orphans

Miss H. W. Hinckley and Miss E. Hanover, agents of the Children's Aid Society and Bureau of Information of Philadelphia, arrived here this morning, and in twenty minutes had established a transfer agency. Miss Hinckley said, "There are hundreds of children here who are apparently without parents. We want all of them given to us, and we will send them to the various homes and orphanages of the State, where they shall be maintained for several months to await the possibility of the reappearance of their parents when they will be returned to them. If after the lapse of a month they do not reclaim their little ones, we shall do more than we ordinarily do in the way of providing good homes for children in their cases. Think of it, in the house adjoining us are seven orphans, all of one family. We have been here only a half hour, but we have already found scores. We shall stay right here till every child has been provided for."

THE WOMEN AND CHILDREN

New Johnstown will be largely a city of childless widowers. One of the peculiar things a stranger notices is the comparatively small number of women seen in the streets. Of the throngs who walked about the place searching for dear friends there is not one woman to ten men. Occasionally a little group of two or three women with sad faces will pick their way about looking for the morgues. There are a few Sisters of Charity, their black robes the only instance in which the conventional badge of mourning is seen upon the streets, and in the parts of the town not totally destroyed the usual number of women are seen in the houses and yards.

But, as a rule, women are a rarity in Johnstown now. This is not a natural peculiarity of Johnstown nor a mere coincidence, but a fact with a terrible reason behind it. There are so many more men than women among the living in Johnstown now because there are so many more women than men among the dead. Of the bodies recovered there are at least two women to every one man. Besides the fact that their natural weakness made them an easier prey to the flood, the hour at which the disaster came was one when the women would most likely be in their homes and the men at work in the open air or in factory yards, from which escape was easy.

AN ALMOST CHILDLESS CITY

Children also are rarely seen about the town and for a similar reason. They are all dead. There is never a group of the dead discovered that does not contain from one to three or four children for every grown person. Generally, the children are in the arms of the grown persons, and often little toys and trinkets clasped in their hands indicate that the children were caught up while at play and carried as far as possible toward safety.

Johnstown, when rebuilt, will be a city of many widowers and few children. In turning a schoolhouse into a morgue, the authorities probably did a wiser thing than they thought. It will be a long time before the schoolhouse will be needed for its original purpose.

THE FLOOD ON THE FLAT

The flood, with a front of twenty feet high, bristling with all manner of debris, struck straight across the flat, as though the river's course had always been that way. It cut off the outer two-thirds of the city with a line as true and straight as could have been drawn by a survey. On the part over which it swept there remains standing but one building, the brewery. With this exception, not only the houses and stores, but the pavements, sidewalks and curbstones, and the earth beneath for several feet are washed away. The pavements were of cinders from the Iron Works, a bed six inches thick and as hard as stone and with a surface like macadam. Over west of the washed-out portion of the city not even the broken fragments of these pavements are left.

Aside from the few logs and timbers left by the after-wash of the flood, there is nothing remaining upon the outer edge of the flat, including two of the four long streets of the city, except the brewery mentioned before and a grand piano. The water-marks on the brewery walls show the flood reached twenty feet up its sides and it stood on a little higher ground than buildings around it at that.

HAEL: THE FURY OF ONE DAM

Imagine for a moment the fury that our 1889 author has so vividly described all throughout this book. Remember that this fury came from a relatively small dam.

Now compare that to the Grand Canyon in the United States. Something that we in heaven have known for quite a while is finally being admitted by your old earth and young earth scientists. The Grand Canyon was not made over a long period of time, but rather, "a lot of water over a short period of time."

Water from Noah's flood dammed up and dammed up until it burst sometime after the 40 days of rain ended.[1]

FIRST STORE OPENED

The first store was opened today by a grocer named W. A. Kramer, whose stock, though covered with mud and still wet from the flood, has been preserved intact. So far, the greater part of his things have been bought for relics. The other storekeepers are dragging out the debris in their shops

---

[1] So no sooner had these leftover Flood waters been dammed than they would have begun to find and exploit weaknesses in the limestone and other layers making up the plateau.

Whether it happened as the Flood year ended, or soon thereafter, the lakes would have soon breached their dams, washing over the plateau and exploiting any channels already there, rapidly carving through the plateau resulting in a deep canyon very similar to what we see today (https://answersingenesis.org/geology/grand-canyon-facts/when-and-how-did-the-grand-canyon-form/)

and shoveling the mud from the upper stories upon inclined boards that shoot it into the street, but with all this energy it will be weeks before the streets are brought to sight again.

As a proof of this, there was found this morning a passenger car fully half a mile from its depot, completely buried beneath the floor and roofs of other houses. All that could be seen of it by peering through intercepting rafters was one of the end windows over which was painted the impotent warning of "Any person injuring this car will be dealt with according to law."

CURIOUS FINDS OF WORKMEN

The workmen find many curious things among the ruins, and are, it should be said to their credit, particularly punctilious about leaving them alone. One man picked up a baseball catcher's mask under a great pile of machinery, and the decorated front of the balcony circle of the Opera House was found with the chairs still immediately about its semicircle, a quarter of a mile from the theatre's site.

The mahogany bar of a saloon, with its nickel-plated rail, lies under another heap in the city park, and thousands of cigars from a manufactory are piled high in Vine street, and are used as the only dry part of the roadway. Those of the people who can locate their homes have gathered what furniture and ornaments they can find together, and sit beside them looking like evicted tenants.

The Grand Army of the Republic, represented by Department Commander Thomas J. Stewart, have placed a couple of tents at the head of Main street for the distribution of food and clothing. A census of the people will be taken, and the city divided into districts, each worthy applicant will be furnished with a ticket giving his or her number and the number of the district.

THE TALE THE CLOCKS TELL

The clocks of the city in both public and private houses tell different tales of the torrent that stopped them. Some of them ceased to tick the moment the water reached them. In Dibert's banking-house the marble time-piece on the mantel stopped at seven minutes after 4 o'clock. In the house of the Hon. John M. Rose, on the bank of Stony Creek, was a clock in every room of the mansion from the cellar to the attic. Mr. Rose is a fine machinist, and the mechanism of clocks has a fascination for him that is simply irresistible. He has bronze, marble, cuckoo, corner or "grandfather" clocks-all in his house. One of them was stopped exactly at 4 o'clock; still another at 4:10, another at 4:15, and one was not stopped till 9 P. M. The "grandfather" clock did not stop at all, and is still going.

The town clocks, that is the clocks in church towers, are all going and were not injured by the water. The mantel piece clocks in nearly every house show a "no tick" at times ranging from 3:40 to 4:15.

DEATH IN THE JAIL.

This morning a man, in wandering through the skirts of the city, came upon the city jail, and finding the outer door open, went into the gloomy structure. Hanging against the wall he found a bunch of keys and fitting them in the doors opened them one after another. In one cell he found a man lying on the floor in the mud in a condition of partial decomposition. He looked more closely at the dead body and recognized it as that of John McKee, son of Squire McKee, of this city, who had been committed for a short term on Decoration Day for drunkenness. The condition of the cell showed that the man had been overpowered and smothered by the water, but not till he had made every effort that the limits of his cell would allow to save himself. There were no other prisoners in the jail.

ONLY FIFTY SAVED AT WOODVILLE

The number of people missing from Woodville is almost incredible, and from present indications it looks as if only about fifty people in the borough were saved. Mrs. H. L. Peterson, who has been a resident at Woodville for a number of years, is one of the survivors. While looking for Miss Paulsen, of Pittsburg, of the drowned, she came to a coffin which was marked "Mrs. H. L. Peterson, Woodville Borough, PA., age about forty, size five feet one inch. complexion dark, weight about two hundred pounds." This was quite an accurate description of Mrs. Peterson. She tore the card from the coffin and one of the officers was about to arrest her. Her explanations were satisfactory, and she was released.

In speaking of the calamity afterward she said, "The people of Woodville had plenty of time to get out of the town if they were so minded. We received word shortly before two o'clock that the flood was coming, and a Pennsylvania Railroad conductor went through the town notifying the people. I stayed until half-past three o'clock, when the water commenced to rise very rapidly, and I thought it was best to get out of town. I told a number of women that they had better go to the hills, but they refused, and the cause of this refusal was that their husbands would not go with them and they refused to leave alone."

HAEL: GOD WILL FIX THIS

". . . but not the way you expect."

As was stated above, the townspeople had plenty of time to get out had they chosen to.

I have had the opportunity to be a Guardian Angel for men and women that are strong, fervent, and bold pray-ers. And yet, I often see an arrogance that begins to make its way to the surface. This is not an absolute statement, merely an observation from the last 6,000 years or so.

Clyde Smith and his wife Stella were in their upper seventies on that fateful day. In reasonable health, they spent much time working in their garden and tending their chickens. Every afternoon at 1:30, after they put the supper dishes away, they would commence together to read the Word, sing and read a few hymns, and then pray for their friends and family and whatever else seemed to be on their heart.

Upon hearing the news of the oncoming flood, Bro. Clyde and his wife didn't move. They had heard these warnings for years, and even when the dam did break it never caused any real damage. So instead of moving to higher ground the couple continued to sit in their comfortable living room, looking out their front windows. The fire in the grate was nice and toasty, and besides they were having a hallelujah time praying for their family.

They didn't realize it but the Holy Spirit had laid their entire family on their heart to pray for, one last time. As they lifted up each family member they did what Bro. Clyde had been calling "conversational prayer," where he or his wife would bring up a family member and pray about only one thing for them and then pause, and the other person would pray along the same subject for that family member until they exhausted the items on their heart for that person. Then one of them would bring up another relative.

They would pray this way for each family member.

Their Bibles were always open, and one would hear the rustling of pages while they prayed. Sis. Stella listened to her husband pray for their son, Clyde Jr. and their daughter-in-law, Maggie, who had moved to California last summer to do missionary work with the Central Sierra Miwoks, who lived along the drainage area of the Tuolumne and Stanislaus Rivers in the great Central Valley.

As he prayed, Sis. Stella noted that Clyde did not talk to God about visiting them next summer as he always did. She thought this while they were taking their usual 3:30 coffee break. When they returned to the living room she would ask him about not praying for their trip to California which they planned to make next summer.

As her husband stayed by the fire, he found himself in Psalm 123. His eyes fastened upon verse one and the end of verse two, "I lift my eyes to You, the One enthroned in heaven. . . until He shows us favor."

Taking his Bible to the kitchen where Stella stirred a little extra sugar into his coffee, Bro. Clyde smiled at his wife's thoughtfulness and started to read this passage to her when they heard this strange grating sound. It began as a low rumble, but within seconds it quickly grew into what sounded like continuous thunder rolling towards them. Their home started to shake, and they lifted their eyes to look out the back window above the sink.

They both noticed the mountain of debris at the same time. It seemed to be taller than the houses behind them. They were already hugging each other, but just then Clyde felt Stella squeeze him, digging her fingertips into his arm. To not fall down in the rumbling shaking home, they knelt down holding onto the drain board.

By this time the debris wave was above them and as it crashed atop them Stella heard Clyde gently say, "Show us favor."

Our wings were already around them, and the next thing she noticed was that she and Clyde were being carried to heaven where Jesus stood welcoming them.

Excited, they both stood there in the great hall of heaven where they saw family members who had preceded them to heaven. They were in the company of a great cloud of witnesses.[1] But there was a good looking young man among them whom neither of them recognized. He looked somewhat familiar but they both looked at each other with the same unasked question, "which relative is this?"

He noticed their questioning looks and moved forward to hug them and said, "I'm your grandson." And he then paused, some tears began to form in their eyes, and he continued. "I'm Clyde III. My mother gave birth to me a few months after they arrived in California, but shortly after child-birth I arrived here. I don't think they told you for they did not want to worry you."

Clyde put his arms around his grandson, and pulling his wife towards them he simply said, "Thank You, Lord, for the favor You have shown us."

---

[1] Hebrews 12:1

As their eyes teared up again, the Lord did not wipe those wonderful tears away, for they were tears of joy.

TERRIFIC EXPERIENCE OF A PULLMAN CONDUCTOR

Mr. John Barr, the conductor of the Pullman car on the Day Express train that left Pittsburgh at eight o'clock, May 31, gave an account of his experience in the Conemaugh Valley flood, "I was the last one saved on the train," he said. "When the train arrived at Johnstown last Friday, the water was up to the second story of the houses and people were going about in boats. We went on to Conemaugh and had to halt there, as the water had submerged the tracks and a part of the bridge had been washed away. Two sections of the Day Express were run up to the most elevated point.

"About four o'clock I was standing at the buffet when the whistle began blowing a continuous blast, the relief signal. I went out and saw what appeared to be a huge moving mountain rushing rapidly toward us. It seemed to be surmounted by a tall cloud of foam.

SOUNDING THE ALARM

"I ran into the car and shouted to the passengers, 'For God's sake follow me! Stop for nothing!'

"They all dashed out except two. Miss Paulsen and Miss Bryan left the car, but returned for their overshoes. They put them on, and as they again stepped from the car they were caught by the mighty wave and swept away. Had they remained in the car they would have been saved, as two passengers who stayed there escaped.

"One was Miss Virginia Maloney, a courageous, self-possessed young woman. She tied securely about her neck a plush bag, so that her identity could be established if she perished. Imprisoned in the car with her was a maid employed by Mrs. McCullough. They attempted to leave the car, but the water drove them back. They remained there until John Waugh, the porter, and I waded through the water and rescued them.

"The only passengers I lost were the two unfortunate young ladies I have named. I looked at the corpses of the luckless victims brought in during the two days I remained in Johnstown, but the bodies of the two passengers were not among them.

"At Conemaugh the people were extremely kind and hospitable. They threw open their doors and provided us with a share of what little food they had and gave us shelter.

STRIPPED OF HER CLOTHING.

While at Conemaugh, Miss Wayne, of Altoona, who had a miraculous escape, was brought in. She was nude, every article of her clothing having been torn from her by the furious flood. There was no female apparel at hand, and she had to don trousers, coat, vest and hat.

"We had a severe task in reaching Ebensburg," she told everyone. "We were eighteen miles from Conemaugh. We started on Sunday and were nine hours in reaching our destination. At Ebensburg we boarded the train which conveyed us to Altoona, where we were cared for at the expense of the Pennsylvania Railroad Company.

"I had a rough siege. I was in the water twelve hours. The force of the flood can be imagined by the fact that seven or eight locomotives were carried away and floated on the top of the angry stream as if they were tiny chips."

CHAPTER XV
Stories of the Flood

War, death, cataclysm like this, America,
Take deep to thy proud, prosperous heart.

E'en as I chant, lo! out of death, and out of ooze and slime.
The blossoms rapidly blooming, sympathy, help, love,
From west and east, from south and north and over sea,
Its hot spurr'd hearts and hands humanity to human aid moves on;
And from within a thought and lesson yet.

Thou ever-darting globe! thou Earth and Air!
Thou waters that encompass us!
Thou that in all the life and death of us, in action or in sleep.
Thou laws invisible that permeate them and all!
Thou that in all and over all, and through and under all, incessant!
Thou! thou! the vital, universal, giant force resistless, sleepless, calm,
Holding Humanity as in the open hand, as some ephemeral toy,
How ill to e'er forget thee!

---- Walt Whitman ----

HAEL: POETRY

The 1889 author included this Walt Whitman poem in his original work, and I chose to leave it, but my friends, make no mistake, Mr. Whitman was not talking about our Creator as the "giant force. . . holding humanity."

I'm not saying anything negative about this celebrated writer and poet, I just want you to see where his, and presumably the 1889 author's hope is. As humanists their hope is not in the God that I am reminding you of. As I write these anecdotal stories, giving you a behind the scenes look at this tragedy, the Johnstown flood, I hope you are seeing the God of all comfort.[1]

---

[1] 2 Corinthians 1:3e

STORIES OF THE FLOOD

"Are the horrors of the flood to give way to the terrors of the plague?" is the question that is now agitating the valley of the Conemaugh. Today opened warm and almost sultry, and the stench that assails one's senses as he wanders through Johnstown is almost overpowering. Sickness, in spite of the precautions and herculean labors of the sanitary authorities, is on the increase and the fears of an epidemic grow with every hour.

"It is our impression," said Dr. T. L. White, assistant to the State Board of Health, this morning, "that there is going to be great sickness here within the next week. Five cases of malignant diphtheria were located this morning on Bedford street, and as they were in different houses they mean five starting points for disease. All this talk about the dangers of epidemic is not exaggerated, as many suppose, but is founded upon all experience. There will be plenty of typhoid fever and kindred diseases here within a week or ten days in my opinion. The only thing that has saved us thus far has been the cool weather. That has now given place to summer weather, and no one knows what the next few days may bring forth.

FRESH MEAT AND VEGETABLES WANTED

Even among the workmen there is already discernible a tendency to diarrhea and dysentery. The men are living principally upon salt meat, and there is a lack of vegetables. I have been here since Sunday and have tasted fresh meat but once since that time. I am only one of the many. Of course, the worst has passed for the physicians, as our arrangements are now perfected, and each corps will be relieved from time to time. Twenty more physicians arrived from Pittsburgh this morning and many of us will be relieved today. But the opinion is general among the medical men that there will be more need for doctors in a week hence than there is now.

SANITARY WORK

Dr. R. L. Sibbel, of the State Board of Health, is in charge of Sanitary Headquarters. "We are using every precaution known to science," said he this morning, "to prevent the possibility of epidemic. Our labors here have not been confined to any particular channel, but have been extended in various directions. Disinfectants, of course, are first in importance, and they have been used with no sparing hand. The prompt cremation of dead animals as fast as discovered is another thing we have insisted upon. The immediate erection of water-closets [toilets] throughout the ruins for the workmen was another work of the greatest sanitary importance that has been attended to. They! too, are being disinfected at frequent intervals. We have a committee, too, that superintends the burial of the victims at the cemeteries. It is of the utmost importance in this wholesale interment that the corpses should be interred a safe distance beneath the surface in order that their poisonous emanations may not find exit through the crevices of the earth.

"Another committee is making a house-to-house inspection throughout the stricken city to ascertain the number of inhabitants in each standing house, the number of the sick, and to order the latter to the hospital whenever necessary. One great danger is the overcrowding of houses and hovels, and that is being prevented as much as possible by the free use of tents upon the mountain side. So far there is but little contagious disease, and we hope by diligent and systematic efforts to prevent any dangerous outbreak."

DODGING RESPONSIBILITY

It is now rumored that the South Fork Hunting and Fishing Club is a thing of the past. No one admits his membership and it is doubtful if outside the cottage owners one could find more than half a dozen members in the city. Even some of the cottage owners will repudiate their ownership until it is known whether or not legal action will be taken against them. If it were not for the publicity which might follow one could secure a transfer of a large number of shares of the club's stock to himself, accompanied by a good-sized roll of money. It is certain that the cottage owners cannot repudiate their ownership. None of them, however, will occupy the houses this summer.

THE CLUB FOUND GUILTY

Coroner Hammer, of Westmoreland county, who has been sitting on the dead found down the river at Nineveh, concluded his inquests today. His trip to South Fork Dam on Wednesday has convinced him that the burden of this great disaster rests on the shoulders of the South Fork Hunting and Fishing Club of Pittsburgh. The verdict was written tonight, but not all the jury were ready to sign it. It finds the South Fork Hunting and Fishing Club responsible for the loss of life because of gross, if not criminal negligence, and of carelessness in making repairs from time to time. This would let the Pennsylvania Railroad Company out from all blame for allowing the dam to fall so badly out of repair when they got control of the

Pennsylvania Canal and abandoned it. The verdict is what might have been expected after Wednesday's testimony.

THE WORK CONTINUES

Six thousand men were at work on the ruins today. They are paid two dollars a day, and have to earn it. The work seems to tell very little, however, for the mass of debris is simply enormous. The gangs have cleaned up the streets pretty thoroughly in the main part of the city, from which the brick blocks were swept like card houses before a breeze. The houses are pulled apart and burned in bonfires. Nowhere is anything found worth saving.

It is not probable that the mass of debris at the bridge, by which the water is tainted, can be removed in less than thirty days with the greatest force possible to work on it. That particular job is under the control of the State Board of Health. Every day adds to its seriousness. The mass is being cleared by dynamite at the bridge where the current is strongest, and the open place slowly grows larger. Not infrequently a body is found after an explosion has loosened the wreckage.

So called relief corps are still moving to and fro in the city, but the most serious labor of many of the members is to carry a bright yellow badge to aid them in passing the guards while sight-seeing. The militia men are little better than ornamental. The guards do a good deal of changing, to the annoyance of workers who want to get into the lines, but they rarely stop anyone. The soldiers do a vast deal of loafing. A photographer who had his camera ready to take a view among the ruins was arrested today and made to work for an hour by General Hastings' order. When his stent was done he did not linger, but went at once.

SIGNS OF IMPROVEMENT

"What is the condition of the valley now?" I asked Colonel Scott.   ·

"It is improving with every hour. The perfect organization which has been effected within the past day or two has gradually resolved all the chaos and confusion into a semblance of order and regulation."

"Are many bodies being discovered now?"

"Very few; that is to say, comparatively few. Of course, as the waters recede more and more between the banks, we have come upon bodies here and there, as they were exposed to sight. The probabilities are that there will be a great many bodies yet discovered under the rubbish that covers the streets, and our hope and expectation is that the majority of all the dead may be recovered and disposed of in a Christian manner."

"How about the movement to burn the rubbish, bodies and all?"

"I do not think that will be done, at least only as a last extremity. While there is great anxiety in regard to the sanitary condition, all possible precautions are being taken, and we hope to prevent any disease until we shall have time to thoroughly overhaul the wreck."

CONSIDERATION FOR THE DEAD.

"The greatest consideration is being given to this matter of the recovery of the dead and treatment of the bodies after discovery. I think an impression has gone abroad that the dead are being handled here very much as one would handle cord wood, but this is a great mistake. As soon as possible after discovery they are borne from public gaze and taken to the Morgue, where only persons who have lost relatives or friends are admitted. Of course, the general exclusion is not applied to attendants, physicians and representatives of the press, but it is righteously applied to careless sight-seers. We have no room for sight-seers in Johnstown now. It is earnest workers and laborers we want, and of these we can hardly have too many."

SPECULATING IN DISASTER

Some long-headed men are trying to make a neat little stake quietly out of the disaster. A syndicate has been formed to buy up as much real estate as possible in Johnstown, trusting to get a big block as they got one today, for one-third of the valuation placed on it a week ago. The members of the syndicate are keeping very much in the background and conducting their business through a local agent.

I asked Adjutant General Hastings today what he thought of the situation.

"It is very good so far as reported," was the reply. "Bodies are being gradually recovered all the time, but of course not in the large number of the first few days. Last night we arrested several ghouls that were wandering amid the wreck on evil intent, and they were promptly taken to the guard house. This morning they were given the choice of imprisonment or going to work at two dollars a day, and they promptly chose the latter. We are getting along very well in our work, and very little tendency to lawlessness, I am happy to say, is observed."

Succor for the Living

The Red Cross flag now flies over the society's own camp beside the Baltimore and Ohio tracks, near the bridge to Kernville. The tents were pitched this morning and the camp includes a large supply tent, mess tent and offices. Miss Clara Barton, of Washington, is, of course, in charge, and the work is being rapidly gotten into shape. I found Miss Barton at the camp this morning.

"The Red Cross Society will remain here," she said, "so long as there is any work to do. There is hardly any limit to what we will do. Much of the present assistance that has been extended is, of course, impulsive and ephemeral. When that is over there will still be work to do, and the Red Cross Society will be here to do it. We are always the last to leave the field.

"We need and can use to the greatest advantage all kinds of supplies, and shall be glad to receive them. Money is practically useless here as there is no place to buy what we need."

Dr. J. Wilkes O'Neill, of Philadelphia, surgeon of the First Regiment, is here in charge of the Philadelphia division of the Red Cross Society. He is assisted by a corps of physicians, nurses and attendants. Within two hours after establishing the camp this morning about forty cases, both surgical and medical, were treated. Diphtheria broke out in Kernville today. Eleven cases were reported, eight of which were reported to be malignant. The epidemic is sure to extend. There are also cases of ulcerated tonsillitis. The patients are mostly those left homeless by the flood and are fairly well situated in frame houses. The doctors do not fear an epidemic of pneumonia. The Red Cross Society has established a hospital camp in Grubbtown for the treatment of contagious diseases. An epidemic of typhoid fever is feared, two cases having appeared. The camp is well located in a pleasant spot near fine water. It is supplied with cots, ambulances and some stores. They have an ample supply of surgical stores, but need medical stores badly.

Serving Out the Rations

At the commissary station at the Pennsylvania Railroad depot there was considerable activity. A crowd of about one thousand people had gathered about the place after the day's rations. The crowd became so great that the soldiers had to be called up to guard the place until the Relief Committee was ready to give out the provisions. Several carloads of clothing arrived this morning and was to be disposed of as soon as possible. The people were badly in need of clothing, as the weather had been very chilly since Saturday.

B. F. Minnimun, a wealthy contractor of Springfield, Ohio, arrived this forenoon with a dispatch from Governor Foraker offering 2,000 trained laborers for Johnstown, to be sent at once if needed. The dispatch, further stated that if anything else was needed Ohio stood ready to respond promptly to the call.

WHAT CLARA BARTON SAID

"It is like a blow on the head, there are no tears, they are stunned, but, ah, sir, I tell you they will awake after a while and then the tears will flow down the hills of this valley from thousands of bleeding hearts, and there will be weeping and wailing such as never before."

That is what Clara Barton, president of the National Red Cross, said this afternoon as she stood, in a plain black gown on the bank of Stony Creek directing the construction of the Red Cross tents, and she looked motherly and matronly, while her voice was trembling with sympathy.

"You see nothing but that dazed, sickly smile that calamity leaves," she went on, "like the crazy man wears when you ask him, 'How came you here?' 'Something happened,' he says, and that he alone knows, all the rest is blank to him. Here they give you that smile, that look and say 'I lost my father, my mother, my sisters,' but they do not realize it yet. The Red Cross intends to be here in the Conemaugh Valley when the pestilence comes to them, and we are making ready with all our heart, with all our soul, with all our strength. The militia, the railroad, the Relief Committees and everybody is working for us. The railroad has completely barricaded us so that none of our cars can be taken away by mistake."

When the great wave of death swept through Johnstown the people who had any chance of escape ran hither and thither in every direction. They did not have any definite idea where they were going, only that a crest of foaming waters as high as the housetops was roaring down upon them through the Conemaugh and that they must get out of the way of that. Some in their terror dived into the cellars of their houses and clambered over the adjoining roofs to places of safety. But the majority made for the hills, which girt the town like giants. Of the people who went to the hills, the water caught some in its whirl.

The others clung to trees and roots and pieces of debris which had temporarily lodged near the banks, and managed to save themselves. These people either stayed out on the hills wet, and in many instances walked all night, or they managed to find farmhouses which sheltered them. There was a fear of going back to the vicinity of the town. Even the people whose houses the water did not reach abandoned their homes and began to think of all of Johnstown as a city buried beneath the water. But in the houses which were thus able to afford shelter there was not food enough for all. Many survivors of the flood went hungry until the first relief supplies arrived from Pittsburgh.

STRUGGLING TO LIFE AGAIN

From all this fright, destitution and exposure is coming a nervous shock, culminating in insanity, pneumonia, fever and all the other forms of disease. When these people came back to Johnstown on the day after the wreck of the town they had to live in sheds, barns and in houses which had been but partially ruined. They had to sleep without any covering, in their wet clothes, and it took the liveliest kind of skirmishing to get anything to eat. Pretty soon a citizen's committee was established, and nearly all the male survivors of the flood were immediately sworn in as deputy sheriffs. They adorned themselves with tin stars, which they cut out of pieces of the sheets of metal in the ruins, and pieces of tin with stars cut out of them are now turning up continually, to the surprise of the Pittsburgh workmen who are endeavoring to get the town in shape.

The women and children were housed, so far as possible, in the few houses still standing, and some idea of the extent of the wreck of the town may be gathered from the fact that of 300 prominent buildings only 16 are uninjured. For the first day or so people were dazed by what had happened, and for that matter they are dazed still. They went about helpless, making vague inquiries for their friends, and hardly feeling the desire to eat anything. Finally, the need of creature comforts overpowered them, and they woke up to the fact that they were faint and sick.

REFUGEES IN THEIR OWN CITY

Now this is to some extent changed by the arrival of tents and by the systematic military care for the suffering. But the daily life of a Johnstown man who is a refugee in his own city is still aimless and wandering. His property, his home, in nine cases out of ten, his wife and children, are gone. The chances are that he has hard work to find the spot where he and his family once lived and were happy. He meditates on suicide, and even looks on the strangers who have flocked in to help him and to put him and his town on their feet again with a kind of sullen anger. He has frequent conflictswith the soldiers and with the sightseers, and he is crazy enough to do almost anything.

The first thing that Johnstown people do in the morning is to go to the relief stations and get something to eat. They go carrying big baskets, and their endeavor is to get all they can. There has been a new system every day about the manner of dispensing the food and clothing to the sufferers. At first the supplies were placed where people could help themselves. Then they were placed in yards and handed to people over the fences. Then people had to get orders for what they wanted from the citizens' committee and their orders were filled at the different relief stations. Now the matter has been arranged this way, and probably finally. The whole matter of receiving and dispensing the relief supplies has been placed in the hands of the Grand Army of the Republic men.

WOMEN TOO PROUD TO BEG

The Grand Army men have made the Adams Street Relief Station a central relief station and all the others at Kernville, the Pennsylvania depot, Cambria City and Jackson and Somerset Streets, substations. The idea is to distribute supplies to the substations from the central station and thus avoid the jam of crying and excited people at the committee's headquarters. The Grand Army men have appointed a committee of women to assist in their work. The women go from house to house ascertaining the number of people lost from there in the flood and the exact needs of the people. It was found necessary to have some such committee as this, for there were women actually starving who were too proud to take their places in lines with the other women with bags and baskets. Some of these people were rich before the flood.

Now they are not worth a dollar. One man who was reported to be worth $100,000 before the flood now is penniless and has to take his place in the line along with others seeking the necessaries of life.

Though the Adams street station is now the central relief station, the most imposing display of supplies is made at the Pennsylvania Railroad freight and passenger depots. Here on the platform and in the yards, are piled up barrels of flour in long rows three and four barrels high. Biscuits in cans and boxes by the carload, crackers under the railroad sheds in bins, hams by the hundred strung on poles, boxes of soap and candles, barrels of kerosene oil, stacks of canned goods and things to eat of all sorts and kinds are here to be seen.

No Fear of a Food Famine

The same sight is visible at the Baltimore and Ohio Railroad and there is now no fear of a food famine in Johnstown, though of course everybody will have to rough it for weeks. What is needed most in this line are cooking utensils. Johnstown people want stoves, kettles, pans, knives and forks. All the things that have been sent so far have been sent with the evident idea of supplying an instant need, and that is right and proper. But it would be well now if instead of some of the provisions that are sent, cooking utensils should arrive. Fifty stoves arrived from Pittsburgh this morning, and it is said more are coming. At both the depots where the supplies are received and stored a big rope line encloses them in an impromptu yard so as to give room to those having the supplies in charge to walk around and see what they have got. On the inside of this line, too, stalk back and forth the soldiers with their rifles on their shoulders, and by the side of the lines pressing against the ropes there stands every day from daylight until dawn a crowd of women with big baskets who make piteous appeals to the soldiers to give them food for their children at once before the order of the relief committee.

Where Death Rules

The following letters from a young woman to her mother, written immediately after the disaster at Johnstown from her home in New Florence, a few miles west of that place, though not intended for publication, picture in graphic manner the agony of suspense sustained by those who escaped the flood, and give side pictures of the scenes following the disaster. They were received in Philadelphia:

Hours of Suspense
New Florence, PA

> My Darling Mother: I am nearly crazed, and thought I would try and be quiet and write to you, as it always comforts me to feel you are near your child, though many miles are now between us. I have said my prayers over and over again all day long, and tonight I am going to spend in the watch-tower, and am trying to be quiet and brave, although my heart is just wrung with anguish. Andrew sent me word from Johnstown this afternoon about half-past three he was safe and would be home shortly. Well, he has never come, and I have had many reports of the work train, but no one seems to know anything definite about him. I have telegraphed and

telegraphed, but no news yet, and all I can find out is he was seen on the bridge just before it went down. I am trying to be brave.

GOOD NEWS AT LAST
SUNDAY MORNING

You see, dearest mother, I could not write, and new I am happy, though tired, for Andrew is home and safe, and I thank God for the great mercy he has shown his child. I won't dwell on my anxiety, it can better be imagined than described. From the letter I had from him at Johnstown, written at 9 A. M. Friday, until 6:30 last evening, I never knew whether he was living or dead. Thomas, our man, brought the news. God bless him, and it nearly cost him his life to do it, poor man. Andrew got separated from the party, and was close to the bridge when it was carried away, but escaped by going up the mountain.

He tried to signal to his men he was safe, but could not make them see him, nor could those men that were with him, all communication was impossible. Thomas left him at nine o'clock Friday night on the mountain and tried to get home. He got a man to ferry him across the river above Johnstown, and the boat was upset, but all managed to get ashore, and Thomas walked all night and all yesterday, and came straight to me and told me my husband was safe, and an hour later I had a telegram from Andrew. He had walked from the Conemaugh side to Bolivar. The bridge at Nineveh was the only bridge left standing. He took the first train home from Bolivar and got home about 9:30.

I telegraphed you in the morning, or rather Uncle Clem, that I was safe and Andrew reported safe, though now they tell me every one here thought he was lost and Thomas with him. Thomas's wife was met at the station and informed of his death by some of the men, and six hours afterwards Thomas came home, yet more dead than alive, poor man. It is very hard to write, as all the country people and men have been here to tell me how glad they are "I got my husband safely back, and that I am a powerful sight lucky young woman."

Well, mother darling, make your mind easy about your children now. Andrew is safe and well, though pretty well exhausted, and his feet are so sore and swollen he can hardly stand, and can't wear anything but rubbers, as his mountain shoes he cut to pieces. He left early this morning, but will be back tonight. I cannot begin to tell you of the horrors, as the papers do not half picture the distress. New Florence was not flooded, though some of the people left the place on Friday night and went up on Squirrel Hill.

HAEL: PITY OR PITIFUL

I know that some of you will be disgruntled with me for my comments here, but as I am reading this woman's telegrams to her mother I am almost getting anxious myself. The purpose of this book of my anecdotal stories behind the scenes is to give you glimpses of God in the midst of tragedy.

Now I don't know this woman and purposely did not look in the records and annals of her life.

But let me tell you what I heard in her writing. I heard a woman who is "blessed by God" because He did for her what she worried so much He would not do.

Did this young woman just tell us much more about herself than she realizes? I don't want to speculate anymore because it would not be fair. Let me merely ask you, is God your friend when He does not give you what you want? She continues and I think atones for herself a bit. You decide.

SCENES AT THE RIVER

I went down to the river once, and that was enough, as I knew Andrew would not like me to see the sorrow, for which there was no help. I went just after the bridge fell, saw Centreville flooded and the people make a dash for the mountain. Yesterday two hundred and three bodies were taken from the river near here, and yet every train takes away more. The freight cars have taken nothing but human freight, and wagon load after wagon load of dead bodies have been right in front of the house. There was a child about Nellie's age, with light hair, dead in the wagon, with her hands clasped, saying her prayers, and her blue eyes staring wide open. By her side lay a man with a pipe in his mouth, naked children, and a woman with a baby at her breast. Oh, the terror on their faces. Two women and three men were rescued here, and a German family of mother, four children and father. I had them all on my hands to look after; no one could make them understand, and how I ever managed it I don't know, but I did. They lost two children and their home, but had a little money and were going to his brother's, at Hazleton. They got here in the night and left at noon, and it would have done your heart good to see them eat, one was a baby five weeks old.

HELP NEEDED

Now, mother, I want you to go around among the family and get me everything in the way of clothes you possibly can, and get Uncle Clem to express them to me. I should also like money, and as much as you can get can be used. I am pretty well cleaned out of everything, as all the cattle and stock have been lost and nothing can be bought here, and all I have in the way of provisions is some preserves, chocolate, coffee, olives and crackers. We can't starve, as we have the chickens.

I got the last meat from the butcher's yesterday, and he said he didn't expect to have any more for a week, so I told Uncle Clem I would not mind having two hams from Pittsburgh, and was very grateful for his telegram. I telegraphed him in the morning, also Uncle White at Germantown, so that they might know I was all right, but from Auntie's telegram I judge Uncle Clem's telegrams were the only ones that got through. If I find I need provisions I will let you know, but do not think I will need anything for myself, and the poor are being fed by the relief supplies, and what is needed now is money and clothes.

HELPERS

There's not a house in the place that is not in trouble from the loss of some dear, one, nor one that does not hold or shelter some one or more of the sufferers. Tell everybody anything you can get can be used, and by the time you get this letter I will know of more cases to provide for, so take everything you can get, and don't worry about me, for I am all right now that Andrew is safe. This letter has been written by instalments, as I have been interrupted so many times, so pardon the abruptness of it, and please send it to Germantown, as I have too much to do now.

My hands and heart are both full. Milk is as scarce as wine, as the pasturage was all on the other side, and cows were lost, and bread is as scarce as can be, and instead of a dozen eggs, we only get one a day. I am proud of New Florence, as all it has done to help the

347

sufferers no one knows, and as for Mr. Bennett, he is one in a thousand. Mr. Hay's son has worked like a Trojan. Tell Cousin Hannah that the new tracks will be sure to be straight, as Andrew will superintend the whole business. With heart full of love to one and all and a kiss to the children. Lovingly,

Bett.

THE AWFUL AFTER SCENES
NEW FLORENCE, PA.
SUNDAY NIGHT

My Darling Mother: This is my second letter to you today. It is after 11 o'clock, and one of the men has just brought me word that Andrew will be home, he thought, by 1 o'clock; so I am waiting up for him, so as to give him his dinner, and I have been through so much I cannot go to bed until I know he is safe home again. I put him up a good lunch, and know he cannot starve.

Oh the horrors of today! I have only had one pleasant Sunday here, and that was the one after we were married. I have had a very busy day, as I have been through our clothes, and routing out everything possible for the sufferers and the dead, and the cry today for linen sheets, etc., was something awful. I have given away all my underclothes, excepting my very best things and all my old ones I made into face-cloths for the dead. Today they took five little children out of the water. They were playing "Ring around a rosy," and their hands were clasped in a clasp which even death did not loosen, and their faces were still smiling.

One man identified his wife among those who came ashore here, and Rose said that he was nearly crazy, and that her face was the most beautiful thing she ever saw, and that she had very handsome pearls in her ears and was so young looking. The dead are all taken from here to Johnstown and Nineveh and other places, where they will be most likely to be identified, about thirty have been identified here and taken away. I feel hardened to a great deal, and feel God has been so merciful to me I must do all I can for the unfortunate ones. I hope soon to have some help from you all, for I have given willingly of my little and my means are exhausted. I expect we will have to live on ham and eggs next week, but we are thankful to have that, as I would rather live low and give all I can, than not to live. All I care about is that Andrew gets enough to

348

eat, as he needs a great deal to keep his strength up, working as hard as he does. Now I will close as it is nearly time for him to be home. Lovingly,

BETT.

HAEL: WOULD SHE SMILE

As Bett writes above of the children smiling, even in death, I wonder what this woman would look like in death. Just curious.

Do you think I'm being too hard on her? Well, I'm not perfect, I'm only an angel.

FEEDING THE HUNGRY

There are over 30,000 people at Johnstown who must be fed from the outside world. Of these 18,000 are natives of the town that a week ago had 29,500 inhabitants, all the others are dead or have gone away. Over 12,000 people are here clearing the streets, burying the dead, attending the sick, and feeding and sheltering the homeless, all these people have to be fed at least three times a day, for days are very long in Johnstown just now. They begin at five o'clock in the morning, two hours before the whistles in the half mired Cambria Iron Company's building blow, and end just about the time the sun is going down. If the people who are on the outside and who are engaged in the labor of love of sending the food that is keeping strength in Johnstown's tired arms and the clothing that is covering her nakedness could understand the situation as it is they would redouble their efforts. Johnstown cannot draw on the country immediately around about her, for that was drained days ago. To be safe, there should be a week's supply of food ahead. At no time has there been a day's supply or anything like it.

A CRISIS IN THE COMMISSARY

Twice within the last forty-eight hours the commissary department at the Pennsylvania Railroad Depot, where nearly 10,000 people are furnished with food, have been in state of mind bordering on panic. They had run out of food; people who had trudged down the hill with expectant faces and empty baskets had to trudge back again with hearts heavy and baskets still empty. That was the case on Wednesday night. Then the Citizens'

Committee had to send to the refugee camp, the smallest food station in the city, and take away 1500 loaves of bread. The bread supply in the central portion of the town had suddenly given out and there was a clamoring crowd demanding to be fed.

The same thing happened again last night. It was not so bad as on the night before, but there were anxious faces enough among the men under the direction of Major Spangler, who realized the awful responsibility of providing the mouths of the thousands with food. The supply had given out, but fortunately not until almost everybody had been supplied. Telegrams announced that eight carloads of provisions had been shipped from the West and were somewhere in the line between Pittsburgh and Johnstown. At midnight nothing could be heard of them. The delay was maddening. If the food did not arrive it meant fully 10,000 breakfastless and possibly dinnerless people in Johnstown today, with consequent suffering and possible disorder among the rough and rowdy element.

THE DANGER TIDED OVER

Before daylight the expected cars came in from Ohio and Pittsburgh and the danger was over for the time being. This serves, however, to show the perilous condition the town is in, living as it is in a hand-to-mouth fashion. It should be remembered that the only direct access to Johnstown from the West is by way of the Pennsylvania, which is handicapped as she has never been before, and from the East and South, of the Baltimore and Ohio. If the Pennsylvania were opened through to the East a steady stream of 200 cars already loaded for the sufferers would pour over the Alleghenies, but the Pennsylvania does not see light ahead much more clearly than yesterday. The terrible breaks and washouts will require days yet to repair, and supplies that come from the interior of the State must come by means of wagons.

DISTRIBUTING SUPPLIES.

Inside the warehouse a score of volunteers and Pittsburgh policemen break open the boxes and pile the goods in separate heaps; the women's clothing, the men's, the children's and the different sizes being placed in regular order. Then the barriers are opened and the crowd surges in like depositors making a run on a savings bank. The police keep good order and the ubiquitous Tumblestone and his assistants dole out the goods to all who have orders. Special orders call for stoves, mattresses and blankets.

If the Philadelphians could see the faces of the people they are helping before and after they have passed the distribution windows they would feel well repaid for their visible sympathy. Chairman Scott says the class of goods from Philadelphia have been of the highest quality. "We have been delighted with the thought and excellence of the selections and amiable nature of the contributions. The two miles of track lying between here and Morrellville are still blocked with cars stretched from one end to the other, and fresh arrivals are coming in daily over the Baltimore and Ohio." Although it is impossible to say how much has been received from Philadelphia, Mr. Tumblestone says that so far as many as eighteen freight cars, each filled from the sides to the roof, have arrived from the Quaker City, and their contents have been distributed.

A Cool Request

This remark showed the greatest sang-froid [excessive composer or coolness] known to be exhibited during the flood, but the most irreverent was that of an old man who was saved by E. B. Entworth, of the Johnson works. On Saturday morning Mr. Entworth rowed to a house near the flowing debris at the bridge, and found a woman, with a broken arm, and a baby. After she had got into the boat she cried, "Come along, grandpap." Whereupon an old man, chilled but chipper, jumped up from the other side of the roof, slid down into the boat, and said, "Gentlemen, can any of you give me a chew of tobacco?"

Tracks that were Laid in a Hurry

If Pennsylvania Railroad trains ever ran over tougher looking tracks than those used now through Johnstown it must have been before people began to ride on it. The section from the north end of the bridge to the railroad station has a grade that wabbles between 50 and 500 feet to the mile and jerks back and forth sideways as though laid by a gang of intoxicated men on a dark night. When the first engine went over it everybody held his breath and watched to see it tumble. These eccentricities are being straightened out, however, as fast as men and broken stones can do it.

The railroad bridge at Johnstown deserves attention beyond that which it is receiving on account of the way it held back the flood. It is one of the most massive pieces of masonry ever set up in this country. In a general way it is solid masonry of cut sandstone blocks of unusual size, the whole nearly 400 feet long, forty wide, and averaging about forty deep. Seven arches of about fifty feet span are pierced through it, rising to within a few feet of the top and leaving massive piers down to the rock beneath. As the bridge crosses the stream diagonally, the arches pierce the mass in a slanting direction, and this greatly adds to the heavy appearance of the bridge. There has been some disposition to find fault with the bridge for being so strong, the idea being that if it had gone out there would have been no heaping up of buildings behind it, no fire, and fewer deaths. This is probably unfair, as there were hundreds of persons saved when their houses were stopped against the bridge by climbing out or being helped out upon the structure. If the bridge had gone, too, the flood would have taken the whole instead of only half of Cambria City.

CHILDHOOD'S PEACEFUL SLEEP

In the midst of all, a girl of six or seven, with a light shawl thrown over her figure, slept as peacefully as if she lay in the comfortable embrace of her own crib at home. She was little Bertha Reed, who had been sent out from Chicago in the care of the conductor on a trip to Brooklyn, where she was to meet her aunt. At Pittsburgh she was taken in charge by a Miss Harvey, a relative. She was a passenger on the Chicago limited, the last train to get safely across the bridge at South Fork. She was a model of patience and cheerfulness through all the discomforts and drawbacks of the voyage, and her innocent prattle made every man and woman love her.

It might have been supposed that if one were to waken any of these sleeping passengers to obtain their names and ask them of the disaster they might surly have resented it. But they didn't. Now and then one of them would half-sleepily hand out his ticket under the mistaken notion that the reporter was the conductor. Another shake brought them round, and they answered everything as kindly as if the unavoidable breaking in upon their comfort were a matter of no concern whatever. Sometimes it would seem that great sorrow must have a chastening effect upon everyone.

FROM ALL PARTS OF THE WORLD

It was a strange gathering altogether, and made one think again of the remark so often repeated in "No Thoroughfare," "How small the world is." All the ends of the earth had sent their people to meet at the disaster, and the tide of human life flows on as recklessly as the current of any sea or river. Here weary, sleepy and sad, was Jacob Schmidt, of Aspen, Colorado. He had been a passenger on the Pittsburgh Day Express. He was standing on the platform when the flood came and by a lurching of the car he was thrown into the boiling torrent. He managed to seize a floating plank and was saved, but all his money and other valuables were lost. That was a particularly hard loss to him, because he was on his way to South Africa to seek his fortune. Behind him was R. B. Jones, who had come from the other side of the globe, in particular from Sydney, Australia, and met the others at Altoona. He was on the way for a visit to his parents in York County. He was on the Chicago Limited and just escaped the danger.

In a front car was Peter Sherman, of Pawtucket, Rhode Island. He was tall and broad shouldered and his sun browned face was shaded by a big soft hat. He was on his way from Texarkana, way down in Texas, and he too was at Conemaugh. He was a passenger on the first section of the Day Express. He had not slept a wink on the way down from Altoona, and he told his story spiritedly.

He said, "I heard a voice in the car crying the reservoir is burst, run for your lives! I got up and made a rush for the door. A poor little cripple with two crutches sat in front of me and screamed to me to save him or he would be drowned. I grabbed him up under one arm and took his crutches with my free hand. As we stepped from the car the water was coming. I made my way up the hill toward a church. The water swooped down on us and was soon up to my knees. I told the cripple I could not carry him further; that we should both be lost. He screamed to me again to save him, but the water was gaining rapidly on us. He had a grip of my arm, but finally let go, and I laid him, hopefully, on the wooden steps of a house. I managed to reach the high land just in time. I never saw the cripple afterwards, but I learned that he was drowned."

A Great Loss

A tall, heavily built man, with tattered garments, walked along the platform with the help of a cane. His face was covered with a beard, and his head was bowed so that his chin almost touched his breast. One foot was partially covered by a cut shoe, while on the other foot he wore a boot from which the heel was missing. This was John Stephens, a foreman at the Johnson Steel Rail Works at Woodvale. He was a big, strong man, but his whole frame trembled as he said: "Yes, I am from Johnstown. I lost my wife and three children there, so I thought I would leave."

It was only by the greatest effort that Mr. Stephens kept the tears back. He then told his experience in this way: "I was all through the war. I was at Fair Oaks, at Chancellorsville, in the Wilderness, and many other battles, but never in my life was I in such a hot place as I was on Friday night. I don't know how escaped, but here am I alone, wife and children gone. I was at the office of the company on Friday. We had been receiving telephonic messages all morning that the dam was unsafe. No one heeded them. I did not know anything about the dam. The bookkeeper said there was not enough water up there to flood the first floor of the office. I thought he knew, so I didn't send my family to the hills.

"I don't know what time it was in the afternoon that I saw the flood coming down the valley. I was standing at the gate. Looking up the valley I saw a great white crowd moving down upon us. I made a dash for home to try to get my wife and children to the hills. I saw them at the windows as I ran up to the house. That is the last time I ever saw their faces. No sooner had I got into the house than the flood struck the building. I was forced into the attic. It was a brick house with a slate roof. I had intended to keep very cool, but I suppose I forgot all about that."

SWEPT DOWN THE STREAM

"It seemed a long time, but I suppose it was not more than a second before the house gave way and went tumbling down the stream. It turned over and over as it was washed along. I was under the water as often as I was above it. I could hear my wife and children praying, although I could not see them. I did not pray. They were taken and I was left for some purpose, I suppose. My house finally landed up against the stone railway bridge. I was then pinned down to the floor by a heavy rafter or something. Somehow or other I was lifted from the floor and thrown almost out upon the bridge. Then some people got hold of me and pulled me out and took me over to a brickyard. My eyes and nose were full of cinders. After I reached the brickyard I vomited fully a pint of cinders which I had swallowed while coming through that awful stream of water. I can't tell you what it was like. No one can understand it unless he or she passed through it."

"Did you find your wife and children?"

"No. I searched for them all of Saturday, Sunday and Monday, but could find no trace of them. I think they must have been among those who perished in the fire at the bridge. I would have stayed there and worked had it not been the place was so near my old home that I could not stand it. I thought I would be better off away from there where I could not see anything to recall that horrible sight."

Mr. Stephens above never did find his family, and afterwards he became very bitter. He was first bitter about his wife and children praying, and God not saving them, compared to him who did not pray and yet he was saved.

His conclusion: "You don't exist, God!"

When John Stephens thought of the bookkeeper that made so little reference to any danger from the dam, he was glad that the bookkeeper died, for Mr. Stephens would have surely killed him, the way he was thinking.

His conclusion: "You don't exist, God!"

He sent a telegram to his mother-in-law in Philadelphia to tell her of the news and started back to work. Within a few days came a reply. "In spite of all, glad you are well. Come home to us as soon as you can. God knows why He has allowed this." Right then and there he decided he would never go back to those religious nuts again.

His conclusion: "You don't exist, God!"

Some three years later, John Stephens, who had remained in Johnstown, had a visitor at his boarding house. As a foreman he made good money, but from the date of the flood onwards he paid for his room and board and then spent every remaining dollar on drink in one of the many taverns that were rebuilt almost immediately.

By now his tall and muscular physique had reduced slightly, but only slightly. Still larger and stronger than most men, he often wondered how he kept his job as a foreman, and then drowned his wondering in beer.

On this evening his visitor, the Methodist minister Rev. Chapman, had an older man by his side. Reverend Chapman looked at Mr. Stephens with some trepidation, for the last time he came by, John nearly threw him out the door. Rev. Chapman was the pastor for him, his wife and children before the flood. In that instant at the door John recalled his last meeting with the Rev. Chapman. He had mentioned the word "God" and John went "crazy" telling the reverend that "God doesn't exist!" and reached for him to throw him out the upper story window.

John didn't recognize the older man standing next to him, perhaps it was because he was somewhat drunk. But the moment he spoke the angry foreman broke down.

"John, we are worried for you, son," said his father-in-law.

The big man started to shake, not with rage, but with uncontrollable anguish.

355

As the Reverend Chapman backed away out of fear, Bro. Homer Calhoun stepped forward and grabbed his son-in-law under the arms and moved him to his bed. There John heaved with sobs, slept, and then awakened from nightmares hollering to his wife and kids, yelling at the bookkeeper and yelling at God.

Bro. Homer stayed with John Stephens all night long, even though he had a nice room in a hotel downtown. The next morning being Sunday, John didn't have to work so he let Bro. Homer convince him to go to breakfast at the hotel.

Hardly a word was spoken during breakfast, and when they walked back to John's boarding house they started to walk near the Methodist Church. John stopped abruptly and went in the opposite direction going around the block so as to not walk by his old church.

Stopping in front of the boarding house John wanted to hug his father-in-law but could not. He wanted to thank him for breakfast and call him dad, but he could not. With Bro. Homer watching his hurting son-in-law, John turned and went up the steps. When he got to the top he turned around and simply said, "Thank you."

Bro. Homer smiled and replied, "I plan to stay here for a while, son."

They nodded to each other and parted ways.

The next morning Bro. Homer awaited his son-in-law outside his boarding house as he went off to work. In his two hands were two mugs of coffee. He gave one to his son-in-law without saying a word and turned and went back to his hotel. This went on every morning and on Friday, a bit angry, his son-in-law asked, "Why are you doing this, old man? Why are you here?"

Smiling, a hearty sincere smile, Bro. Homer simply asked, "Do you want to have dinner with me tonight?"

John Stephens, the big foreman, just grunted and turned away.

That night his father-in-law was at his work place when John exited the building. "I thought I'd catch you, son, before you went out for a drink."

With a smirk the foreman replied, "Good thinking. Okay, where do you want to go?"

"Well, I've been eating at the hotel every night," said his father-in-law, "and I would like to go somewhere different. Do you like the rebuilt Opera House restaurant just around the corner from my hotel?"

John Stephens seemed startled for a moment, visibly shaken, and said, "I've never been there."

Bro. Homer immediately turned and headed to John's boarding house so John could change.

Upon arriving at the restaurant John seemed to roll his shoulders and almost crouch as he entered the doors. He looked around as if almost scared to be there.

Bro. Homer pretended like he did not notice and acquired a quiet table for two in a corner of the restaurant. For an hour they ate in silence and he observed his son-in-law looking around the restaurant.

Finally, he asked, "Why do you keep looking around, son?"

Without looking at his father-in-law he simply replied, "the owners of this establishment also had a restaurant before the flood, and . . ." His throat started to constrict and he got choked up.

"I know, son," brother Homer said, reaching across the table and setting his hand on the big man's now heaving shoulders. She wrote to mother and told her about it. She said that you two would go every Friday and have a little date, letting the kids stay with a care giver."

John said nothing, by now back in control of his emotions, and just looked down at his meal and ate quietly.

As they left the restaurant heading back to the boarding house John was getting angry and blurted out, "Why are you doing this, old man? Why can't you leave me alone?"

And as calm as ever, Homer merely replied, "Can you take tomorrow off? I want to tell you a story."

John had now mounted the steps and turned to look at Bro. Homer. Sighing he said, "I'll try, but I can't promise anything. Come by tomorrow with coffee and we will go to the plant and I will ask."

The next morning his father-in-law was waiting for him when he exited his boarding house, cup of coffee in hand, but Bro. Homer was a bit more sobered. John caught the change but said nothing.

John Stephen's supervisor didn't know who Homer was and knew not to ask his favorite foreman, but he could tell that since this unknown man had been around, John's attitude had been different. More than happy to see his foreman with a man like Bro. Homer, John's supervisor gave him the day off and any others he would want.

Later that morning they were seated on Bro. Homer's balcony outside his room.

"I hope you don't mind us eating here, but what I want to share with you is difficult and I fear I need some privacy," the older man said.

Just grunting his assent John sipped more coffee.

Beginning Homer said, "Something happened last year that sobered me to what you are going through." As Homer paused, it wasn't because he was weighing his words, it was because he struggled to say them.

"Do you remember my next-door neighbor, son?" Homer continued.

"Yes, I think you and he were always out fishing together, working on each other's garden or playing cards at night," John chuckled for the first time. "I remembered mom, or, um, your wife," John corrected. "I seem to remember she used to get real mad at you two for playing cards."

Homer smiled a bit, seemingly in a different world though in the same room.

"How is that old goat?" John asked, feeling a bit more relaxed with his father-in-law.

The silence that ensued seemed like it lasted forever. Grabbing his mug of coffee slowly and then putting it to his lips Homer drank down the last swallow and then refilled it.

Still not saying a word, he refocused on his son-in-law and with a tear falling down his cheek he said, "He was murdered not 10 months ago.

"I was very angry at God, John. At times I think I still am angry at Him."

John set his bite of breakfast down as the gravity of what he saw in his father-in-law's face hit him.

For the first time in a long time, the big foreman softened a bit and put a knowing hand on another man out of sympathy. "I understand." John said and paused and then said again, "I understand."

They sat there in silence for a few minutes and then the old man started to smile, gently, and hesitantly. "Son, God took me through a journey that I never expected to go through and then He taught me something I never knew I didn't know."

John sat silently listening to his father-in-law who told of the murder and its senselessness, the capture of the culprit and his execution. And then Bro. Homer looked up and said, "Son, John, would you forgive me?"

The younger man sat back and sat up not knowing why he was being asked for forgiveness.

358

The older man went on, "John, I had no idea the pain you were going through with the loss of your wife and children. Mom and I were very angry at you for not recognizing that we grieved for them too. I was so angry at you for being selfish." The old man faltered for a moment and then continued. "Son, forgive me. I am the one who was so selfish."

They both sat there in silence for a time as John filled his father-in-law's mug with more coffee.

"The last few months," the older man went on, "I have been crying out to the Lord for my sin of lack of empathy towards you and selfishness on my part. I have been prostrate before the Lord for the last two months every morning, and then ten days ago I told your mother-in-law I needed to go and see you."

He smiled, "Do you know what she said to me? She said, 'I know, it's about time that you do!'"

And the two men chuckled together.

"I don't know why God spared your life and not my daughter's or my grandchildren's, but He did. And that tells me that He is not done with you, my son. And so here is my prayer for you." And with those words the older man grabbed the younger man's massive hand, closed his eyes, and said, "Lord, God of heaven, You are the One who spoke the words and the worlds leapt into existence.[1] You are the One whose throne is above the heavens and is sovereign over all.[2] And yet You are the One who inclines His ear to us,[3] though thousands of angels are worshipping You.[4] Father, You have comforted me, so that I could comfort my son, John. My prayer for him is simple. I trust You to comfort him so that he can then comfort others in the self-same way.[5] Use that gentle spirit in him that I have always seen. Cause him to be a gentle comforter to others."

Over time God used John in the mill where he worked. When there were accidents he volunteered to tell the families of the situation. He went back to church and volunteered to help the poor, the widows and the orphans. He stopped spending his money on drink, began saving, became a compassionate, gentle Christian and was known as a giant Teddy Bear.

"And all because You took my family from me," he would say to the Lord in private, when no one else was there to hear him.

---

[1] Genesis 1
[2] Psalm 103:19
[3] Psalm 40:1
[4] Revelation 5:11
[5] 2 Corinthians 1:4

One day, many years later he found Ephesians 5:20, a verse he'd read many times but never truly saw. It basically says, "thank the Lord FOR everything." Sobered for a few days by the meaning of the verse, by its implication, and by the requirement now upon him, he got on his knees, and couldn't say a word, all he could do was cry. After a few minutes, back in control of his emotions, he looked at the verse again, and again his throat constricted and he started to cry. This went on for nearly an hour when finally, in a whispered, tear stained voice he stammered, "Thank You, Lord for the death of my family." After a pause he continued, "I miss them, Lord. I don't know why You did this, but I accept Your word, Your truth, and Your hope."

God comforted this man in a way that no one else ever could. Many years later he was carried across Jordan and saw Jesus, the Author and Finisher of John's faith.[1]

Also standing there were his wife and kids, his mother-in-law and then a massive line of people that he had either comforted directly or through his comforting of their families.

As he went through the great line of people, he missed the man he most looked forward to seeing. And then John saw Homer at the end of the line. They nodded to one another, hugged, and then Homer said, as tears flowed, I'm very proud of you, son.

HOW THE SURVIVORS LIVE

With a view of showing the character of living in and about Johnstown, how the people pass each day and what the conveniences and deprivations of domestic life experienced under the new order of things so suddenly introduced by the flood are, an investigation of a house-to-house nature was made today. As a result, it was noted that the degrees of comfort varied with the people as the types of human nature. As remarked by a visitor:

"The calamity has served to bring to the surface every phase of character in man, and to bring into development traits that had before been but dormant. Generally speaking all are on the same footing so far as need can be concerned. Whether houses remain to them or not, all the people have to be fed, for even should they have money, cash is of no account, provisions cannot be bought, people who still have homes nearly all of them furnish quarters for some of the visitors. Militia officers,

---

[1] Hebrews 12:2

committeemen, workmen, etc., must depend upon the supply stations for food."

AT PROSPECT

The best preserved borough adjoining Johnstown is Prospect, with its uniformly built gray houses, rising tier upon tier against the side of the mountain, at the north of Johnstown. There are in the neighborhood of 150 homes here, and all look as if but one architect designed them. They are large, broad gabled, two-story affairs, with comfortable porches, extending all the way across the front, each being divided by an interior partition, so as to accommodate two families. The situation overlooked the entire horseshoe-shaped district, heretofore described.

Nearly every householder in Prospect is feeding not only his own family, but from two to ten others, whom he has welcomed to share what he has. Said one of these, "We are all obliged to go to the general department for supplies, for we could not live otherwise. Our houses have not been touched, but we have given away nearly everything in the way of clothing, except what we have on. There were two little stores up here, but we purchased all they had long ago. It does not matter whether the people are rich or poor, they are all compelled to take their chances. In Prospect are the quarters of the Americus Club, of Pittsburgh, an organization which is widely spoken of as having distinguished itself by furnishing meals to any and every hungry person who applied."

AN INCIDENT

As two newspaper men were about to descend the hill, after visiting a number of points, a little woman approached and made an inquiry about the running of trains. She was one of the survivors and wished to reach Clearfield, where her grown-up sons were. "I'd walk it if I could," she said, "but it's too far, and I'm too old now." She was living with her friends, who have taken care of her since her home was swept away.

A DISTRIBUTING POINT

At the base of the long flight of wooden steps that lead to Prospect is the path extending across to the Pennsylvania Railroad station. Here is one of the principal distributing points. Three times each day a remarkable sight is here to be witnessed. Along the track at the eastern end, from the station platform back as far as the freight house, standing upon railroad ties, resting upon piles of lumber, and trying to hold their places in the line of succession in any position possible, crowds of people wait to be served. Aged, decrepit men and women and little girls and boys hold baskets, boxes, tin cans, wooden buckets, or any receptacle handy in which they may carry off provisions for the day.

SAD SIGHTS

The women have, many of them, tattered or ill-fitting clothing, taken at random when the first supply of this character arrived, their heads covered with thin shawls or calico sun shades. They stand there in the chilly morning wind that blows through the valley along the mountains, patiently waiting their turn at the provision table, making no complaint of cold feet and chilled bodies. In the line are people who, ten days ago, had sufficient of this world's goods to enable them to live comfortably the remainder of their lives. They are massed in solidly.

Guards of soldiers stand at short intervals to keep them back and preserve the lines, and sentries march up and down the entire length of the station challenging the approach of any one who desires to pass along the platform. For a distance of about one hundred feet to the railroad signal tower are piled barrels of flour, boxes of provisions, and supplies of all descriptions. Under the shed of the station an incongruous collection of clothing is being arranged to allow of convenient distribution. While they waited for the signal to commence operations, a guard entered into conversation with a woman in the line. She was evidently telling a story of distress, for the guard looked about hastily to a spot where canned meats and bread were located and made a movement as if to obtain a supply for the woman, but the eyes of brother soldiers and a superior officer were upon him and he again assumed his position. It is said to be not unusual for the soldiers, under cover of dusk, to overstep their duty in order to serve some applicant who, through age or lack of physical strength, is poorly equipped to bear the strain. All sorts of provisions are asked for. One woman asks boldly for ham, canned chicken, vegetables and flour. Another approaches timidly and would be glad to have a few loaves of bread and a little coffee.

NO DISCRIMINATION

Before the complete system was introduced, complaints were made of discrimination by those dealing out supplies, but under the present order of things the endeavor is made to treat everybody impartially. Provisions are given out in order, so that imposition is avoided. It would seem that there could be no imposition in any case, however. The people who are here, and who are able to get within the lines at all, have a reason for their presence, and this is not curiosity. They are here for anything but entertainment, and there is no possibility of purchasing supplies. All must needs apply at the commissary department.

A big distributing point for clothing is at the Baltimore and Ohio Railroad station, in the Fourth Ward, known as Harpville, on the east bank of the Stony Creek. A rudely constructed platform extends over a washed-out ditch, partially filled with debris. In the vicinity is a large barn and several smaller outhouses, thrown in a tumble-down condition. Piled against them are beams and rafters from houses smashed into kindling wood. All about the station are boxes, empty and full, scattered in confusion, and around and about these crowds are clustered as best they can. A big policeman stands upon a raised platform made of small boxes, and as he is supplied with goods from the station he throws about in the crowds socks, shoes, dresses, shirts, pantaloons, etc., guessing as rapidly as possible at proportion and speedily getting rid of his bundle. Around the corner, on a street running at right angles with the tracks, is the provision department. These two are sample stations. They are scattered about at convenient points, and number about ten in all.

CHAPTER XVI
Order Out of Chaos

By slow degrees and painful labor, the barren place where Johnstown stood begins again to look a little like the habitations of a civilized community. Daily a little is added to the cleared space once filled with the concrete rubbish of this town, daily the number of willing workers who are helping the town to rise again increases. Today the great yellow plain which was filled with the best business blocks and residences before the flood is covered with tents for soldiers and laborers and gangs of men at work. The wrecks are being removed or burned up. Those houses which were left only partially destroyed are beginning to be repaired. Still, it will be months, very likely years, before the pathway of the flood ceases to be perfectly plain through the town. Its boundaries are as plainly marked now as if drawn on a map, where the flood went it left its ineffaceable track. Nearly one-half of the triangle in which Johnstown stood is plainly marked, one angle of the triangle pointing to the east and directly up the Conemaugh Valley, from which the flood descended. Its eastern side was formed by the line of the river. The second angle pointed toward the big stone arch bridge, which played such an important part in the tragedy. The western ran along the base of the mountain on the bank of Stony Creek, and the third angle was toward Stony Creek Valley.

HAEL: GOD'S GRACE

Surprising little plague continued after the clean-up. There were apparently only forty deaths due to contagious diseases, contracted from the mayhem of the flood. A testimony to the concern taken by your state and local committees. One has even said, that when things calmed down, "there was a break-out of good health" after the flood.[1]

WORKING ON THE STONE BRIDGE DEBRIS

By seven o'clock the whole valley was full of people and the scene was a most animated one. The various sections of the flooded territory were full

---

[1] Thank you to Richard Burkert, President and CEO of the Johnstown Area Heritage Association for some of these facts.

of men busy in searching for the dead, removing and burning the debris. At eight o'clock this morning five bodies had been taken from the mass at the stone bridge. A large force of men have been working all day on this part of the wreck, but so great is the quantity of wreckage to be gone over and removed that while much work is done very slow progress is being made. The continued falling of the river renders the removal of the debris every day more arduous, and where a few days ago the timbers when loosened would float away, now they have to be moved by hand, making the work very slow.

A most welcome arrival this morning was Dr. B. Bullen of disinfectant fame. He brought with him fifty barrels more of his disinfectant. The doctor will take charge of the disinfecting of the dangerous sections of the flooded district and notably at the stone bridge. Twenty-five barrels have already been used with most favorable results. Dr. Bullen was a former resident of Johnstown and lost thirty relatives in the flood, among them three brothers-in-law, three uncles and two aunts.

Eight Days Later

The Cambria Iron Company's Works presented a busy scene today. At least nine hundred men are at work, and most rapid progress is being made in clearing away the wreck. It is said that the works will start up in about three weeks.

There is little change in the situation. Everyone is working with the one end in view, to clear away the wreckage and give the people of Johnstown a chance to rebuild. The laborers working at the Cambria Iron Works and on the Pennsylvania Railroad seem to be making rapid progress. This is no doubt for the reason that these men are more used to this kind of work. About ten o'clock the rain was over, and the sun came out with its fierce June heat.

A number of charges of dynamite were fired during the day, and each time with good effect. The channels through to the bridge are almost clear of debris, and each charge of dynamite has loosened large quantities of the wreckage.

This is the eighth day since the demon of destruction swept down the valley of the Conemaugh, but the desolation that marks its angry flight is still visible in all its intensity and horror. The days that have been spent by weary toilers whose efforts were steeled by grief have done little to repair the devastation wrought in one short hour by the potent fury of the elements. To the watchers on the mountain side all seems yet chaos and confusion. The thousand fires that spot the valley show that the torch is being used to complete the work of annihilation where repair is impossible and the smoke curls upward. It reminds one of the peace offerings of ancient Babylon.

Uncle Sam's Men on Hand

The corps of government engineers that arrived last night has already demonstrated the valuable assistance which it is capable of rendering in these times of emergency. With but a few hours rest, those men were up ere sunrise this morning, and by eight o'clock a pontoon bridge had been stretched across the river at Kernville. Acting in conjunction with the Pennsylvania military authorities they are pursuing their labors at various other points, and by sundown it is confidently expected that pontoon bridges will be erected at all places where the necessities of traffic demand. It is the fact, probably not generally known. that the great government of the United States owns only 500 feet of pontoon bridges, and that these are the same that were used by the federal forces in the civil war, twenty-five years ago. The bridges that are to be used at Johnstown were brought from West Point and Willet's Point, where they have been for years used in the ordinary course of instruction in the military and engineer corps.

Stone Bridge Affair Continues

Affairs at the tremendous stone bridge wreckage pile seem to have resolved themselves into a state of almost hopelessness. It is amazing the routine into which everything has fallen in this particular place. Every morning at seven o'clock a score of Lilliputs come mechanically from huts and tents or the bare hillside, and wearily and weakly go to work clearing away this mass, and at the rate they are now proceeding it will actually be months before the debris is cleared away and the last body found. Fortunately the wind is blowing away from us or we would have olfactory evidence that what is not found is far worse than what has been exposed.

Then it may be good business and good policy to have these few workers fool around the edge of the wreckage for five or ten minutes adjusting a dynamite blast, then hastily scramble away and consume as much more time before a tremendous roar announces the ugly work is done, but the onlookers doubt it. Sometimes, when an extra-large shot is used, the water, bits of wood and iron, and other shapes more fearfully suggestive, fly directly upward in a solid column at least three hundred feet high, only to fall back again in almost the same spot, to be tugged and pulled at or coaxed to float down an unwilling current that is falling so rapidly now that even this poor mode of egress will soon be shut entirely off.

The fact of the matter is simply this, they are not attempting to recover bodies at the bridge, but as one blast tears yards of stuff into flinders it is shoved indifferently into the water, be it human or brute, stone, wood or iron, to float down toward Pittsburgh or to sink to the bottom, maybe a few yards from where it was pushed off from the main pile.

Up in the center of the town the debris is piled even higher than at the stone bridge, but the work is going on fairly well. The men seem to be working more together and enter into the spirit of the thing. Besides this, horses and wagons can get at the wrecks, and it really looks as if this part of the ruins has been exaggerated, and some of the foremen there say that at the present rate of work going on through the town, all the bodies that ever will be recovered will be found within the next ten days. As to the condition these bodies are in, that has become almost a matter of indifference, except as to to effect upon the health of the living.

FRAGMENT OF A BIBLE

"What is that you have there? A piece of a Bible? Yes, you will find lots of leaves lying around. There is a story, I don't know how true it is, that many people have thrown their Bibles away since the flood, declaring that their belief, after the horrors they have witnessed, is at an end. I can hardly credit this. But there is one curious thing that is certain, and everybody has noticed it. Books and Bibles have been found in the rubbish all over the town, and in a great many instances they are open at some passage calling attention to flood and disaster. I have found these myself a dozen times. It is a remarkable coincidence, to say the least.

"Some people may find a warning in all this. I don't pretend to say, but as we walk along here let me tell you of a conversation I had with a man who was worth nearly $20,000 before the flood. He has lost every cent, and is glad enough to get his daily meals from the supplies sent here.

"'I don't know what to think of Johnstown,' he said. 'We have been called a wicked place. Perhaps all this is a judgment. Just when we have been most prosperous some calamity has come upon us. We were never more prosperous than when this flood over whelmed us,'

"It is now 6 o'clock. See, the workmen are knocking off and are going to the river to wash up. Now, out comes the baseball, for recreation always follows work here. Dusk settles down over the valley. An engine nearby begins to throb, and electric lights spring up here and there. All over the town the flames of the great bonfires leap out of the gloom. From the camps of the workmen come ribald songs and jests. The presence of death has no effect on the living.

"The songs gradually die away, and the singers drop off into a deep sleep. The town becomes as silent as the graveyards which have been filled with its victims. Not a sound is heard save the crackling of the flames and the challenges of the sentries to some belated newspaper man or straggler.

"And thus, another day draws to a close in ill-fated Johnstown."

HAEL: THE LOSS OF FAITH

Much of this narrative I deleted, but I believe that the writer gave a few points of graphic description that were helpful. I especially like his unconfirmed story of the Bibles and the loss of faith, not because it was a corroborated story by his own admission, but because it is true. We see this even in the 21ˢᵗ century church.

As we have watched you, strengthened you, helped you, and lived with you in various ways, we see that this phenomenon of a loss of faith is rooted in one thing: pride.

Basically, your bent, like the evil one himself who said, "I will make myself like the Most High,"[1] is what you struggle with. It is a submission issue. Forgive me, but the plain truth is you do not want to submit to God, UNLESS He will do what you want Him to do.

The author who introduced me to the world likes to ask his congregations to do this: "Get a blank sheet of paper and write across the top, 'God's Will for My Life' and then sign it, blank!"

Let God fill in what He wants.

There is a mode of praying today that has its mind set on "giving God advice." I'm embarrassed for you to write it, but it is true, isn't it?

I would like to share with you a story of a most pitiful Christian. I have tried to keep from introducing him to you, but our 1889 author referred to him earlier. I will not point out where, suffice to say that his belief system did not live itself out the way he expected.

---

[1] Isaiah 14:14

While he did not choose to be angry with Jehovah, he did choose to no longer believe in his god.

The lower case "g" above is not an accident. Rather, it is an accurate description as you will soon see. Let's call the man Mr. Beatty. He believed a system of theology which said that Jehovah never wants him ill and never wants him poor which all led him to define precious scriptural promises with a selfish bent as often as he could.

On May 31st, 1889, Mr. Beatty's theology came crashing down upon his head, quite literally.

You know that we as angels do not know men's hearts, right? Only God knows that. However, after being around as long as we have, we can be pretty accurate when we speculate on a person's salvation based on the works we see and based upon our view of his or her life.

When this man's theology of "greed" could not hold up, he abandoned his faith. Why? Because his faith was no longer convenient for him.

Don't leave this story! You might be surprised that there is some application to you who are "right-thinking" Christians (yes, my putting that in quotations means that I am being sarcastic for the problem is NOT merely in greedy Christians).

He suffered from what many of you suffer from. He never gave God his entire heart and soul. His commitment to God was conditioned on whether or not God did what he expected.

My friends, Mr. Beatty is not in heaven.

THE NINTH DAY

Governor Beaver has assumed the command. He arrived in Johnstown yesterday, the 8th, and will take personal charge of the work of clearing the town and river. For that purpose, $1,000,000 from the State Treasury will be made available immediately. This action means that the State will clear and clean the town.

It was a day of prayer but not a day of rest in Johnstown. Faith and works went hand in hand. The flood smitten people of the Conemaugh, though they met in the very path of the torrent that swept their homes and families into ruin, offered up their prayers to Almighty God and besought His divine mercy. But all through the ruin-choked city the sound of the pick and the shovel mingled with the voice of prayer, and the challenge of the sentinel rang out above the voice of supplication. There was no cessation in the great task the flood has left them with its legacy of woe. Four charges of dynamite last night completed the wreck of the Catholic Church of St. John, which had been left by the flood in a worthless but dangerous condition.

The thousands of laborers continued their work just as on any week day, except that there was no dynamite used on the gorge and that the Cambria Iron Works were closed. There was the usual reward of the gleaners in the harvest-field of death, fifty-eight bodies having been recovered. The most of those have been in Stony Creek, up which they were carried by the back rush of the current after the bridge broke the first wave.

Roman Catholic services were held in the open air.

FATHER SMITH'S EXHORTATION

When the mass was over and Father Troutwine, who conducted it, had retired, Father Smith stood before them. "We have had enough of death lately," he said in a voice full of sympathy, "the calamity that has visited us is the greatest in the history of the United States. You must not be discouraged. Other places have been visited by disaster at times, yet we know that they have risen again. You must not look on the fearful past. The lives of the lost cannot be restored."

Here he paused because they were weeping around him, and his own voice was broken, but continuing with an effort, he told them to reflect for consolation upon the manner in which their friends had gone to death. "They had looked to God," he said, and wafted in prayers and acts of contrition, their souls had left their bodies and appeared at the throne in heaven. "Surely never such prayers fell save from the lips of saints, and the lost of the valley are saints today while you mourn for them. God, who measures the acts of men by their opportunities, had pardoned their sins. You who are left living must go to work with a will. Be men, be women. The eyes of the world are upon you, the eyes of all civilized nature. They listen, they wait to see what you are going to do."

Father Smith closed by telling them that the coming fast days of this week need not be observed in the midst of such destitution as this, and they might eat without sinning any food that would give them life and strength. When the father had finished the congregation filed slowly out past the high pile of coffins, for St. Columba's was a morgue in the days just passed.

THE PROTESTANT SERVICES

Chaplain Maguire held service in the camp of the 14th today. His pulpit was a dry goods box with the lid missing. It had been emptied of its freight into the wide lap of suffering. Before him stood the blue-coated guardsmen in a deep half circle. There was a shed at his back and a group of flood survivors, some in old clothing of their own, some in the new garments of charity. They were for the most part members of the Methodist congregation of Johnstown to which he had preached for three years.

"I hunted a long time yesterday for the foundations of my little home," he said, "but they were swept away, like the dear faces of the friends who used to gather around my table. But God doesn't own this side alone; He owns the other side too, and all is well whether we are on this side or the other. Are your dear ones saved or lost? The only answer to that question is found in whether they trusted in God or not. Trust in the Lord and verily ye shall dwell in the land and be fed."

It was not a sermon. Nobody had words or voice for preaching. Others spoke briefly and prayed. They sang, "Jesus, Lover of My Soul."

A SONG IN THE WATERS

The shrill treble of the weeping women in the shed was almost lost in the strong bass of the soldiers. "Cora Moses, who used to sing in our church choir, sang that beautiful hymn as she drifted away to her death amid the wreck," said the chaplain. "She died singing it. There was only the crash of buildings between the interruption of the song of earth and its continuation in heaven."

HAEL: MARTYRS' END

If you have ever read Foxes' Book of Martyrs, you will see very graphic descriptions of deaths that all throughout the ages we have had to watch our charges endure. I confess to you that sometimes the sight of the way they were going to die made us want to bolt into humanity's eyesight, unbind our charge, saving them, and then, forgive me, but we want to completely wipe out the person or persons preparing to kill him or her.

We had the same desire at this flood. The desire to save was so strong, but the choice to obey our Creator, your Lord and Savior was far greater.

Cora Moses reminds me of the Martyrs from antiquity who, when burned at the stake would sing until their lips fell off, or would raise hands in praise until they were merely stumps of charcoaled limbs.

You know already, if you have made it this far in the book, that one of us had our wings around that dear woman comforting her, until we were able to carry her to Jesus who welcomed her into the kingdom, saying to her, "Well done, Cora, My good and faithful servant." And she immediately entered into the joy of her Lord.[1]

DR. BEALE'S ADDRESS

Dr. Beale, whose own Presbyterian Church was one of the first morgues opened and who has lived among dead bodies ever since is the cheeriest man in Johnstown *[this is Hael, and he is an incredible pray-er]*. He made a prayer and an address. It was all straight-from-the-shoulder kind of talk, garbed in homely phrase.

In the address he said, "I have been asked to say something about this disaster and its magnitude, but I haven't the heart. Besides I haven't the words. If I was the biggest truth teller in the world I could not tell the tale."

Then the preacher went hammer and tongs at the practical teachings of the flood. "That night in Alma Hall when we thought we would all die I heard men rail on God in prayer and pledge themselves to lead better lives if life was given them. Since then I heard those same men cursing and swearing in these streets. Brethren, there was no real prayer in any of those petitions put up by those of godless lives that night. They were merely crying out to a higher power for protection. They were like the death-bed fears of the infidel, for I have seen seventeen infidels die and everyone showed the white feather. Nay, those prayers were unsanctified by the spirit, but let us who are here now living, dedicate ourselves to the service of Almighty God. There were those who were to be dedicated that night. I know one who, when it came, sent his family up the staircase, and taking up his Bible from his parlor table, opened at the 46th Psalm, first verse, and, following them, read, and the waters followed him closely. And through the flood he read the word of God and there was peace in that house while terror was all around it.

---

[1] Matthew 25:23

MOTHERING THE ORPHANS

Dr. Beale announced that Miss Walk wanted twenty-five children for the Northern Home and then began shaking hands with his congregation and pressing on them the lessons of his sermon. "Ah, old friend," he said, to a sandy moustached man in the grand army uniform, "You came safe out of the flood, now give that big heart of yours to Jesus."

The Baptist congregation also held an open-air service. The unfortunate Episcopal congregation is quite disorganized by the loss of their church and rector. They held no service, yet in a hundred temporary houses of the homeless the beautiful old litany of the faith was read by the devout churchmen.

THE DINNER "SHAD" JONES COOKED

The Sunday dinner was a great success. The bill of fare was vegetable soup, cold ham, beans, canned corn, pickled tripe and black coffee. It is worthy of note that the table in the officers' quarters did not have a delicacy upon it which was not shared by the men. The commissary ran short and had to borrow from the work men's supplies. The dinner today was cooked by "Shad" Jones, a negro man known to every traveling man who has ever stopped at Johnstown, for his ability to hold four eggs in his mouth and swallow a drink of water without cracking a shell. He lost his wife in the flood and the 14th has adopted him.

On this, the ninth day, the waters began to give up their dead. Stony Creek first showed their white faces and lifeless bodies floating on the surface, and men in skiffs went after them with their grappling rods. Several of them were taken ashore during the afternoon and carried to the Presbyterian Church morgue, which was the nearest. Then, too, the dead among the wreckage on shore came to light just the same as on other days. Their exhumation excites no notice here now. Dr. Beale, keeper of the records of morgues, counted the numbers on his finger tips and said there were more than fifty found today in Johnstown alone.

In one dead man's pocket was $3,133.62. He was Christopher Kimble, an undertaker and finisher, who, when he saw the water coming, rushed down stairs to the safe to save his gold and there he was lost. Several bodies were taken from the human raft burned beyond all recognition.

The body of Miss Bessie Bryan, the young Philadelphian, was identified today as it lay in a coffin by a grave from which it had been exhumed in Grand View Cemetery. "Returning home from a wedding in Pittsburgh with her friend, Miss Paulsen, caught by the flood on the Day Express, found dead and buried twice," will be the brief record of her wild sad fate.

WHISKEY AND RIOTING

Lieutenant Wright, Company 1, with a detail of ninety-eight men, was called to the banks of Stony Creek over the raft tonight, to protect the employees of the Philadelphia Gas Company. There they found a gang of rioters. The rioters this afternoon found a barrel of whiskey in the field of debris, and before the militia could destroy it they had managed to take a large quantity of it up on the mountain. Tonight they came down to the camp intoxicated, attacked the cook, cleared the supper table and were managing things with a high hand when a messenger was dispatched for the guard. Before Lieutenant Wright's men reached there they had escaped. The Beaver Falls gang was surprised this afternoon by the militia, and gallons of whiskey, which they had hidden, were destroyed, A dozen saloons were swept into the creek at the bridge, and it is supposed that a hundred or more barrels are buried beneath the raft.

Among the most interesting relics of the flood is a small gold locket found in the ruins of the Hurlbut house yesterday. The locket contains a small coil of dark brown hair, and has engraved on the inside the following remarkable lines : "Lock of George Washington's hair, cut in Philadelphia while on his way to Yorktown, 1781" Mr. Benford, one of the proprietors of the house, states that the locket was the property of his sister, who was lost in the flood, and was presented to her by an old lady in Philadelphia, whose mother and herself cut the hair from the head of the "Father of His Country."

MILLIONS OF MONEY FOR JOHNSTOWN

Never before in our country has there been such a magnificent exhibition of public sympathy and practical charity. As the occasion was the most urgent ever known, so the response has been the greatest. All classes have come to the rescue with a generosity, a thoughtfulness and heartfelt pity sufficient to convince the most stubborn misanthrope that religion is not dead and charity has not, like the fabled gods of Greece, forsaken the earth.

The following lines, cut from one of our popular journals, aptly represents the public feeling, and the warm sympathy that moved every heart:

I stood with a mournful throng
 On the brink of a gloomy grave,
In a valley where grief had found relief
 On the breast of an angry wave!
I heard a tearful song
 That told of an orphan's love-
'Twas a song of woe from the valley below,
 To the Father of Heaven above!

'Twas the wail of two lonely waifs-
 Two children who prayed for bread!
'Twas a pitiful cry, a mournful sigh
 From the home of the silent dead!
'Twas a sad and soulful strain
 It made the teardrops start;
'Twas an echo of pain, a weird refrain-
 And a song that touched my heart.

Poor, fatherless, motherless waifs,
 Come, dry your tearful eyes!
Not in vain, not in vain, have ye sung your refrain,
 Its echo has pierced the skies!
The angels are watching you there,
 For your "home" is now above,
And your Father is He who forever shall be
 A Father of infinite love!

Blest be the noble throng,
 With generous impulse stirred,
Who are bringing relief to the Valley of Grief.
 Where the orphan's song was heard!
Peace to them while they live,
 Peace when their souls depart,
For a friend in need is a friend indeed
 And a friend that reaches my heart!

RELIEF FUNDS STARTED

Great interest is being taken in the Herald fund for the Johnstown
sufferers. In the city, employees of all sorts of business houses, and of

railroad, steamboat and other companies, are striving to see who can collect the most money.

In the country, ministers, little girls, school children and busy workers are all collecting for the fund. It is being boomed by rich and poor, far and near.

With the checks for hundreds of dollars yesterday came this note, enclosing a dime:

NEW YORK, June 8, 1889.

MR. EDITOR:

1 am a little orphan girl.   I saved ten cents, it is all 1 have, but I should like to send it to the sufferers of the flood.

ANNIE ABEL

HAEL: SHE GAVE ALL SHE HAD

Interesting isn't it, that God views sacrifice differently than the world does. As you read about men and women giving hundreds and thousands of dollars, do not forget God's view.

Jesus and His disciples were standing watching people put their money into the treasury. It is simple and short, from Mark 12:41-44:

Sitting across from the temple treasury, He watched how the crowd dropped money into the treasury. Many rich people were putting in large sums. And a poor widow came and dropped in two tiny coins worth very little. Summoning His disciples, He said to them, "I assure you: This poor widow has put in more than all those giving to the temple treasury. For they all gave out of their surplus, but she out of her poverty has put in everything she possessed—all she had to live on."

Is that not exciting? As far as Jesus is concerned, she gave MORE than the rich man.

God isn't interested in how fat your wallet is, He is interested in the size of your heart.

ALTOONA TO THE RESCUE.

Altoona has been so hemmed in by floods and the like, and her representatives have been so busy, that they had but little to say of the prompt action and excellent work done by open handed citizens of that beautiful interior Pennsylvania city. Altoona first became alarmed by the non-arrival and reported loss of the Day Express east on the Pennsylvania Railroad Friday afternoon. Soon the station was thronged with an anxious crowd, and the excitement became intense as the scant news came slowly in. Saturday the anxiety was relieved by a telegram from Ebensburg, which a blundering telegraph operator made "three hundred lost," instead of "three thousand." That was soon corrected by later news, and the citizens immediately were called upon to meet for action. The Mayor presided, and at once $2,600 was subscribed and provisions offered. By three o'clock that afternoon a car had been loaded and started for Ebensburg, thirty-two miles away in charge of a committee. At Ebensburg that evening ten teams were secured after much trouble and the supplies sent overland seventeen miles to the desolated valley. The night was an awful one for the committee in charge. The roads were badly washed and all but impassible. The hours dragged on. At last, Sunday morning, the wagons drove into desolate Conemaugh. There were no cheers to greet them, no cries of pleasure. The wretched sufferers were too wretched, too dazed for that. They simply crowded around the wagons, pitifully begging for bread or anything to eat.

The committee report: "Impostors have not bothered us much, and, singular enough, the ones that have were chiefly women, though to-day we sent away a man who we thought came too frequently. On questioning he owned up to having fifteen sacks of flour and five hams in his house. On Tuesday we began to keep a record of those who received supplies, and we have given out supplies to fully 550 families, representing 2,500 homeless people. Our district is only for one side of the river. On the other is a commissary on Adams street, near the Baltimore and Ohio Railway station, another at Kernville, a third at Cambria City, a fourth at Morrellville and a fifth at Cambria. The people are very patient, though, of course, in their present condition they are apt to be querulous.

WANTED A BETTER DRESS

One woman who came for a dress indignantly refused the one I offered her. "I don't want that," she said. "I lost one that cost me $20, $15 for the cloth and $5 for making, and I want a $20 dress. You said you would make our losses good," and she did not take the dress.

A clergyman came to me and begged for anything in the shape of foot covering. I had nothing to give him. Men stand about ready to work, but barefooted. The clothing since the first day or two, when we got only worn stuff, fit only for bandages, has been good, and is now of excellent quality. Most of the children's garments are outgrown clothes, good for much service. Pittsburgh has sent from thirty to forty car loads of supplies, all of good quality and available, and in charge of local commissary men who had sense enough to go home when they turned over their supplies and did not stay and eat up the provisions they brought.

ORDER OUT OF CHAOS

The final acts in the great calamity, the horror which wrung the heart of the world, can be briefly told.

For many weeks the gigantic work of clearing away the ruins went on. Then came the very serious question, what could be done to repair the almost infinite damage, restore the homes of thousands, and render Johnstown fit for habitation as they were before the dreadful disaster occurred.

Temporary bridges were constructed for the passage of trains until permanent ones could be built. Cambria Iron Works resumed operations on June 10th.

The Relief Committee have decided to erect a hundred portable houses to shelter the survivors. The houses will be twelve by twenty-six feet, will be large enough to accommodate six persons each. And each house will be furnished with everything necessary to do housekeeping.

FIRE ADDED TO FLOOD

Fire broke out on the 24th of June, and for a time threatened to reduce to ashes that part of the town which had been spared by the angry waters. Some children were playing that they were workmen and attempted to burn up some loose rubbish.

The fire crackled, leaped up with threatening glare, reached out its red tongue for fresh fuel and jumped from one building to another. The progress of the flames was finally stayed by blowing up buildings. Twenty-five houses were destroyed.

A LATER REPORT

More than six weeks after the catastrophe, another careful recorder made these observations:

"Though the work already accomplished is great, as much or more remains undone. Only the lumber has been removed from the debris, while sand, dirt, bricks and stones form a mass several feet thick over the whole town. Railroad cars and wrecked houses that were washed away from their foundations are still seen in various parts of town.

"The rivers are half filled with debris, which have withstood all efforts to move it. The people themselves have shelter for the present in one-story, ten-by-twenty houses without plastering or any other provision for against the elements."

A NEW CITY

Throughout the summer months the work of removing the vast masses of debris caused by the flood was carried forward vigorously. Where the accumulation was greatest dynamite was finally brought into use. Some persons objected to this, just as before they objected to applying the torch. Love clings even to its dead, and shrinks from any disfigurement of the form that was cherished tenderly in life.

It was not uncommon after a heavy blast to see whole bodies, or fragments of bodies, suddenly brought into view. The spectacle was appalling, and would have been even more so but for the fact that death had become commonplace.

As fast as the streets and building sites could be cleared of the immense deposits with which they were overlaid, new dwellings were erected.

Thus, it will be seen that the stricken city is taking on a new life, is slowly rising from the terrible disaster, and bids fair in due time to fully recover from the deadly shock. For such a consummation all persons will devoutly wish, and will rejoice at every sign of the restored businesses, homes, industries and domestic comforts.

MARK S MIRZA, A NOTE FROM THE AUTHOR

Do you have a particularly meaningful death in your memory?

What I mean by that is, do you have a particularly sweet memory of a loved one?

I do, and I'd like to share it with you.

Over a decade ago my mother went to be with the Lord. It wasn't a surprise, and it was something we all planned for, as did she. She wouldn't let us wear black, and she wanted a pine box (it was a nice pine box, of course).

I remember getting the call from my family and getting on a plane that day. I remember the funeral, the crying, the smiling, the story telling and the laughing.

But there is one scene that will forever remain in my mind, and even now, will often bring me to tears.

Mom had had cancer for a number of years and at this particular Christmas her organs were beginning to shut down. When the day came for my wife and I to drive back to the airport my mom and dad walked us to the door and we hugged for the last time. And of course, we knew that it would be the last time, this side of Jordan.

When we finally left each other's embrace she said something, choosing her words very purposefully, she said, "I love you forever."

Naida and I went to the car. I loaded the luggage and helped Naida into the passenger seat, I walked around the car, opened the driver's side door and turned to look at the house. My mom was still at the front porch and we just stood there staring at each other, neither of us moved. We stood there for a few long moments before I got into the car and drove off.

Even now I have a few strong sobs that are stuck in my throat and want to get out.

Why am I sharing this memory with you? I suppose that it is because, like these men, women, boys and girls that you have just read about, I too have a hope relative to my loved ones. And I am confident, confident beyond words, that this hope will be realized one day.

When I enter glory, among other people, my mom will be standing there, next to Jesus welcoming me into heaven along with Him.

Truly, death has lost its sting. If you don't mind I'll plagiarize Chaplain Maguire from the Protestant Memorial in Johnstown, on June 9th, 1889.

"God doesn't merely own this side alone; He owns the other side too, and all is well whether we are on this side or the other."

Chaplain Maguire, nine days after the tragic flood in Johnstown continued, "Are your dear ones saved or lost?"

I would like to ask you, not about your "dear ones" as Chaplain Maguire did, but let me ask you. Are you saved or lost?

Chaplain Maguire concluded. "The only answer to that question is found in whether [you] trust in God or not. Trust in the Lord and verily ye shall dwell in the land and be fed."

HAEL: PARTING WORDS FROM OUR CREATOR

God Our Refuge[1]
For the choir director.
A song of the sons of Korah. According to Alamoth.

God is our refuge and strength, a helper who is always found in times of trouble.

Therefore, we will not be afraid, though the earth trembles and the mountains topple into the depths of the seas,

Though its waters roar and foam and the mountains quake with its turmoil.

Selah

There is a river—its streams delight the city of God, the holy dwelling place of the Most High.

God is within her; she will not be toppled. God will help her when the morning dawns.

Nations rage, kingdoms topple; the earth melts when He lifts His voice.

The Lord of Hosts is with us; the God of Jacob is our stronghold.

Selah

Come, see the works of the Lord, who brings devastation on the earth.

---

[1] Psalm 46 (HCSB)

He makes wars cease throughout the earth. He shatters bows and cuts spears to pieces; He burns up the chariots.

"Stop your fighting—and know that I am God, exalted among the nations, exalted on the earth."

Yahweh of Hosts is with us; the God of Jacob is our stronghold.

Selah